D1186560

EVERYMAN,
I WILL GO WITH THEE,
AND BE THY GUIDE,
IN THY MOST NEED
TO GO BY THY SIDE

IVO ANDRIĆ

THE
BRIDGE ON
THE DRINA

TRANSLATED FROM THE SERBO-CROAT
BY LOVETT F. EDWARDS

WITH AN INTRODUCTION
BY MISHA GLENNY

EVERYMAN'S LIBRARY
Alfred A. Knopf New York London Toronto
402

THIS IS A BORZOI BOOK
PUBLISHED BY ALFRED A. KNOPF

First included in Everyman's Library, 2021
Иво Андрић, На Дрини ћуприја / Ivo Andrić, Na Drini ćuprija,
originally published in 1945 by the Prosveta
Publishing Company, Belgrade
© The Ivo Andrić Foundation, Beograd, Serbia

Translation by Lovett F. Edwards first published in the UK by George Allen
and Unwin Ltd, London, 1959 and in the USA by The Macmillan Company,
New York, 1959. It is reprinted in the USA with the permission of Scribner,
a Division of Simon & Schuster, Inc.

Introduction copyright © 2021 by Misha Glenny
Bibliography and Chronology copyright © 2021 by Everyman's Library

www.randomhouse.com/everymans
www.everymanslibrary.co.uk

ISBN: 978-0-593-32022-8 (US)
978-1-84159-402-6 (UK)

A CIP catalogue reference for this book is available from the British Library

Library of Congress Cataloging-in-Publication Data

Names: Andrić, Ivo, 1892-1975, author. | Edwards, Lovett Fielding,
translator. | Glenny, Misha, writer of introduction.
Title: The bridge on the Drina / Ivo Andrić; translated from the
Serbo-Croat by Lovett F. Edwards; with an introduction by Misha Glenny.

Other titles: Na Drini ćuprija. English
Description: New York: Alfred A. Knopf, 2021. | Series: Everyman's Library; 402 |
"This is a Borzoi book" | Includes bibliographical references. |
Summary: "A hardcover edition of Nobel Prize-winning author Ivo Andrić's historical novel
about the Balkans, first published in 1945, translated from the Serbo-Croatian by Lovett F. Edwards,
with a new introduction by Misha Glenny, a bibliography, and a chronology of the author's life
and times" – Provided by publisher.
Identifiers: LCCN 2021024248 | ISBN 9780593320228 (hardcover)
Subjects: LCGFT: Novels.
Classification: LCC PG1418.A6 N313 2021 | DDC 891.8/2352–dc23
LC record available at https://lccn.loc.gov/2021024248

Typography by Peter B. Willberg

Book design by Barbara de Wilde and Carol Devine Carson

Typeset in the UK by Input Data Services Ltd, Isle Abbotts, Somerset

Printed and bound in Germany by GGP Media GmbH, Pössneck

C O N T E N T S

———

INTRODUCTION

But the bridge still stood, the same as it had always been, with the eternal youth of a perfect conception, one of the great and good works of man, which do not know what it means to change and grow old and which, or so it seemed, do not share the fate of the transient things of this world.

Ivo Andrić was no run-of-the-mill Nobel laureate. He was the only individual personally acquainted with both Gavrilo Princip and Adolf Hitler, the two men whose actions triggered the First and Second World Wars respectively. One could easily adapt Andrić's own biography into a novel as it encapsulates many of the fateful and sometimes fatal dilemmas which people from Central and South-Eastern Europe faced through much of the twentieth century.

After his death in 1975 and again following the wars in Croatia and Bosnia which finally ended in 1995, literary critics and writers from Andrić's home country have engaged in intense discussion about the writer's literary merits. Contributions to this debate range from the obsequious to the vitriolic. Throw in equally serious reflections about linguistic, political and cultural identity and this discussion becomes hard to understand for those without a decent grasp of the politics and culture of Bosnia, Croatia and Serbia, not to mention the former Yugoslavia in both its royalist and communist variants. The issue is complicated still further because none of the five countries which Andrić might have called his 'home country' exists any more (the last one collapsed in 1991).

Ivo Andrić was born in 1892 in Travnik. This town built into the hills of central Bosnia not far from Mount Vlašić, now a popular tourist destination, commands little attention outside the country. Nonetheless, it played an important part in the country's history because from the late seventeenth to the mid-nineteenth century, it was the capital of the Ottoman province of Bosnia and seat of the administrative rulers, the viziers. As a consequence for such a small settlement it has an unusual array of architectural riches, some of whose foundations stretch back to the fifteenth century. Both Andrić's parents were Catholics, which in the context of Bosnia meant they were Croats. Travnik was a mixed town, consisting mainly of Catholics and Muslims, whom Andrić usually refers to as Turks in his writing even though the great majority were actually Slavs who had converted to Islam, along with smaller communities of Orthodox Serbs and Sephardic Jews. Andrić never disguised his Croat origins but many years later when he moved to Belgrade, he designated himself a Serb, albeit with no confessional affiliation.

He was born a subject of the Ottoman Empire but in a province which the Sultan in Istanbul, Abdülhamid II, controlled only in name. In 1878, fourteen years before Andrić's birth, the Austro-Hungarian Empire had secured the right to occupy Bosnia and Herzegovina as a result of decisions taken at the Congress of Berlin. The Sultan may still have ruled in name but Kaiser Franz Joseph I was now the *de facto* ruler. Vienna's subsequent decision to annex the two provinces in 1908, stripping the Sultan of his nominal suzerainty, was a key moment in the events leading up to the outbreak of the First World War.

Andrić recognizes this great symbolic break. 'The year 1908,' he wrote in *The Bridge on the Drina*, 'brought with it great uneasiness and a sort of obscure threat which thenceforward never ceased to weigh upon the town.' Yet for Andrić Habsburg rule had already had a profound impact on Bosnia, especially on its economic and social life.

In fact this had begun much earlier, about the time of the building of the railway line and the first years of the new century. With the rise in prices and the incomprehensible but always perceptible fluctuations of government paper, dividends and exchanges, there was more and more talk of politics.

Andrić had a nuanced approach to the Austro-Hungarian occupation. He argued that it led to much needed modernization and economic renewal. His interpretation has not always found favour among critics from both Bosnia and Serbia. Yet Andrić was no slavish supporter of the Habsburgs. At key moments in the novel, he identifies future dangers which all the great power manoeuvring implied.

INTRODUCTION

At the time of the original occupation in 1878, Bosnia and Herzegovina was an extremely poor and conservative region. Earlier attempts by a reformist government in Istanbul to break the power of the begs and agas, the Ottoman provincial rulers and landowners, had largely failed. Much of the Catholic, Orthodox and the nominally free Muslim peasantry lived hand to mouth. People's circumstances in the more affluent towns were often precarious, too. Above all, the pace of life was glacial. So when in the wake of Franz Joseph's military occupation of Bosnia and Herzegovina the Habsburg Double Eagle built its nest in every town and in every village, the sudden invasion of hundreds upon hundreds of Habsburg bureaucrats had a severe psychological impact on the Muslims in particular. Men in neatly cut European uniforms brandished their ink and stamps, demanding endless information about the Empire's new peoples; poking their noses into the private lives and habits of families whose word until a few months earlier had been more powerful in Bosnia than even the Sultan's. Snapping orders in strange tongues, they counted houses and measured roads, or more frequently the land upon which new roads and railways would soon be built; they put up signs on buildings and signs on streets in foreign languages. They handed out letters telling young men to report for military service; they indulged in futile administrative rituals about which whole novels have been written; and everywhere they hung portraits of His Imperial and Royal Highness, Franz Joseph I.

Andrić recalls this period in *The Bridge on the Drina* when Muslim elders gather (on the bridge of course) to discuss Vienna's decision to hold a census:

As always, Alihodja was the first to lose patience.
'This does not concern the Schwabes'* faith, Muderis Effendi; it concerns their interests . . . We cannot see today what all this means, but we shall see it in a month or two, or perhaps a year. For, as the late lamented Shemsibeg Branković used to say: "The Schwabes' mines have long fuses!" This numbering of houses and men, or so I see it, is necessary for them because of some new tax, or else they are thinking

---

* The colloquial word for German speakers.

of getting men for forced labour or for their army, or perhaps both. If you ask me what we should do, this is my opinion. We have not got the army to rise at once in revolt. That God sees and all men know. But we do not have to obey all that we are commanded. No one need remember his number nor tell his age. Let them guess when each one of us was born.

As successive Sultans had discovered in the previous hundred years, Bosnia's Muslim landowners and administrators were very practised at passive resistance. Nonetheless, the rapid changes introduced by Vienna contributed to what a distinguished historian of Bosnia has called 'a widespread sense of alienation and fear among Bosnian Muslims'. The psychological distress occasioned by these changes was 'a major cause of Muslim emigration to Istanbul and other parts of the Ottoman Empire . . . during the era of the Double Eagle.'[1]

For all the imperialist disdain towards local traditions which the new regime evinced, Habsburg rule introduced significant investment in health, education and transport that benefited the local population. Progress, however, often fell victim to the competitive rancour between the Empire's two governments in Vienna and Budapest who had established an unwieldy system of joint control over Bosnia.

The new circumstances undoubtedly benefited young Ivo. With an absent father, his hard-working if barely literate mother dispatched her two-year-old son to his father's sister and her husband in the eastern part of Bosnia, specifically the small town of Višegrad. Ivo's uncle was a minor Habsburg official, meaning the family had an income and economic security of sorts. Where Travnik's population was predominantly Catholic or Muslim, the primarily Muslim town of Višegrad had a large Orthodox Serbian minority, especially in the surrounding villages. It was during these early years that Andrić learned the unique rhythms and vocabulary of Serbian folk tradition and Ottoman Bosnian together with the mythology and history of the region which he would later draw upon to fashion his great work, *The Bridge on the Drina*.

Without wanting to overstate their advantages, the Croats were the community that probably benefited most from the

Habsburg occupation. Croatia proper which bordered Bosnia and Herzegovina to the west and the north had long been integral to the Habsburg Empire and so Croats from both sides of the border were suddenly living in what was *de facto* the same state. A large number of the clerks, postmen and stationmasters who were new to Bosnia had arrived from Croatia. They, of course, spoke the local language. Before long the Catholic Church had received permission to establish an archbishopric in Sarajevo, or Vrhbosna, as the Croats called it by an even older name. The growth of Croatian influence also helped young Ivo. When he finished primary school, he returned to his mother in the Bosnian capital and received a scholarship from a Croatian cultural foundation to attend the Gymnasium there. The school itself was a product of Habsburg modernization.

It was at this school that Ivo Andrić met Gavrilo Princip. If Andrić came from modest circumstances, his Serb friend, two years younger, came from a positively deprived home as described by the Serb historian, Vladimir Dedijer:

In the old house the doors are small, and so very low that you can enter the house only by bowing your head. Inside it is dark. The house has no windows; instead of floor only beaten earth. To the left from the door is a stone bench on which a wooden barrel for water was standing . . . Smoke went through a *badza*, a hole in the roof above the open fireplace. The only light in the house came through it.[2]

Together Andrić and Princip belonged to a circle of radicals called Young Bosnia. There were similar radical groups operating in several parts of Europe at the time, most with the shared aim of throwing off imperial rule and replacing it with a nation state. Young Italy and Young Russia provided a particular inspiration for the group in Sarajevo.

The ideology of Young Bosnia was inchoate at best, infused with strains of socialism, anarchism, nationalism, and the Russian *narodniki*'s admiration of the peasantry. With his typical mixture of detachment and intimacy, Andrić looked back on the arrival of this new breed of young nationalists, submerged in political passions, in sleepy Višegrad. He was, of course, looking back at his own youth:

These were a new sort of young men, educated in various cities and states and under various influences. From the great cities, from the universities and schools which they attended, these young men came back intoxicated with that feeling of proud audacity with which his first and incomplete knowledge fills a young man, and carried away by ideas about the rights of peoples to freedom and of individuals to enjoyment and dignity. With every summer vacation they brought back with them free-thinking views on social and religious questions and an enthusiastically revived nationalism which recently, especially after the Serbian victories in the Balkan wars, had grown to a universal conviction and, in many of these youths, to a fanatical desire for action and personal sacrifice.

But in Bosnia, this is where it started to get really complicated. Young Bosnia included members of all four confessions – Orthodoxy, Catholicism, Islam and Judaism – but the majority was Serb. United in their antipathy towards Habsburg rule, they were sometimes divided by different perceptions of where liberation from the Austrian overlord might lead. Yugoslavism had emerged in Serbia and among Croats during the nineteenth century – the idea that you could unite all southern Slavs (excepting Bulgarians who already had their own state) in one country. But whereas Croatia and Bosnia were under foreign occupation, their neighbour to the east, Serbia, was an independent kingdom and the bulk of the Young Bosnians, who were Orthodox, i.e. Serbs, believed that Serbia would play the role that Piedmont had played in unifying Italy.

So at the outset, different communities conceived the Yugoslav idea in different ways which would prove problematic in the future. Nonetheless, if one could argue that Ivo Andrić supported any ideology, it was Yugoslavism and it was at the Gymnasium in Sarajevo in the run-up to the First World War that he absorbed this. Fortunately for literature, he was obsessed by ideas and writing and less inclined to engage in conspiratorial activities than his schoolfriends like Princip. Andrić had long departed Sarajevo to study in Krakow, southern Poland, via Zagreb and Vienna, when a conspiratorial Serbian nationalist group, the Black Hand, provided Young Bosnia with the weapons that would kill Archduke Franz Ferdinand on 28 June 1914 in Sarajevo.

Although not directly connected to the assassination, Andrić
was arrested in Split in Croatia on his way back to Sarajevo
and spent the next three years in Austro-Hungarian prisons, an
experience which he would often visit in his writing both figura-
tively and literally. He had also seemingly undergone a change
in his political attitude. Before the war, he had engaged in
political, philosophical and literary debate. True, he was careful
to couch any political messages that infused his early prose in
metaphors sufficiently complex to fool the dunderheads of the
Imperial censors but not the careful reader. Now, Andrić began
the process of distancing his stories from contemporary political events. Furthermore, his own political engagement faded
quickly. Andrić's one steadfast commitment was to the idea of
Yugoslavia and with the formation of the Kingdom of Serbs,
Croats and Slovenes (SHS) in December 1918 that wish was
fulfilled. Never mind that the Yugoslav royal family was actually Serbian and the Croats and Slovenes would quickly tire of
the centralization of political and economic power in Belgrade
which characterized the first Yugoslav entity.

Despite its many faults, Andrić appeared committed to supporting this first Yugoslavia as he would the second communist
version after the Second World War. In the 1920s, he secured a
position in the Yugoslav Foreign Ministry and represented his
country in many capitals and provincial centres from Rome,
Trieste and Bucharest to Graz, Geneva and Berlin. His favour-
ite posting was to Madrid where he was able to indulge in his
boundless passion for the work of Goya. Indeed, there is some
evidence to suggest that as a writer Andrić hoped to achieve for
literature that which Goya had for art.

In an amusing satire published to acclaim in Belgrade, the
author, Svetislav Basara, speculates that Andrić exploited his
several chronic lung conditions (including tuberculosis) in order
to advance his progress around the consuls and embassies of
Europe:

As soon as Andrić complained to the Ministry of Foreign Affairs of the
Kingdom of SHS about the climate at his posting, he was transferred to
a place whose climate was not necessarily any better than the previous
one but was nonetheless a place that Andrić was keen to visit . . . The

history of Andrić's illnesses is in fact a travelogue. His brilliant career left a much deeper impression on the world of clinical pathology than it did on diplomacy.[3]

Scurrilous and unfair though this assessment might be, it does point to a truth about Andrić. He used his natural intelligence and diligence to succeed as a diplomat while devoting his extensive spare time to writing and absorbing as much as he could about European culture and literature. During the Austrian occupation of Bosnia he taught himself German with the help of the famous small yellow paperbacks of Reclam, the publishing house which to this day produces cheap versions of German and world literature, a fact he references in *The Bridge on the Drina*. But he also learned Polish, Italian, Spanish, Romanian and French and was able to read and translate from Russian and English.

These influences, along with the very specific language of his Bosnian homeland and Serbian and Croatian literary traditions, are evident throughout his writing. In some of the close descriptive passages in *The Bridge on the Drina* there are echoes of *The Magic Mountain* by Thomas Mann, a writer whom Andrić admired hugely. But he succeeds in blending these European traditions effortlessly with the cadences and vocabulary of the Bosnian language's mixed heritage.

Andrić understood Bosnia as a country where East and West meet and it is surely no coincidence that the image of the bridge is probably the most persistent metaphor throughout his work. In 1925 he published his story 'The Bridge at Žepa' – Žepa was another small town in eastern Bosnia – which in many respects anticipates his great novel by almost two decades. Indeed, in 1933 he published an essay entitled 'Bridges':

Of all the things that people strive to achieve or build during their lives, I can think of nothing better or more valuable than bridges. They are more important than houses; more sacred and more useful than churches. They belong to everyone and are of use to everyone, carefully constructed at a place where you encounter the greatest number of human needs, more durable than other buildings and never in the service of anything secret or evil . . .

In the end, everything that speaks to our life – thoughts, efforts, observations, smiles, words, sighs – all these push towards the other side of the river to which they are directed as towards a goal – and only on the far bank does life acquire its real meaning. Everything has something that must be overcome or bridged: disorder, death or meaninglessness. Because everything is transition, the bridge whose ends become lost in eternity, and by comparison all earthly bridges are mere children's toys, pale symbols. AND ALL OUR HOPE LIES ON THE OTHER SIDE.

Andrić failed to convince everyone of his perception of Bosnia as a bridge between East and West but there is hope and optimism evident in his literature that is often obscured by the bleakness of much of his vision.

Andrić's influence within the Foreign Ministry accelerated after Yugoslavia's proto-fascist Prime Minister, Milan Stojadinović, appointed him head of its political section, the most senior position in the civil service. If subsequent accusations of Andrić being politically compromised hold true then it is in this period (1935–41) that much of the evidence lies. Apart from his involvement with plans to annex Albania, there was his support for Stojadinović's policy of cosying up to Hitler's Germany. Against that was the ever starker evidence that Britain and France and then, following the Molotov–Ribbentrop pact, Stalin's Russia, clearly had no intention of coming to anybody's aid in Central and South-Eastern Europe. With Germany's rapidly developing military might, Andrić believed with some justification that the only way of preserving Yugoslavia was to ensure that his country did not antagonize Hitler.

Andrić probably did not understand that the thinking of his Prime Minister, Stojadinović, had evolved to such a degree that he was giving up on Yugoslavia and planning a secret deal with Italy to carve up large parts of Croatia which would fall under Rome's control and create instead a Greater Serbia. And at this point the British did intervene, persuading the Prince Regent Paul to force Stojadinović's resignation and bring together leading Serb and Croat politicians to bolster Yugoslavia's domestic integrity. This was a signal to Hitler that Britain's influence over Yugoslavia was suddenly growing. 'In order to convince Berlin that the removal of Stojadinović was for purely internal Yugoslav reasons and did not signal a move away from Berlin,' wrote Michael Martens in his exemplary biography of Andrić, 'Paul hit upon a persuasive argument: he would send Stojadinović's top man and most trusted adviser as Yugoslav Ambassador to Hitler – Ivo Andrić.'

Martens describes the preposterous courtly uniform which Andrić was obliged to wear when presenting his credentials to Hitler. Later Andrić spoke only very rarely about his encounters with the Nazi leader but he did say that what struck him most about that first meeting was that 'his hand was cold and a little damp'. Martens continues the story:

Only later did he learn . . . that Hitler was possibly already ill at the time. 'And still later, as I remembered this meeting and that handshake, I had the following thought: perhaps he, the merciless and aggressive dictator, was more a product of his illness than his ideas . . .' [4]

Andrić also got to know other key figures in the Nazi leadership including some of the leading cultural apologists for Hitler's regime. The Germans considered Andrić to be a highly competent and largely disinterested interlocutor although Andrić would almost certainly have argued that his sole loyalty during this period was to his country.

There followed perhaps the greatest stroke of luck in Andrić's life. When the new Yugoslav government finally agreed with Andrić's assessment that the two countries should enter into a formal pact (meaning that Yugoslavia would *de facto* have joined the Axis), Prince Regent Paul sent a trusted middleman to negotiate the deal, bypassing Andrić who in terms of protocol should have been Berlin's interlocutor. With a little bit of spin when the communists took over after the war, Andrić did little to counter the idea that he had objected to the deal. The Nazi–Yugoslav pact was never implemented as a coup in Belgrade led to Prince Paul's fall. As a consequence, Hitler decided to invade Yugoslavia in early April 1941.

The Germans offered Andrić, whom they admired, the opportunity to escape to Switzerland where he might have been able to spend the war in peace. But again, to his subsequent credit, Andrić refused and instead returned to Belgrade, soon to be bombarded, invaded and occupied by the very people with whom the writer had just spent two very intense years. Over the next three years, he stayed either in the very centre of Belgrade (a stone's throw from Belgrade's great Art Deco icon, the Moskva Hotel) or in Sokobanja, a small town in eastern Serbia surrounded by gorgeous countryside. In these two places with remarkable self-discipline and as unspeakable brutality swirled around him, Andrić wrote the trilogy at whose centre was *The Bridge on the Drina*. First in the trilogy was another great novel, *The Travnik Chronicle*, better known in English as either *The Bosnian Chronicle* or by its original subtitle *The Days of the Consuls*. The final novel, *The Woman from Sarajevo*, is to my mind one of his bleakest works and that is saying something. Regardless of how one views Andrić, this endeavour was an act of extraordinary single-mindedness.

*

The Bridge on the Drina spans four hundred years. On first reading, it can strike the reader as a disconnected chronicle of events. Indeed, some critics have suggested that the book is little more than a series of short stories. But a slow meditative reading of this engrossing novel uncovers manifold themes, moods and characters which connect to one another in surprising ways.

As an inanimate object, it is probably inappropriate to consider the bridge as a character even if at times it seems to come alive. Yet the bridge certainly frames and guides the entire book. From the start of the novel, Andrić focuses on its very centre:

. . . where it widened out into two completely equal terraces placed symmetrically on either side of the roadway and making it twice its normal width. This was the part of the bridge known as the *kapia*. Two buttresses had been built on each side of the central pier which had been splayed out towards the top, so that to right and left of the roadway there were two terraces daringly and harmoniously projecting outwards from the straight line of the bridge over the noisy green waters far below. The two terraces were about five paces long and the same in width and were boarded . . . by a stone parapet. Otherwise, they were open and uncovered. That on the right as one came from town was called the *sofa*.

It is here on the *kapia* and the stone seats of the *sofa* that so many of the events, intrigues, rumours, flirtations and deaths take place. The *kapia* exerts a fascination on all who visit or pass by it. Apart from the opening chapters, we watch from the bridge a variety of characters confront, overcome and succumb to the challenges which the different stages of life present. As politics, tradition and mythology shift so do the opportunities and pitfalls, although a certain essence runs through the text like the Drina itself.

Despite its long span, the chronological framework of the novel is fairly straightforward. The first half of the book takes place during the Ottoman period stretched across some 350 years. The second half from Chapter XI onwards deals with the much shorter period from the consolidation of Austro-Hungarian power following the Congress of Berlin until the outbreak of the First World War in 1914, which of course was triggered by Franz Ferdinand's assassination. Višegrad, the small town where the bridge crosses the River Drina, is one of the first victims of that war.

The novel begins with the story of Mehmed Pasha Sokollu, Grand Vizier of the Ottoman Empire (1565–79), the man who decides to build the bridge. It ends with its partial destruction in 1914 when a huge amount of explosives which the Austrian military built into the structure is detonated after a Serbian shell hits the target.

Sokollu was an extraordinary figure. He was born to a poor Serbian peasant family in eastern Bosnia in a village on a tributary of the Drina not far to the south of Višegrad. Andrić dates the beginning of the story from 1516 when as a ten-year-old boy, Sokolović, as the Serbs know him, was swept up in the *devşirme* or 'blood tax', the Ottoman cull of Christian boys who were forced to convert to Islam and grew up as loyal servants to the Sultan in his military or civil service. Sokollu never forgets that first trip to Istanbul and the surly, slow ferryman responsible for the young lad's traumatic crossing of the troubled Drina. Unlike many boys caught up in the blood tax (while on one level they were obviously victims, on another level the *devşirme* offered potentially extraordinary advancement, wealth and power as in his case), Sokollu wanted to give something back to his home region. His idea was that the bridge at Višegrad over the fast-moving Drina would be a link between the East and West. At the time, the Ottoman Empire under the direction of Suleyman the Magnificent had been conquering large parts of the Balkans and even Central Europe. So the bridge was in part something to link different parts of the Ottoman Empire, in part a tool to aid its expansion. But it was also intended to benefit the people of eastern Bosnia.

Children dominate the opening of the story, including a legend still widespread today. According to this, every night a mischievous spirit, or *vila*, would undo the work of the bridge's stonemason to prevent its completion. To placate the spirit, the mason realized he would have to immure two peasant twins still at their mother's breast into the structure of the bridge. The mason installed a little grate so that the mother could continue to feed the imprisoned children.

While youth defines the opening of the story, death and one ageing man, Alihodja Mutevelić, closes the novel. Some Bosnian critics have argued that Andrić's characterization of the country's Muslims is universally negative. But although Alihodja is not a particularly likeable character, he makes ever more acute observations, rather like a Greek chorus. For all the modernization which the Austro-Hungarians introduced, the novel tracks how everything from 1878 was leading towards the most devastating explosion – literally in the case of the bridge and metaphorically with regard to the First World War.

Michael Martens highlights that Andrić wrote this novel in the middle of the Second World War as the Jews from Salonika and Skopje were being sent via Belgrade to their ultimate destination in Auschwitz. The cattle trucks were moving on a Balkan rail network largely constructed by the Austrians. In the novel Alihodja makes one of the most chillingly accurate observations when the railway comes to Višegrad: 'The time will come when the Schwabes will make you ride where you don't want to go and where you never even dreamt of going.'

Andrić was lucky to survive the Nazi occupation of Serbia.

But he was equally fortunate not to fall foul of the new communist regime which assumed power after the war. The second Yugoslavia experienced an extremely bloody birth as the Communist party meted out retribution in the wake of four years of occupation and brutal civil war. Despite his association with Stojadinović, Andrić could boast of an association with Princip and Young Bosnia while his friendship with leading cultural figures of the new regime also offered him a certain protection. Marshal Tito, the undisputed dictator of communist Yugoslavia, never cared for Andrić and his work. But as the writer's fame grew thanks to his trilogy of novels, Tito recognized that in a turbulent world, especially after Yugoslavia broke with the rest of the communist bloc in 1948, Andrić was a valuable element in what is now called 'soft power'. Once he was awarded the Nobel Prize, primarily for *The Bridge on the Drina*, in 1961, his position as one of communist Yugoslavia's greatest talents was unassailable.

Since the appalling destruction of Bosnia, in particular, as Yugoslavia collapsed into war in the 1990s, several leading critics from Bosnia have denounced Ivo Andrić and his work. The most forthright of these has suggested that Andrić laid the ideological ground for the genocide of Bosnia's Muslims between 1992 and 1995. Much but not all of this is based on two pieces of work by Andrić. The first is his hastily written dissertation from 1924 which he needed to complete in order to continue within the Foreign Ministry. If anything justifies the criticism, it is this document. The second is a short story of just nine pages entitled *Letter from the Year 1920*, in which Andrić describes Bosnia as a country that is drenched in hate and argues that this hatred is part of its unchangeable essence. Except for one brief hint, it does not, however, imply that Islam is any more responsible for this than Bosnia's other three confessions. But even a cursory reading reveals that these are not Andrić's thoughts. They are those of a doctor from a mixed Sarajevo marriage in the aftermath of the First World War. Andrić intends this ironically as becomes clear when having 'escaped' Bosnia, the doctor is eventually killed tending patients on the Republican side in the Spanish Civil War. 'Thus ended the life of the man who was on the run from hatred,' he concludes. This is no condemnation of

INTRODUCTION

Muslim traditions in Bosnia or anywhere else. It is a condemnation of us all.

Misha Glenny

1   Robert J. Donia, *Islam under the Double Eagle: The Muslims of Bosnia and Hercegovina, 1878–1914*, New York, 1981, p. 182.
2   Vladimir Dedijer, *The Road to Sarajevo*, London, 1967, p. 187.
3   Svetislav Basara, *Kontraendorfin*, Belgrade, 2020, pp. 22–23.
4   Michael Martens, *Im Brand der Welten: Ivo Andrić. Ein europäisches Leben*, Vienna, 2019, p. 201, p. 205.

SELECT BIBLIOGRAPHY

There are very few book-length studies of Andrić in English but the most important is Celia Hawkesworth's *Ivo Andrić: Bridge Between East and West* (Bloomsbury, London, 2000).

A more academic study which focuses on Andrić's relationship with Yugoslavia is Vanita Singh Mukerji, *Ivo Andrić: A Critical Biography* (McFarland, Jefferson, NC and London, 1990).

The most recent and thorough biography of Andrić is in German: Michael Martens, *Im Brand der Welten: Ein europäisches Leben*, Paul Zsolnay, Vienna, 2019, which is also published in Serbo-Croat.

In English the bulk of critical work on Andrić is to be found in academic journals. One of the most succinct which engages with the political controversy concerning Andrić since the Bosnian war of the 1990s is again by Celia Hawkesworth: *Ivo Andrić as Red Rag and Political Football* (The Slavonic and East European Review, Vol. 80, No. 2, April 2002), https://www.jstor.org/stable/4213436

On Bosnian, Yugoslav and Balkan history:

Bosnia: A Cultural History by Ivan Lovrenović, Saqi Books, London, 2001; New York University Press, 2001.

A Concise History of Bosnia by Cathie Carmichael, Cambridge University Press, 2015.

A History of Yugoslavia by Marie-Janine Calic, Purdue University Press, West Lafayette, IN, 2019.

Yugoslavia as History: Twice there was a Country, by John R. Lampe, Cambridge University Press, 2000.

The Balkans: Nationalism, War and the Great Powers, 1804–2012 by Misha Glenny, Granta, London, 2012.

The Balkans: From the End of Byzantium to the Present Day by Mark Mazower, Phoenix Press, London, 2002.

History of the Balkans, Vols 1 & 2, by Barbara Jelavich, Cambridge University Press, 1983.

CHRONOLOGY

DATE	AUTHOR'S LIFE	LITERARY CONTEXT
1875		
1876		Walt Whitman: *Memoranda During the War.* Herbert Spencer: *The Principles of Sociology.* George Eliot: *Daniel Deronda.*
1877		Ivan Turgenev: *Virgin Soil.*
1878		Henrik Ibsen: *A Doll's House.* Thomas Hardy: *The Return of the Native.*
1881		Eugen Kumičić: *Olga and Lina.*
1882		Ibsen: *An Enemy of the People.* Whitman: *Specimen Days.*
1883		Friedrich Nietzsche: *Thus Spake Zarathustra* (to 1892). Guy de Maupassant: *Une Vie.*
1884		Joris-Karl Huysmans: *À Rebours.* Maupassant: *Miss Harriet.* Ion Luca Caragiale: *The Lost Letter* (play). Émile Zola: *Germinal.*
1885		Silvije Kranjčević: *Folk Songs.* Alexander Herzen: *My Past and Thoughts.* Karl Marx: *Das Kapital* Vol. II (published posthumously).

Revolt against Ottoman rule in Herzegovina and Bosnia (to 1878). Ottoman state declares itself bankrupt.

Bulgarian uprising suppressed by Ottomans. Serbia and Montenegro declare war on the Ottoman Empire. First Ottoman constitution promulgated by Sultan Abdul Hamid II.

Russia joins war on Serbia's behalf.

Russian victory marks end of Russo-Turkish War. Treaty of Berlin: to counterbalance Russia's new influence in the Balkans, the great powers of Europe place Bosnia and Herzegovina – while still notionally part of the Ottoman Empire – under Austro-Hungarian occupation, prompting vigorous resistance from local Bosnian forces. Recognition of the newly independent states of Romania, Serbia and Montenegro. Bulgaria becomes a principality under nominal Ottoman sovereignty (achieving full independence in 1908). Britain acquires Cyprus. First Ottoman Parliament prorogued and constitution allowed to lapse.

Abdul Hamid II set ups the OPDA (Ottoman Public Debt Administration), a European controlled institution within the Ottoman treasury, to service government debt (to 1914).

Austro-Hungarian statesman Béni Kállay is appointed Common Finance Minister of Bosnia-Herzegovina (to 1903). Public works programme: factories developed, agriculture promoted, schools built. Nevertheless, Kállay fails to insulate his new domain from the growing nationalist movements of Croatian, Serbian and Yugoslav ('South Slav') peoples. Triple Alliance of Germany, Austria-Hungary and Italy.

Orient Express begins operating between Paris and Constantinople.

Sarajevo tramway opens, one of the oldest in Europe (electrified 1895). Serbo-Bulgarian War.

DATE	AUTHOR'S LIFE	LITERARY CONTEXT
1886		Nietzsche: *Beyond Good and Evil.* Ksaver Šandor Gjalski: *Under Old Roofs.*
1887		Gjalski: *In the Night.*
1888		Ante Kovačić: *In the Registrar's Office.* Anton Chekhov: 'The Steppe'.
1890		Josip Kozarac: *Dead Capital.* Knut Hamsun: *Hunger.* Ibsen: *Hedda Gabler.* Maupassant: *L'Inutile Beauté.*
1891		Janko Leskovar: *The Thought of Eternity.* Selma Lagerlöf: *Gösta Berling's Saga.* Aleksa Šantić: *Poems.* Leo Tolstoy: *The Kreutzer Sonata.* Oscar Wilde: *The Picture of Dorian Gray; Salome.* Hardy: *Tess of the D'Urbervilles.*
1892	Ivo Andrić is born (9 October) to Antun and Katarina Andrić in Travnik, Bosnia, during a visit to relatives. He is soon taken to the family home in Sarajevo.	Antun Matoš: 'The Power of Conscience'. Pyotr Kropotkin: *The Conquest of Bread.* Gerhart Hauptmann: *The Weavers* (play). Hugo von Hofmannsthal: *The Death of Titian.* Arthur Conan Doyle: *The Adventures of Sherlock Holmes.* Wilde: *Lady Windermere's Fan.* Maurice Maeterlinck: *Pelléas et Mélisande* (play).
1893		Josip Draženović: *Sketches from a Coastal Small Town Life.* Zola: *Le Docteur Pascal* concludes Rougon-Macquart series.
1894	Antun dies of tuberculosis, a hereditary burden of the Andrić family. Faced with penury, Katarina entrusts Ivo to his father's sister, Ana, and her husband, Ivan Matkovšćik, in Višegrad. They raise him in the Catholic faith, while his mother works in Sarajevo.	Kozarac: *Tena.* Hamsun: *Pan.* Ioan Slavici: *Mara* (to 1906).

CHRONOLOGY

Great Powers recognize Bulgarian unification with Ottoman province of Eastern Rumelia.

Wilhelm II dismisses Bismarck.

Franco-Russian Alliance. Gladstone's last ministry in Britain (to 1894).

Benz's four-wheel car.

Dreyfus case begins in France.

DATE	AUTHOR'S LIFE	LITERARY CONTEXT
1895		Vladimir Vidrić: *Equinox* (play).
		Richard Strauss's *Four Last Songs*.
		Henryk Sienkiewicz: *Quo Vadis*.
		Kálmán Mikszáth: *St Peter's Umbrella*.
		Theodor Fontane: *Effi Briest*.
		Frank Wedekind: *Earth Spirit*.
		Tolstoy: *Master and Man*.
		Wilde: *The Importance of Being Earnest*; *An Ideal Husband*.
		Sigmund Freud: *Studies on Hysteria*.
1896		Fontane: *The Poggenpuhl Family*.
		Anton Chekhov: *The Seagull*.
1897		Bram Stoker: *Dracula*.
		Schnitzler: *La Ronde*.
		August Strindberg: *Inferno*.
		Edmond Rostand: *Cyrano de Bergerac*.
1898		Josip Murn: *Fin de siècle* (series of poems).
		Stefan Żeromski: *The Labours of Sisyphus*.
		George Bernard Shaw: *Plays Pleasant and Unpleasant*.
		H. G. Wells: *The War of the Worlds*.
1899		Vjenceslav Novak: *The Last Stipančićs*.
		Oton Župančič: *The Goblet of Inebriation* (poems).
		Władysław Reymont: *The Promised Land*.
		Milorad J. Mitrović: *Book About Love* (poems).
		Henry James: *The Awkward Age*.
		Tolstoy: *Resurrection*.
1900		Milan Begović: *Boccadoro Book* (poems).
		Vladimir Nazor: *Slavic Legends*.
		Matoš: *New Fragments*.

CHRONOLOGY

Freud's *Studies on Hysteria* inaugurates psychoanalysis. Marconi demonstrates radio transmission. Lumière brothers' *cinématographe.*

Uprising in Crete against Ottoman rule.

Vienna Secession formed. Queen Victoria's Diamond Jubilee.

Assassination of Empress Elizabeth of Austria in Geneva. First German Navy Law: arms race with Britain begins. The Curies discover radium.

Planck's quantum theory.

DATE	AUTHOR'S LIFE	LITERARY CONTEXT
1900 cont.		Freud: *The Interpretation of Dreams*.
		Władysław Orkan: *Tenant Farmers*.
1901		Lagerlöf: *Jerusalem* (to 1902).
		Jovan Dučić: *Poems, Book 1*.
		Gabriele D'Annunzio: *Francesca da Rimini*.
		Stanisław Wyspiański: *The Wedding* (play).
		Anton Fogazzaro: *Little Old World*.
		Thomas Mann: *Buddenbrooks*.
		Strindberg: *The Dance of Death*.
		Chekhov: *Three Sisters*.
		Nietzsche: *The Will to Power*.
1902		Kranjčević: *Spasms* (poems).
		Šantić: *Emina* (poem).
		Ivo Vojnović: *Dubrovnik Trilogy*.
		Petar Kočić: *From the Mountain and Below the Mountain* (stories).
		Rainer Maria Rilke: *The Book of Pictures*.
		Kropotkin: *Mutual Aid: A Factor of Evolution*.
		Maxim Gorky: *The Lower Depths*.
		Joseph Conrad: *The Heart of Darkness*.
		James: *The Wings of the Dove*.
1903	Returns to his mother in Sarajevo and enrols at Great Sarajevo Gymnasium, the oldest secondary school in Bosnia, after receiving a stipend from the Croat cultural group Napredak (Progress).	Vidrić: *Dubrovnik Trilogy*. Ante Pavičić: *Waves of Thought and Emotion* (poems). Milan Rakić: *Poems* (to 1924, inspired by French Symbolism). Orkan: *In the Mountain Valleys*. Mitrović: *Commemorative Songs*. Hauptmann: *Rosa Bernd*.
1904		James: *The Golden Bowl*.
		Reymond: *The Peasants* (to 1909).
		Conrad: *Nostromo*.
		Wederkind: *Pandora's Box*.

CHRONOLOGY

HISTORICAL EVENTS

Death of Queen Victoria; accession of Edward VII.

Lenin: *What is to be done?* Balfour becomes Prime Minister in Britain (to 1905).

Stephan Burián von Rajecz replaces deceased Kállay as Common Finance Minister. Murder of Serbian king Aleksandar Obrenović; election of Peter I. Ilinden Uprising of Macedonians against the Ottoman Empire. Mass protests against Hungarian governor in Croatia. Wright brothers' first successful powered flight.

Entente Cordiale between Britain and France. Russo-Japanese War.

DATE	AUTHOR'S LIFE	LITERARY CONTEXT
1904 cont.		Chekhov: *The Cherry Orchard*. Kočić: *From the Mountain and Below the Mountain II* (stories).
1905		E. M. Forster: *Where Angels Fear to Tread*. Heinrich Mann: *Professor Unrat*.
1906		Janko Kamov: *The Drained Swamp* (to 1909). Lagerlöf: *The Wonderful Adventures of Nils*. John Galsworthy: *The Man of Property* (first volume of *The Forsyte Saga*). Shaw: *The Doctor's Dilemma*. Gorky: *The Mother*.
1907		Šantić: *Under the Fog* (verse dramatization). Vojislav Ilić: *Collected Poems* (published posthumously). Rilke: *New Poems* (to 1908). Conrad: *The Secret Agent*.
1908		Vladimir Nazor: *Veli Jože*. Župančič: *Duma* (poems). Dučić: *Poems, Book 2*. Żeromski: *The Wages of Sin*. Anatole France: *L'Île des Pingouins*. Arnold Bennett: *The Old Wives' Tale*.
1909	Following the Annexation Crisis and high treason trial in Zagreb, Andrić becomes a fierce advocate for the liberation of the South Slav peoples from the Austro-Hungarian Empire.	Matoš: *Tired Tales*. Milutin Nehajev: *Escape*. Vladimir Ćorović: *Serbian Folk Tales*. Andre Ady: *On the Chariot of Elijah*. Maeterlinck: *L'Oiseau bleu*. Marinetti's Futurist manifesto.
1910	Chosen as President of the Croatian Progressive Organization (CPO).	Matoš: 'Our People and Lands'. Kočić: *Howls from Snakes* (stories). Župančič: *The Blacksmith's Song* (poems).

C H R O N O L O G Y

First organized general strike in Bosnia-Herzegovina. Emerging Serbian intelligentsia press for a democratic government. Serb-Croat coalition in Croatia. First Russian Revolution.

Out of three major populations in Bosnia-Herzegovina (Muslims, Croats, Serbs) Muslims become the first to establish a political party – the Muslim National Organization (MNO), demanding religious and political autonomy under the sovereignty of the sultan. Austro-Serbian customs war – the 'Pig War' (to 1911). Algeciras Crisis: Austria-Hungary supports Germany against France. Launch of HMS *Dreadnought*, first modern battleship.

Universal suffrage for males over 24 introduced in Austrian territories. Founding of Serbian National Organization, which declares rights of Serbs to national sovereignty, self-determination, property rights and parliamentary rule. Russia joins Entente Cordiale (Britain and France) to form the Triple Entente. Picasso and Braque pioneer Cubism.

Critical year in the history of South Slavs. The Bomb Affair (May) leads to severing of relations between Serbia and Montenegro. Young Turk Revolution (July) brings a constitutional government – the Committee of Union and Progress – to power in the Ottoman Empire; Young Turk influence threatens to spread to Bosnia-Herzegovina. The MNO demand a constitution (Sept.). The Annexation Crisis: on 7 October, Austria-Hungary announces annexation of Bosnia-Herzegovina, officially ending the 125-year rule of Ottoman Empire and angering Muslims and Serbs, and alarming the Triple Entente and Triple Alliance. Montenegro and Serbia object; latter initiates secret discussions with Ottoman Empire to take action.
Ottoman Empire recognizes annexation on 26 February, in exchange for financial compensation. Serbia and Russia back down; Austria's annexation of Bosnia-Herzegovina is recognized by Great Powers. Student riots throughout empire. Zagreb treason trials: 53 Serbs put on trial in Croatia for collaborating with Serbia to form an independent state. Muslims of Bosnia-Herzegovina are granted cultural and religious autonomy. Pan-Slav Congress in Russia.

Constitution promulgated for Bosnia-Herzegovina. Bitter resentment among Serb and South Slav nationalists leads to formation of revolutionary groups such as Mlada Bosna ('Young Bosnia') dedicated to overthrowing Habsburg Empire, especially active in schools and universities. Government crushes peasant strikes. Albanian revolts against Ottoman rule (to 1912).

DATE	AUTHOR'S LIFE	LITERARY CONTEXT
1910 cont.		Forster: *Howards End*. Rilke: *The Notebooks of Malte Laurids Brigge*.
1911	Chosen as President of the new Serb-Croat Progressive Youth (SCPY). Publishes his first two poems, 'At Dusk' and 'Gentle and Good Moonlight', in *Bosanska vila*.	Ivan Kozarac: *Devil's Blood*. Conrad: *Under Western Eyes*. Šantić: *Poems*. Stanislav Vinaver: *Mjeća*.
1912	Elected as one of the leaders of the student strike committee in Sarajevo. On 29 February he gives a moving speech at Sarajevo's railway station, in which he praises the Young Croat Luka Jukić for his attempt to assassinate Ban Cuvaj. Begins studies at the Royal University in Zagreb, where he promptly joins student activists and takes part in demonstrations.	Josip Kosor: *Passion's Furnace* (play). Veljko Petrović: *Patriotic Poems*. Svetozar Ćorović: *The Despot* (play). Žeromski: *The Faithful River*. Carl Jung: *The Psychology of the Unconscious*. France: *Les Dieux ont soif*.
1913	Transfers to the University of Vienna, where he attends lectures in history, philosophy and South Slavic literature, but the city's climate takes a toll on his health. After contracting pneumonia, he asks to be transferred on medical grounds.	Nazor: *Istrian Tales*. Šantić: *On the Old Hearths*. Alain-Fournier: *Le Grand Meaulnes*. Gorky: *My Childhood*. D. H. Lawrence: *Sons and Lovers*. Marcel Proust: *À la recherche du temps perdu* (to 1927).
1914	Completes his fourth semester at the Faculty of Philosophy at Jagiellonian University in Cracow. Publishes six prose poems in the anthology *Hrvatska mlada Lirika* (New Croatian lyrical verse). Learning of the Archduke's assassination, he decides to return home. On 4 August, a week after Austria-Hungary declares war on Serbia, he is arrested and jailed in Split, and moved to a prison in Maribor. Plagued by tuberculosis in cramped and dark prison quarters, Andrić intensively writes prose poems.	James Joyce: *Dubliners*. Lawrence: *The Prussian Officer*. France: *La Révolte des Anges*. Shaw: *Pygmalion*.

CHRONOLOGY

The Diet passes law guaranteeing peasant serfs long-term loans for voluntary redemption, but they are still obligated to deliver a third of their harvest to the landlord. Moroccan Crisis (July–Sept.) brings Europe to the brink of war. Formation of the Black Hand, a secret military organization in Serbia aiming to unite South Slavs in a 'Greater Serbia'.

Political tension on the rise among progressive youth in South Slavic lands. In an attempt to bring stability to Croatia, the Ban (viceroy) Slavko Cuvaj is given emergency powers to establish order. Students strike throughout Croatia. Young Bosnians (made up of Serbs and Croats) pour onto Sarajevo streets in anti-Hungarian demonstrations, joined by Muslims (Feb.). Ten students are expelled from school. Tormented by police, the Serb-Croat Progressive Youth (SCPY) dissipates. Tension heightened by First Balkan War: Serbia, Montenegro, Bulgaria and Greece attack Ottoman Empire. The *Titanic* sinks.

Second Balkan War breaks out over division of Macedonia: Austria-Hungary alarmed by Serbian victory. In May, the governor of Bosnia-Herzegovina, Oskar Potiorek, declares a state of emergency, dissolves parliament, closes Serb cultural associations and suspends civil courts.

Archduke Francis Ferdinand, the heir to the Habsburg throne, is assassinated on a trip to Sarajevo (28 June) by Gavrilo Princip, a member of Mlada Bosna, with some assistance from inside Serbia. Austria-Hungary declares war on Serbia one month later; outbreak of World War One. Austrian invasion into Serbia.

IVO ANDRIĆ

DATE	AUTHOR'S LIFE	LITERARY CONTEXT
1915	Released from prison in March due to lack of evidence, Andrić is exiled to a Franciscan monastery in Ovčarevo, where he meets and befriends Fra Alojzije Perčinlić. He spends his time reading the monastic chronicles on the history of local Catholic and Orthodox churches, which later inspires his doctoral thesis.	Župančič: *Ciciban* (poems). Tomáš Masaryk: *The Problem of Small Nations in the European Crisis.* Franz Kafka: *The Metamorphosis.* Ford Madox Ford: *The Good Soldier.* Lawrence: *The Rainbow.*
1916	Transferred to Zenica prison.	Jan Kasprowicz: *The Book of the Poor.* Ivana Brlić-Mažuranić: *Croatian Fairy Tales.* Joyce: *The Portrait of the Artist as a Young Man.*
1917	Andrić is finally freed when Emperor Charles I issues amnesty to political prisoners (July). Returns to Visegrád. A couple of hospital stints follow ongoing ill health.	Dragutin Domjanić: *Statuettes and Popular Songs.* Miroslav Krleža: *Three Symphonies.* Milutin Bojić: *Poems of Pain and Pride.* Ulderiko Donadini: *Whirlwind.* Freud: *Introduction to Psychoanalysis.*
1918	Founds Yugoslav journal *Književni jug* (Literary South) with other nationalist writers. Enrols in the Faculty of Philosophy at Zagreb University to complete his studies. Publishes *Ex Ponto*, a lyrical prose work written during his internment.	Wacław Berent: *Stoning Alive.* Srdan Tucic: *The Liberators.* Hermann Sudermann: *Lithuanian Stories.* Tristan Tzara's Dada manifesto. Oswald Spengler: *The Decline of the West* (to 1923).
1919	In need of a greater income to sustain himself and his ageing family, Andrić takes up a secretarial position in the Ministry of Religion in Beograd.	Nehajev: *Big City.* Milutin Uskoković: *Newcomers.* Karl Kraus: *The Last Days of Mankind* (play). Somerset Maugham: *Home and Beauty.*
1920	Publishes *Nemiri* (Unrest). Begins five-year association with literary and political journal *Nova Europa* (New Europe). Assigned as consular to Royal	Antun Šimić: *Metamorphosis* (poems). Tin Ujević: *Cry of Silver.* György Lukács: *The Theory of the Novel.*

CHRONOLOGY

Fall of Premysl to Russians (March) after 133-day siege. Gallipoli landings (April). Italy enters war on side of Entente (May). Austro-Hungarian forces occupy Serbia and capture Belgrade (Oct.). Bulgaria joins Central Powers and immediately attacks Serbia. Surrender of Serbia and Macedonia (Dec.).

Romania allies with Entente. Central Powers occupy Bucharest. Death of Franz Joseph, aged 86; succeeded by Karl I (King Karl IV) of Hungary. Lloyd George becomes British Prime Minister (to 1922).

February Revolution in Russia. Abdication of Nicholas II (March). Corfu Declaration (July) calls for a unified Yugoslav state (the Kingdom of Serbs, Croats and Slovenes) after the war. Bolshevik (October) Revolution (the Tsar and his family are assassinated the following year). Russia pulls out of war. Civil war in Russia and Ukraine (to 1921). Battle of Caporetto: Italian army decisively defeated. United States enters war.

President Wilson's Fourteen Points for world peace (Jan.). Allies recognize territorial aspirations of Czechs, South Slavs and Romanians, all of whom announce their secession (Oct.). Bosnia-Herzegovina throws off Habsburg rule: creation of the Kingdom of Serbs, Croats and Slovenes, colloquially known as Yugoslavia ('Land of the South Slavs'). November Revolution in Germany; abdication of Wilhelm II.

Treaty of Versailles (June) imposes punitive peace terms on Germany. Treaty of St Germain (Sept.): Austro-Hungarian Empire dissolved. Short-lived socialist uprisings in Germany and Italy; socialist city administration in Vienna (to 1927). Dismantling of the Ottoman Empire; Turkish War of Independence. Bauhaus school of design founded in Germany. First non-stop transatlantic flight.

Creation of Little Entente with Czechoslovakia and Romania as part of the French security system.
League of Nations founded.

xxxvii

DATE	AUTHOR'S LIFE	LITERARY CONTEXT
1920 cont.	Yugoslav Mission at the Vatican. In Italy, he writes some of his finest stories, such as 'The Journey of Alija Djerzeles', 'Mustafa Madžar' and 'The Bridge on the Žepa'. Transferred to Yugoslav consulate in Bucharest.	Vinaver: *Pantologija*; *Manifesto of the Expressionist School.* Miloš Crnjanski: *The Journal of Čarnojević*; *The Explanations of Sumatra.* Wells: *The Outline of History.*
1921		Dinko Šimunović: *Youth.* Kosor: *The Invincible Ship* (play). Rastko Petrović: *The Burlesque of Mr Perun the God of Thunder.* Luigi Pirandello: *Six Characters in Search of an Author.* Petrović: *Changing Spring* (stories). Aldous Huxley: *Chrome Yellow.* Maugham: *The Circle.*
1922	Sent to consulate in Trieste.	Joyce: *Ulysses.* Donadini: *Bogeyman.* T. S. Eliot: *The Waste Land.* Katherine Mansfield: *The Garden Party.* Virginia Woolf: *Jacob's Room.* Andrei Bely: *Petersburg.* Breton: *Surrealist Manifesto.* Karel Čapek: *The Markropulos Affair.*
1923	Because of continuing bouts of tuberculosis he requests a transfer to consulate in Graz. Loses his job on arrival due to the new stipulation of a doctoral degree.	Jaroslav Hašek: *The Good Soldier Švejk.* Šimunović: *Vinčić Family.* Ksaver Šandor Gjalski: *The Love of Lieutenant Milić.* Rilke: *The Duino Elegies*; *Sonnets to Orpheus.* Italo Svevo: *Confessions of Zeno.* Shaw: *Saint Joan.*
1924	Influential friends intervene. Andrić is retained in consulate as a day worker, while he focuses on his Ph.D. at Graz University. Completes dissertation on spiritual life in Bosnia under the Ottoman Empire; awarded a Doctor of Philosophy.	Šantić: *Poems.* Žeromski: *Seedtime.* Vladimir Stanimirović: *Exodus: The Albanian Odyssey in Three Acts.* Antoni Lange: *Miranda.* T. Mann: *The Magic Mountain.* Ford: *Parade's End* (to 1928).

CHRONOLOGY

HISTORICAL EVENTS

The Vidovan Constitution is approved – the first constitution of the Kingdom of Serbs, Croats and Slovenes.

USSR formally established.

Proclamation of the Republic of Turkey with Kemal Atatürk as the first President.

First Labour government in Britain, with Ramsay MacDonald as Prime Minister. Death of Lenin.

DATE	AUTHOR'S LIFE	LITERARY CONTEXT
1924 cont.	Transferred to the Ministry of Foreign Affairs in Belgrade. Publishes *Stories I (Pripovetke I)* in a prestigious collection of the Serbian Literary Guild (Srpska književna zadruga).	
1925	Mother dies.	Fran Galović: *From My Hills.* August Cesarec: *The Emperor's Kingdom.* Woolf: *Mrs Dalloway.* Kafka: *The Trial.* F. Scott Fitzgerald: *The Great Gatsby.*
1926	Named Vice Consul in Marseilles, before being assigned to consulate general in Paris. While in France he travels and researches the Paris archives, material he later uses for *Bosnian Chronicle (Travnička hronika)*. Becomes a member of the Serbian Academy of Arts and Sciences.	Đuro Sudeta: *Houses in the Valley.* Milan Begović: *Adventurer at the Door.* Viktor Car Emin: *New Struggle.* Kafka: *The Castle.* Wells: *The World of William Clissold.*
1927	Aunt dies.	V. Ćorović: *Bosnia and Herzegovina* (history). Woolf: *To the Lighthouse.* Joseph Roth: *The Wandering Jews.* Herman Hesse: *Steppenwolf.*
1928	Leaves France for new post as Vice Consul to Yugoslav legation in Madrid. He is especially inspired by Spain, writing essays on Goya and Simon Bolivar, and begins *The Devil's Yard (Prokleta avlija)*.	Stanimirović: *The Field Hospital* (poems). Gustav Krklec: *Trip to Heaven* (poems). Cesarec: *Golden Youth.* Huxley: *Point Counter Point.* Eugene O'Neill: *Strange Interlude.*
1929	Sent to Brussels as secretary of the Yugoslav legation for Belgium and Luxembourg.	Eric Maria Remarque: *All Quiet on the Western Front.* Robert Graves: *Goodbye to All That.* Alfred Döblin: *Berlin Alexanderplatz.* Ernest Hemingway: *A Farewell to Arms.* Jean Cocteau: *Les Enfants terribles.*

Locarno Pact guarantees existing Franco-German frontier.
Hitler: *Mein Kampf.*

General Strike in Britain. Germany admitted to League of Nations.
Television demonstrated by J. L. Baird.

The Jazz Singer – first 'talkie'.

Kellogg-Briand Pact, outlawing war and providing for peaceful settlement of
disputes. First Five-Year Plan in USSR. Stalin *de facto* dictator and object of
nationwide cult.

Suspension of the constitution by King Alexander Karadjordjević, and
declaration of royal dictatorship; SHS is renamed 'Kingdom of Yugoslavia'.
Division of Bosnia and Herzegovina into four administrative districts called
banovine. Founding of Croat fascist Ustaša movement. Wall Street Crash:
beginning of worldwide Depression. Forcible collectivization of agriculture
in USSR.

DATE	AUTHOR'S LIFE	LITERARY CONTEXT
1930	Posted to Geneva as a secretary of the permanent delegation of the Kingdom of Yugoslavia at the League of Nations.	Sudeta: *Mor.* Freud: *Civilisation and Its Discontents.* Roth: *Job.* Robert Musil: *The Man Without Qualities* (to 1924). Noel Coward: *Private Lives.*
1931	Made head of the Political Department of the Ministry of Foreign Affairs. Publishes *Stories (Pripovetke)* in Serbian Literary Guild (Srpska književna zadruga).	Vladimir Nazor: *Fantasies and Grotesque* (poems).
1932		Krleža: *The Return of Philip Latinowicz.* Ujević: *Cry on the Promenade.* Dučić: *The Treasure of Emperor Radovan: A Book About Destiny.* Roth: *The Radetzky March.* Huxley: *Brave New World.* Wells: *The Work, Wealth and Happiness of Mankind.*
1933		V. Ćorović: *History of Yugoslavia.* Slavko Kolar: *Either we are or not.* Cesarec: *Fugitives.*
1934		Vjekoslav Majer: *Songs of a Worried European.* Nikola Šop: *Jesus and My Shadow.* Halldór Laxness: *Independent People.* Miklós Bánffy: *The Transylvanian Trilogy* (to 1940).
1935		Đuro Arnold: *Threshold of Eternity.*
1936	Publishes *Stories II (Pripovetke II)* in Serbian Literary Guild (Srpska književna zadruga).	Krleža: 'Balade Petrice Kerempuha'. Klaus Mann: *Mephisto.* Kolar: *We are for justice.*
1937	Named assistant to Milan Stojadinović, the minster of foreign affairs and prime minister.	Ivo Kozarčanin: *Someone Else's Wife; Man Alone.* Nabokov: *The Gift.*

CHRONOLOGY

Introduction of sham democratic system in Yugoslavia.

Nazis largest party in German Reichstag. Lausanne Conference: German war reparations suspended indefinitely by Allies and repudiated by Hitler in 1933. Geneva Conference on disarmament (to 1934). Famine in Ukraine (to 1934). Cockcroft and Walton split the atom.

Hitler becomes German Chancellor and is granted dictatorial powers. Germany and Japan leave League of Nations. US President Franklin Roosevelt announces 'New Deal'.

Death of President Hindenburg; German plebiscite approves Hitler taking sole power as Führer. Night of the Long Knives: Hitler purges opponents. Comintern calls for formation of 'Popular Front' against Fascism. Murder of Kirov (Dec.) gives Stalin pretext for launching his 'Great Terror'. Rome Protocols signed by Italy, Austria and Hungary.

Nuremberg Laws in Germany debar Jews from public life. Germany openly rearming.
Popular Front wins election in Spain, prompting Fascist military coup and Spanish Civil War (to 1939). Popular Front win French election; Léon Blum becomes first socialist premier. Hitler marches into demilitarized Rhineland. Rome–Berlin Axis signed. Moscow show trials (to 1938). Abdication crisis in Britain.
German attack on Basque city of Guernica.

DATE	AUTHOR'S LIFE	LITERARY CONTEXT
1938		Krleža: *The Edge of Reason.* Oskar Davičo: *Poems.* Dobriša Cesarić: *Saved World.* Roth: *The Emperor's Tomb.* Evelyn Waugh: *Scoop.* Jean-Paul Sartre: *Nausea.* Jean Giraudoux: *Ondine.*
1939	Named Yugoslavia's minister to Germany. Becomes a regular member of the Croatian Academy of Arts and Sciences.	Davičo: *Hana* (poems). Emin: *Hero of the Sea.* Joyce: *Finnegans Wake.* Arthur Koestler: *The Gladiator.*
1940		Isidora Sekulić: *The Chronicle of a Small Town Cemetery.* Vjekoslav Kaleb: *On the Rock.* Greene: *The Power and the Glory.* Hemingway: *For Whom the Bell Tolls.*
1941	After Axis invasion of Yugoslavia, the German government refuses to permit Andrić and his diplomatic staff to go to neutral Switzerland. Yugoslav diplomatic personnel are sent to Belgrade, where Andrić is kept under surveillance. Here, he devotes himself to writing and refuses all invitations to publish.	Petrović: *The Sixth Day.* Bertolt Brecht: *Mother Courage and Her Children* first performed. Rebecca West: *Black Lamb and Grey Falcon.*
1942		Kaleb: *Outside of Things.* Waugh: *Put Out More Flags.* Albert Camus: *The Stranger.*
1943		T. Mann: *Joseph and His Brothers.* Hesse: *The Glass Bead Game.* Šop: *For the Late Table.* Sartre: *Being and Nothingness.* Laxness: *Iceland's Bell.* Brecht: *The Life of Galileo* first performed.
1944	Writes his war diary on the eleven bombings of Belgrade by Allies. His public life resumes in October, after the liberation of Belgrade.	Eliot: *Four Quartets.* Sartre: *Huis Clos.*
1945	Publishes three novels written during war: *The Bridge on the Drina (Na Drini Cuprija); Bosnian Chronicle (Travnička hronika)* and	Ivan Kovačić: *Fire and Roses* (poems). George Orwell: *Animal Farm.* Waugh: *Brideshead Revisited.*

CHRONOLOGY

Germany annexes Austria (March). Munich Conference (Sept.): Britain, France and Italy agree on the transfer of Sudetenland from Czechoslovakia to Germany. First Vienna Award: Germany and Italy agree that Slovakia and part of Ruthenia should be returned to Hungary (Nov.). Kristallnacht pogrom in Germany (Nov.).

Hitler occupies Czechoslovakia (March). Hungary follows Germany in leaving League of Nations. 'Pact of Steel' between Italy and Germany (May). Serb–Croat Settlement to create the autonomous Banovina of Croatia (Aug.). Germans invade Poland (1 Sept.). Britain and France declare war on Germany (3 Sept.).
German armies advancing throughout Europe. Churchill Prime Minister in Britain (May). Fall of France (June). Battle of Britain. USSR annexes Baltic states (June). Hungary, Italy and Japan sign Hitler's Tripartite Pact (Nov.).

Germans invade USSR (June). German-led Axis invasion of Yugoslavia (April); surrender of Yugoslav army. Founding of the Independent State of Croatia – the Ustaša – under Ante Pavelić. German military government in Serbia, under Milan Nedić. Two organized resistance movements emerge: Serb royalists under Draža Mihailović (Chetniks) and the Yugoslav communist partisans under Josip Broz Tito; their sharply divergent aims lead to civil war. Start of Ustaša's mass extermination of Jews and Roma. Japanese bomb Pearl Harbor: USA enters the war. Hungary at war with USA and Britain (Dec.).

Battle of Sutjeska. First meeting of the Antifascist Council of the People's Liberation Front of Yugoslavia in Bihać (AVNOJ). Wannsee Conference co-ordinates Hitler's 'Final Solution'. Allies defeat Rommel at El Alamein. Battle of Neretva (Jan.). Russian victory at Stalingrad. Hungarian Second Army in Russia is almost annihilated. Germans surrender in North Africa. Fall of Mussolini. Allies invade Italy. Second meeting of AVNOJ in Jajce (Nov.). Announcement of creation of federal and socialist Yugoslavia; Allied recognition of Tito.

March of the People's Liberation Army into Belgrade. D-Day landings in France and Allied advance to German border (June–Dec.).

Yalta Conference of Churchill, Roosevelt and Stalin (4–11 Feb.). Fall of Budapest (16 Feb.). The whole of Hungary in Soviet hands by April. Mussolini killed by partisans. Fall of Berlin (2 May). Partisans liberate Sarajevo (April). VE day: unconditional surrender of Germany (8 May).

xlv

DATE	AUTHOR'S LIFE	LITERARY CONTEXT
1945 cont.	*The Woman from Sarajevo* (*Gospođica*), as well as *Selected Short Stories*.	Sartre: *The Age of Reason*.
1946	Adapting to the new political situation of Communist Yugoslavia, Andrić is chosen to serve as a representative in the Republican Assembly of Bosnia-Herzegovina (to 1950).	Desanka Maksimović: *The Poet and His Native Land* (poems).
1947		T. Mann: *Doctor Faustus*. Camus: *The Plague*.
1948	*New Stories* (*Nove pripovetke*).	Petrović: *A Quail in the Hand*. Laxness: *The Atom Station*.
1949		Orwell: *Nineteen Eighty-Four*.
1950		Davičo: *Cherry Behind the Wall* (poems). Mihailo Lalić: *The Wedding*.
1951		Marguerite Yourcenar: *Memoirs of Hadrian*. J. D. Salinger: *Catcher in the Rye*.
1952		Wisława Szymborska: *That's Why We Are All Alive* (poems).
1953		Ranko Marinković: *Hands*. Davičo: *A Man of Man*. Czesław Miłosz: *The Captive Mind*. Gombrowicz: *Diaries* (to 1969). Samuel Beckett: *Waiting for Godot*. Saul Bellow: *The Adventures of Augie March*.
1954	Publishes short novel *The Devil's Yard* (*Prokleta avlija*). Becomes a member of the League of Communists of Yugoslavia.	Dobrica Ćosić: *Koreni*.
1955		Lalić: *Separation*.
1956		Ivan Slamnig: *Alley After the Ceremony*; *Landslide*. Marinković: *Gloria* (play).

CHRONOLOGY

HISTORICAL EVENTS

Proclamation of the creation of the Democratic Federal Yugoslavia (DFJ). Land reform and state purchasing programme for agricultural produce. Trieste crisis.
Constitution of the Federal People's Republic of Yugoslavia (FNRJ), partitioned into six equal constituent republics, undergoing the same social, economic and political change; nationalization of large landholdings, banks and means of production.

Paris Peace Conference: recognition of Yugoslavia's borders (annexation of Istria without Trieste).
Blockade of Berlin (to 1949). State of Israel founded.

Break with Stalin; Yugoslavia expelled from Cominform. NATO and COMECON formed. Beginning of Cold War. USSR tests its first nuclear bomb. Communist People's Republic of China founded.
Introduction of socialist self-management system in Yugoslavia. Cazin peasant uprising.

Communist Party of Yugoslavia renamed the League of Communists of Yugoslavia. Accession of Elizabeth II in Britain.

Constitutional reform incorporating self-management system. Death of Stalin. European Court of Human Rights set up in Strasbourg.

Novi Sad agreement on a written Serbo-Croatian language in two variants. Vietnam War begins.

Declaration in Moscow by Khrushchev and Tito on the right of every country to pursue socialism in its own way. Bandung Conference. USSR and its Eastern European satellites sign the Warsaw Pact.
Soviets invade Hungary. Suez crisis.

DATE	AUTHOR'S LIFE	LITERARY CONTEXT
1956 cont.		Miodrag Bulatović: *The Devils Are Coming.*
1957	Receives Charter from the Federation of Writers and the Alliance of Publishers.	Lalić: *The Mountain of Cries* (to 1962). Vladan Desnica: *The Spring of Ivan Galeb.* Branko Miljković: *I Wake Her in Vain* (poems). Alain Robbe-Grillet: *Jealousy.*
1958	Marries Milica Babić, a costume designer at the National Theatre in Belgrade.	Zaim Topčić: *Lump of Sun.* Giuseppe Tomasi di Lampedusa: *The Leopard.* Boris Pasternak: *Doctor Zhivago.*
1959		Miljković: *Death Against Death* (poems). Günter Grass: *The Tin Drum.* William Burroughs: *Naked Lunch.*
1960	Publishes short story collection *Faces* (*Lica*).	Miljković: *The Origin of Hope* (poems). Radomir Konstantinović: *Exodus.* Lalić: *The Pursuit.* Witold Gombrowicz: *Pornography.* John Updike: *Rabbit, Run.*
1961	Awarded the Nobel Prize for Literature.	Antun Šoljan: *Traitor.* Miljković: *The Shining Blood* (poems). Joseph Heller: *Catch-22.*
1962		Topčić: *Black Snows.* Crnjanski: *The Second Book of Migration.* Alexsandr Solzhenitsyn: *One Day in the Life of Ivan Denisovich.*
1963		Irena Vrkljan: *Time of Friendship.*
1964		Maksimović: *I Seek Clemency.* Bellow: *Herzog.* Hemingway: *A Moveable Feast.*
1965		Marinković: *Cyclops.* Šoljan: *Short Trip.* Crnjanski: *Lament Over Belgrade.* Borislav Pekić: *The Time of Miracles.* Gombrowicz: *Cosmos.*

CHRONOLOGY

Foundation of European Economic Community.

Castro seizes power in Cuba.

'Muslim' first used as a term denoting national identity in Yugoslavia census. John F. Kennedy elected US President. Erection of Berlin Wall. Yuri Gagarin becomes first man in space.

Cuban Missile Crisis.

Federal People's Republic of Yugoslavia renamed the Socialist Federal Republic of Yugoslavia (SFRY). Assassination of John F. Kennedy. Eighth Party Congress of the League of Communists. Introduction of market-economy reforms and the federalization of the constitution. Khrushchev deposed and replaced by Brezhnev.

DATE	AUTHOR'S LIFE	LITERARY CONTEXT
1966	*Love in the Town: Short Stories* (*Ljubav u kasabi: pripovetke*).	Mak Dizdar: *Stone Sleeper* (to 1971). Meša Selimović: *Death and the Dervish*. Vrkljan: *The room, this frightful garden* (poems). Szymborska: *101 Poems*. Mikhail Bulgakov: *The Master and the Margarita* (to 1967) published posthumously.
1967		Bulatović: *Hero on a Donkey*. Szymborska: *No End of Fun* (poems). Gabriel García Márquez: *One Hundred Years of Solitude*.
1968	*Aska and the Wolf: Short Stories* (*Aska i vuk: Pripovetke*).	Solzhenitsyn: *The First Circle*.
1969		Konstantinović: *Small Town Philosophy*. Szymborska: *Couldn't Have* (poems).
1970		Selimović: *The Fortress*. Pekić: *The Pilgrimage of Arsenije Njegovan*. Borislav Pekić: *The Houses of Belgrade*.
1971		Dizdar: *Blue River*. Ivo Brešan: *Hamlet performance in the village of Mrduša Donja* (play). Stjepan Čuić: *Stalin's Picture and Other Stories*. Crnjanski: *A Novel of London*. Camus: *A Happy Death*.
1972		Slamnig: *Better Half of Courage*. Danilo Kiš: *Hourglass*.
1973		Lalić: *The Luck of War*. Solzhenitsyn: *The Gulag Archipelago* (to 1975).
1974		Šoljan: *Port*.
1975	Dies 13 March. His will bequeaths his possessions to the state – as a cultural and humanitarian	Bulatović: *People with Four Fingers*. Bellow: *Humboldt's Gift*.

1

CHRONOLOGY

Mao launches 'Cultural Revolution' in China.

'Declaration on the Status and Name of the Croatian Literary Language.'
Arab–Israeli Six-Day War.

Student unrest in US and throughout Europe. Albanian uprising in
Kosovo and West Macedonia. Bosnian Central Committee decrees that
'the Muslims are a distinct nation'. Soviet-led invasion of Czechoslovakia.
Assassination of Martin Luther King, Jr. Nixon US President.
Americans land first man on the moon.

Islamic Declaration by Alija Izetbegović.

Croatian Spring. Constitutional amendment expanding the federalization
of Yugoslavia. Ousting from power of party leadership in Zagreb. Brezhnev
visits Belgrade.

Ousting from power of party leadership in Belgrade; political purge in
party. USSR and USA sign Strategic Arms Limitation Treaty (SALT).

New passage in constitution granting greater authority to the republics and
autonomous provinces; Tito confirmed as president for life.
End of Vietnam War. USSR and Western powers sign Helsinki Agreement.

DATE	AUTHOR'S LIFE	LITERARY CONTEXT
1975 cont.	endowment – and provides for an annual prize to be awarded to the best short-story collection.	Primo Levi: *The Periodic Table*.
1976	Three additional books by Andrić are published: *The House on Its Own* (*Kuća na osami*); *Signs by the Roadside* (*Znakoui pored pumi*), and the novel *Omer Pasha Latas* (*Omerpaša Latas*).	Kiš: *A Tomb for Boris Davidovich*.
1977		Predrag Matvejević: *Literature and Its Social Function*; *Those Windmills*.
1978		Pekić: *The Golden Fleece* (to 1986).
1980	The Ivo Andrić Endowment sponsors an international meeting in Belgrade to discuss the work of Andrić in the context of European literature and culture.	Umberto Eco: *The Name of the Rose*.

C H R O N O L O G Y

HISTORICAL EVENTS

Death of Mao Tse-Tung.

Charter 77 signed by 241 Czechoslovak intellectuals.

Tito dies, succeeded by Lazar Koliševski. Growing economic problems and national tensions.

NOTE

ON THE PRONUNCIATION OF SERBO-CROAT NAMES

Andrić's novel is published both in the Cyrillic and Latin (Croat) alphabets. I have used the Croatian spelling throughout. The language is strictly phonetic. One sound is almost always designated by one letter or (in Croat) combination of letters.

Generally speaking, the foreigner cannot go far wrong if he uses 'continental' vowels and English consonants, with the following exceptions:

c is always ts, as in ca*ts*.

č is ch as in *ch*urch.

ć is similar but softer, as t in the Cockney pronunciation of tube.

Many family names end in ć. For practical purposes, the foreigner may regard č and ć as the same.

dj is the English j in judge – the English j in fact.

dž is practically the same, but harder. It is usually found in words of Turkish origin.

j is always soft, the English y.

r is sometimes a vowel, strongly rolled. Hence such strange looking words as vrh (summit).

š is sh as in *sh*ake.

ž is zh as z in azure.

Other variations do not occur in this book. In a few cases I have left the conventionally accepted English spelling, instead of insisting pedantically on Serbo-Croat versions: e.g. Sanjak (Serbo-Croat: Sandžak), Belgrade (Serbo-Croat: Beograd), etc. In the case of purely Turkish names, I have sometimes transliterated them phonetically, as the Croat version is equally arbitrary.

The use of the original names retains dignity and flavour. Attempts to adapt them to English phonetics (in itself an ungrateful task) results in such monstrosities as Ts(e)rnche – for Crnče.

Lovett F. Edwards

THE BRIDGE
ON THE DRINA

CHAPTER I

FOR THE GREATER part of its course the river Drina flows through narrow gorges between steep mountains or through deep ravines with precipitous banks. In a few places only the river banks spread out to form valleys with level or rolling stretches of fertile land suitable for cultivation and settlement on both sides. Such a place exists here at Višegrad, where the Drina breaks out in a sudden curve from the deep and narrow ravine formed by the Butkovo rocks and the Uzavnik mountains. The curve which the Drina makes here is particularly sharp and the mountains on both sides are so steep and so close together that they look like a solid mass out of which the river flows directly as from a dark wall. Then the mountains suddenly widen into an irregular amphitheatre whose widest extent is not more than about ten miles as the crow flies.

Here, where the Drina flows with the whole force of its green and foaming waters from the apparently closed mass of the dark steep mountains, stands a great clean-cut stone bridge with eleven wide sweeping arches. From this bridge spreads fanlike the whole rolling valley with the little oriental town of Višegrad and all its surroundings, with hamlets nestling in the folds of the hills, covered with meadows, pastures and plum-orchards, and criss-crossed with walls and fences and dotted with shaws and occasional clumps of evergreens. Looked at from a distance through the broad arches of the white bridge it seems as if one can see not only the green Drina, but all that fertile and cultivated countryside and the southern sky above.

On the right bank of the river, starting from the bridge itself, lay the centre of the town, with the market-place, partly on the level and partly on the hillside. On the other side of the bridge, along the left bank, stretched the Maluhino Polje, with a few scattered houses along the road which led to Sarajevo. Thus the bridge, uniting the two parts of the Sarajevo road, linked the town with its surrounding villages.

Actually, to say 'linked' was just as true as to say that the sun rises in the morning so that men may see around them and finish their daily tasks, and sets in the evening that they may be able to sleep and rest from the labours of the day. For this great stone bridge, a rare structure of unique beauty, such as many richer and busier towns do not possess ('There are only two others such as this in the whole Empire,' they used to say in olden times) was the one real and permanent crossing in the whole middle and upper course of the Drina and an indispensable link on the road between Bosnia and Serbia and further, beyond Serbia, with other parts of the Turkish Empire, all the way to Stambul. The town and its outskirts were only the settlements which always and inevitably grow up around an important centre of communications and on either side of great and important bridges.

Here also in time the houses crowded together and the settlements multiplied at both ends of the bridge. The town owed its existence to the bridge and grew out of it as if from an imperishable root.

In order to see a picture of the town and understand it and its relation to the bridge clearly, it must be said that there was another bridge in the town and another river. This was the river Rzav, with a wooden bridge across it. At the very end of the town the Rzav flows into the Drina, so that the centre and at the same time the main part of the town lay on a sandy tongue of land between two rivers, the great and the small, which met there and its scattered outskirts stretched out from both sides of the bridges, along the left bank of the Drina and the right bank of the Rzav. It was a town on the water. But even though another river existed and another bridge, the words 'on the bridge' never meant on the Rzav bridge, a simple wooden structure without beauty and without history, that had no reason for its existence save to serve the townspeople and their animals as a crossing, but only and uniquely the stone bridge over the Drina.

The bridge was about two hundred and fifty paces long and about ten paces wide save in the middle where it widened out into two completely equal terraces placed symmetrically on either side of the roadway and making it twice its normal width. This was the part of the bridge known as the *kapia*. Two buttresses had been built on each side of the central pier which had been splayed out towards the top, so that to right and left of the roadway there were two terraces daringly and harmoniously projecting outwards from the straight line of the bridge over the noisy green waters far below. The two terraces were about five paces long and the same in width and were bordered, as was the whole length of the bridge, by a stone parapet. Otherwise, they were open and uncovered. That on the right as one came from the town was called the *sofa*. It was raised by two steps and bordered by benches for which the parapet served as a back; steps, benches and parapet were all made of the same shining stone. That on the left, opposite the *sofa*, was similar but without benches. In the middle of the parapet, the stone rose higher than a man and in it, near the top, was inserted a plaque of white marble with a rich Turkish inscription, a *tarih*, with a carved chronogram which told in thirteen verses the name of the man who built the bridge and the year in which it was built. Near the foot of this stone was a fountain, a thin stream of water flowing from the mouth of a stone snake. On this part of the terrace a coffee-maker had installed himself with his copper vessels and Turkish cups and ever-lighted charcoal brazier, and an apprentice who took the coffee over the way to the guests on the *sofa*. Such was the *kapia*.

On the bridge and its *kapia*, about it or in connection with it, flowed and developed, as we shall see, the life of the townsmen. In all tales about personal, family or public events the words 'on the bridge' could always be heard. Indeed on the bridge over the Drina were the first steps of childhood and the first games of boyhood.

The Christian children, born on the left bank of the Drina, crossed the bridge at once in the first days of their lives, for they were always taken across in their first week to be christened. But all the other children, those who were born on the right bank and the Moslem children who were not christened at all, passed, as had once their fathers and their grandfathers, the main part of their childhood on or around the bridge. They fished around it or hunted doves under its arches. From their very earliest years, their eyes grew accustomed to the lovely lines of this great stone structure built of shining porous stone, regularly and faultlessly cut. They knew all the bosses and concavities of the masons, as well as all the tales and legends associated with the existence and building of the bridge, in which reality and imagination, waking and dream, were wonderfully and inextricably mingled. They had always known these things as if they had come into the world with them, even as they knew their prayers, but could not remember from whom they had learnt them nor when they had first heard them.

They knew that the bridge had been built by the Grand Vezir, Mehmed Pasha, who had been born in the nearby village of Sokolović, just on the far side of one of those mountains which encircled the bridge and the town. Only a Vezir could have given all that was needed to build this lasting wonder of stone (a Vezir – to the children's minds that was something fabulous, immense, terrible and far from clear). It was built by Rade the Mason, who must have lived for hundreds of years to have been able to build all that was lovely and lasting in the Serbian lands, that legendary and in fact nameless master whom all people desire and dream of, since they do not want to have to remember or be indebted to too many, even in memory. They knew that the *vila* of the boatmen had hindered its building, as always and everywhere there is someone to hinder building, destroying by night what had been built by day, until 'something' had whispered from the waters and counselled Rade the Mason to find two infant children, twins, brother and sister, named

Stoja and Ostoja, and wall them into the central pier of the bridge. A reward was promised to whoever found them and brought them hither.

At last the guards found such twins, still at the breast, in a distant village and the Vezir's men took them away by force; but when they were taking them away, their mother would not be parted from them and, weeping and wailing, insensible to blows and to curses, stumbled after them as far as Višegrad itself, where she succeeded in forcing her way to Rade the Mason.

The children were walled into the pier, for it could not be otherwise, but Rade, they say, had pity on them and left openings in the pier through which the unhappy mother could feed her sacrificed children. Those are the finely carved blind windows, narrow as loopholes, in which the wild doves now nest. In memory of that, the mother's milk has flowed from those walls for hundreds of years. That is the thin white stream which, at certain times of year, flows from that faultless masonry and leaves an indelible mark on the stone. (The idea of woman's milk stirs in the childish mind a feeling at once too intimate and too close, yet at the same time vague and mysterious like Vezirs and masons, which disturbs and repulses them.) Men scrape those milky traces off the piers and sell them as medicinal powder to women who have no milk after giving birth.

In the central pier of the bridge, below the *kapia*, there is a larger opening, a long narrow gateway without gates, like a gigantic loophole. In that pier, they say, is a great room, a gloomy hall, in which a black Arab lives. All the children know this. In their dreams and in their fancies he plays a great role. If he should appear to anyone, that man must die. Not a single child has seen him yet, for children do not die. But Hamid, the asthmatic porter, with bloodshot eyes, continually drunk or suffering from a hangover, saw him one night and that very same night he died, over there by the wall. It is true that he was blind drunk at the time and passed the night on the bridge under the open sky in a temperature

of −15°C. The children used to gaze from the bank into that
dark opening as into a gulf which is both terrible and fasci-
nating. They would agree to look at it without blinking and
whoever first saw anything should cry out. Open-mouthed
they would peer into that deep dark hole, quivering with
curiosity and fear, until it seemed to some anaemic child that
the opening began to sway and to move like a black curtain,
or until one of them, mocking and inconsiderate (there is
always at least one such), shouted 'The Arab' and pretended
to run away. That spoilt the game and aroused disillusion
and indignation amongst those who loved the play of imagination, hated irony and believed that by looking intently
they could actually see and feel something. At night, in
their sleep, many of them would toss and fight with the Arab
from the bridge as with fate until their mother woke them
and so freed them from this nightmare. Then she would
give them cold water to drink 'to chase away the fear' and
make them say the name of God, and the child, overtaxed
with daytime childish games, would fall asleep again into
the deep sleep of childhood where terrors can no longer take
shape or last for long.

Up river from the bridge, in the steep banks of grey chalk,
on both sides of the river, can be seen rounded hollows, always
in pairs at regular intervals, as if cut in the stone were the
hoofprints of some horse of supernatural size; they led downwards from the Old Fortress, descended the scarp towards
the river and then appeared again on the farther bank, where
they were lost in the dark earth and undergrowth.

The children who fished for tiddlers all day in the summer
along these stony banks knew that these were hoofprints of
ancient days and long dead warriors. Great heroes lived on
earth in those days, when the stone had not yet hardened and
was soft as the earth and the horses, like the warriors, were of
colossal growth. Only for the Serbian children these were the
prints of the hooves of Šarac, the horse of Kraljević Marko,
which had remained there from the time when Kraljević
Marko himself was in prison up there in the Old Fortress

and escaped, flying down the slope and leaping the Drina, for at that time there was no bridge. But the Turkish children knew that it had not been Kraljević Marko, nor could it have been (for whence could a bastard Christian dog have had such strength or such a horse!) any but Djerzelez Alija on his winged charger which, as everyone knew, despised ferries and ferrymen and leapt over rivers as if they were water-courses. They did not even squabble about this, so convinced were both sides in their own belief. And there was never an instance of any one of them being able to convince another, or that any one had changed his belief.

In these depressions which were round and as wide and deep as rather large soup-bowls, water still remained long after rain, as though in stone vessels. The children called these pits, filled with tepid rainwater, wells and, without distinction of faith, kept the tiddlers there which they caught on their lines.

On the left bank, standing alone, immediately above the road, there was a fairly large earthen barrow, formed of some kind of hard earth, grey and almost like stone. On it nothing grew or blossomed save some short grass, hard and prickly as barbed wire. That tumulus was the end and frontier of all the children's games around the bridge. That was the spot which at one time was called Radisav's tomb. They used to tell that he was some sort of Serbian hero, a man of power. When the Vezir, Mehmed Pasha, had first thought of building the bridge on the Drina and sent his men here, everyone submitted and was summoned to forced labour. Only this man, Radisav, stirred up the people to revolt and told the Vezir not to continue with this work for he would meet with great difficulties in building a bridge across the Drina. And the Vezir had many troubles before he succeeded in overcoming Radisav for he was a man greater than other men; there was no rifle or sword that could harm him, nor was there rope or chain that could bind him. He broke all of them like thread, so great was the power of the talisman that he had with him. And who knows what might have happened and whether the Vezir would ever have been able to build the bridge, had he not found some of his men who were wise and skilful, who bribed and questioned Radisav's servant. Then they took Radisav by surprise and drowned him while he was asleep, binding him with silken ropes for against silk his talisman could not help him. The Serbian women believe that there is one night of the year when a strong white light can be seen falling on that tumulus direct from heaven; and that takes place sometime in autumn between the greater and lesser feasts of the Virgin. But the children who, torn between belief and unbelief, remained on vigil by the windows overlooking Radisav's tomb have never managed to see this heavenly fire, for they were all overcome by sleep before midnight came. But there had been travellers, who knew nothing of this, who had seen a white light falling on the tumulus above the bridge as they returned to the town by night.

The Turks in the town, on the other hand, have long told that on that spot a certain dervish, by name Sheik Turhanija, died as a martyr to the faith. He was a great hero and defended on this spot the crossing of the Drina against an infidel army. And that on this spot there is neither memorial nor tomb, for such was the wish of the dervish himself, for he wanted to be buried without mark or sign, so that no one should know who was there. For, if ever again some infidel army should invade by this route, then he would arise from under his tumulus and hold them in check, as he had once done, so that they should be able to advance no farther than the bridge at Višegrad. And therefore heaven now and again shed its light upon his tomb.

Thus the life of the children of the town was played out under and about the bridge in innocent games and childish fancies. With the first years of maturity, when life's cares and struggles and duties had already begun, this life was transferred to the bridge itself, right to the *kapia*, where youthful imagination found other food and new fields.

At and around the *kapia* were the first stirrings of love,

the first passing glances, flirtations and whisperings. There too were the first deals and bargains, quarrels and reconciliations, meetings and waitings. There, on the stone parapet of the bridge, were laid out for sale the first cherries and melons, the early morning *salep* and hot rolls. There too gathered the beggars, the maimed and the lepers, as well as the young and healthy who wanted to see and be seen, and all those who had something remarkable to show in produce, clothes or weapons. There too the elders of the town often sat to discuss public matters and common troubles, but even more often young men who only knew how to sing and joke. There, on great occasions or times of change, were posted proclamations and public notices (on the raised wall below the marble plaque with the Turkish inscription and above the fountain), but there too, right up to 1878, hung or were exposed on stakes the heads of all those who for whatever reason had been executed, and executions in that frontier town, especially in years of unrest, were frequent and in some years, as we shall see, almost of daily occurrence.

Weddings or funerals could not cross the bridge without stopping at the *kapia*. There the wedding guests would usually preen themselves and get into their ranks before entering the market-place. If the times were peaceful and carefree they would hand the plum-brandy around, sing, dance the *kolo* and often delay there far longer than they had intended. And for funerals, those who carried the bier would put it down to rest for a little there on the *kapia* where the dead man had in any case passed a good part of his life.

The *kapia* was the most important part of the bridge, even as the bridge was the most important part of the town, or as a Turkish traveller, to whom the people of Višegrad had been very hospitable, wrote in his account of his travels: 'their *kapia* is the heart of the bridge, which is the heart of the town, which must remain in everyone's heart'. It showed that the old masons, who according to the old tales had struggled with *vilas* and every sort of wonder and had been compelled to wall up living children, had a feeling not only for the permanence and beauty of their work but also for the benefit and convenience which the most distant generations were to derive from it. When one knows well everyday life here in the town and thinks it over carefully, then one must say to oneself that there are really only a very small number of people in this Bosnia of ours who have so much pleasure and enjoyment as does each and every townsman on the *kapia*.

Naturally winter should not be taken into account, for then only whoever was forced to do so would cross the bridge, and then he would lengthen his pace and bend his head before the chill wind that blew uninterruptedly over the river. Then, it was understood, there was no loitering on the open terraces of the *kapia*. But at every other time of year the *kapia* was a real boon for great and small. Then every citizen could, at any time of day or night, go out to the *kapia* and sit on the *sofa*, or hang about it on business or in conversation. Suspended some fifteen metres above the green boisterous waters, this stone *sofa* floated in space over the water, with dark green hills on three sides, the heavens, filled with clouds or stars, above and the open view down river like a narrow amphitheatre bounded by the dark blue mountains behind.

How many Vezirs or rich men are there in the world who could indulge their joy or their cares, their moods or their delights in such a spot? Few, very few. But how many of our townsmen have, in the course of centuries and the passage of generations, sat here in the dawn or twilight or evening hours and unconsciously measured the whole starry vault above! Many and many of us have sat there, head in hands, leaning on the well-cut smooth stone, watching the eternal play of light on the mountains and the clouds in the sky, and have unravelled the threads of our small-town destinies, eternally the same yet eternally tangled in some new manner. Someone affirmed long ago (it is true that he was a foreigner and spoke in jest) that this *kapia* had had an influence on the fate of the town and even on the character of its citizens. In those endless sessions, the stranger said, one must search for the key to the inclination of many of our townsmen to reflection and dreaming and one of the main reasons for that melancholic serenity for which the inhabitants of the town are renowned.

In any case, it cannot be denied that the people of Višegrad have from olden times been considered, in comparison with the people of other towns, as easy-going men, prone to pleasure and free with their money. Their town is well placed, the villages around it are rich and fertile, and money, it is true, passes in abundance through Višegrad, but it does not stay there long. If one finds there some thrifty and economical citizen without any sort of vices, then he is certainly some newcomer; but the waters and the air of Višegrad are such that his children grow up with open hands and widespread fingers and fall victims to the general contagion of the spendthrift and carefree life of the town with its motto: 'Another day another gain.'

They tell the tale that Starina Novak, when he felt his strength failing and was compelled to give up his role as highwayman in the Romania Mountains, thus taught the young man Grujić who was to succeed him:

'When you are sitting in ambush look well at the traveller who comes. If you see that he rides proudly and that he wears a red corselet and silver bosses and white gaiters, then he is from Foča. Strike at once, for he has wealth both on him and in his saddlebags. If you see a poorly dressed traveller, with bowed head, hunched on his horse as if he were going out to beg, then strike freely, for he is a man of Rogatica. They are all alike, misers and tight-fisted but as full of money as a pomegranate. But if you see some mad fellow, with legs crossed over the saddlebow, beating on a drum and singing at the top of his voice, don't strike and do not soil your hands for nothing. Let the rascal go his way. He is from Višegrad and he has nothing, for money does not stick to such men.'

All this goes to confirm the opinion of that foreigner. But none the less it would be hard to say with certainty that this opinion is correct. As in so many other things, here too it is not easy to determine what is cause and what effect. Has the *kapia* made them what they are, or on the contrary was it imagined in their souls and understandings and built for them according to their needs and customs? It is a vain and superfluous question. There are no buildings that have been built by chance, remote from the human society where they have grown and its needs, hopes and understandings, even as there are no arbitrary lines and motiveless forms in the work of the masons. The life and existence of every great, beautiful and useful building, as well as its relation to the place where it has been built, often bears within itself complex and mysterious drama and history. However, one thing is clear; that between the life of the townsmen and that bridge, there existed a centuries-old bond. Their fates were so intertwined that they could not be imagined separately and could not be told separately. Therefore the story of the foundation and destiny of the bridge is at the same time the story of the life of the town and of its people, from generation to generation, even as through all the tales about the town stretches the line of the stone bridge with its eleven arches and the *kapia* in the middle, like a crown.

CHAPTER II

NOW WE MUST go back to the time when there was not even a thought of a bridge at that spot, let alone such a bridge as this.

Perhaps even in those far-off times, some traveller passing this way, tired and drenched, wished that by some miracle this wide and turbulent river were bridged, so that he could reach his goal more easily and quickly. For there is no doubt that men had always, ever since they first travelled here and overcame the obstacles along the way, thought how to make a crossing at this spot, even as all travellers at all times have dreamed of a good road, safe travelling companions and a warm inn. Only not every wish bears fruit, nor has everyone the will and the power to turn his dreams into reality.

The first idea of the bridge, which was destined to be realized, flashed, at first naturally confused and foggy, across the imagination of a ten-year-old boy from the nearby village of Sokolovići, one morning in 1516 when he was being taken along the road from his village to far-off, shining and terrible Stambul.

Then this same green and awe-inspiring Drina, this mountain river 'which often grew angry', clamoured there between barren and naked, stony and sandy banks. The town even then existed, but in another form and of different dimensions. On the right bank of the river, on the crest of a precipitous hill, where now there are ruins, rose the well preserved Old Fortress, with widespread fortifications dating from the time of the flowering of the Bosnian kingdom, with casements and ramparts, the work of one of the powerful Pavlović nobles. On the slopes below this fortress and under its protection stood the Christian settlements, Mejdan and Bikovac, and the recently converted Turkish hamlet of Dušče. Down on the level ground between the Drina and the Rzav, where the real town later spread, were only the town meadows, with a road running through them, beside which was an old-fashioned inn and a few huts and water-mills.

Where the Drina intersected the road was the famous Višegrad ferry. That was a black old-fashioned ferryboat and on it a surly, slow old ferryman called Jamak, whom it was harder to summon when awake than any other man from the deepest sleep. He was a man of giant stature and extraordinary strength, but he had suffered in the many wars in which he had won renown. He had only one eye, one ear and one leg (the other was wooden). Without greeting and without a smile, he would moodily ferry across goods and passengers in his own good time, but honestly and safely, so that tales were told of his reliability and his honesty as often as of his slowness and obstinacy. He would not talk with the passengers whom he took across nor would he touch them. Men threw the copper coins that they paid for the crossing into the bottom of the black boat where they lay all day in the sand and water, and only in the evening would the ferryman collect them carelessly in the wooden scoop which he used to bale out the boat and take them to his hut on the river bank.

The ferry only worked when the current and height of the river were normal or a little higher than normal, but as soon as the river ran cloudy or rose above certain limits, Jamak hauled out his clumsy bark, moored it firmly in a backwater and the Drina remained as impassable as the greatest of oceans. Jamak then became deaf even in his one sound ear or simply went up to the Fortress to work in his field. Then, all day long, there could be seen travellers coming from Bosnia who stood on the farther bank in desperation, frozen and drenched, vainly watching the ferry and the ferryman and from time to time yelling long drawn summonses:

'O-o-o-o-o. . . . Jama-a-a-k. . . .'

No one would reply and no one would appear until the

waters fell, and that moment was decided by Jamak himself, dark and unrelenting, without discussion or explanation.

The town, which was then little more than a hamlet, stood on the right bank of the Drina on the slopes of the steep hill below the ruins of the one-time fortress, for then it did not have the size and shape it was to have later when the bridge was built and communications and trade developed.

On that November day a long convoy of laden horses arrived on the left back of the river and halted there to spend the night. The aga of the janissaries, with armed escort, was returning to Stambul after collecting from the villages of eastern Bosnia the appointed number of Christian children for the blood tribute.

It was already the sixth year since the last collection of this tribute of blood, and so this time the choice had been easy and rich; the necessary number of healthy, bright and good-looking lads between ten and fifteen years old had been found without difficulty, even though many parents had hidden their children in the forests, taught them how to appear half-witted, clothed them in rags and let them get filthy, to avoid the aga's choice. Some went so far as to maim their own children, cutting off one of their fingers with an axe.

The chosen children were laden on to little Bosnian horses in a long convoy. On each horse were two plaited panniers, like those for fruit, one on each side, and in every pannier was put a child, each with a small bundle and a round cake, the last thing they were to take from their parents' homes. From these panniers, which balanced and creaked in unison, peered out the fresh and frightened faces of the kidnapped children. Some of them gazed calmly across the horses' cruppers, looking as long as they could at their native land, others ate and wept at the same time, while others slept with heads resting on the pack-saddles.

A little way behind the last horses in that strange convoy straggled, dishevelled and exhausted, many parents and relatives of those children who were being carried away for ever to a foreign world, where they would be circumcised, become Turkish and, forgetting their faith, their country and their origin, would pass their lives in the ranks of the janissaries or in some other, higher, service of the Empire. They were for the most part women, mothers, grandmothers and sisters of the stolen children.

When they came too close, the aga's horsemen would drive them away with whips, urging their horses at them with loud cries to Allah. Then they would fly in all directions and hide in the forests along the roadsides, only to gather again a little later behind the convoy and strive with tear-filled eyes to see once again over the panniers the heads of the children who were being taken from them. The mothers were especially persistent and hard to restrain. Some would rush forward not looking where they were going, with bare breasts, and dishevelled hair, forgetting everything about them, wailing and lamenting as at a burial, while others almost out of their minds moaned as if their wombs were being torn by birth-pangs, and blinded with tears ran right on to the horsemen's whips and replied to every blow with the fruitless question: 'Where are you taking him? Why are you taking him from me?' Some tried to speak clearly to their children and to give them some last part of themselves, as much as might be said in a couple of words, some recommendation or advice for the way. . . .

'Rade, my son, don't forget your mother. . . .'

'Ilija, Ilija, Ilija!' screamed another woman, searching desperately with her glances for the dear well-known head and repeating this incessantly as if she wished to carve into the child's memory that name which would in a day or two be taken from him forever.

But the way was long, the earth hard, the body weak and the Osmanlis powerful and pitiless. Little by little the women dropped back exhausted by the march and the blows, and one after the other abandoned their vain effort. Here, at the Višegrad ferry, even the most enduring had to halt for they were not allowed on the ferry and were unable to cross the water. Now they could sit in peace on the bank and weep, for no one persecuted them any longer. There they waited as if turned to stone and sat, insensible to hunger, thirst and cold, until on the farther bank of the river they could see once more the long drawn out convoy of horses and riders as it moved onward towards Dubrina, and tried once more to catch a last glimpse of the children who were disappearing from their sight.

On that November day in one of those countless panniers a dark-skinned boy of about ten years old from the mountain village of Sokolovići sat silent and looked about him with dry eyes. In a chilled and reddened hand he held a small curved knife with which he absent-mindedly whittled at the edges of his pannier, but at the same time looked about him. He was to remember that stony bank overgrown with sparse, bare and dull grey willows, the surly ferryman and the dry water-mill full of draughts and spiders' webs where they had to spend the night before it was possible to transport all of them across the troubled waters of the Drina over which the ravens were croaking. Somewhere within himself he felt a sharp stabbing pain which from time to time seemed suddenly to cut his chest in two and hurt terribly, which was always associated with the memory of that place where the road broke off, where desolation and despair were extinguished and remained on the stony banks of the river, across which the passage was so difficult, so expensive and so unsafe. It was here, at this particularly painful spot in that hilly and poverty-stricken district, in which misfortune was open and evident, that man was halted by powers stronger than he and, ashamed of his powerlessness, was forced to recognize more clearly his own misery and that of others, his own backwardness and that of others.

All this was summed up in that physical discomfort that the boy felt on that November day and which never completely left him, though he changed his way of life, his faith, his name and his country.

What this boy in the pannier was later to become has

been told in all histories in all languages and is better known in the world outside than it is amongst us. In time he became a young and brave officer at the Sultan's court, then Great Admiral of the Fleet, then the Sultan's son-in-law, a general and statesman of world renown, Mehmed Pasha Sokolli, who waged wars that were for the most part victorious on three continents and extended the frontiers of the Ottoman Empire, making it safe abroad and by good administration consolidated it from within. For these sixty odd years he served three Sultans, experienced both good and evil as only rare and chosen persons may experience them, and raised himself to heights of power and authority unknown to us, which few men reach and few men keep. This new man that he had become in a foreign world where we could not follow even in our thoughts, must have forgotten all that he had left behind in the country whence they had once brought him. He surely forgot too the crossing of the Drina at Višegrad, the bare banks on which travellers shivered with cold and uncertainty, the slow and worm-eaten ferry, the strange ferryman, and the hungry ravens above the troubled waters. But that feeling of discomfort which had remained in him had never completely disappeared. On the other hand, with years and with age it appeared more and more often; always the same black pain which cut into his breast with that special well-known childhood pang which was clearly distinguishable from all the ills and pains that life later brought to him. With closed eyes, the Vezir would wait until that black knife-like pang passed and the pain diminished. In one of those moments he thought that he might be able to free himself from this discomfort if he could do away with that ferry on the distant Drina, around which so much misery and inconvenience gathered and increased incessantly, and bridge the steep banks and the evil water between them, join the two ends of the road which was broken by the Drina and thus link safely and for ever Bosnia and the East, the place of his origin and the places of his life. Thus it was he who first, in a single moment behind closed eyelids, saw the firm graceful silhouette of the great stone bridge which was to be built there.

That very same year, by the Vezir's order and at the Vezir's expense, the building of the great bridge on the Drina began. It lasted five years. That must have been an exceptionally lively and important time for the town and the whole district, full of change and of events great and small. But for a wonder, in the town which remembered for centuries and discussed every sort of event, including all those directly connected with the bridge, not many details of the commencement of the operation were preserved.

The common people remember and tell of what they are able to grasp and what they are able to transform into legend. Anything else passes them by without deeper trace, with the dumb indifference of nameless natural phenomena, which do not touch the imagination or remain in the memory. This hard and long building process was for them a foreign task undertaken at another's expense. Only when, as the fruit of this effort, the great bridge arose, men began to remember details and to embroider the creation of a real, skilfully built and lasting bridge with fabulous tales which they well knew how to weave and to remember.

CHAPTER III

IN THE SPRING of that year when the Vezir had made his decision to build, his men arrived in the town to prepare everything necessary for the construction work on the bridge. There were many of them, with horses, carts, various tools and tents. All this excited fear and apprehension in the little town and the surrounding villages, especially among the Christians.

At the head of this group was Abidaga, who was responsible to the Vezir for building the bridge; with him was the mason, Tosun Effendi. (There had already been tales about this Abidaga, saying that he was a man who stopped at nothing, harsh and pitiless beyond measure.) As soon as they had settled in their tents below Mejdan, Abidaga summoned the local leaders and all the principal Turks for a discussion. But there was not much of a discussion, for only one man spoke and he was Abidaga. Those who had been summoned saw a powerfully built man, with green eyes and an unhealthy reddish face, dressed in rich Stambul clothes, with a reddish beard and wonderfully upturned moustaches in the Magyar fashion. The speech which this violent man delivered to the notables astonished them even more than his appearance: 'It is more than likely that you have heard tales about me even before I came here and I know without asking that those tales could not have been pleasant or favourable. Probably you have heard that I demand work and obedience from everyone, and that I will beat and kill anyone who does not work as he should and does not obey without argument; that I do not know the meaning of "I cannot" or "There isn't any", that wherever I am heads will roll at the slightest word, and that in short I am a bloodthirsty and hard man. I want to tell you that those tales are neither imaginary nor exaggerated. Under my linden tree there is no shade. I have won this reputation over long years of service in which I have devotedly carried out the orders of the Grand Vezir. I trust in God that I shall carry out this work for which I was sent and when at the completion of the work I go hence, I hope that even harsher and darker tales will go before me than those which have already reached you.'

After this unusual introduction to which all listened in silence and with downcast eyes, Abidaga explained that it was a matter of a building of great importance, such as did not exist even in richer lands, that the work would last five, perhaps six, years, but that the Vezir's will would be carried out to the fineness of a hair and punctual to a minute. Then he laid down his first requirements and what he therefore expected from the local Turks and demanded from the *rayah* – the Christian serfs.

Beside him sat Tosun Effendi, a small, pale, yellowish renegade, born in the Greek islands, a mason who had built many of Mehmed Pasha's bequests in Stambul. He remained quiet and indifferent, as if he were not hearing or did not understand Abidaga's speech. He gazed at his hands and only looked up from time to time. Then they could see his big black eyes, beautiful and short-sighted eyes with a velvety sheen, the eyes of a man who only looks to his work and does not see, does not feel and does not understand anything else in life or in the world.

The notables filed out of the small stuffy tent, troubled and downcast. They felt as if they were sweating under their new ceremonial clothes and each one of them felt fear and anxiety taking root in him.

A great and incomprehensible disaster had fallen upon the town and the whole of the district, a catastrophe whose end could not be foreseen. First of all began the felling of the forests and the transport of the timber. So great a mass of scaffolding arose on both banks of the Drina that for long the people thought that the bridge would be built of wood. Then the earthworks began, the excavations, the revetting of the chalky banks. These were mostly carried out by forced labour. So everything went on until the late autumn, when work was temporarily stopped and the first part of the construction completed.

All this was carried out under Abidaga's supervision and that of his long green staff which has passed into legend. Whomever he pointed at with this staff, having noticed that he was malingering or not working as he should, the guards seized; they beat him on the spot and then poured water over his bleeding and unconscious body and sent him back to work again. When in late autumn Abidaga left the town, he again sent for the notables and told them that he was going away to another place for the winter, but that his eye would still be on them. All would be responsible for everything. If it were found that any part of the work had been damaged, if a single stick were missing from the scaffolding, he would fine the whole town. When they ventured to say that damage might be caused by floods, he replied coldly and without hesitation that this was their district and the river too was theirs as well as whatever damage it might cause.

All the winter the townsmen guarded the material and watched the construction works like the eyes in their head. And when with the spring Abidaga once again appeared, with Tosun Effendi, there came with them Dalmatian stone-masons, whom the people called 'Latin masters'. At first there were about thirty of them, led by a certain Mastro Antonio, a Christian from Ulcinj. He was a tall, handsome man of keen eye, bold glance and hooked nose, with fair hair falling to his shoulders and dressed like a noble in the western manner. His assistant was a negro, a real negro, a young and merry man whom the whole town and all the workmen soon nicknamed 'the Arab'.

If in the previous year, judging from the mass of scaffolding, it seemed as if Abidaga had intended to build the bridge of wood, it now seemed to everyone that he wanted to build a new Stambul here on the Drina. Then began the hauling of stone from the quarries which had already been opened up in the hills near Banja, an hour's walk from the town.

Next year a most unusual spring broke near the Višegrad ferry. Besides all that which sprang up and flowered every year at that time, there arose out of the earth a whole settlement of huts; new roads made their appearance and new approaches to the water's edge. Countless oxcarts and packhorses swarmed on all sides. The men from Mejdan and Okolište saw how every day, like a sort of harvest, there grew there by the river a restless swarm of men, beasts and building material of every kind.

On the steep banks worked the master stone-masons. The whole area took on a sort of yellowish colour from the stone-dust. And a little farther along, on the sandy plain, local workers were slaking lime and moving, ragged and pale, through the white smoke which rose high from the kilns. The roads were torn to pieces by the overloaded carts. The ferry worked all day, taking from one bank to the other building material, overseers and workmen. Wading in the spring waters up to their waists, special workmen drove in piles and stakes and put in position gabions filled with clay, intended to break the current.

All this was watched by those who up till then had lived peacefully in their scattered houses on the slopes near the Drina ferry. And it would have been well for them had they been able only to watch, but the work soon became so extensive and its impetus so great that it drew into the whirlpool everything alive or dead, not only in the town but also from great distances away. With the second year the number of workers had grown to such an extent that they equalled all the male inhabitants of the town. All carts, all horses and oxen worked only for the bridge. Everything that could creep or roll was taken and pressed into service, sometimes paid but sometimes by force. There was more money than before, but high prices and shortages increased more rapidly than the money flowed in, so that when it reached men's hands it was already half eaten away. Even worse than the rise in prices and the shortages was the unrest, disorder and insecurity which now enveloped the town as a consequence of the incursion of so many workmen from the outer world. Despite all Abidaga's severity, there were frequent clashes among the workers, and many thefts from the gardens and courtyards. The Moslem women had to keep their faces veiled even when they went into their own yards, for the gaze of the countless workers, local and foreign, might come from anywhere and the Turks of the town kept the practices of Islam very strictly, the more so since they were all recently converted and there was scarcely one of them who did not remember either a father or a grandfather who was a Christian or a recently converted Turk. Because of this the older persons who followed the law of Islam were openly indignant and turned their backs on this chaotic mass of workers, draft animals, wood, earth and stone which grew ever larger and more complicated on both sides of the ferry and which, in the underpinning operations, broke into their streets, their courtyards and their gardens.

At first they had all been proud of the great bequest which the Vezir was to erect in their district. Then they had not realized, as they now saw with their own eyes, that these glorious buildings involved so much disorder and unrest, effort and expense. It was a fine thing, they thought, to belong to the pure ruling faith; it was a fine thing to have as a countryman the Vezir in Stambul, and still finer to imagine the strong, costly bridge across the river, but what was happening now in no way resembled this. Their town had been turned into a hell, a devil's dance of incomprehensible works, of smoke, dust, shouts and tumult. The years passed, the work extended and grew greater, but there was no end or thought of end to be seen. It looked like anything you like, but not a bridge.

So thought the recently converted Turks of the town and, in private among themselves, avowed that they were fed up to the teeth with lordship and pride and future glory and had had more than enough of the bridge and the Vezir.

They only prayed Allah to deliver them from this disaster and restore to them and their homes their former peace and the quietness of their humble lives beside the old-fashioned ferry on the river.

All this affected the Turks, but even more it affected the Christian *rayah* of the whole Višegrad district, with this difference, that no one asked their opinion about anything, nor were they even able to express their indignation. It was now the third year since the people had been on forced labour for the new bridge, they themselves and all their horses and oxen. And that too not only for the local *rayah* but also all those from the nearby districts. Everywhere Abidaga's guards and horsemen seized the *rayah* from the villages and even the towns and drove them away to work on the bridge. Usually they surprised them while sleeping and pinioned them like chickens. Through all Bosnia, traveller told traveller not to go to the Drina, for whoever went there was seized, without question of who or what he was or where he was going, and was forced to work for at least a few days. The young men in the villages tried to run away into the forests, but the guards took hostages from their houses, often women, in place of those who fled.

This was the third autumn that the people had been forced to labour on the bridge and in no way could it be seen that the work was progressing or that the end of their misfortune was in sight. Autumn was already in full spate; the roads were breaking up from the rains, the Drina was rising and troubled, and the bare stubble full of slow-winged ravens. But Abidaga did not halt the work. Under the wan November sun the peasants dragged wood and stone, waded with bare feet or in sandals of freshly slaughtered hide along the muddy roads, sweating with strain or chilled by the wind, folding around themselves cloaks full of new holes and old patches, and knotting up the ragged ends of their single shirts of coarse linen, blackened by rain, mud and smoke, which they dared not wash lest they fall to pieces in the water. Over all of them hovered Abidaga's green staff, for

Abidaga visited both the quarries at Banja and the works around the bridge several times each day. He was filled with rage and fury against the whole world because the days were growing shorter and the work had not progressed as quickly as he wished. In a heavy surcoat of Russian fur and high boots, he climbed, with red congested face, over the scaffolding of such piers as already arose from the waters, visited forges, barracks and workers' huts and swore at everyone he came across, overseers and contractors alike.

'The days are short. Always shorter. You sons of bitches, you are eating your bread for nothing!'

He burst out in fury, as if they were to blame because it dawned late and darkened early. Before twilight, that relentless and implacable Višegrad twilight, when the steep hills seemed to close in over the town and each night fell quickly, as heavy and deaf as the last, Abidaga's fury rose to its height; and having no one left on whom to vent his wrath, he turned it on himself and could not sleep for thinking of so much work not being done and so many people malingering and wasting time. He ground his teeth. He summoned the overseers and worked out how, from then on, it would be possible to make better use of the daylight and exploit the workers more effectively.

The people were sleeping in their huts and stables, resting and restoring their forces. But all did not sleep; they too knew how to keep vigil, to their own profit and in their own manner. In a dry and spacious stable a fire was burning, or more exactly had been burning, for now only a few embers glowing in the half-lit space remained. The whole stable was filled with smoke and the heavy, sour smell of wet clothes and sandals and the exhalations of about thirteen human bodies. They were all pressed men, peasants from the neighbourhood, Christian *rayah*. All were muddy and wet through, exhausted and careworn. They resented this unpaid and pointless forced labour while up there in the villages their fields awaited the autumn ploughing in vain. The greater number were still awake. They were drying their gaiters by the fire, plaiting sandals or only gazing at the embers. Amongst them was a certain Montenegrin, no one knew from where, whom the guards had seized on the road and had pressed for labour for several days, though he kept telling them and proving to them how wearisome and hard this work was for him and how his honour could not endure this work for slaves.

Most of the wakeful peasants, especially the younger ones, gathered around him. From the deep pocket of his cloak the Montenegrin drew out a *gusle*, a tiny primitive fiddle, clumsy and as small as the palm of a man's hand, and a short bow. One of the peasants went outside and mounted guard before the stable lest some Turk should chance to come along. All looked at the Montenegrin as if they saw him for the first time and at the *gusle* which seemed to disappear in his huge hands. He bent over, the *gusle* in his lap, and pressed its head under his chin, greased the string with resin and breathed heavily on the bow; everything was moist and slack. While he occupied himself with these petty tasks, calmly and self-confidently as if he were alone in the world, they all looked at him without a movement. At last the first notes wailed out, sharp and uneven. The excitement rose. The Monte-negrin found the key and began to sing through his nose and accompany himself with the *gusle*. Everyone was intent, awaiting the wonderful tale. Then, suddenly, after he had more or less attuned his voice to the *gusle*, the Montenegrin threw back his head proudly and violently so that his Adam's apple stood out in his scrawny neck and his sharp profile was outlined in the firelight, and sang in a strangled and constrained voice: A-a-a-a- a-a-a-a- and then all at once in a clear and ringing tone:

> 'The Serbian Tsar Stefan
> Drank wine in fertile Prizren,
> By him sat the old patriarchs,
> Four of them, the old patriarchs;
> Next them were nine bishops

And a score of three-tailed Vezirs
And the ranks of Serbian nobles.
Wine was served by Michael the cup-bearer
And on the breast of his sister Kandosia
Shone the light of precious stones. . . .'

The peasants pressed closer and closer around the singer but without making the slightest noise; their very breathing could be heard. They half closed their eyes, carried away with wonder. Thrills ran up and down their spines, their backs straightened up, their breasts expanded, their eyes shone, their fingers opened and shut and their jaw muscles tightened. The Montenegrin developed his melody more and more rapidly, even more beautiful and bolder, while the wet and sleepless workmen, carried away and insensible to all else, followed the tale as if it were their own more beautiful and more glorious destiny.

Among the countless peasants pressed for hard labour was a certain Radisav from Unište, a small village quite close to the town. He was a smallish man, dark-faced, with restless eyes, a little bent, and walked quickly, spreading out his legs and moving his head and shoulders from left to right, right to left, as if sowing wheat. He was not as poor as he appeared to be, nor as simple as he made himself out. His family were known as the Heraci; they had good land and there were many males in the house, but almost the whole village had been converted to Islam over the past forty years so that they were lonely and isolated. This small, bowed Radisav had been scurrying about from one stable to the next these autumn nights 'sowing' revolt and had insinuated himself among the peasants like an eel, whispering and counselling with one only at a time. What he said was roughly this:

'Brother, we have had enough of this. We must defend ourselves. You can see for yourself that this building work will be the death of all of us; it will eat us all up. Even our children will have to do forced labour on the bridge, if there are any of us left. For us this work means extermination and nothing less. A bridge is no good to the poor and to the *rayah*, but only for the Turks; we can neither raise armies nor carry on trade. For us the ferry is more than enough. So a few of us have agreed among ourselves to go by night, at the darkest hour, and break down and spoil as much as possible of what has been done, and to spread the rumour that it is a *vila*, a fairy, who is destroying the works at the bridge and who does not want any bridge over the Drina. We shall see if this will be of any help. We have no other way and something must be done.'

There were, as always, some who were fainthearted and unreliable, who thought this to be a sterile idea; since the cunning and powerful Turks would not be turned away from their intention they would have to do forced labour even longer since God so willed. They should not make bad worse. But there were also those who felt that anything was better than to go on slaving and to wait until even the last rag of clothing fell from a man and the last ounce of strength be wasted by the heavy labour and Abidaga's short commons; and that they must follow anyone who was willing to go to extremes. These were for the most part young men, but there were also serious married men, with families, who agreed, though without enthusiasm or fire, and who said worriedly:

'Come and let's break it down; may his blood eat him up before he eats us up. And if that does not help. . . .'

And at that point they waved their hands in desperate resolution.

So in these first autumn days the rumour began to spread, first among the workers and then in the town itself, that the *vila* of the waters had intervened in the work on the bridge, that she destroyed and pulled down overnight what had been built by day and that the whole scheme would come to nothing. At the same time, inexplicable damage began to appear over night in the revetments and even in the masonry itself. The tools which the masons had up till then left on the piers began to get lost and disappear, the revetments to break down and be carried away by the waters.

The rumour that the bridge would never be finished spread far afield. Both Turks and Christians spread it and little by little it took form as a firm belief. The Christian *rayah* were jubilant, whispering it stealthily and soundlessly but from a full heart. The local Turks, who had earlier looked on the Vezir's building work with pride, began to wink disdainfully and wave their hands. Many of the converted Turks who, in changing faith, had not found what they had hoped for, but had continued to sit down to a meagre supper and go about with patched elbows, heard the rumour and repeated with enjoyment the story of the great lack of success and found some sort of proud satisfaction in the thought that not even Vezirs could carry out everything they had a mind to do. It was already being said that the foreign *maestri* were preparing to leave and that there would be no bridge there where no bridge had ever been before and where it should never have been begun. All these tales blended and spread quickly.

The common people easily make up fables and spread them quickly, wherein reality is strangely and inextricably mixed and interwoven with legend. The peasants who listened at night to the *gusle* player said that the *vila* who was destroying the bridge had told Abidaga that she would not cease her work of destruction until twin children, Stoja and Ostoja by name, should be walled into the foundations. Many swore that they had seen the guards who were searching for such a pair of children in the villages (the guards were indeed going around the villages but they were not looking for children but listening for rumours and interrogating the people in order to try and find out who were those unknown persons who were destroying the bridge).

A short time before, it had happened that in a village above Višegrad a poor stuttering half-witted girl, who was a servant, became pregnant, she herself would not say, or could not say, by whom. It was a rare and almost unheard-of event that a girl, and such a girl, should conceive and still more so that the father should remain unknown. The story was noised far abroad. In good time the girl gave birth, in some stable or other, to twins, both stillborn. The women from the village who helped her at the birth, which was exceptionally difficult, at once buried the children in a plum-orchard. But on the third day after, the unfortunate mother got up and began to look for her children everywhere in the village. In vain they explained to her that the children had been born dead and had been buried. Finally, in order to be rid of her incessant questionings, they told her, or rather explained to her by gestures, that her children had been taken away to the town, down there where the Turks were building the bridge. Weak and distraught, she wandered down into the town and began to range around the ferry and the construction works, looking fearfully into the eyes of the men there and asking in incomprehensible stutterings for her children. The men looked at her in amazement or drove her away so that she should not hinder them at their work. Seeing that they did not understand what she wanted, she unbuttoned her coarse peasant shift and showed them her breasts, painful and swollen, on which the nipples had already begun to crack and showed all bloody from the milk that flowed from them irresistibly. No one knew how to help her and explain to her that her children had not been walled up in the bridge, for to all kind words and assurances, curses and threats, she only stuttered miserably and with sharp distrustful glances peered into every corner. Finally they gave up persecuting her and allowed her to wander about the construction work, avoiding her with a sorrowful compassion. The cooks gave her some of the workers' porridge which had got burnt at the bottom of the cauldrons. They called her mad Ilinka and, after them, the whole town did so. Even Abidaga himself passed by her without cursing her, turning his head away superstitiously, and ordered that she be given alms. So she went on living there, a harmless idiot, by the construction works. And because of her the story remained that the Turks had walled her children into the bridge. Some believed it and others not, but none the less it was repeated all the more and noised afar.

Meanwhile the damage went on, now less now more, and parallel with it the rumours spread even more obstinately that the *vilas* would not permit a bridge to be built across the Drina.

Abidaga was furious. It enraged him that anyone could be found who dared to undertake anything against his work or his intentions despite his proverbial harshness which he cultivated as a special subject for pride. Also all these people disgusted him, the Moslems as much as the Christians; slow and unskilled in their work, they were quick enough for raillery and lack of respect and knew only too well how to find mocking and corrosive words for everything they did not understand or did not know how to do. He posted guards on both banks of the river. The damage to the earthworks then ceased, but damage to the construction work in the river itself continued. Only on moonlit nights was there no damage. That confirmed Abidaga, who did not believe in the *vila*, in his belief that this particular *vila* was not invisible and did not descend from on high. For a long time he would not, or could not, believe those who said it was due to peasant cunning, but now he was convinced that that was exactly what it was. And that excited him to still greater fury. But he none the less knew that he must appear calm and hide his fury if he wanted to snare these pests and finish once and for all with these tales about *vilas* and about stopping work on the bridge, which might become dangerous. He summoned the chief of the guards, a certain man from Plevlje, who had grown up in Stambul, a pale and unhealthy man.

The two men were instinctively hostile to one another, but at the same time were continually drawn together and came into conflict. Between them incomprehensible feelings of hatred, repulsion, fear and distrust were woven permanently. Abidaga, who was mild and pleasant towards no one, displayed an unconcealed repulsion towards this pale-faced renegade. All that he did or said drove Abidaga into a frenzy and provoked him to curse and humiliate him, but the more that the man from Plevlje abased himself and was obsequious, the greater grew Abidaga's repulsion. From the first day of their meeting the leader of the guards was superstitiously and terribly afraid of Abidaga and this fear became in time an oppressive nightmare which never left him. At every step and movement, often in his dreams, he would think: what will Abidaga say about this? In vain he tried to please him and do what he wished. Everything that came from him Abidaga accepted with disdain. And that incomprehensible hatred hampered and disconcerted the man from Plevlje and made him still stiffer and clumsier. He believed that, because of Abidaga, he would one day lose not only his job and his position, but also his head. Therefore he lived in a state of permanent agitation and passed from dull discouragement to a feverish and cruel zeal. When now, pale and stiff, he stood before Abidaga, the latter spoke to him in a voice hoarse with anger.

'Listen, blockhead, you are clever with these sons of sows, you know their language and all their monkey-tricks. Yet for all that you are incapable of finding out what scab it is who has dared to spoil the Vezir's work. That is because you are a scab yourself, the same as they are, and the only worse scab is whoever made you leader and a chief and has found nobody to reward you as you deserve. So I will do so, since there is no other. Know that I will put you under the earth so that you will not throw as much shadow as even the tiniest blade of grass. If all damage to the works does not cease within three days, if you do not catch whoever is doing this and do not put an end to all these silly stories about *vilas* and about stopping the work, then I will put you living on a stake on the highest part of the staging, that all may see you and take fright and get some sense into their heads. I swear this by my life and my faith, which I do not swear by lightly. Today is Thursday. You have till Sunday. Now go to the devil who sent you to me. Go! March!'

Even without this oath the man from Plevlje would have believed Abidaga's threat, for even in his dreams he used to shudder at his words and at his glance. Now he went out in

one of his fits of panic-stricken terror and at once set desperately to work. He summoned his own men and, passing
suddenly from dull torpor to mad rage, he began to curse
them.

'Blind good-for-nothings!' raged the man from Plevlje, as
if he were already placed alive upon the stake and yelling in
the face of each of the guards. 'Is it thus that you keep watch
and look after the Sultan's interests? You are quick and lively
enough when you go to the cooking pots, but when you are
on duty your legs are leaden and your wits are dull. My face
burns because of you. But you will do no more slacking in
my employ. I will massacre all of you; not a single one of
you will keep his head on his shoulders if in two days this
business does not end and if you do not seize and kill these
bastards. You have still two days to live. I swear it by my faith
and the Koran!'

He went on shouting in this way for a long time. Then,
not knowing what else to say to them or with what more to
threaten them, he spat at them one by one. But when he had
played himself out and freed himself from the pressure of his
fear (which had taken the form of rage) he set to work at once
with desperate energy. He spent the night cruising up and
down the banks with his men. At one time during the night
it seemed to them that something was knocking at that part
of the staging which was farthest out in the river and they
rushed thither. They heard a plank crack and a stone fall into
the river, but when they got to the spot they indeed found
some broken scaffolding and a part of the masonry torn away
but no trace of the miscreants. Faced with that ghostly emptiness the guards shivered from superstitious fright and from
the darkness and moisture of the night. They called to one
another, peered into the blackness, waved lighted torches,
but all in vain. The damage had been done again, and they
who had done it had not been caught and killed, as though
in very truth they were invisible.

The next night the man from Plevlje arranged his ambush
better. He sent some of his men over to the farther bank

also and when night fell he hid guards in the scaffolding right out to the end and he himself with two others sat in a boat which he had drawn unnoticed in the darkness to the left bank. Thence in a few strokes they could be at one of the two piers on which construction had begun. In this way he could fall on the miscreants from two sides, so that they could not escape unless they had wings or could go under water.

All that long cold night the man from Plevlje lay in the boat covered with sheepskins, tormented by the dark thoughts whirling in his head; would Abidaga really carry out his threat and take his life which, under such a chief, was in any case no life but only terror and torment? But along the whole of the construction works not a murmur could be heard except the monotonous lapping and lisping of the unseen waters. Thus it dawned and the man from Plevlje felt in all his stiffened body that his life was darkening and shortening.

On the next, the third and last night, there was the same vigil, the same arrangements, the same fearful listening. Midnight passed. The man from Plevlje was seized with a mortal apathy. Then he heard a slight splash and then, louder, a blow on the oak beams which were placed in the river and on which the staging rested. There was a sharp whistle. But the leader's boat had already moved. Standing upright, he peered into the darkness, waving his hands and shouting in a hoarse voice:

'Row, row. . . .'

The men, half awake, rowed vigorously, but a strong current caught the boat earlier than it should have. Instead of reaching the staging, the boat turned down river. They were unable to make way against the current and it would have swept them far away had not something unexpectedly checked them.

There, right in the middle of the main current, where there were neither beams nor scaffolding, their boat struck something heavy and wooden which echoed dully. Only

then did they realize that on the scaffolding above them
the guards were struggling with something. The guards,
local renegades, were all shouting at once; they fell over one
another in the darkness in a medley of broken and incomprehensible cries:

'Hold there, don't let go!'

'Hey, fellows, here!'

'It's me! . . .'

Between the shouts some heavy object or human body
could be heard splashing into the water.

The man from Plevlje was for some moments uncertain
where he was or what was happening, but as soon as he had
come to his senses he began to pull with an iron hook at
the end of a long pole at the beams on which his boat had
struck and succeeded in pulling the boat upstream nearer and
nearer the scaffolding. Soon he was up to the oak piles and,
taking heart, shouted at the top of his voice:

'Lights! Light a torch there! Throw me a rope!'

At first no one answered. Then, after much shouting, in
which no one listened to or could understand anyone else, a
weak torch glimmered uncertainly and fitfully above. This
first spark of light only confused the eyes even more and
mingled in an uneasy whirl, men, things and their shadows
with the red reflections on the water. But then another torch
flamed in another hand. The light steadied and men began
to pull themselves together and recognize one another. Soon
everything became clear and explicable.

Between the boat of the man from Plevlje and the scaffolding lay a small raft made of only three planks; at the
front was an oar, a real raftsman's oar, only shorter and
weaker. The raft was moored with a bark cord to one of
the beams under the scaffolding and was held thus against
the swift waters which splashed about it and tried with all
their force to pull it away downstream. The guards on the
staging helped their leader to cross the raft and climb up to
them. All were haggard and out of breath. On the planks a
Christian peasant was lying. His breast was heaving quickly

and violently and his eyes, starting out of his head, showed fear-stricken whites.

The oldest of the four guards explained to their excited leader that they had been keeping watch at various points on the staging. When they heard the sound of oars in the darkness, they had thought it was their leader's boat, but they had been clever enough not to show themselves and to wait and see what would happen. Then they saw two peasants who approached the piers and with some difficulty moored their raft to one of them. They let them climb up and come among them and then they attacked them with axes, overcame them and bound them. One, who had been struck unconscious by a blow from an axe, they had bound easily, but the other one, after pretending to be half-dead, had slipped from their grasp like a fish through the planks into the water. The frightened guard halted in his story and the man from Plevlje screamed:

'Who let him go? Tell me who let him go, or I shall chop you all into small pieces, all of you.'

The men stood silently and blinked at the red flickering light while their leader kept turning around as if searching the darkness, and shouting insults at them such as they had never heard him use by day. Then, suddenly, he started, leant over the bound peasant as if over a precious hoard, and began to mutter through his teeth in a thin lachrymose voice:

'Guard him, guard him well! You bastards, if you let him go, not a single one of you will keep his head on his shoulders.'

The guards crowded round the peasant. Two more hurried to join them, crossing the ferry from the farther bank. The man from Plevlje ordered them to bind the prisoner more securely. So they carried him like a corpse slowly and carefully to the bank. The man from Plevlje went with them, not looking where he was treading and never taking his eyes from the bound man. It seemed to him that he was growing in stature with every step, that only from that moment was he beginning to live.

On the bank new torches were lighted and began to flare

up. The captive peasant was taken into one of the workmen's barracks where there was a fire, and was bound tightly to a post with ropes and chains taken from the hearth.

It was Radisav of Unište himself.

The man from Plevlje calmed down a little; he no longer screamed or swore, but he was unable to keep still. He sent guards along the banks to look for the other peasant who had leapt into the water, though it was clear that on so dark a night, if he had not drowned, it would be impossible to find or catch him. He gave order after order, went out, came in again and then once again went back, drunk with excitement. He began to interrogate the bound peasant, but soon left off doing that also. All that he did was only to master and conceal his nervousness, for in fact he had only one thought in his head; he was waiting for Abidaga. He had not long to wait.

As soon as he had slept out his first sleep Abidaga, as was his habit, waked shortly after midnight and, no longer able to sleep, stood by his window and looked out into the darkness. By day he could see from his balcony at Bikavac the whole river valley and all the construction works, with the barracks, mills, stables and all that devastated and littered space around them. Now in the darkness he sensed their presence and thought with bitterness how slowly the work was proceeding and how, sooner or later, this must reach the Vezir's ears. Someone would be sure to see to that. If no one else, then that smooth, cold and crafty Tosun Effendi. Then it might chance that he might fall into disgrace with the Vezir. That was what prevented him from sleeping, and even when he did fall asleep he trembled in his dreams. His food seemed poison to him, men seemed odious and his life dark when he even thought of it. Disgrace – that meant that he would be exiled from the Vezir's presence, that his enemies would laugh at him (Ah! Anything but that!), that he would be nothing and nobody, no more than a rag, a good-for-nothing, not only in the eyes of others but also in his own. It would mean giving up his hard won fortune or, if he managed to keep it, to eke it out stealthily, far from Stambul, somewhere in the obscure provinces, forgotten, superfluous, ridiculous, wretched. No, anything but that! Better not to see the sun, not to breathe the air. It would be a hundred times better to be nobody and to have nothing. That was the thought that always came back to him and several times a day forced the blood to beat painfully in his skull and his temples, but even at other times never completely left him but lay like a black cloud within him. That was what disgrace meant to him, and disgrace was possible every day, every hour, since everyone was working to bring it on him. Only he alone worked against it and defended himself; it was one man against everyone and everything. That had now lasted fifteen years, from the first time that the Vezir had entrusted him with a great and important task. Who could endure it? Who could sleep and be at peace?

Although it was a cold damp autumn night, Abidaga opened the casement and looked into the darkness, for the closed room seemed stifling to him. Then he noticed that there were lights and movements on the scaffolding and along the banks. When he saw that there were more and more of them, he thought that something unusual must have happened, dressed and woke his servant. Thus he arrived at the lighted stable just at the moment when the man from Plevlje no longer knew what further insults to use, whom to order and what to do to shorten the time.

The unexpected arrival of Abidaga completely bewildered him. So much had he longed for this moment, yet now that it had come he did not know how to profit from it as he had hoped. He stuttered in excitement and forgot all about the bound peasant. Abidaga only gazed through him disdainfully and went straight up to the prisoner.

In the stable they had built up a big fire to which the guards kept adding fresh faggots so that even the most distant corner was lit up.

Abidaga stood looking down at the bound peasant for he was much the taller man. He was calm and thoughtful.

Everyone waited for him to speak, while he thought to himself; so this is the one with whom I have had to struggle and fight, this is what my position and my fate depended upon, this wretched half-witted renegade from Plevlje and the incomprehensible and obdurate opposition of this louse from the *rayah*. Then he shook himself and began to give orders and to question the peasant.

The stable filled with guards, and outside could be heard the voices of the awakened overseers and workmen. Abidaga put his questions through the man from Plevlje.

Radisav first said that he and another man had decided to run away and that therefore they had prepared a small raft and set off downstream. When they pointed out to him the senselessness of this story since it was impossible in the darkness to go down the turbulent river full of whirlpools, rocks and shoals, and that those who want to run away do not climb on the scaffolding and damage the works, he fell silent and only muttered sullenly:

'Well, I am in your hands. Do what you like.'

'You will soon find out what we like,' Abidaga retorted briskly.

The guards took away the chains and stripped the peasant to the buff. They threw the chains into the heart of the fire and waited. As the chains were covered with soot, their hands were blackened and great patches were left on themselves and on the half-naked peasant. When the chains were almost red hot, Merdjan the Gipsy came up and took one end of them in a long pair of tongs, while one of the guards took the other end.

The man from Plevlje translated Abidaga's words.

'Perhaps now you will tell the whole truth.'

'What have I got to tell you? You know everything and can do what you like.'

The two men brought the chains and wrapped them round the peasant's broad hairy chest. The scorched hair began to sizzle. His mouth contracted, the veins in his neck swelled, his ribs seemed to stand out and his stomach muscles to contract and relax as when a man vomits. He groaned from the pain, strained at the ropes which bound him and writhed and twisted in vain to lessen the contact of his body with the red hot iron. His eyes closed and the tears flowed down his cheeks. They took the chain away.

'That was only a beginning. Isn't it better to talk without that?'

The peasant only breathed heavily through his nose, and remained silent.

'Who was with you?'

'His name was Jovan, but I do not know either his house or his village.'

They brought the chains again and the burning hair and skin sizzled. Coughing from the smoke and writhing from the pain, the peasant began to speak jerkily.

Those two alone had come to an agreement to destroy the work on the bridge. They thought that it had to be done and they had done it. No one else had known anything about it or had taken part in it. At first they had set out from the banks in various places and been quite successful, but when they saw that there were guards on the scaffolding and along the banks, they had thought of binding three planks together to make a raft and thus, unnoticed, approach the work from the river. That had been three days ago. On the first night they had nearly been caught. They only just got away. So the next night they had not gone out at all. When they tried again that same night with the raft, there had happened what had happened.

'That is all. So it was, and so we worked. Now do what you will.'

'No, no, that is not what we want. Tell us who made you do this! What you have suffered up till now is nothing to what you will get later on!'

'Well, do what you like.'

Merdjan then came nearer with a pair of pincers. He knelt in front of the bound man and began to tear the nails off his naked feet. The peasant remained silent and clenched his teeth but a strange trembling shook his whole body up to the waist even though he was bound which showed that the pain must have been exceptionally great. After a few moments the peasant forced a few muttered words through his teeth. The man from Plevlje, who had been hanging on his every word and waiting eagerly for some sort of admission, made a sign with his hand to the gipsy to stop and at once asked:

'What was that? What did you say?'

'Nothing. I only said: why in the name of God do you waste your time torturing me?'

'Tell us who made you do it?'

'Who made me do it? Why, the devil.'

'The devil?'

'The devil. Certainly that same devil who made you come here and build the bridge!'

The peasant spoke softly, but clearly and decisively.

The devil! A strange word, said so bitterly in so unusual a situation. The devil! The devil is certainly somewhere in this thought the man from Plevlje, standing with bowed head as if the bound man were questioning him and not he the bound man. The words touched him on a sensitive spot and awoke in him all of a sudden all his anxieties and fears, in all their strength and terror, as if they had never been swept away by the capture of the culprit. Perhaps indeed all this, with Abidaga and the building of the bridge and this mad peasant, was the devil's work. The devil! Perhaps he was the only one to fear. The man from Plevlje shivered and shook himself. At that moment the loud and angry voice of Abidaga brought him to himself.

'What's the matter with you? Are you asleep, good-for-nothing?' shouted Abidaga, striking his right boot with his short leather whip.

The gipsy was still kneeling with the pincers in his hand and looking upwards with black shining eyes, frightened and humble, at the tall figure of Abidaga. The guards piled up the fire which was already roaring. The whole place shone; it was like a furnace but somehow solemn. What that evening had seemed a gloomy and undistinguished building all at once was transformed, became larger, widened out. In the stable and around it reigned a sort of solemn emotion and a special silence as there is in places where one extracts the truth, a living man is tortured or where fateful things occur. Abidaga, the man from Plevlje and the bound man moved and spoke like actors and all the others went on tiptoe with lowered eyes, not speaking save when forced to and then only in a whisper. Everyone wished to be somewhere else, only not to be in this place nor at this work, but since that was not possible, they all lowered their voices and moved as little as they could, as if to get as far away as possible from this affair.

Seeing that the interrogation was going slowly and did not give any hope of results, Abidaga with impatient movements and loud oaths went out of the stable. After him reeled the man from Plevlje, followed by the guards.

Outside it was growing light. The sun had not yet risen, but the whole horizon was clear. Deep among the hills the clouds lay in long dull purple bands and between them could be seen the clear sky almost green in colour. Scattered patches of mist lay over the moist earth out of which peeked the tops of the fruit trees with sparse yellowish leaves. Still striking at his boot with his whip, Abidaga gave orders. The criminal should continue to be interrogated, especially about those who had helped him, but he should not be tortured beyond endurance lest he die. Everything must be made ready so that at noon that same day he should be impaled alive on the outermost part of the construction work at its highest point, so that the whole town and all the workers should be able to see him from the banks of the river; Merdjan was to get everything ready and the town-crier to announce the execution through all the quarters of the town, so that at midday all the people might see what happened to those who hindered the building of the bridge, and that the whole male population, both Turks and *rayah*, from children to old men, must gather on one or other of the banks to witness it.

The day which was dawning was a Sunday. On Sunday work went on as on any other day, but this day even the overseers were distrait. As soon as it was broad daylight, the news spread about the capture of the criminal, his torture and his execution which was to take place at midday. The hushed and solemn mood of the stable spread over the whole area about the building works. The men on forced labour worked silently, each one avoided looking his neighbour in the eyes, and each man looked only to the work before him as if that were the beginning and the end of his world.

An hour before noon the people of the town, for the most part Turks, had collected on a level space near the bridge. Children were hoisted on to high blocks of building stone which were lying about. The workmen swarmed around the narrow benches where the meagre rations which kept them alive were usually distributed. Chewing at them, they were silent and looked uneasily about them. A little later Abidaga appeared, accompanied by Tosun Effendi, Mastro Antonio and one or two of the more prominent Turks. All stood on a small dry hummock between the bridge and the stable where the condemned man was. Abidaga went once more to the stable, where he was told that everything was ready; lying there was an oak stake about eight feet long, pointed as was necessary and tipped with iron, quite thin and sharp, and all well greased with lard. On the scaffolding were the blocks between which the stake would be embedded and nailed, a wooden mallet for the impalement, ropes and everything else that was needed.

The man from Plevlje was distraught, his face earthen in colour and his eyes bloodshot. Even now he was not able to endure Abidaga's flaming glances.

'Listen, you! If everything is not as it should be and if you disgrace me in public, neither you nor your bastard of a gipsy will ever appear before me again, for I will drown you both in the Drina like a pair of blind puppies.'

Then, turning to the shivering gipsy, he said more kindly:

'You will get six grosh for the job, and another six if he stays alive till nightfall. See to it!'

The *hodja* called out from the main mosque in the market-place in a clear sharp voice. Uneasiness spread among the assembled people and a few moments later the door of the stable opened. Ten guards were drawn up in two ranks, five on either side. Between them was Radislav, barefooted and bareheaded, alert and stooping as ever, but he no longer 'sowed' as he walked but marched strangely with short steps, almost skipping on his mutilated feet with bleeding holes where the nails had been; on his shoulders he carried a long white sharpened stake. Behind him was Merdjan with two other gipsies who were to be his helpers in the execution of the sentence. Suddenly from somewhere or other the man from Plevlje appeared on his bay and took his place at the head of the procession, which only had to go about a hundred paces to reach the first scaffolding.

The people craned their necks and stood on tiptoe to see the man who had hatched the plot and destroyed the building work. They were all astonished at the poor miserable appearance of the man they had imagined to be quite different. Naturally, none of them knew why he hopped in so droll a manner and took abrupt little steps, and none of them could see the burns from the chains which crossed his chest like great belts, for his shirt and cloak hid them. Therefore he seemed to all those there too wretched and too insignificant to have done the deed which now brought him to execution. Only the long white stake gave a sort of gruesome grandeur to the scene and kept everyone's eyes fixed on it.

When they reached the spot on the bank where the excavation work began, the man from Plevlje dismounted and with a sort of solemn and theatrical air gave the reins to a groom, then disappeared with the others in the steep muddy track which led down to the water's edge. A little later the people saw them again as they appeared in the same order on the staging, climbing upwards slowly and carefully. On the narrow passages made of planks and beams the guards

closely surrounded Radisav and kept him very near them
lest he should leap into the river. They dragged their way
along slowly and climbed even higher till they reached the
top. There, high above the water, was a boarded space about
the size of a small room. On it, as on a raised stage, they took
their places, Radisav, the man from Plevlje and the three
gipsies, with the rest of the guards posted around them on
the staging.

The people watching moved uneasily and shifted about.
Only a hundred paces separated them from those planks,
so that they could see every man and every movement, but
could not hear words or distinguish details. The people and
the workmen on the left bank were about three times farther
away, and moved around as much as they could and made
every effort to try to see and hear better. But they could
hear nothing and what they could see seemed at first only
too ordinary and uninteresting and at the end so terrible that
they turned their heads away and many quickly went home,
regretting that they had ever come.

When they ordered Radisav to lie down, he hesitated a
moment and then, looking past the gipsies and guards as if
they were not there, came close up to the man from Plevlje
and said almost confidentially as if speaking to a friend, softly
and heavily:

'Listen, by this world and the next, do your best to pierce
me well so that I may not suffer like a dog.'

The man from Plevlje started and shouted at him, as if
defending himself from that too intimate approach:

'March, Vlach! You who are so great a hero as to destroy
the Sultan's work now beg for mercy like a woman. It will be
as it has been ordered and as you have deserved.'

Radisav bent his head still lower and the gipsies came up
and began to strip off his cloak and his shirt. On his chest the
wounds from the chains stood out, red and swollen. Without
another word the peasant lay down as he had been ordered,
face downward. The gipsies approached and the first bound
his hands behind his back; then they attached a cord to each

of his legs, around the ankles. Then they pulled outwards and to the side, stretching his legs wide apart. Meanwhile Merdjan placed the stake on two small wooden chocks so that it pointed between the peasant's legs. Then he took from his belt a short broad knife, knelt beside the stretched-out man and leant over him to cut away the cloth of his trousers and to widen the opening through which the stake would enter his body. This most terrible part of the bloody task was, luckily, invisible to the onlookers. They could only see the bound body shudder at the short and unexpected prick of the knife, then half rise as if it were going to stand up, only to fall back again at once, striking dully against the planks. As soon as he had finished, the gipsy leapt up, took the wooden mallet and with slow measured blows began to strike the lower blunt end of the stake. Between each two blows he would stop for a moment and look first at the body in which the stake was penetrating and then at the two gipsies, reminding them to pull slowly and evenly. The body of the peasant, spreadeagled, writhed convulsively; at each blow of the mallet his spine twisted and bent, but the cords pulled at it and kept it straight. The silence from both banks of the river was such that not only every blow but even its echo from somewhere along the steep bank could be clearly heard. Those nearest could hear how the man beat with his fore-head against the planks and, even more, another and unusual sound, that was neither a scream, nor a wail, nor a groan, nor anything human; that stretched and twisted body emitted a sort of creaking and cracking like a fence that is breaking down or a tree that is being felled. At every second blow the gipsy went over to the stretched-out body and leant over it to see whether the stake was going in the right direction and when he had satisfied himself that it had not touched any of the more important internal organs, he returned and went on with his work.

From the banks all this could scarcely be heard and still less seen, but all stood there trembling, their faces blanched and their fingers chilled with cold.

For a moment the hammering ceased. Merdjan now saw that close to the right shoulder muscles the skin was stretched and swollen. He went forward quickly and cut the swollen place with two crossed cuts. Pale blood flowed out, at first slowly then faster and faster. Two or three more blows, light and careful, and the iron-shod point of the stake began to break through at the place where he had cut. He struck a few more times until the point of the stake reached level with the right ear. The man was impaled on the stake as a lamb on the spit, only that the tip did not come through the mouth but in the back and had not seriously damaged the intestines, the heart or the lungs. Then Merdjan threw down the mallet and came nearer. He looked at the unmoving body, avoiding the blood which poured out of the places where the stake had entered and had come out again and was gathering in little pools on the planks. The two gipsies turned the stiffened body on its back and began to bind the legs to the foot of the stake. Meanwhile Merdjan looked to see if the man were still alive and carefully examined the face that had suddenly become swollen, wider and larger. The eyes were wide open and restless, but the eyelids were unmoving, the mouth was wide open but the two lips stiff and contracted and between them the clenched teeth shone white. Since the man could no longer control some of his facial muscles the face looked like a mask. But the heart beat heavily and the lungs worked with short, quickened breath. The two gipsies began to lift him up like a sheep on a spit. Merdjan shouted to them to take care and not shake the body; he himself went to help them. Then they embedded the lower, thicker end of the stake between two beams and fixed it there with huge nails and then behind, at the same height, buttressed the whole thing with a short strut which was nailed both to the stake and to a beam on the staging.

When that too had been done, the gipsies climbed down and joined the guards, and on that open space, raised a full eight feet upright, stiff and bare to the waist, the man on the stake remained alone. From a distance it could only be guessed that the stake to which his legs had been bound at the ankles passed right through his body. So that the people saw him as a statue, high up in the air on the very edge of the staging, high above the river.

A murmur and a wave of movement passed through the onlookers on the banks. Some lowered their eyes and others went quickly home without turning their heads. But the majority looked dumbly at this human likeness, up there in space, unnaturally stiff and upright. Fear chilled their entrails and their legs threatened to give way beneath them, but they were still unable to move away or take their eyes from the sight. And amid that terrified crowd mad Ilinka threaded her way, looking everyone in the eyes and trying to read their glances to find from them where her sacrificed and buried children were.

Then the man from Plevlje, Merdjan and a pair of guards went up to the impaled man and began to examine him more closely. Only a thin trickle of blood flowed down the stake. He was alive and conscious. His ribs rose and fell, the veins in his neck pulsed and his eyes kept turning slowly but unceasingly. Through the clenched teeth came a long drawn-out groaning in which a few words could with difficulty be distinguished.

'Turks, Turks, . . .' moaned the man on the stake, 'Turks on the bridge . . . may you die like dogs . . . like dogs.'

The gipsies picked up their tools and then, with the man from Plevlje, came down from the staging to the bank. The people made way for them and began to disperse. Only the children on the high blocks of stone and the bare trees waited a little longer, not knowing if this were the end or whether there would be more, to see what would happen next with that strange man who hovered over the waters as if suddenly frozen in the midst of a leap.

The man from Plevlje approached Abidaga and reported that everything had been carried out correctly and satisfactorily, that the criminal was still alive and that it seemed that he would go on living since his internal organs had not been damaged. Abidaga did not reply but only gave a sign with his hand to bring his horse and began to say goodbye to Tosun Effendi and Mastro Antonio. Everyone began to disperse. Through the market-place the town-crier could be heard announcing that the sentence had been carried out and that the same or a worse punishment awaited anyone who would do the like in future.

The man from Plevlje remained in perplexity on the level space which had now suddenly emptied. His servant held his horse and the guards waited for orders. He felt that he ought to say something but was not able to because of the wave of feeling that only now began to rise within him and choke him. Only now did he become conscious of all that he had forgotten since he had been too busy carrying out the sentence. He remembered Abidaga's threat that it would have been he who would have been placed upon the stake had he not succeeded in catching the criminal. He had escaped that horror, but only by a hair and only at the last moment. But things had turned out otherwise. The sight of that man, who was hanging, bound and still alive, over the river filled him with terror and also with a sort of painful joy that such a fate had not been his and that his body was still undamaged, was free and able to move. At that thought burning pains shot through his chest and spread into his legs and arms and forced him to move about, to smile and to speak, just to prove to himself that he was healthy, that he could move freely, could speak and laugh aloud, could even sing if he so wished, and not merely mutter useless curses from a stake, awaiting death as the only happiness which could still be his. His hands and arms moved of their own volition, his lips opened and from them flowed unwittingly a strangled laugh and a copious flow of words:

'Ha, ha, ha, Radisav, thou mountain *vila*, why so stiff? . . . Why not go on and undermine the bridge? . . . Why writhe and groan? Sing, *vila*! Dance, *vila*!'

Astonished and bewildered, the guards watched their leader dance with outstretched arms, heard him sing and choke with laughter and with strange words, saw the white foam oozing more and more from the corners of his lips. And his bay horse, in fear, cast sidelong glances at him.

CHAPTER IV

ALL THOSE WHO had been present at the execution of the sentence spread terrible reports through the town and the surrounding villages. An indescribable fear gripped the townsmen and the workers. Slowly and gradually a full consciousness of what had happened in their midst in the course of a short November day came home to them. All conversation centred on the man who, high up there on the scaffolding, was still alive on the stake. Everyone resolved not to speak of him; but what good was that when their thoughts turned continually to him and all glances centred on the spot?

The peasants coming from Banja carting stone in their bullock carts turned their eyes away and curtly ordered their oxen to make haste. The workers at work along the banks and on the staging called to one another in hushed voices and as little as they could. The overseers themselves, with their wooden staves in their hands, were subdued and less brutal. The Dalmatian stone-masons clenched their jaws, turned their backs on the bridge and struck angrily with their chisels which in the universal stillness sounded like a flock of woodpeckers.

Twilight came quickly and the workers hurried to their hovels in the wish to get as far as possible from the staging. Before it was quite dark, Merdjan and a trusted servant of Abidaga once more climbed the staging and definitely confirmed that Radisav was even then, four hours after the sentence had been carried out, alive and conscious. Consumed with fever, he rolled his eyes slowly and painfully, and when he saw the gipsy below him, he began to groan more loudly. In this groaning, which showed his life was ebbing, it was possible to distinguish only a few isolated words:

'The Turks . . . the Turks . . . the bridge!'

Having satisfied themselves, they returned to Abidaga's house at Bikavac, telling everyone whom they met on their way that the criminal was still alive; and since he ground his teeth and spoke well and clearly from the stake there was every hope that he would live until noon the next day. Abidaga too was satisfied and gave orders that Merdjan was to be paid his promised reward.

That night everything living in the town and about the bridge slept in fear. Or rather those who could slept but there were many to whom sleep would not come.

The next day which was a Monday dawned a sunny November morning. There was not an eye in the whole town or about the building work that did not turn towards that intricate criss-cross of beams and planks over the waters, at the farther end of which, upright and apart, was the man on the stake. Many who, on waking, had thought that they had dreamt all that had taken place the day before upon the bridge, now rose and with fixed eyes looked at the continuance of this nightmare which remained there stark in the sun.

Amongst the workers there was still that hush of the day before, filled with pity and bitterness. In the town there was still that whispering and anxiety. Merdjan and that same servant of Abidaga's climbed up the scaffolding once more and examined the condemned man; they spoke to each other, lifted their eyes and looked upwards into the face of the peasant and then, suddenly, Merdjan pulled at his trousers. From the way in which they made their way downwards to the bank and walked silently through the men at work, everyone realized that the peasant had at last died. Those who were Serbs felt a certain easing of the spirit, as at an invisible victory.

Now they looked more boldly up at the scaffolding and the man who had been condemned. They felt as if fate, in their continual wrestling and measuring of forces with the Turks, had now inclined to their side. Death was the greatest trump in the game. Mouths till then contracted in fear now began to open. Muddy, wet, unshaven and pale, rolling great blocks of Banja stone with pinewood levers, they halted for a moment to spit on their palms and say to each other in hushed voices:

'May God pardon him and have mercy upon him!'

'Ah, the martyr! It is hard for such as we!'

'Don't you see that he has become a saint?'

And everyone glanced up at the dead man who stayed there as upright as if he had been marching at the head of a company. Up there, so high, he no longer seemed terrible or pitiful to them. On the other hand, it was now clear to all of them how he was exalted and set apart. He no longer stood on the earth, his hands held to nothing, he did not swim, did not fly; he no longer had any weight. Freed from all earthly ties and burdens, he was no longer a prey to troubles; no one could do anything more against him, neither rifle nor sword, nor evil thoughts, nor men's words, nor Turkish courts. Naked to the waist, with arms and legs bound, his head thrown back against the stake, that figure no longer seemed to bear any likeness to a human body which grows and then rots away, but seemed to be raised on high, hard and imperishable as a statue which would remain there forever.

The men on forced labour turned and crossed themselves stealthily.

In Mejdan the women hurried through the courtyards to whisper to each other for a moment or so and weep, and then at once rushed back to see if the luncheon had burnt. One of them lighted an ikon-lamp. Quickly, in all the houses, ikon-lamps hidden away in the corners of the rooms began to glow. The children, blinking in this solemn atmosphere, looked at the brightness and listened to the broken and incomprehensible sentences of their elders: 'Defend us, O Lord, and protect us!', 'Ah, martyr, he is chosen before God as if he had built the greatest of churches!', 'Help us, O Lord, Thou Holy One, drive away the enemy and do not let him rule longer over us!'; and incessantly asked who was the martyr and who was building a church and where. The small boys were especially inquisitive. Their mothers hushed them:

'Be quiet, my soul! Be quiet and listen to mother. As long as you are alive keep away from those accursed Turks.'

Before it began to darken, Abidaga once more went around the construction work and, satisfied with the result of this terrible example, ordered that the peasant be taken down from the stake.

'Throw the dog to the dogs!'

That night, which fell suddenly as soft and moist as spring, there began an incomprehensible murmuring, a coming and going among the workers. Even those who had not wanted to hear of destruction and resistance were now ready to make sacrifices and do all that they could. The man on the stake had become an object of general attention as if he had been holy. Some hundreds of exhausted men, moved by an inner force made up of pity and ancient custom, instinctively joined in an effort to get the corpse of the martyred man, to prevent it from being profaned and to give it Christian burial. After cautious whispered consultations in the huts and stables, the men on forced labour collected among themselves the considerable sum of seven grosh with which to bribe Merdjan. To carry out this work they chose three of the craftiest among them and succeeded in getting in touch with the executioner. Wet and tired from their labours, the three peasants bargained, slowly and cunningly, going round and round the point. Frowning, scratching his head and stuttering intentionally, the oldest of the peasants said to the gipsy:

'Well, it's all over now. It was so fated. Still, you know it is, a human being, one of God's creations . . . it shouldn't . . . you know what I mean . . . it shouldn't be eaten by beasts or torn to bits by dogs.'

Merdjan, who knew well enough what was in the wind, defended himself, more sorrowfully than obstinately.

'No. Don't even speak of it. You'll get me well roasted. You don't know what a lynx that Abidaga is!'

The peasant was troubled, frowned and thought to himself: 'He is a gipsy, a thing without cross or soul, one cannot call him either friend or brother, and one cannot take his word by anything in heaven or earth', and held his hand in the shallow pocket of his cloak tightly grasping the seven grosh.

'I know that very well. We all know that it is not easy for you. Only, no one can blame you. Here we have got together four grosh for you which, as we see it, should be enough. . . .'

'No, no, my life is dearer to me than all the treasure in the world. Abidaga would never let me live; that one sees everything, even when he is asleep. I am dead at the mere thought of it!'

'Four grosh, even five, but that's all we can do! We could even find that much,' went on the peasant, paying no heed to the gipsy's laments.

'I dare not, I dare not. . . .'

'Very well then. . . . . Since you have got your orders to throw the . . . the body . . . to the . . . to the dogs, you will throw it. But what happens after that is none of your affair, nor will anyone ask you about it. So you see if we, for example, should take that . . . that body . . . and should bury it somewhere according to our law but, let us say, stealthily so that not a living soul will know . . . then you will, for example, say next day that the dogs have . . . have carried away that . . . that body. No one will be any the worse and you will have got your share. . . .'

The peasant spoke carefully and with circumspection, only he halted with a strange uneasiness before the word 'body'. . . .

'Am I to lose my head for five grosh? No, no, n-o-o-.'

'For six,' added the peasant calmly.

The gipsy drew himself up, spread out his arms, and assumed an expression of moving sincerity, as only men who do not distinguish truth from lies can do. He stood before the peasant as though he were the judge and the peasant the criminal.

'Let it be on my head, since that is my fate, and let my *chai* remain a widow and my children beggars; if you give me seven grosh, take the body away, but no one must see and no one must know.'

The peasant shook his head, regretting deeply that this scab must get everything right down to the last farthing, as if the gipsy had been able to see into his closed fist!

Then they came to an agreement, down to the last detail. Merdjan was to bring the corpse, when he had taken it from the scaffolding, to the left bank of the river and there, as soon as it grew dark, was to throw it down on a stony patch near the road, so that it could be seen both by Abidaga's servants and by anyone who might be passing by. The three peasants would be hidden in a thicket, a little farther on. As soon as darkness fell, they would take the corpse, carry it away and bury it, but in a hidden place and without any visible trace, so that it would seem quite likely that the dogs had dragged it away overnight and eaten it. Three grosh were to be paid in advance and four more when the job was finished.

That same night everything was carried out according to the agreement.

At twilight Merdjan brought the corpse and threw it on the roadside. (It no longer resembled that body which all had looked at for the past two days, upright and stiff upon the stake; this was once again the old Radisav, small and bowed, only now without blood or life.) Then he went back at once with his assistants by the ferry to the town on the other bank. The peasants waited in the thicket. One or two late workers passed, and a Turk on his way home to the town. Then the whole countryside became quite still and dark. Dogs began to appear, those powerful, mangy, hungry cowardly curs without masters or homes. The peasants con-cealed in the undergrowth threw stones at them and drove them away. They ran with tails between their legs but only for twelve paces or so from the corpse where they waited to see what would happen next. Their eyes could be seen glowing and shining. When it was clear that night had really fallen and there was no longer any likelihood that anyone else would come along, the peasants came out of their hiding place carrying a pick and shovel. They had also brought two planks with them on which they placed the corpse and so carried it away. There in a gully caused by the spring and autumn rains rushing down the hill into the Drina, they removed the larger stones which formed the bed of a dry watercourse, and dug out a deep grave quickly, silently, without words and without noise. In it they placed the cold, stiff, twisted body. The oldest of the peasants leapt into the pit, crossed himself carefully a few times, lit first a piece of tinder and then a small candle of twisted wax, shielding the light with his two hands; he placed it above the head of the dead man and crossed himself, repeating three times quickly and aloud, 'In the Name of the Father, the Son and the Holy Spirit.' The two men with him crossed themselves in the darkness above. The peasant then made a movement with his hands over the dead man as if pouring from his empty hand the unseen wine and said twice, softly and reverently:

'Peace with the saints, O Christ, for the soul of Thy slave.'

Then he whispered a few more words, disconnected and incomprehensible, but sounding like prayers, solemn and reverent, while the two men above the grave crossed themselves continually. When he had ended, they lowered the two planks so that they formed a sort of roof over the dead man. Then the peasant crossed himself once more, extinguished the candle and climbed out of the grave. Then, slowly and carefully, they replaced the earth in the grave, treading it down well so that no swelling could be seen. When that was done, they put back the stones, like the bed of the stream, across the freshly dug earth, crossed themselves once more and went back home, making a wide detour so as to rejoin the road at a point as far away as possible.

That night there fell a dense soft rain without wind, and in the morning that dawned the whole river valley was filled with milky mist and a heavy moisture. In a sort of white resplendence which now rose and now fell, the sun could be seen somewhere struggling with the mists which it was unable to pierce. All was ghostly, new and strange. Men suddenly appeared out of the mist and equally suddenly were lost in it. In such weather, early in the morning, there passed through the market-place a simple country cart and on it two guards watching the man from Plevlje, their leader until the day before, bound and under arrest.

From the previous day, when in the access of unexpected emotion at finding himself still alive and not on the stake he had begun to dance before them all, he had never calmed down. All his muscles twitched, he could no longer keep still, but was constantly tormented by the irresistible urge to prove to himself and show others that he was still healthy, whole and capable of movement. At intervals he would remember Abidaga (that was the black spot in his new joy!) and would fall into a dark reverie. But while he was in this mood, fresh forces would collect within him which drove him irresistibly to wild and spasmodic movements like a madman. He would get up again and begin to dance, spreading out his arms, clicking his fingers and twisting like a dancer, showing by sudden and lively actions that he was not on the stake and gasping to the rhythm of his dance:

'See . . . see . . . I can do this . . . and that . . . and that! . . .'

He refused to eat and would suddenly break off every conversation that he began and start to dance, affirming childishly at every movement:

'See, see, I can do this . . . and this. . . .!'

When that night they finally decided to tell Abidaga what had happened, he replied coldly and abruptly:

'Take the madman to Plevlje and let them keep him chained up in his own house there, so that he does not play the fool round here. He was not the man for a job like that!'

So was it done. But as their leader was unable to keep still, his guards were forced to bind him to the cart in which he was sitting. He wept and defended himself and as long as he was able to move any part of his body, he struggled and shouted: 'See, see!' Finally they had to bind his arms and his legs, so that now he sat in the cart upright like a sack of wheat swaddled in ropes. But, since he was no longer able to move, he began to imagine that they were impaling him on the stake and writhed and resisted with desperate cries:

'Not me, not me! Catch the *vila*! No, Abidaga!'

From the last houses on the outskirts of the town, people rushed out excited by his cries, but the cart with the guards and the sick man was swiftly lost to sight in the thick mist along the Dobruna road through which the sun could just be glimpsed.

The unexpected and pitiable departure of the man from Plevlje instilled still greater fear into men's bones. It began to be whispered that the condemned peasant had been innocent and that this had preyed on the mind of the man from Plevlje. Among the Serbs in Mejdan the women began to tell how the *vilas* had buried the dead body of the hapless Radisav below Butkovo Stijene and how at night a plenteous light fell upon his grave, thousands and thousands of lighted candles which flamed and quivered in a long line reaching from heaven to earth. They had seen them through their tears.

All sorts of things were whispered and believed, but fear was stronger than all else.

Work on the bridge was carried on quickly, smoothly and without interruption or hindrance. It went on somehow or other until the beginning of December when an unexpectedly hard frost came, against which even Abidaga's power could do nothing.

There were unheard-of frosts and blizzards in that first half of December. The stones froze into the ground and the wood cracked. A fine crystalline snow covered everything, tools and whole huts, and the next day a capricious wind would drive it to another side and bury another part. Work ceased of itself and the fear of Abidaga paled and finally disappeared. Abidaga tried to fight against it for some days but finally gave way. He dismissed the workers and stopped the work. In the midst of the heaviest snowfall he rode away with his men. That same day Tosun Effendi set out on a peasant's sleigh heaped with straw and blankets, and after him Mastro Antonio, in the opposite direction. And all that camp of forced labourers dispersed into the villages and the deep valleys without a sound and as imperceptibly as water soaked up by the earth. The building works remained like a discarded toy.

Before setting out Abidaga again summoned the leading Turks. He was depressed by his angry impotence and told them, as in the previous year, that he left everything in their hands and that theirs was the responsibility.

'I am going away but my eyes remain here. Take heed; better that you cut off a score of disobedient heads than that a single nail of the Sultan's should be lost. As soon as spring breaks I shall be here once more and shall call everyone to account.'

The leaders promised everything as they had the year before and dispersed to their homes, filled with anxiety and wrapped in their cloaks, capes and shawls, thanking God to themselves that God had given winter blizzards to the world and had in that way shown that His power was able to put a limit to the power of the mighty.

But when spring broke again, it was not Abidaga who came, but a new representative of the Vezir, Arif Beg, together with Tosun Effendi. What he had so much feared had happened to Abidaga. Someone, someone whom he knew well and had worked near him, had sent to the Grand Vezir detailed and accurate reports of his work on the Višegrad bridge. The Vezir had been accurately informed that for those two years between two and three hundred workmen had been summoned for forced labour every day without a single para of pay and very often bringing their own food, and that Abidaga had taken the Vezir's money for himself (the amount of money that he had up till then managed to embezzle was also reckoned). He had covered up his dishonesty, as is so often the case in life, by excessive zeal and exaggerated severity, so that the people of the whole district, not only the *rayah* but also the Turks, instead of giving thanks for this great bequest, cursed both the hour when it had been begun and the man for whom it was being built. Mehmed Pasha, who had been struggling all his life with the peculations and dishonesty of his officials, had ordered his unworthy servant to reimburse the whole sum and take what remained of his fortune and his harem and go at once to a small town in Anatolia, and never to let himself be heard of again unless he wanted a worse fate to befall him.

Two days after Arif Beg, Mastro Antonio also arrived from Dalmatia with the first workers. Tosun Effendi presented him to the new chief, and on a warm sunny April day they inspected the construction works and settled the order for the first work. After Arif Beg had withdrawn, leaving the other two alone on the bank, Mastro Antonio looked attentively at the face of Tosun Effendi who, even on so sunny a day, was huddled up in a wide black mantle.

'This is quite another sort of man. Thanks be to God! I only ask myself who was so smart and so brave as to inform the Vezir and have that animal removed?'

Tosun Effendi only looked straight in front of him and said quietly:

'There is no doubt, this one is better.'

'It must have been someone who knew Abidaga's affairs well and who had access to the Vezir and enjoyed his trust.'

'Certainly, certainly, this one is better,' replied Tosun Effendi without looking up and wrapping his mantle even more closely around him.

So the work began under the new chief, Arif Beg.

He was, indeed, quite a different sort of man. Exceptionally tall, stooping, bald, with salient cheekbones and slit-like black laughing eyes, the people at once nicknamed him Misir-Baba – Old Baldie. Without shouting, without a staff, without big words or visible effort, he gave orders and set everything in order good-humouredly and casually with confident authority; he never overlooked anything or lost track of anything. But he also brought with him a feeling of strict attention to everything that was the Vezir's will or order, but like a calm, normal and honest man who had nothing to be afraid of and nothing to conceal, so that he had no need to frighten or persecute anyone. The work went on at the same speed (since speed was what the Vezir wanted), faults were punished with similar severity, but unpaid forced labour was stopped from that day. All the workers were paid and received rations in flour and salt, and all went quicker and better than in Abidaga's time. Also, mad Ilinka vanished; during the winter she had disappeared somewhere into the villages.

The construction work grew and extended.

It could now be seen that the Vezir's bequest was not for a bridge only, but also for a *han* or caravanserai, in which travellers from afar who intended to cross the bridge could find shelter for themselves, their horses and their goods should they arrive at nightfall. On Arif Beg's order the construction of this caravanserai was commenced. At the entry to the market-place, 200 paces from the bridge, just where the road to Mejdan began to rise steeply, there was a level space on which until then the Wednesday stock-market had been held. On this level space the building of the new *han* began. Work went on slowly, but from the very start it could be seen that it would be a solid and grandiose building conceived on a grand scale. The people scarcely even noticed how, slowly but surely, a great stone *han* was rising, for their attention was wholly centred on the building of the bridge.

What was now being done on the Drina was so complicated, all the work so interlocked and complex, that the loungers in the town, who watched the building work from the two banks as if it were some natural phenomenon, could no longer follow it with understanding. There were always fresh embankments and trenches running in various directions, and the river was divided and split up into side-currents and backwaters and its main course moved from one to another. Mastro Antonio brought from Dalmatia especially skilled cordwainers and collected all the hemp even from the districts around. In special buildings the master-workmen twisted ropes of exceptional strength and thickness. Greek carpenters, according to designs of their own or those drawn up by Tosun Effendi, built huge wooden cranes with pawls, erected them on rafts and thus, with these ropes, raised even the heaviest blocks of stone and transported them to the piers which, one by one, began to rise out of the bed of the river. The transport of each one of these huge blocks from the banks to its position in the foundations of the bridge-piers lasted four days.

Watching all this, day after day, year after year, the towns-people began to lose count of time and of the real intentions of the builders. It seemed to them that the construction had not moved an inch forward but was becoming more and more complicated and involved in auxiliary and subsidiary workings, and the longer it lasted the less it looked like what it was intended to be. Men who do not work themselves and who undertake nothing in their lives easily lose patience and fall into error when judging the work of others. The Višegrad Turks again began to shrug their shoulders and wave their hands when they talked of the bridge. The Christians remained silent, but watched the building work with secret and hostile thoughts, wishing for its failure as for that of every Turkish undertaking. It was about this time that the *iguman* of the monastery at Banja near Priboj wrote on the last blank page of one of his sacred books: 'Be it known that about this time Mehmed Pasha undertook the building of a bridge over the Drina at Višegrad. And great oppression fell upon the Christian people with hard labour. From the sea came master-masons. For three years they built and many *aspers* were spent in vain. They divided the waters into two and into three but they were unable to complete the bridge.'

Years passed; summer and autumn, winter and spring, fol-lowed one another; the workers and the master-masons came and went. Now the whole Drina was conquered, not by the bridge but by the wooden scaffoldings which looked like a complicated and senseless conglomeration of pine beams and planks. From both banks rose high wooden cranes fastened on to firmly fixed rafts. On both sides of the river fires smoked, on which lead was being melted in order to be poured into the holes in the stone blocks binding them invisibly to one another.

At the end of the third year occurred one of those accidents without which great buildings are rarely completed. The central pier, which was a little higher and wider at the top than the others, since on it the *kapia* was to rest, was just being completed. During the transportation of a great stone block, work suddenly came to a stop. The workmen swarmed about the great rectangular stone which, held by thick ropes, hung above their heads. The crane had not been able to lift it accurately over its place. Mastro Antonio's assistant, the Arab, rushed impatiently to the spot and began with loud angry cries (in that strange composite language which had been evolved in the course of years between these men from all parts of the world) to give orders to those handling the crane on the waters below. At that moment, for no known reason, the ropes gave way and the block fell, first by one corner and then with its full weight on to the excited Arab who had not even troubled to look above his head but only down at the water. By a strange chance the block fell exactly into position, but in its fall it caught the Arab and crushed the whole lower part of his body. Everyone began to rush around, to give the alarm, to shout for help. Mastro Antonio arrived quickly. The young negro, after his first unconsciousness, had come to himself; he groaned through clenched teeth and looked, sad and frightened, into Mastro Antonio's eyes. Frowning and pale, Mastro Antonio gave orders to summon the workmen, bring tools and try to lift the block. But all was in vain. A flow of blood suddenly poured out, the young man's breath came short and his eyes glazed over. Within half an hour he died, feverishly clutching Mastro Antonio's hands in his.

The Arab's funeral was a solemn event which was long remembered. All the Moslem males turned out to escort

him and each for a few paces carried the bier on which lay
only the upper half of the young body, for half had remained
under the stone block. Mastro Antonio raised over his grave
a fine memorial, made of the same stone from which the
bridge was built. The death of this young man, whom he
had befriended as a child living in poverty in Ulcinj, where a
few negro families still lived, had shaken him. But the work
did not cease even for a moment.

That year and the next the winter was mild and work went
on until mid-December. The fifth year of the work began.
Now that wide irregular circle of wood, stone, auxiliary
equipment and all sorts of material began to contract.

On the level space beside the Mejdan road the new *han*,
freed from its scaffolding, already stood. It was a large building, constructed of the same sort of stone of which the bridge
was made. Work was still going on both inside and out, but
already from a distance it could be seen how much it excelled
in size, the harmony of its lines and the solidity of its construction, anything that had ever been built or even thought
of in the town. That building of clear, yellowish stone, with
its roof of dark red tiles and a row of finely carved windows,
seemed to the townsmen a thing unheard of, which from
now on must become an integral part of their everyday life.
Built by a Vezir, it looked as though only Vezirs could inhabit
it. The whole building shone with a sense of grandeur, taste
and luxury which bewildered them.

About the same time all that formless mass of criss-cross
beams and supports over the river began to be reduced in
size and to thin out and through it emerged, more and more
clearly, the bridge itself, of lovely Banja stone. Individual
workers and small groups were still employed on jobs which
seemed to the people senseless and unconnected with the
main construction, but by now it was clear even to the most
doubting of the townsmen that out of all this work the bridge
itself rose, to a single design and a faultless reckoning, over
and above all these individual jobs. First the lesser arches,
both in height and in span, which were nearest to the banks

appeared and then, one by one, the others were revealed until even the last of them was freed of its scaffolding, showing the whole bridge with all its eleven arches, perfect and wondrous in its beauty, like a new and strange feature in the townsmen's eyes.

Quick to respond to good or evil, the people of Višegrad were now ashamed of their doubts and lack of belief. They no longer tried to conceal their wonder or to restrain their enthusiasm. Passage across the bridge was not yet permitted, but they collected on both banks, especially on the right one where the market-place and the greater part of the town were, and watched the workers passing across it and how they worked at smoothing the stones of the parapet and the raised seats of the *kapia*. The Višegrad Turks watched this work by another's hand at another's expense to which for a full five years they had given every sort of name and prophesied the worst of futures.

'*Ama*, but I always told you,' a little Moslem *hodja* from Dušče said excitedly and gleefully, 'that nothing escapes the Sultan's hand and that these men of sense would finally put up what they had in mind, but you kept saying: they won't do this, or they can't do that. Now you see they have built it, and what a bridge they have built, what convenience and what beauty!'

Everyone approved his words, though no one really remembered when he said them, and they all knew very well that he too had ridiculed the building and the man who had been building it. All of them were sincerely enraptured.

'Eh, fellows, fellows, see what is rising here, in this town of ours!'

'See how great is the Vezir's power and foresight. Wherever he turns his eyes there is profit and blessing.'

'Yet all this is nothing,' added the gay and lively little *hodja*, 'there will be still finer things. You see how they are grooming and decorating it like a horse for a fair.'

So they competed in expressions of enthusiasm, searching for new, better and more high-flown words of praise. Only

Ahmedaga Sheta, the rich grain merchant, a sullen man and a miser, still looked askance at the work and those who praised it. Tall, yellow and wizened, with black piercing eyes and thin lips that looked as if they were glued together, blinking in the fine September sun, he alone did not renounce his earlier opinion (for certain men are filled with unreasonable hate and envy greater and stronger than anything that other men can imagine). To those who enthusiastically praised the greatness and permanence of the bridge, saying that it was stronger than any fortress, he retorted disdainfully:

'Just wait till the floods, one of our real Višegrad floods! Then you will see what will be left of it!'

All of them argued bitterly with him and praised those who had been working on the bridge, especially Arif Beg, who with the smile of a great lord always on his lips had created such a work as though it had been child's play. But Sheta was firmly determined not to acknowledge anything of anyone:

'Yes, indeed. But if it had not been for Abidaga with his green staff and his tyranny and oppression, I ask you what could Old Baldie have done to finish the bridge despite his smile and his hands clasped behind his back?'

Offended at the universal enthusiasm as if it had been a personal insult, Sheta departed angrily to his shop, to sit in his usual place where he could see neither sun nor bridge, nor hear the murmur and the movement of the excited throng.

But Sheta was an isolated example. The joy and enthusiasm of the citizens continued to grow and spread to the surrounding villages. In the early days of October, Arif Beg ordered a great feast for the completion of the bridge. This man of lordly manners, of unrelenting severity and strict honesty, who had spent all the monies confided to him for the purpose for which they were intended and had kept nothing for himself, was regarded by the people as the chief personage in this achievement. They spoke more of him than of the Vezir himself. So his feast turned out rich and brilliant.

The overseers and workers received gifts in money and clothing and the feast, in which anyone who wished could take part, lasted two days. The Vezir's health was celebrated in meat and drink, in music, dancing and song; horse and foot races were arranged, and meat and sweetstuffs divided amongst the poor. On the square which linked the bridge with the market-place, *halva* was cooked in cauldrons and served piping hot to the people. That *halva* even got as far as the villages around the town and whoever ate it wished good health to the Vezir and long life to his buildings. There were children who went back fourteen times to the cauldrons until the cooks, recognizing them, drove them away with their long wooden spoons. One gipsy child died after eating too much hot *halva*.

Such things were long remembered and spoken about when tales were told of the creation of the bridge, the more so since, it seems, generous Vezirs and honest officials in later years died out and such feasts became rarer and rarer and at last completely unknown, until in the end they passed into legend with the *vilas*, with Stoja and Ostoja and similar wonders.

While the feast lasted, and in general all those early days, the people crossed the bridge countless times from one bank to the other. The children rushed across while their elders walked slowly, deep in conversation or watching from every point the new views open to them from the bridge. The helpless, the lame and the sick were brought on litters, for no one wanted to be left out or renounce their share in this wonder. Even the least of the townsmen felt as if his powers were suddenly multiplied, as if some wonderful, superhuman exploit was brought within the measure of his powers and within the limits of everyday life, as if besides the well-known elements of earth, water and sky, one more were open to him, as if by some beneficent effort each one of them could suddenly realize one of his dearest desires, that ancient dream of man – to go over the water and to be master of space.

The Turkish youths formed a round dance, a *kolo*, around the cauldrons of *halva* and then led the dance across the bridge, since it seemed to them that they were flying and not treading the solid earth. The dance wound round in circles about the *kapia*, the dancers beating their heels and stamping on the new flagstones as if to test the stoutness of the bridge. Around that winding, circling *kolo* of young bodies tirelessly leaping up and down in the same rhythm, the children played, running in and out between the dancing feet as if through a moving fence, standing in the centre of this *kolo* which was being danced for the first time in their lives on that bridge about which there had been so much talk for years, and even on the *kapia*, wherein, it was said, the unlucky Arab was imprisoned and showed himself of nights. Enjoying the young men's *kolo*, they were none the less overcome by that fear which the Arab himself, when he had been alive and working on the bridge, had always instilled into the children of the town. On that high, new and strange bridge, it seemed to them that they had long forsaken their mothers and their homes and were wandering in lands of black people, marvellous buildings and strange dances; they trembled, but were unable to keep their thoughts from the Arab or to abandon the wonderful new *kapia*. Only some fresh marvel could have distracted their attention.

A certain Murat, known as 'the dumb one', a dim-witted youth from the noble family of Turković from Nezuke, who was often the butt of the town, suddenly climbed on to the stone parapet of the bridge. There were shrieks from the children, startled cries from the older people, but the idiot, as though under a spell, with outstretched arms and head flung back, went along the narrow stones, step by step, as though he were not flying above the waters and the depths but taking part in a wonderful dance. Parallel with him walked a crew of urchins and nondescripts urging him on. On the farther side of the bridge his brother Aliaga waited for him and spanked him like a small child.

Many people went far down the river, half an hour's

walk, to Kalata or Mezalin, and looked thence at the bridge, standing out white and delicate with its eleven arches, like a strange arabesque on the green waters amid the dark hills.

About this time too a great white plaque was brought, with an engraved inscription, and built into the *kapia*, into that wall of reddish stone which rose a good six feet from the parapet of the bridge. The people gathered around the inscription and looked at it until some seminarist or koranic student was found who would, with more or less ability, for a coffee or a slice of water-melon or even for the pure love of Allah, read the inscription as best he could.

A hundred times those days they spelt out the verses of the *tarih*, written by a certain Badi, which gave the name and title of the man who had made the bequest as well as the fortunate year 979 AH, that is to say 1571 in the Christian calendar, when it was completed. This Badi for good money wrote easy and sonorous verses and knew well how to foist them upon great men who erected or restored great buildings. Those who knew him (and who were somewhat envious of him) used to say mockingly that the vault of heaven was the one and only building on which there was not a *tarih* from Badi's pen. But he, despite all his fine earnings, was a poor famished devil continually at odds with that special sort of penury that often goes with verse writing like a kind of curse and which no amount of pay or salary can assuage.

Because of their literary shortcomings, their thick heads and lively imaginations, each of the local scholars read and interpreted in his own way Badi's *tarih* on the stone plaque which, as every text once revealed to the public, stood there, eternal on the eternal stone, always and irrevocably exposed to the looks and interpretations of all men, wise or foolish, evil or well-intentioned. Each one of these listeners remembered those lines which best suited his ear and his temperament. So what was there, engraved on the hard stone in the sight of all men, was repeated from mouth to mouth, often changed and corrupted into nonsense.

On the stone was written:

'See how Mehmed Pasha, the greatest among the wise and
    great of his time,
Mindful of the testament of his heart, by his care and toil
Has built a bridge over the River Drina,
Over this water, deep and swift-flowing.
His predecessors had not been able to put up anything.
I pray that by the Mercy of Allah this bridge will be firm
And that its existence will be passed in happiness
And that it will never know sorrow.
For in his lifetime he poured out gold and silver for his
    bequest
And no man can say that fortune has been wasted
Which has been spent to such an end.
Badi, who has seen this, when the bridge was completed
    gave this *tarih*.
"May Allah bless this building, this wonderful and
    beautiful bridge".'

But at last the people had eaten their fill and had wondered
enough, walked enough and had listened to the verses of the
inscription to their hearts' content. The nine days' wonder
became a part of their everyday life and they crossed the
bridge hurriedly, indifferently, anxiously, absent-mindedly
as the tumultuous waters that flowed beneath it, as if it were
only one of the countless roads that they and their beasts trod
beneath their feet. And the plaque with the inscription fell as
silent as any other stone.

Now the road from the left bank of the river was directly
connected with that end of the road on the level space on the
farther side. Gone was the dark, worm-eaten ferry with its
eccentric ferryman. Far below the last arches of the bridge
there remained that sandy rock and the steep banks equally
difficult to ascend or descend and on which travellers had
waited so despairingly and had called so vainly from one
bank to the other. All that, together with the stormy river,
had been surmounted as if by magic. Men now passed far
above, as if on wings, straight from one high bank to the

CHAPTER IV   75

other, along the wide strong bridge which was as firm and
lasting as a mountain and which echoed under horses' hooves
as if it were made only of a thin plaque of stone.

Gone too were those wooden water-mills and the hovels
in which travellers in case of need had spent the night. In
their place stood the firm and luxurious caravanserai which
received the travellers who daily grew more numerous. They
entered the *han* through a wide gateway of harmonious lines.
On each side was a large window with a grille, not of iron
but carved in a single block of limestone. In the wide rectangular court was space for merchandise and baggage and
around it were ranged the doors of thirty-six rooms. Behind,
under the hillside, were the stables; to general amazement
they too were of stone, as if built for the Sultan's stud. There
was not such another *han* from Sarajevo as far as Adrianople.
In it every traveller might remain for a day and a night and
receive, free of all cost, fire, shelter and water for himself, his
servants and his beasts.

All this, as the bridge itself, was the bequest of the Grand
Vezir, Mehmed Pasha, who had been born more than sixty
years before up there behind the mountains in the hillside
village of Sokolovići, and who in his childhood had been
taken away with a crowd of other Serbian peasant boys as
blood tribute to Stambul. The expenses for maintaining the
caravanserai came from the *vakuf*, the religious endowment,
which Mehmed Pasha had founded from the rich properties
seized in the newly-conquered territories of Hungary.

Thus many troubles and inconveniences disappeared with
the erection of the bridge and the foundation of the *han*.
There disappeared too that strange pain which the Vezir in
his childhood had brought from Bosnia, from the Višegrad
ferry; those dark shooting pains which from time to time
had seemed to cut his breast in two. But it was not fated
that Mehmed Pasha should live without those pangs or long
enjoy in his thoughts his Višegrad bequest. Shortly after the
final completion of the work, just when the caravanserai had
begun to work properly and the bridge to become known to

the world, Mehmed Pasha once again felt the 'black knife' in his breast. And that for the last time.

One Friday, when he went with his suite to the mosque, a ragged and half-demented dervish approached him with his left hand stretched out for alms. The Vezir turned and ordered a member of his suite to give them. But the dervish then drew a heavy butcher's knife from his right sleeve and violently stabbed the Vezir between the ribs. His suite cut the dervish down, but the Vezir and his murderer breathed their last at the same moment. The dead assassin, big, red-faced, lay with outstretched arms and legs as if still exalted by the impulse of his senseless blow; and beside him the Grand Vezir, with his robe unbuttoned on his chest and his turban flung far away. In the last years of his life he had grown thin and bowed, almost withered and coarser in feature. And now with half-bared chest, bareheaded, bleeding, twisted and crumpled, he looked more like an ageing and battered peasant of Sokolovići than the dignitary who until a short time before had administered the Turkish Empire.

Months and months passed before the reports of the Vezir's assassination reached the town and then not as a clear and definite fact but as a secret whisper which might or might not have been true. For in the Turkish Empire it was not permitted to spread reports or to gossip about bad news and tragic events even when they had taken place in a nearby country, much less so when they took place on its own soil. Furthermore, in this case, it was in no one's interest to talk much about the Grand Vezir's death. The party of his adversaries, which had at last succeeded in overthrow-ing him, hoped that with his solemn funeral every livelier memory of him would also be buried. And Mehmed Pasha's kin, collaborators and supporters in Stambul had for the most part no objection to saying as little as possible about the one-time Grand Vezir, for in this way their own chances of conciliating the new rulers and having their own past over-looked were increased.

But the two fine buildings on the Drina had already begun

to exercise their influence on trade and communications, on the town of Višegrad and the whole country around, and they went on doing so without regard for the living or the dead, for those who were rising or those who were falling. The town soon began to move downwards from the hillside to the water's edge and expand and develop more and more about the bridge and around the caravanserai, which the people called the Stone Han.

Thus was born the bridge with its *kapia* and so the town developed around it. After that, for a period of more than 300 years, its role in the development of the town and its significance in the life of the townspeople was similar to that which we have described above. And the significance and substance of its existence were, so to speak, in its permanence. Its shining line in the composition of the town did not change, any more than the outlines of the mountains against the sky. In the changes and the quick burgeoning of human generations, it remained as unchanged as the waters that flowed beneath it. It too grew old, naturally, but on a scale of time that was much greater not only than the span of human existence but also than the passing of a whole series of generations, so that its ageing could not be seen by human eye. Its life, though mortal in itself, resembled eternity for its end could not be perceived.

CHAPTER V

THE FIRST CENTURY passed, a time long and mortal for men and for many of their works, but insignificant for great buildings, well conceived and firmly based, and the bridge with its *kapia* and the nearby caravanserai stood and served as they had on their first day. So too would a second century have passed over them, with its changes of seasons and human generations, and the buildings would have lasted unchanged; but what time could not do, the unstable and unpredictable influence of faraway affairs did.

At that time, at the end of the seventeenth century, much was sung, spoken and whispered about Hungary, whence the Turkish armies after a hundred years of occupation were about to withdraw. Many Bosnian *spahis* (landowners who held their lands on military tenure) had left their bones on Hungarian soil, defending their properties in the battles preceding the withdrawal. They were, it might be thought, the lucky ones for many of the other *spahis* returned as bare as a finger to their former Bosnian homeland, where there awaited them sparse soil and a straitened and penurious life after the rich lordliness and spaciousness of life on the great Hungarian estates. The far off and uncertain echo of all this penetrated as far as Višegrad, but no one there could ever have imagined that distant Hungary, a land of legend, could have any connection with the real, everyday life of the town. But with the Turkish retreat from Hungary there remained outside the frontiers of the Empire also those properties of the *vakuf* (the religious endowment) from the revenues of which the caravanserai at Višegrad was maintained.

Both the people of the town and the travellers who had made use of the Stone Han for the past 100 years had become accustomed to it and had never even considered by what means it had been maintained, how the revenues had been founded, or from what source they came. All had made use of it, profiting by it as from a blessed and fertile roadside orchard which was both nobody's and everybody's; they repeated mechanically 'peace to the Vezir's soul' but did not stop to think that the Vezir had died 100 years before, nor did they ask who now preserved and defended the imperial lands and the *vakuf*. Who could ever have dreamt that the affairs of the world were in such dependence upon one another and were linked together across so great a distance? So at first no one in the town even noticed that the income of the *han* had dried up. The attendants worked and the *han* received travellers as before. It was thought that the money for its upkeep had been delayed, as had happened before. But the months passed and even the years, and the money did not come. The *mutevelia* (the administrator of the bequest), Dauthodja Mutavelić, for the people so called him after his appointment and the nickname stuck, applied to everyone he could think of, but received no reply. The travellers had to look after their own needs and cleaned up the *han* as much as they found necessary for their own convenience, but as each one went his way he left behind manure and disorder for others to clean up and put right, even as he himself had tidied up whatever he had found dirty and in disorder. But after each traveller there remained just a little more dirt than he himself had found.

Dauthodja did all that he could to save the *han* and keep it going. First he spent his own money and then he began to borrow from his relatives. So he patched things up from year to year and kept the precious building in its former beauty. To those who reproached him for ruining himself trying to preserve what could not be preserved, he replied that he was investing the money well for he gave it as a loan to God and that he, the *mutevelia*, should be the last to desert this bequest which it seemed all others had deserted and abandoned.

This wise and godfearing, stubborn and obstinate man,

whom the town long remembered, allowed no one to turn him from his vain effort. Working devotedly, he had long become reconciled to the idea that our destiny on this earth lies in the struggle against decay, death and dissolution and that man must persevere in this struggle, even if it were completely in vain. Sitting before the *han* which was falling into dissolution before his eyes, he replied to all those who tried to dissuade him or pitied him:

'There is no need to feel sorry for me. For all of us die only once, whereas great men die twice, once when they leave this world and a second time when their lifework disappears.'

When he was no longer able to pay day-labourers, he himself, old as he was, rooted up the weeds around the *han* with his own hands and carried out minor repairs to the building. So it was that death overtook him one day when he had climbed up to repair a cracked slate on the roof. It was natural that a small town *hodja* could not maintain what a Grand Vezir had founded and which historical events had sentenced to disaster.

After Dauthodja's death the *han* rapidly began to fall into ruins. Signs of decay appeared everywhere. The gutters began to crack and to smell nasty, the roof to let in the rains, the doors and windows the winds, and the stables to be choked with manure and weeds. But from without the perfect building still looked unchanged, calm and indestructible in its beauty. Those great arched windows on the ground floor, with grilles as delicate as lace cut in soft stone from a single block, looked peacefully out upon the world, but the simpler windows on the floor above already showed signs of poverty, neglect and internal disorder. Little by little travellers began to avoid spending the night in the town or, if they did, stayed at Ustamujić's inn and paid for their night's lodging. They came more and more rarely to the caravanserai, even though they had not to pay but only to wish peace to the Vezir's soul. At last, when it become clear that the money would never come, everyone abandoned any pretence to care for the building, even the new *mutevelia*, and the caravanserai stayed mute and deserted and fell into ruin and disrepair as do all buildings in which no one lives and which no one looks after. Wild grasses, weeds and thistles grew around it. Ravens nested on the roof and crows gathered there in dense black flocks.

Thus before its time and unexpectedly forsaken (all such things seem to happen unexpectedly) the Vezir's Stone Han began to disintegrate and fall to pieces.

But if the caravanserai, due to unusual circumstances, was forced to betray its mission and fall into ruin before its time, the bridge, which needed neither supervision nor maintenance, remained upright and unchanged, linking the two banks and bearing across the river burdens dead and alive, as it had in the first days of its existence.

In its walls the birds nested and in the invisible cracks opened by time grew little tufts of grass. The yellowish porous stone of which the bridge was built hardened and contracted under the alternate influence of moisture and of heat. Eternally beaten by the winds which blew up and down the river valley, washed by the rains and dried by the fierce heats of summer, that stone in time turned white with the dull whiteness of parchment and shone in the twilight as if lighted from within. The great and frequent floods, which were a heavy and continual menace to the town, were unable to do anything against it. They came every year, in spring and autumn, but all were not dangerous and fateful to the town beside the bridge. Every year, once or perhaps twice, the Drina rose in tumult and its muddied waters roared down, bearing through the arches of the bridge torn-up fences from the fields, uprooted stumps of trees, and dark earthy waters filled with leaves and branches from the riverside forests. The courtyards, gardens and storerooms of the houses nearest the river suffered. But everything ended there. At irregular intervals of between twenty and thirty years came great floods which were afterwards remembered as one remembers insurrections or wars and were long used as a date from which to reckon time, to calculate the ages of citizens or the term of men's lives ('Five or six years before the great flood. . . .' 'During the great flood. . . .').

After these great floods little movable property remained in that larger part of the town which lay on the low sandy strip between the Drina and the Rzav. Such a flood threw the whole town several years back. That generation spent the rest of its life in repairing the damage and the misfortune left by the 'great flood'. To the end of their lives men, talking amongst themselves, recalled the terror of that autumn night when, in the chill rain and hellish wind, to the light of an occasional lantern, they would take out their goods, each from his own shop, and carry them to higher ground at Mejdan and there store them in the shops and warehouses of others. When the next day, in the cloudy dawn, they looked down from the hillside on the town that they loved as strongly and as unconsciously as their own blood, and saw the darkened muddied waters rushing through the streets at roof level, they would try to guess whose house it was from which the foaming waters were noisily tearing the roof plank by plank and whose house still remained upright.

On feast days and festivals and during the nights of Ramazan the grey-haired toilworn and anxious fathers of families would grow lively and talkative when the conversation turned to the greatest and hardest event of their lives, to the 'great flood'. After the interval of fifteen or twenty years in which they had once more restored their fortunes and their homes, the flood was recalled as something great and terrible, near and dear to them; it was an intimate bond between the men of that generation who were still living, for nothing brings men closer together than a common misfortune happily overcome. They felt themselves closely bound by the memory of that bygone disaster. They loved to recall memories of the hardest blow dealt them in their lives. Their recollections were inexhaustible and they repeated them continually, amplified by memory and repetition; they looked into one another's eyes, sclerotic and with yellowing whites, and saw there what the younger men could not even suspect. They were carried away by their own words and drowned all their present everyday troubles in the recollection of those greater ones which they had experienced so long ago.

Sitting in the warm rooms of their homes through which that flood had at one time passed, they recounted for the hundredth time with special enjoyment moving and tragic scenes. And the more harrowing and painful the recollection the greater pleasure was there in recollecting it. Seen through tobacco smoke or a glass of plum-brandy, such scenes were often transformed by distance and imagination, magnified and embellished, but not one of them ever noticed that this was so and would have sworn that it had in fact so happened, for they all shared in this unconscious exaggeration.

Thus there still lived a few old men who remembered the last 'great flood', about which they could still speak among themselves, repeating to the younger men that there were no longer such disasters as in time past, but no such blessings and good living either.

One of the very greatest of all these floods, which occurred in the second half of the eighteenth century, was especially long remembered and became the subject of countless tales.

In that generation, as the older men later said, there was practically no one who remembered the last great flood well. None the less, on those rainy autumn days all were on the alert, knowing that 'the waters were hostile'. They emptied the warehouses closest to the river and wandered by night, by the light of lanterns, along the banks to listen to the roar of the waters, for the older men affirmed that they could tell by some special moaning of the waters whether the flood to come would be one of those ordinary ones which visited the town every year and caused minor damage, or whether it would be one of those, happily rare, which flooded both the bridge and the town and carried away everything that was not on firm foundations. Next day the Drina did not rise and the town that night slept soundly, for men were tired out from lack of sleep and the excitement of the night before. So it was that the waters deceived them. That night the Rzav rose suddenly in a manner never before remembered and, red with mud, piled up at its confluence with the Drina. Thus the two rivers overwhelmed the whole town.

Suljaga Osmanagić, one of the richest Turks in the town, then owned a thoroughbred Arab horse, a chestnut of great value and beauty. As soon as the reinforced Drina began to rise, two hours before it overflowed into the streets, this chestnut began to neigh and did not calm down until it had awakened the stable-boys and its owner and until they had taken it out of its stall which was beside the river. So the greater part of the inhabitants were awakened. Under the chill rain and the raging wind of the dark October night began a flight and a saving of all that could be saved. Half-dressed, the people waded up to their knees, carrying on their backs their wakened and complaining children. At every moment dull crashes could be heard when the tree stumps which the Drina washed down from the flooded forests struck against the piers of the stone bridge.

Up at Mejdan, which the waters had never in any circumstances been able to reach, windows were all alight and flickering lanterns danced and quivered in the darkness. All the houses were open to welcome those who had suffered and who came drenched and despondent with their children or their most precious belongings in their arms. In the stables burned fires by which those unable to find a place in the houses could dry themselves.

The leading merchants of the town, after they had placed the people in the houses, Turkish in Turkish homes and Christian and Jewish in Christian homes, gathered in the great ground-floor room of Hadji Ristić's house. There were the *mukhtars* (the Moslem leaders) and the *kmets* (the Christian headmen) of all the quarters, exhausted and wet to the skin, after having wakened and moved to safe quarters all their fellow citizens. Turks, Christians and Jews mingled together. The force of the elements and the weight of common misfortune brought all these men together and bridged, at least for this one evening, the gulf that divided one faith from the other and, especially, the *rayah* from the Turks: Suljaga Osmanagić, Petar Bogdanović, Mordo Papo, the big, taciturn and witty parish priest Pop Mihailo, the fat and serious Mula Ismet, the Višegrad *hodja*, and Elias Levi, known as Hadji Liacho, the Jewish rabbi well known even far beyond the town for his sound judgement and open nature. There were about ten others, from all three faiths. All were wet, pale, with clenched jaws, but outwardly calm; they sat and smoked and talked of what had been done to save the people and of what still remained to be done. Every moment younger people entered, streaming with water, who reported that everything living had been taken to Mejdan and to the fortress and put in houses there, Turkish and Christian, and that the waters down in the valley were still rising and invading street after street.

As the night passed – and it passed slowly and seemed enormous, growing greater and greater like the waters in the valley – the leaders and rich men of the town began to warm themselves over coffee and plum-brandy. A warm and close circle formed, like a new existence, created out of realities and yet itself unreal, which was not what it had been the day before nor what it would be the day after, but like a transient island in the flood of time. The conversation rose and strengthened and changed subject. They avoided speaking of past floods known only in tales, but spoke of other things that had no connection with the waters and with the disaster which was at that moment taking place.

Desperate men make desperate efforts to appear calm and indifferent, almost casual. By some tacit superstitious agreement and by the unwritten but sacred laws of patronal dignity and business order which have existed since olden times, each considered it his duty to make an effort and at that moment at least externally to conceal his fear and his anxieties in face of a disaster against which he could do nothing and to talk in a light tone about unrelated things.

But just as they began to grow calm in this conversation

and to find in it a moment of forgetfulness, and thereby the rest and energy that they would need so greatly in the day to come, a man entered, bringing with him Kosta Baranac. That young merchant was wet through, muddied to the knees and dishevelled. Dazzled by the light and confused by the numbers present, he looked at them as if in a dream, wiping the water from his face with his open hand. They made room for him and offered him plum-brandy, which he was unable to raise to his lips. His whole body shivered. A whisper ran through the room that he had tried to leap into the dark current that now flowed in a sandy torrent immediately above the spot where his barns and granaries had been.

He was a young man, a recent settler, who had been brought to the town twenty years before as an apprentice, but had later married into a good family and become a merchant. A peasant's son, he had in the last few years by daring speculation and ruthless exploitation become rich, richer than many of the leading families of the town. But he was not used to loss and was unable to support disaster. That autumn he had bought large quantities of plums and walnuts, far beyond his real resources, reckoning that in winter he would be able to control the price of both dried plums and walnuts and so clear his debts and make a good profit, as he had done in previous years. Now he was ruined.

Some time was to pass before the impression made on them by the sight of this ruined man could be dispelled, since all of them, some more some less, had been hit by this flood and only by inborn dignity had they been able to control themselves better than this upstart.

The oldest and most prominent amongst them once again turned the conversation to casual matters. They began to tell long stories of former times, which had no sort of connection with the disaster that had drawn them hither and surrounded them on all sides.

They drank hot plum-brandy and embarked on recollections of earlier days, about the eccentric characters of the town and every kind of strange and unusual event. Pop

Mihailo and Hadji Liacho set the example. When the talk inevitably returned to earlier floods, they recalled only what was pleasant or comical, or at least seemed so after so many years, as if they wanted to cast a spell upon the waters and to defy the flood.

They talked of Pop Jovan, who had once been parish priest here, who his parishioners had said was a good man but did not have 'a lucky hand' and that God had paid little heed to his prayers.

At the time of the summer droughts which often ruined the whole harvest, Pop Jovan had regularly led a procession and read the prayers for rain, but the only result was still greater drought and stifling heat. When one autumn, after such a dry summer, the Drina began to rise and threaten a general flood, Pop Jovan had gone out to the banks, collected the people, and began to read a prayer that the rain should cease and the waters recede. Then a certain Jokić, a drunkard and ne'er-do-well, reckoning that God always did exactly the opposite from what Pop Jovan prayed for, shouted:

'Not that one, father! Read the summer one, the one for rain; that will help the waters dry up.'

Fat and well-fed Ismet Effendi spoke of his predecessors and their struggles with the floods. At one of these disasters long ago a pair of the Višegrad *hodjas* went out to read a prayer to stay the disaster. One of these *hodjas* had a house in the lower part of the town, the other one on the hillside where the waters could not reach. The first to read was the *hodja* from the house on the hillside but the waters showed no sign of receding. Then a gipsy whose house was already half disintegrated in the waters shouted:

'*Ama*, fellows, let the *hodja* from the market-place, whose house is under water like ours, read. Can't you see that that fellow from the hill only reads with half his heart?'

Hadji Liacho, red-faced and smiling, with riotous tufts of white hair showing from under his unusually shallow fez, laughed at everything and said mockingly to the priest and *hodja*:

'Don't talk too much about prayers against floods, or else our people might remember and drive all three of us out in this downpour to read prayers for them.'

So they ranged story against story, all insignificant in themselves but each with a meaning for them and their generation though incomprehensible to others; harmless recollections which evoked the monotonous, pleasant yet hard life of the townsmen, their own life. Though all these things had changed long ago they still remained closely bound up with their lives, although far from the drama of that night which had brought them together in that fantastic circle.

Thus the town's leaders, accustomed from childhood to misfortunes of every kind, dominated the night of the great flood and found enough strength in themselves to jest in face of the disaster which had come upon them and thus mastered the misery that they were not able to avoid.

But within themselves they were all greatly anxious and each of them, beneath all the jokes and laughter at misfortune, as if under a mask, turned over and over in his mind anxious thoughts and listened continually to the roar of the waters and the wind from the town below, where he had left all that he possessed. The next day in the morning, after a night so spent, they looked down from Mejdan to the plain below where their houses were under water, some only half submerged and others covered to the roof. Then for the first and last time in their lives they saw their town without a bridge. The waters had risen a good thirty feet, so that the wide high arches were covered and the waters flowed over the roadway of the bridge which was hidden beneath them. Only that elevated part on which the *kapia* had been built showed above the surface of the troubled waters which flowed about it like a tiny waterfall.

But two days later the waters suddenly fell, the skies cleared and the sun broke through, as warm and rich as it does on some October days in this fertile land. On that lovely day the town looked pitiable and terrible. The houses of the gipsies and the poorer folk on the banks were bent

over in the direction of the current, many of them roofless
and with the mud and clay of their walls washed away, dis-
playing only a black trellis of willow branches so that they
looked like skeletons. In the unfenced courtyards the houses
of the richer townsmen gaped open with staring windows;
on each a line of reddish mud showed how deeply it had
been flooded. Many stables had been washed away and granaries overturned. In the lower shops there was mud to the
knees, and in that mud all the goods that had not been taken
away in time. In the streets were whole trees rooted up and
brought there by the waters from no one knew where, and
the swollen corpses of drowned animals.

That was their town, to which they must now descend
and go on with their lives. But between the flooded banks,
above the waters which still raged noisily, stood the bridge,
white and unchanged in the sun. The waters now reached
halfway up the piers and the bridge seemed as if it were in
some other and deeper river than that which usually flowed
beneath it. Along the parapet still remained deposits of mud
which had now dried and were cracking in the sun, and on
the *kapia* was piled up a whole heap of small branches and
rubbish from the river. But all that in no way altered the
appearance of the bridge, which alone had passed through
the flood unaltered and emerged from it unscathed.

Every man in the town set to work at once to repair the
damage and no one had time to think of the meaning of
the victory of the bridge, but going about his affairs in that
ill-fated town in which the waters had destroyed or at least
damaged everything, he knew that there was something
in his life that overcame every disaster and that the bridge,
because of the strange harmony of its forms and the strong
and invisible power of its foundations, would emerge from
every test unchanged and imperishable.

The winter which then began was a hard one. Everything
that had been stored in courtyards and barns, wood, wheat,
hay, the flood had carried away; houses, stables and fences
had to be repaired and fresh goods had to be obtained on

credit to replace those which had been destroyed in warehouses and shops. Kosta Baranac, who had suffered more than any, because of his overbold speculations with plums, did not outlive the winter, but died of mortification and shame. He left his young children almost penniless and a number of small but widespread debts in all the villages. He was recalled in the memory of the town as a man who had overtaxed his strength.

But by the next summer the recollection of the great flood had begun to pass into the memory of the older men, where it would live long, while the younger people sat singing and talking on the smooth white stone *kapia* over the water which flowed far below them and accompanied their songs with its murmurings. Forgetfulness heals everything and song is the most beautiful manner of forgetting, for in song man feels only what he loves.

So, on the *kapia*, between the skies, the river and the hills, generation after generation learnt not to mourn overmuch what the troubled waters had borne away. They entered there into the unconscious philosophy of the town; that life was an incomprehensible marvel, since it was incessantly wasted and spent, yet none the less it lasted and endured 'like the bridge on the Drina'.

CHAPTER VI

AS WELL AS floods there were also other onslaughts on the
bridge and its *kapia*. They were caused by the development
of events and the course of human conflicts; but they could
do even less than the unchained waters to harm the bridge
or change it permanently.

At the beginning of last century Serbia rose in revolt.
This town on the very frontier of Bosnia and Serbia had
always been in close connection and permanent touch with
everything that took place in Serbia and grew with it 'like a
nail and its finger'. Nothing that happened in the Višegrad
district – drought, sickness, oppression or revolt – could be a
matter of indifference to those in the Užice district, and vice
versa. But at first the affair seemed distant and insignificant;
distant, because it was taking place on the farther side of the
Belgrade *pashaluk*, insignificant since rumours of revolt were
no sort of novelty. Ever since the Empire had existed there
had been such rumours, for there is no rule without revolts
and conspiracies, even as there is no property without work
and worry. But in time the revolt in Serbia began to affect
the life of the whole Bosnian *pashaluk* more and more, and
especially the life of this town which was only an hour's
march from the frontier.

As the struggle in Serbia grew, more and more was
demanded from the Bosnian Turks. They were asked to
send men to the army and to contribute to its equipment
and supply. The army and the commissariat sent into Serbia
passed to a great extent through the town. That brought
in its train expenses and inconveniences and dangers not
only for the Turks, but especially for the Serbs who were
suspected, persecuted and fined in those years more than
ever before. Finally, one summer, the revolt spread to these

districts. Making a detour around Užice, the insurgents came to within two hours' march of the town. There, at Veletovo, they destroyed Lufti Beg's fortified farmhouse by cannon fire and burnt a number of Turkish houses at Crniče.

There were in the town both Turks and Serbs who swore that they had heard with their own ears the rumbling of 'Karageorge's gun' (naturally with completely opposite feelings). But even if it were a matter for doubt whether the echo of the Serb insurrectionists' gun could be heard as far as the town, for a man often thinks that he can hear what he is afraid of or what he hopes for, there could be no doubt about the fires which the insurgents lit by night on the bare and rocky crest of Panos between Veletovo and Gostilje, on which the huge isolated pines could be counted from the town with the naked eye. Both Turks and Serbs saw the fires clearly and looked at them attentively, although both pretended not to have noticed them. From darkened windows and from the shadows of dense gardens, both took careful note of when and where they were lighted and extinguished. The Serbian women crossed themselves in the darkness and wept from inexplicable emotion, but in their tears they saw reflected those fires of insurrection even as those ghostly flames which had once fallen upon Radisav's grave and which their ancestors almost three centuries before had also seen through their tears from that same Mejdan.

Those flickering and uneven flames, scattered along the dark background of the summer night, wherein skies and mountains merged, seemed to the Serbs like some new constellation in which they eagerly read bold presentiments and, shivering, guessed at their fate and at coming events. For the Turks they were the first waves of a sea of fire which was spreading there in Serbia and which, even as they watched, splashed against the mountains above the town. In those summer nights the wishes and the prayers of both circled around those flames, but in different directions. The Serbs prayed to God that these saving flames, like those which they had always carried in their hearts and carefully concealed, should spread to these mountains, while the Turks prayed to Allah to halt their progress and extinguish them, to frustrate the seditious designs of the infidel and restore the old order and the peace of the true faith. The nights were filled with prudent and passionate whisperings in which pulsed invisible waves of the most daring dreams and wishes, the most improbable thoughts and plans which triumphed and broke in the blue darkness overhead. Next day at dawn, Turks and Serbs went out to work and met one another with dull and expressionless faces, greeted one another and talked together with those hundred or so commonplace words of provincial courtesy which had from times past circulated in the town and passed from one to another like counterfeit coin which none the less makes communication both possible and easy.

When, soon after the feast of St Elias, the fires disappeared from Panos and the revolt was pushed back from the Užice district, once again neither the one side nor the other showed their feelings. And it would really be difficult to say what were the true feelings of either side. The Turks were gratified that the revolt was now far away from them and hoped that it would be entirely extinguished and would end there where all godless and evil enterprises ended. But none the less that gratification was incomplete and overshadowed for it was hard to forget so close a danger. Many of them for long after saw in their dreams those fantastic insurgent fires like a shower of sparks on all the hills around the town or heard Karageorge's gun, not as a distant echo but as a devastating cannonade which brought ruin with it. The Serbs, however, as was natural, remained disillusioned and disappointed after the withdrawal of the fires on Panos but in the depth of their hearts, in that true and ultimate depth which is revealed to no one, there remained the memory of what had taken place and the consciousness that what has once been can be again; there remained too hope, a senseless hope, that great asset of the downtrodden. For those who rule and must oppress in order to rule must work according to reason; and if, carried away by their passions or driven by an adversary, they go beyond the limits of reasonable action, they start down the slippery slope and thereby reveal the commencement of their own downfall. Whereas those who are downtrodden and exploited make equal use of their reason and unreason for they are but two different kinds of arms in the continual struggle, now underground, now open, against the oppressor.

In those times the importance of the bridge as the one sure link between the Bosnian *pashaluk* and Serbia was greatly increased. There was now a permanent military force in the town, which was not disbanded even in the long periods of truce, and which guarded the bridge over the Drina. To carry out this task as well as possible with the minimum of labour, the soldiers began to erect a wooden blockhouse in the centre of the bridge, a monstrous erection crude in shape, position, and the material of which it was made (but all the armies of the world put up, for their own special aims and momentary needs, buildings such as this which, later on, from the point of view of normal peaceful life appear both absurd and incomprehensible). It was a real two-storeyed house, clumsy and hideous, made of rough beams and unplaned planks, with a free passage like a tunnel beneath it. The blockhouse was raised up and rested on stout beams, so that it straddled the bridge and was supported only at its two ends on the *kapia*, one on the left and the other on the right terrace. Beneath it there was a free passage for carts, horses and pedestrians, but from above, from the floor on which the guards slept and to which led an uncovered stairway, it was possible to inspect all who passed, to examine papers and baggage and, at any moment, should the need arise, to stop them.

That indeed altered the appearance of the bridge. The lovely *kapia* was concealed by the wooden structure which squatted over it with its wooden beams like some sort of gigantic bird.

The day the blockhouse was ready it still smelt strongly of resinous wood and steps echoed in its emptiness. The guards at once took up their quarters. By dawn on the first day the blockhouse, like a trap, already claimed its first victim.

In the low and rosy sun of early morning there collected beneath it the soldiers and a few armed townsmen, Turks, who mounted guard around the town by night and so helped the army. In the midst of this group stood a little old man, a vagabond religious pilgrim, something between a monk and a beggar, but mild and peaceful, somehow clean and sweet in his poverty, easy and smiling despite his white hair and lined face. He was an eccentric old fellow named Jelisije from Čajniče. For many years he had been wandering about, always mild, solemn and smiling, visiting churches and monasteries, religious meetings and festivals; he prayed, did penance and fasted. Earlier the Turkish authorities had paid no attention to him and regarded him as a feeble-minded and religious man, letting him go where he would and say what he liked. But now, due to the insurrection in Serbia, new times had come and harsher measures prevailed. A few Turkish families had arrived in the town whose property had been destroyed by the insurgents; they spread hatred and called for vengeance. Guards were everywhere. Supervision was intensified, the local Turks were anxious, filled with rancour and ill-will and looked on everyone bloodthirstily and with suspicion.

The old man had been travelling along the road from Rogatica and by bad luck was the first traveller on the day when the blockhouse had been completed and the first guards had taken up their posts there. In fact he had chosen the very worst time, for the day had not fully dawned. He bore before him, as a man carries a lighted candle, a sort of thick stick decorated with strange signs and letters. The blockhouse swallowed him up like a spider does a fly. They interrogated him curtly. They demanded who he was, what he was doing and whence he came, and commanded him to explain the decorations and writing on his staff. He replied freely and openly, even to questions that had not been asked him, as if speaking before the Last Judgment of God and not before a group of evil Turks. He said that he was no one and nothing, a traveller on this earth, a transient in a transient world, a shadow in the sun, but that he passed his few and short days in prayer and in going from monastery to monastery, until he had visited all the holy places, all the bequests and the tombs of the Serbian tsars and nobles. As to the signs and letters on his staff they represented the times of Serbian freedom and greatness, past and future. For, said the old man, smiling gently and timidly, the day of resurrection was coming soon and, judging from what he had read in books and from what might be seen on the earth and in the skies, it was now quite near. The kingdom was reborn, redeemed by trials and founded on truth.

'I know that it is not pleasant, gentlemen, for you to have to listen to these things and that I should not even speak of them before you, but you have stopped me and told me that I should tell you the whole truth, wherever it may lead. God is truth and God is One! And now, I beg you, let me go on my way for I am due today at Banja, at the Monastery of the Holy Trinity.'

The interpreter Shefko translated, struggling in vain to find in his poor knowledge of the Turkish language equivalents for abstract ideas. The Captain of the Guard, a sickly Anatolian, still only half awake, listened to the confused and disconnected words of the translator and from time to time threw a glance at the old man who, without fear or evil thoughts, looked back at him and confirmed with his eyes that everything was just as the interpreter had said, though he knew not a word of Turkish. Somewhere in the back of his mind it was clear to the Captain that this man was some sort of half-witted infidel dervish, a good-natured and harmless madman. And in the old man's staff, which they had already cut through in several places thinking that it was hollow and that messages were concealed in it, they found nothing. But in Shefko's translation the old man's words seemed suspicious, smelled of politics and seditious intent. The Captain, for his part, would have let this poor dim-witted creature go his way, but the rest of the soldiers and civil guards had gathered together there and were listening to the interrogation. There was his sergeant Tahir, an evil man, sullen and rheumy-eyed, who had already several times slandered him to his chief and accused him of lack of care and severity. Then too there was that Shefko, who in his translation was obviously putting the worst possible construction on the old man's exalted phrases and who loved to stick his nose into everything and carry tales even when there was nothing in them, and was ever ready to give or to confirm an evil report. Then too there were those Turks from the town, volunteers, who went their rounds sullenly and self-importantly, arrested suspicious characters and interfered needlessly in his official duties. They were all there. And all of them, these days, were as if drunk with bitterness, from desire for vengeance and longed to punish and to kill whomsoever they could, since they could not punish or kill those whom they wished. He did not understand them, nor did he approve of them, but he saw that they were all agreed that the blockhouse must have its victim this first morning. He suspected that because of their intoxication of bitterness he might be the one to suffer if he opposed their wishes. The thought that he might have unpleasantness because of this mad old fool seemed to him intolerable. And the old man with his tales of the Serbian Empire would not in any case get very far among the Turks of the district who, these days, were like a swarm of angry bees. Let the troubled waters carry him away, even as they had brought him here. . . .

As soon as the old man had been bound and the Captain was preparing to go into the town so as not to have to watch the execution, some Turkish policemen and a few civilians appeared, leading a poorly dressed Serbian youth. His clothing was torn and his face and hands scratched. This was a certain Mile, a poor devil from Lijesko, who lived quite alone in a water-mill at Osojnica. He might have been nineteen at most, strong and bursting with health.

That morning before sunrise Mile placed some barley in the mill to be ground and then opened the big millrace and went into the forest to cut wood. He brandished his axe and cut the soft alder branches like straws. He enjoyed the morning freshness and the ease with which the wood fell before his axe. His own movements were a pleasure to him. But his axe was sharp and the thin wood too frail for the force that was in him. Something within him swelled his breast and drove him to shout aloud at each movement. His cries became more and more frequent and connected. Mile who, like all men of Lijesko, had no ear and no idea of how to sing, sang and shouted in the thick and shady forest. Without thinking of anything and forgetting where he was, he began to sing what he had heard others singing.

At that time, when Serbia had risen in revolt, the people had made of the old song:

> 'When Alibeg was a young beg
> A maiden bore his standard . . .'

a new song:

> 'When Karageorge was a young beg
> A maiden bore his standard . . .'

In that great and strange struggle, which had been waged in Bosnia for centuries between two faiths, for land and power and their own conception of life and order, the adversaries had taken from each other not only women, horses and arms but also songs. Many a verse passed from one to the other as the most precious of booty.

This song, then, was one recently sung among the Serbs, but stealthily and in secret, in closed houses, at family feasts or in distant pastures where a Turk might not set foot for years at a time and where a man, at the price of loneliness and poverty in the wilds, might live as he wished and sing what he liked. And it was just this song that Mile, the mill attendant, had thought fit to sing in the forest just below the road along which the Turks of Olujac and Orahovac passed on their way to the market in the town.

Dawn had just touched the crests of the mountains and there, in that shady place, it was still quite dark. Mile was all wet with the dew but warm from a good night's sleep, hot bread and work. He brandished his axe and struck the slender alder near its root but the tree only bent and bowed like a young bride who kisses the hand of the '*kum*' who leads her to marriage. The alder was sprinkled with cold dew like a fine rain and remained bent, for it could not fall because of the thickness of the greenery around. Then he cut off the green branches with his axe in one hand as if playing. While he was doing this he sang at the top of his voice pronouncing certain of the words with enjoyment. 'Karageorge' was something vague but strong and daring; 'maiden' and 'standard' were also things unknown to him, but things which in some way answered to his most intimate dreams; to have a girl of his own and to bear a standard. In any case there was a sweetness in pronouncing such words. And all the strength within him drove him on to pronounce them clearly and countless times over. His utterance of them seemed to renew his strength making him repeat them still more loudly.

So sang Mile at the break of day until he had cut and trimmed the branches for which he had come. Then he went down the wet slope dragging his fresh burden behind him. There were some Turks in front of the mill. They had tethered their horses and were waiting for someone. There were ten of them. He felt himself again, as he had been before he had set out to get the wood, clumsy, ragged and embarrassed, without Karageorge before his eyes, without a girl or a standard near him. The Turks waited until he had put down his axe, then fell on him from all sides and after a short struggle bound him with a halter and took him to the town. On their way they beat him and kicked him in the groin, asking him where was his Karageorge now and saying evil words about his girl and his standard.

Under the blockhouse on the *kapia* where they had just bound the half-witted old man some of the town ne'er-do-wells had joined the soldiers even though it had only just dawned. Amongst them were a number of refugees from Serbia whose homes there had been burnt down. All were armed and wore a solemn expression as though a great event or a decisive battle were in question. Their emotion rose with the rising sun. The sun rose rapidly, amid shining mists down there on the skyline above Goleš. The Turks waited for the terrified youth as if he had been a revolutionary leader, though he was ragged and miserable and had been brought from the left bank of the Drina where there was no insurrection.

The Turks from Olujac and Orahovac, exasperated by the arrogance which they were unable to believe was not intentional, bore witness that the young man had been singing in a provocative manner beside the road songs about Karageorge and the infidel fighters. He, frightened, in wet rags, scratched and beaten, his eyes filled with emotion that made him seem to squint, watched the Captain as if he were hoping for salvation from him. As he came rarely to the town he had not known that a blockhouse was being erected on the bridge; therefore everything seemed to him strange and unreal as if he had wandered in his sleep into a strange town filled with evil and dangerous men. Stuttering and keeping his eyes on the ground, he swore that he had never sung anything and that he had never struck a Turk, that he was a poor man, who looked after the water-mill, that he was cutting wood and did not know why he had been brought here. He shivered from fear and was really unable to understand what had happened and how, after that exalted mood down there by the freshness of the stream, he had suddenly found himself bound and beaten here on the *kapia*, the centre of all interest, before so many people to whom he had to answer. He had himself quite forgotten that he had ever sung even the most innocent of songs.

But the Turks stood by their words; that he had been singing insurrectionist songs at the moment they had been passing and that he had resisted them when they wanted to bind him. Each of them confirmed this on oath to the Captain who interrogated them:

'Do you swear by Allah?'

'I swear by Allah.'

'Is that the truth?'

'That is the truth.'

So thrice repeated. Then they put the young man beside Jelisije and went to waken the headsman who, it seemed, slept very soundly. The old man looked at the youth who, confused and ashamed, blinked since he was not used to being the centre of attention in broad daylight on the bridge surrounded by so many people.

'What is your name?' the old man asked.

'Mile,' said the youth humbly, as if he were still replying to the Turkish questions.

'Mile, my son, let us kiss,' and the old man leant his grey head on Mile's shoulder. 'Let us kiss and make the sign of the Cross. In the Name of the Father and of the Son and of the Holy Ghost. In the Name of the Father and of the Son and of the Holy Ghost. Amen.'

So he crossed himself and the youth in words only, for their hands were bound, quickly, for the executioner had already arrived.

The headsman, who was one of the soldiers, rapidly finished his task and the first comers, who descended the hills because of market day and went across the bridge, could see the two heads placed on fresh stakes on the blockhouse and a bloodstained place, sprinkled with gravel and smoothed down, on the bridge where they had been beheaded.

Thus the blockhouse began its work.

From that day onwards all who were suspected or guilty of insurrection, whether caught on the bridge itself or somewhere on the frontier, were brought to the *kapia*. Once there they rarely got away alive. The heads of those connected with the revolt, or simply those who were unlucky, were exposed on stakes placed around the blockhouse and their bodies thrown from the bridge into the Drina if no one appeared to ransom the headless corpse.

The revolt, with shorter or longer periods of truce, lasted for years and in the course of those years the number of those thrown into the river to drift down to 'look for another, better and more reasonable land' was very great. Chance had decreed, that chance that overwhelms the weak and un-mindful, that these two simple men, this pair from the mass of unlearned, poverty-stricken and innocent, should head the procession, since it is often such men who are first caught up in the whirlpool of great events and whom this whirlpool irresistibly attracts and sucks down. Thus the youth Mile and the old man Jelisije, beheaded at the same moment and in the same place, united as brothers, first decorated with their heads the military blockhouse on the *kapia*, which from then onwards, as long as the revolt lasted, was practically never without such decoration. So these two, whom no one before then had ever seen or heard of, remained together in memory, a memory clearer and more lasting than that of so many other, more important, victims.

So the *kapia* disappeared under this bloodstained block-house of ill repute and with it vanished also all meetings, conversations, songs and enjoyment. Even the Turks passed that way unwillingly while only those Serbs who were forced to crossed the bridge hastily and with lowered heads.

Around the wooden blockhouse, whose planks with time became first grey and then black, was quickly created that atmosphere that always surrounds buildings in permanent use by the army. The soldiers' washing hung from the beams and rubbish was tipped from the windows into the Drina, dirty water and all the refuse and filth of barrack life. On the white central pier of the bridge remained long dirty streaks which could be seen from afar.

The job of headsman was for long always carried out by the same soldier. He was a fat and dark-skinned Anatolian with dull yellowish eyes and negroid lips in a greasy and earthen-coloured face, who seemed always to be smiling, with the smile of a well-nourished and good-humoured man. He was called Hairuddin and was soon known to the whole town and even beyond the frontier. He carried out his duties with satisfaction and conscientiousness; and certainly he was exceptionally swift and skilful at them. The townsmen used to say that he had a lighter hand than Mushan the town barber. Both old and young knew him, at least by name, and that name excited awe and curiosity at the same time. On sunny days he would sit or lie all day long on the bridge in the shade under the wooden blockhouse. From time to time he would rise to inspect the heads on the stakes, like a market-gardener his melons. Then he would lie down again on his plank in the shade, yawning and stretching himself, heavy, rheumy-eyed and good-humoured, like an ageing sheepdog. At the end of the bridge, behind the wall, the children gathered inquisitively and watched him timidly.

But when his work was in question, Hairuddin was alert and precise to the minutest detail. He disliked anyone to interfere with his work, a thing which happened more and more often as the insurrection developed. When the insurgents burnt some of the villages above the town, the anger of the Turks passed all measure. Not only did they arrest all insurgents and spies, or those whom they considered such, and brought them to the Captain on the bridge, but in their rancour they even wanted to take part in the execution of the sentence.

Thus one day dawn revealed the head of the Višegrad parish priest, that same Pop Mihailo who had found strength to joke with the *hodja* and the rabbi on the night of the great flood. In the general fury against the Serbs he had been killed, even though innocent, and the gipsy children stuck a cigar in his dead mouth.

Hairuddin strongly disapproved of such actions and prevented them whenever he was able.

When one day the fat Anatolian died unexpectedly of

anthrax a new headsman, in truth far less skilful, continued his work and went on doing so for several years, and until the revolt in Serbia had died down there were always two or three heads exposed on the *kapia*. In such times people quickly grow hardened and insensible. They soon became so accustomed to them that they passed them by indifferently and paid no more heed to them, so that they did not at once notice when they ceased to be exhibited.

When the situation in Serbia and on the frontier died down, the blockhouse lost its importance and its reason for existence. But the guard went on sleeping there, although the crossing of the bridge had long been free and without supervision. In every army things change slowly and in the Turkish army more slowly than in any other. And so it would have remained for God alone knows how long had not a fire broken out one night because of a forgotten candle. The blockhouse was made of resinous planks and was still warm after the heat of the day. It burnt to its foundations, that is to say down to the flagstones of the *kapia*.

The excited people of the town watched the huge blaze which lit up not only the bridge but also the mountains around, and was reflected in wavering red light on the surface of the river. When morning broke, the bridge again appeared in its former shape freed from the clumsy wooden monstrosity which had for years concealed its *kapia*. The white stones were tarnished and sooty, but the rains and snows soon washed them clean again. Thus nothing remained of the blockhouse and the bloody events connected with it save a few bitter memories which paled and finally disappeared with that generation, and one oak beam which had not been burnt as it was fixed into the stone steps of the *kapia*.

So the *kapia* once again became for the town what it had formerly been. On the left terrace as one came from the town a coffee brewer once again lit his brazier and set out his utensils. Only the fountain had suffered, for the snake's head from which the water had flowed had been crushed. The people once again began to dally on the *sofa* and pass the time there in conversation, in business deals or in drowsy time-wasting. On summer nights the young men sang there in groups or sat there solitary suppressing their love-yearning or giving way to that vague desire to go out into the distant world to do great deeds and take part in great events which so often torments young people brought up in a narrow milieu. After a score or so of years a new generation grew up which did not even remember the deformed wooden carcass of the blockhouse or the harsh cries of the guard stopping travellers by night, or Hairuddin or the exposed heads which he had cut off with such professional skill. Only some of the old women, driving away the urchins who came to steal their peaches, would shout in loud and angry curses:

'May God send Hairuddin to cut your hair for you! May your mother recognize your head on the *kapia*!'

But the children who ran away over the fences could not understand the real sense of these curses, though they knew, naturally, that they meant nothing favourable.

Thus the generations renewed themselves beside the bridge and the bridge shook from itself, like dust, all the traces which transient human events had left on it and remained, when all was over, unchanged and unchangeable.

CHAPTER VII

TIME PASSED OVER the bridge by years and decades. Those were the few decades about the middle of the nineteenth century in which the Turkish Empire was consumed by a slow fever. Measured by the eye of a contemporary, those years seemed comparatively peaceful and serene, although they had their share of anxieties and fears and knew droughts and floods and epidemics and all manner of exciting events. Only all these things came in their own time, in short spasms amid long lulls.

The border between the two *pashaluks* of Bosnia and Belgrade, which passed just above the town, began in those years to become ever more sharply defined and to take on the appearance and significance of a state frontier. That changed the conditions of life for the whole district and for the town also, influenced trade and communications, and the mutual relations of Turks and Serbs.

The older Turks frowned and blinked in incredulity, as if they wished to drive away this unpleasant apparition. They threatened and discussed and then for months at a time forgot all about the matter, until harsh reality would once again remind them and alarm them once more.

Thus, one spring day one of the Turks from Veletovo, up there on the frontier, sat on the *kapia* and with deep emotion told the leading Turks gathered there what had been happening at Veletovo.

Some time in the winter, the man from Veletovo said, there had appeared above their village the ill-famed Jovan Mičić, the *serdar* of Ruyan, who had come from Arilje with armed men and begun to inspect and mark out the frontier. When they asked him what he intended to do and why he was there, he replied arrogantly that he had to give account to no one, least of all to Bosnian renegades, but if they really wanted to know he had been sent there by the Prince Miloš to find out where the frontier was to run and how much was to be included in Serbia.

'We thought,' said the man from Veletovo, 'that the Vlach was drunk and did not know what he was saying, for we have long known him as a bandit and a rascal. So we refused to let him stay and then forgot all about him. But not more than two months later he came again, this time with a whole company of Miloš' soldiers and a delegate of the Sultan, a soft pale fellow from Stambul. We could not believe our eyes. But the delegate confirmed everything. He lowered his eyes in shame, but he confirmed. Thus, he said, it had been ordered by Imperial decree that Miloš should administer Serbia in the Sultan's name and that the frontier should be marked out, to know exactly to what point his authority stretched. When the delegate's men began to drive in stakes along the crest below Tetrebica, Mičić came and pulled them up and threw them aside. The mad Vlach (may the dogs eat his flesh!) flew at the delegate, shouted at him as if he were a subordinate and threatened him with death. That, he said, was not the frontier; the frontier had been fixed by the Sultan and the Russian Tsar who had given a *ferman* to Prince Miloš. It now ran along the Lim down as far as the Višegrad bridge and thence down the Drina; thus all this land is part of Serbia. This too, he said, is only for a certain time; later it will have to be advanced. The delegate had great trouble in convincing him and then they fixed the frontier above Veletovo. And there it remains, at least for the present. Only from then on we have been filled with doubt and a sort of fear, so that we do not know what to do or where to turn. We have discussed all this with the people of Užice, but they too do not know what has happened nor what to expect. And old Hadji-Zuko who has twice been to Mecca and is now more than ninety years old says that before a generation has passed the Turkish frontier will be withdrawn right to the Black Sea, fifteen days' march away.'

The leading Turks of Višegrad listened to the man from Veletovo. They seemed calm to all outward appearance, but inwardly they were shaken and confused. They squirmed unintentionally at his words and caught hold of the stone seat with their hands, as if some powerful and invisible force were shaking the bridge beneath them. Then, mastering themselves, they sought words to lessen and diminish the importance of this event.

They did not like unfavourable news or heavy thoughts or serious and despondent conversations on the *kapia*, but they could see for themselves that this boded no good; nor could they deny what the man from Veletovo had said or find words to calm and reassure him. So they could scarcely wait for the peasant who had brought this unpleasant news to return to his village in the mountains. That, naturally, would not lessen the anxiety but it would remove it far from them. And when in fact the man went away, they were only too pleased to be able to return to their usual habits, and to go on sitting peacefully on the *kapia* without conversations which made life disagreeable and the future terrifying, and to leave it to time to soften and ease the weight of the events which had taken place over there behind the mountains.

Time did its work. Life went on, to all appearances unchanged. More than thirty years passed since that conversation on the *kapia*. But those stakes which the Sultan's delegate and the *serdar* of Ruyan had planted struck root and brought forth fruit, late-ripening but bitter to the Turks. The Turks had now to abandon even the last towns in Serbia. One summer day the bridge at Višegrad was burdened with a pitiable procession of refugees from Užice.

It was on one of those hot days with long pleasant twilights on the *kapia* when the Turks from the market-place filled both the terraces over the water. On such days melons were brought there on donkey back. The ripe canteloupes and water-melons had been cooled all day long and in the early evening people would buy and eat them on the *sofa*. Usually two of them would bet whether the inside of a certain water-melon were red or white. Then they would cut it open and whoever lost paid for it and they would eat it together, with talk and loud jokes.

The day's warmth still beat up from the stone terraces but with the twilight there was a cool refreshing air from the water. The middle of the river shone, and near the banks under the willows it turned a shadowy dull green. All the hills around were reddened by the sunset, some strongly and others scarcely touched. Above them, filling the whole south-western part of that amphitheatre which could be seen from the *kapia* were summer mists of continually changing colour. These mists are among the most beautiful sights to be seen in summer on the *kapia*. As soon as the daylight grows strong and the sun leaps up, they appear behind the mountains like thick white silvery-grey masses, creating fantastic landscapes, irregular cupolas and countless strange buildings. They remain thus all day long, heavy and unmoving above the hills surrounding the town which swelters in the sun. The Turks who in early evening sat on the *kapia* had those mists always before their eyes like white silken Imperial tents which in their imagination evoked vague shapes of wars and forays and pictures of strange and immeasurable power and luxury, till darkness extinguished and dispersed them and the skies created fresh magic from the stars and moonlight.

Never could the wonderful and exceptional beauty of the *kapia* be better felt than at that hour on such summer days. A man was then as if in a magic swing; he swung over the earth and the waters and flew in the skies, yet was firmly and surely linked with the town and his own white house there on the bank with its plum-orchard about it. With the solace of coffee and tobacco, many of those simple citizens, who owned little more than those houses and the few shops in the market-place, felt at such times the richness of the world and the illimitability of God's gifts. Such a bridge, lovely and strong, could offer all this to men and would continue to offer it for centuries to come.

This was just such an evening, an evening filled with chatter and laughter and jokes among themselves and the passers-by.

The sprightliest and loudest jokes centred on a short but powerful young man of strange appearance. This was Salko Ćorkan, One-eyed Salko.

Salko was the son of a gipsy woman and some Anatolian soldier or officer who had some time been stationed in the town and had left it before this unwanted son had been born. Shortly afterwards, his mother too had died and the child had grown up without anyone of his own. The whole town fed him; he belonged to everybody and nobody. He did odd jobs about the shops and houses, carried out tasks which no one else would do, cleaned the cesspools and street channels, and buried anything that had died or had been brought down by the waters. He had never had a house or occupation of his own. He ate whatever he happened to find, still standing or walking about, slept in attics, and dressed in parti-coloured rags given him by others. While still a child he had lost his left eye. Eccentric, good-humoured, merry and a drunkard, he often worked for the townsmen for a word or a joke instead of pay.

Around Salko had gathered a number of merchants' sons, young men who laughed at him and played crude jokes on him.

The air smelt of fresh melons and roasting coffee. From the great flagstones, still warm from the day's heat, and sprinkled with water, rose moist and scented the special smell of the *kapia* which filled men with freedom from care and evoked lively fancies.

It was the moment between day and night. The sun had set but the great star which rose over Moljevnik had not yet appeared. In such a moment, when even the most ordinary thing took on the appearance of a vision filled with majesty, terror and special meaning, the first refugees from Užice appeared on the bridge.

The men were for the most part on foot, dusty and bowed,

while the women wrapped in their veils were balanced on small horses with small children tied to the saddle-bags or to boxes. Now and again a more important man rode a better horse, but with lowered head and at a funereal pace, revealing even more clearly the misfortune which had driven them hither. Some of them were leading a single goat on a short halter. Others carried lambs in their laps. All were silent; even the children did not cry. All that could be heard was the beat of horseshoes and footsteps and the monotonous chinking of wooden and copper vessels on the overloaded horses.

The appearance of this overtired and destitute procession dampened the gaiety on the *kapia*. The older people remained seated on the stone benches, while the younger stood up and formed living walls on both sides of the *kapia* and the procession passed between them. Some of the townsmen only looked compassionately at the refugees and remained silent, while others greeted them with '*merhaba*', tried to stop them and offer them something. They paid no attention to the offers and scarcely responded to the greetings, but hurried on to reach their post for the night at Okolište while it was still light.

In all there were about 120 families. More than 100 families were going on to Sarajevo where there was a chance of being settled, while fifteen were to stay in the town; they were for the most part those who had relatives there.

One only of these dog-tired men, poor in appearance and apparently alone, stopped for a moment on the *kapia*, drank his fill of water and accepted an offered cigar. He was white all over from the dust of the road, his eyes shone as if in fever and he was unable to keep his glance fixed on any single object. Vigorously puffing out smoke, he looked around him with those shining disagreeable glances, without replying to the timid and humble questions of individuals. He only wiped his long moustaches, thanked them curtly and with that bitterness which overtiredness and a feeling of being outcast leaves in a man he muttered a few words looking at them with one of those sudden unseeing glances.

'You sit here at your ease and do not know what is happening behind Staniševac. Here we are fleeing into Turkish lands, but where are you to flee when, together with us, your turn will come? None of you knows and none of you ever thinks of it.'

He suddenly ceased. Even the little he said was much for those who till then had been so carefree, and yet little enough for his own bitterness which would not allow him to stay silent yet at the same time prevented him from expressing himself clearly. It was he himself who cut short the heavy silence by saying farewell and hurrying away to catch up with the rest of the procession. All stood up to shout good wishes after him.

All that evening the mood on the *kapia* remained heavy. All were silent and downcast. Even Salko sat dumb and motionless on one of the stone steps surrounded by the husks of the water-melons he had eaten for a bet. Depressed and silent he sat there with downcast looks, absent-mindedly, as though he were not looking at the stone before him but at something far distant which he could scarcely perceive. The people began to disperse earlier than usual.

But next day everything was as it had always been, for the townsmen did not like to remember evil and did not worry about the future; in their blood was the conviction that real life consists of calm periods and that it would be mad and vain to spoil them by looking for some other, firmer and more lasting life that did not exist.

In those twenty-five years in the middle of the nineteenth century the plague raged twice at Sarajevo and the cholera once. When this happened the town kept regulations which, according to tradition, had been given by Mohammed himself to the faithful for their guidance in the event of an epidemic: 'While the Pestilence rages in some place do not go there, for you may become infected, and if you are already in the place where it rages then do not depart from that place lest you infect others.' But since men do not observe even the most salutary of regulations, even when they derive from the

Apostle of God himself, if not forced to do so by 'the power of the authorities', then the authorities on the occasion of every 'plague' limited or completely stopped all travel and postal communications. Then life on the *kapia* changed its aspect. The people of the town, busy or at leisure, thoughtful or singing, disappeared, and on the empty *sofa*, as in times of war or revolution, once again sat a guard of several gendarmes. They stopped all travellers coming from the direction of Sarajevo and waved them back with their rifles or shouted loudly to them to retreat. The post they accepted from the messenger but with every measure of precaution. A small fire of 'aromatic woods' was lit on the *kapia* and produced an abundant white smoke. The gendarmes took each individual letter in a pair of tongs and passed it through this smoke. Only such 'purified' letters were sent onward. Goods they did not accept at all. But their main task was not with letters but with living men. Every day a few arrived, travellers, merchants, bearers of news, tramps. A gendarme awaited them at the entry to the bridge and from a distance signalled with his hand that they might not go farther. The traveller would halt, but begin to argue, to justify himself and explain his case. Each of them considered that it was absolutely necessary to let him into the town and each of them swore that he was healthy and had had no connection with the cholera which was there somewhere in Sarajevo. During these explanations the travellers would edge little by little halfway across the bridge and approach the *kapia*. There, other gendarmes would take their part in the conversation and as they talked at several paces distance they all shouted loudly and waved their arms. Those gendarmes also joined in who sat all day on the *kapia* sipping plum-brandy and eating garlic; their service gave them this right for it was believed that both these were good antidotes against infection, and they made abundant use of their privilege.

Many a traveller would grow tired of pleading with and trying to convince the gendarmes and would return downcast, his work unfinished, along the Okolište road. But some were more persistent and persevering and remained there on the *kapia* hoping for a moment of weakness or inattention or some mad and lucky chance. If it so happened that the leader of the town gendarmes, Salko Hedo, were there, then there was no likelihood that the traveller would achieve anything. Hedo was that true conscientious official who does not really see or hear whomever he talks to, and who only considers him in so far as it is necessary to find the place for him set out by the regulations in force. Until he had done this he was deaf and blind and when he had done it he become dumb as well. In vain the traveller would implore or flatter:

'Salik-Aga, I am healthy. . . .'

'Well then, go in health whence you came. Get along, out of my sight. . . .'

There was no arguing with Hedo. But if some of the younger gendarmes were alone, then something might still be done. The longer the traveller stood on the bridge and the more he shouted and talked with them, told all his troubles, why he had set out and all the problems of his life, the more personal and familiar he seemed to become and less and less like a man who might have cholera. In the end, one of the gendarmes would offer to take a message for him to whomever he wished in the town. This was the first step towards yielding. But the traveller knew that the message would never be delivered for the gendarmes, always suffering from a hangover or half drunk as they were, remembered things with difficulty and delivered messages inside out. Therefore he went on indefinitely with his conversation, implored, offered bribes, called upon God and his soul. All this he did until the gendarme whom he had marked down as the most lenient remained alone on the bridge. Then the business was finished somehow or other. The soulful gendarme would turn his face to the raised wall as if to read the ancient inscription on it, with his hands behind his back and the palm of his right hand extended. The persevering traveller would put the agreed sum of money into the gendarme's palm, glance right and left, and then slide across the other half of the bridge and become lost in the town. The gendarme went back to his post, chewed a head of garlic and washed it down with plum-brandy. This filled him with a certain gay and carefree resolution and gave him fresh strength to keep vigil and guard the town from cholera.

But misfortunes do not last forever (this they have in common with joys) but pass away or are at least diminished and become lost in oblivion. Life on the *kapia* always renews itself despite everything and the bridge does not change with the years or with the centuries or with the most painful turns in human affairs. All these pass over it, even as the unquiet waters pass beneath its smooth and perfect arches.

CHAPTER VIII

IT WAS NOT only the wars, pestilences and migrations of the times which broke against the bridge and interrupted life on the *kapia*. There were also other exceptional events which gave their name to the year in which they took place and were long remembered.

Left and right of the *kapia* in both directions, the stone parapet of the bridge had long become smooth and somewhat darker than the rest. For hundreds of years the peasants had rested their burdens on it when crossing the bridge, or idlers had leant shoulders and elbows upon it in conversation while waiting for others or when, solitary and leaning on their elbows, they looked in the depths below them at the waters as they went foaming swiftly past, always new and yet always the same.

But never had so many idle and inquisitive people leant on the parapet and watched the surface of the water, as if to read in it the answer to some riddle, as in the last days of August that year. The water was clouded by the rains though it was only towards the end of summer. In the eddies below the arches a white foam formed, which moved in circles with twigs, small branches and rubbish. But the leisurely and leaning townsmen were not really looking at the waters which they had always known and which had nothing to tell them; but on the surface of the water and in their own conversations they searched for some sort of explanation for themselves and tried to find there some visible trace of an obscure and cruel destiny which, in those days, had troubled and surprised them.

About that time an unusual thing had taken place on the *kapia* which would long be remembered and which was not likely to happen again as long as the bridge and the town on the Drina existed. It had excited and shaken the townspeople and the story of it had passed beyond the town itself, to other places and districts, to become a legend.

This was, in fact, a tale of two Višegrad hamlets, Velje Lug and Nezuke. These two hamlets lay at the extreme ends of that amphitheatre formed about the town by the dark mountains and their green foothills.

The great village of Stražište on the north-eastern side of the valley was the nearest to the town. Its houses, fields and gardens were scattered over several foothills and embowered in the valleys between them. On the rounded flank of one of these hills lay about fifteen houses, buried in plum-orchards and surrounded on all sides by fields. This was the hamlet of Velje Lug, a peaceful, rich and beautiful Turkish settlement on the slopes. The hamlet belonged to the village of Stražište, but it was nearer to the town than to its own village centre, for the men of Velje Lug could walk down to the market-place in half an hour, had their shops there and did business in the town like the ordinary townsmen. Between them and the townsmen there was indeed little or no difference save perhaps that their properties were more solid and lasting for they stood on the firm earth, not subject to floods, and the men there were more modest and did not have the bad habits of the town. Velje Lug had good soil, pure water and handsome people.

A branch of the Višegrad family of Osmanagić lived there. But even though those in the town were richer and more numerous, it was generally considered that they had 'degenerated' and that the real Osmanagićs were those of Velje Lug whence the family had come. They were a fine race of men, sensitive and proud of their origin. Their house, the largest in the district, showing up white on the hillside just below the crest of the hill, turned towards the south-west; it was always freshly whitewashed, with a roof of blackened thatch and fifteen glazed windows. Their house could be seen from afar and was the first to catch the eye of a traveller coming to Višegrad and the last that he saw on leaving it. The last rays of the setting sun behind the Liještan ridge rested there and shone on the white and shining face of this house. The townsmen were long accustomed to look at it from the *kapia* in the early evening and see how the setting sun was reflected from the Osmanagić windows and how the light left them one after the other. As the sun set and the town was in shadow its last rays, falling on one of the windows, as it broke through the clouds, would shine for a few moments longer like a huge red star over the darkened town.

Also well known and esteemed in the town was the head of that house, Avdaga Osmanagić, a bold and fiery man in private life as in business. He had a shop in the market, a low twilit room in which maize, dried plums or pinecones lay scattered over planks and plaited mats. Avdaga only did a wholesale trade, therefore his shop was not open every day, but regularly on market days and throughout the week according to the needs of business. In it was always one of Avdaga's sons, while he himself usually sat on a bench before it. There he chatted with customers or acquaintances. He was a big and imposing man, ruddy in appearance, but with pure white beard and moustaches. His voice was harsh and throaty. For years he had suffered cruelly from asthma. Whenever he grew excited in conversation and raised his voice, and that was a frequent occurrence, he would suddenly choke, his neck tendons stand out, his face grow red and his eyes fill with tears, while his chest creaked, wheezed and echoed like a storm on the hills. When the fit of choking had passed, he would pull himself together, take a deep breath and go on with the conversation where he had left off, only in a changed thin voice. He was known in the town and the surroundings as a man of harsh words, but generous and brave. So he was in everything, even in business, though often to his own hurt. Often by a bold word he would reduce or raise the price of plums or maize even when this was not to his own advantage, only to spite some avaricious peasant or rapacious merchant. His word was universally listened to and accepted in the market-place, though it was known that he was often hasty and personal in his judgements. When Avdaga came down from Velje Lug and sat before his shop he was rarely alone, for men liked to listen to his talk and wanted to hear his opinion. He was always open and lively, ready to speak out and defend what others considered was best passed over in silence. His asthma and attacks of heavy coughing would interrupt his conversation at any moment, but for a wonder this did not spoil it but made it seem the more convincing and his whole manner of expressing himself had a sort of heavy and painful dignity, which it was not easy to resist.

Avdaga had five married sons and an only daughter, who was the youngest of his children and just ripe for marriage. She was called Fata and it was known of her that she was exceptionally beautiful and the very image of her father. The whole town and to some extent even the whole district discussed the question of her marriage. It has always been the case with us that at least one girl in every generation passes into legend and song because of her beauty, her qualities and her nobility. So she was in those few years the goal of all desires and the inaccessible example; imagination flared up at mention of her name and she was surrounded by the enthusiasm of the men and the envy of the women. She was one of those outstanding persons set apart by nature and raised to dangerous heights.

This daughter of Avdaga resembled her father not only in face and appearance but also in quickness of wit and the gift of words. The youths who, at weddings or meetings, sought to win her by cheap flattery or embarrass her by daring jests, knew this well. Her wit was no less than her beauty. Therefore, in the song about Fata the daughter of Avdaga (songs about such exceptional beings spring up of themselves spontaneously) it was sung:

> 'Thou art wise as thou art lovely,
> Lovely Fata Avdagina . . .'

So they sang and spoke in the town, but there were very few who had the courage to ask for the hand of the girl from Velje Lug. And when they had one and all been rejected, a sort of vacuum was created about Fata, an enchanted circle, made of hatred and envy, of unacknowledged desires and of malicious expectation, such a circle as always surrounds beings with exceptional gifts and an exceptional destiny. Such persons, of whom much is said and sung, are rapidly borne away by that especial destiny of theirs and leave behind them, instead of a life fulfilled, a song or a story.

Thus it often happens amongst us that a girl who is much spoken of remains for that very reason without suitors and 'sits out', whereas girls who in no way measure up to her marry quickly and easily. This was not destined for Fata, for a suitor was found who had the audacity to desire her and the skill and endurance to attain his ends.

In that irregular circle formed by the Višegrad valley, exactly on the opposite side from Velje Lug, lay the hamlet of Nezuke.

Above the bridge, not quite an hour's walk upstream, amid that circle of dark mountains whence, as from a wall, the Drina breaks out in a sudden curve, there was a narrow strip of good and fertile land on the stony river bank. This was formed by the deposits brought down by the river and by the torrents which came down from the precipitous slopes of the Butkovo Rocks. On it were fields and gardens and, above them, steep meadows with sparse grass which lost themselves on the slopes in rugged stone crops and dark undergrowth. The whole hamlet was the property of the Hamzić family, who were also known by the name of Turković. On one half lived five or six families of serfs and on the other were the houses of the Hamzić brothers, with Mustajbeg Hamzić at their head. The hamlet was remote and exposed, without sun but also without wind, richer in fruit and hay than in wheat. Surrounded and shut in on all sides by steep hills, the greater part of the day it was in shadow and in silence, so that every call of the shepherds and every movement of the cowbells was heard as a loud and repeated echo from the hills. One path only led to it from Višegrad. When one crossed the bridge coming from the town and left the main road which turned to the right down river, one came upon a narrow stone track to the left across a patch of waste and stony ground up the Drina along the water's edge, like a white selvedge on the dark slopes which ran down to the river. A man on horse or on foot going along that path, when seen from the bridge above, seemed as if he were going along a narrow tree trunk between the water and the stone, and his reflection could be seen following him in the calm green waters.

That was the path which led from the town to Nezuke; and from Nezuke there was no way on, for there was nowhere to go. Above the houses, in the steep slopes overgrown with sparse forest, two deep white watercourses had been cut, up which the shepherds climbed when they took the cattle to their mountain pastures.

There was the great white house of the eldest Hamzić, Mustajbeg. It was in no way smaller than the Osmanagić house at Velje Lug, but it was different in that it was completely invisible in that hollow alongside the Drina. Around it grew fifteen tall poplars in a semi-circle, whose murmur and movement gave life to that spot so shut in and difficult of access. Below this house were the smaller and humbler houses of the remaining pair of Hamzić brothers. All the Hamzićs had many children and all were fair-skinned, tall and slender, taciturn and reserved, but well able to hold their own in business, united and active in all their affairs. Like all the richer people at Velje Lug, they too had their shops in the town where they brought for sale everything that they produced at Nezuke. At all times of the year, they and their serfs swarmed and climbed like ants along that narrow stony track beside the Drina bringing produce to the town or returning, their business concluded, with money in their pockets, to their invisible village among the hills.

Mustajbeg Hamzić's great white house awaited the visitor

as a pleasant surprise at the end of that stony track that seemed as if it led nowhere. Mustajbeg had four daughters and one son, Nail. This Nail-beg of Nezuke, only son of a noble family, was among the first to cast an eye on Fata of Velje Lug. He had admired her beauty at some wedding or other through a half-opened door, outside which a group of young men had been hanging like a bunch of grapes. When he next had the chance of seeing her, surrounded by a group of her friends, he had essayed a daring jest:

'May God and Mustajbeg give you the name of young bride!'

Fata gave a stifled giggle.

'Do not laugh,' said the excited youth through the narrow opening of the door, 'even that marvel will take place one day.'

'It will indeed, when Velje Lug comes down to Nezuke!' replied the girl with another laugh and a proud movement of her body, such as only women like her and of her age can make, and which said more than her words and her laugh.

It is thus that those beings especially gifted by nature often provoke their destiny, boldly and thoughtlessly. Her reply to young Hamzić was repeated from mouth to mouth, as was everything else that she said or did.

But the Hamzićs were not men to be put off or discouraged at the first difficulty. Even when it was a question of minor matters, they did not come to a conclusion hastily so how much less in such a question as this. An attempt made through some relations in the town had no better success. But then old Mustajbeg Hamzić took into his own hands the matter of his son's marriage. He had always had common business dealings with Osmanagić. Avdaga had recently had some serious losses, due to his explosive and proud character, and Mustajbeg had helped him and supported him as only good merchants can help and support one another in difficult moments; simply, naturally and without unnecessary words.

In these cool half-lit shops and on the smooth stone benches before them were settled not only matters of commercial honour but also human destinies. What happened there between Avdaga Osmanagić and Mustajbeg Hamzić, how did Mustajbeg come to ask for the hand of Fata for his only son Nail, and why did the proud and upright Avdaga 'give' the girl? No one will ever know. No one will ever know either exactly how the matter was thrashed out up there at Velje Lug between the father and his lovely only daughter. There could, naturally, be no question of any opposition on her part. One look filled with pained surprise and that proud and inborn movement of her whole body, and then mute submission to her father's wishes, as it was and still is everywhere and always amongst us. As if in a dream, she began to air, to complete and to arrange her trousseau.

Nor did a single word from Nezuke filter out to the outer world. The prudent Hamzićs did not ask other men to confirm their successes in empty words. They had achieved their wish and, as always, were content with their success. There was no need of anyone else to share in their satisfaction, even as they had never asked for sympathy in their failures and their misfortunes.

But none the less people talked of this widely and unthinkingly, as is the habit of men. It was told throughout the town and the country around that the Hamzićs had got what they wanted, and that the lovely, proud and clever daughter of Avdaga, for whom no suitor good enough had been found in all Bosnia, had been outplayed and tamed; that none the less 'Velje Lug would come to Nezuke' even though Fata had publicly proclaimed that it would not. For people love to talk about the downfall and humiliation of those who have been exalted too much or have flown too high.

For a month the people savoured the event and drank in tales of Fata's humiliation like sweet water. For a month they made preparations at Nezuke and at Velje Lug.

For a month Fata worked with her friends, her relations and her servants on her trousseau. The girls sang. She too sang. She even found strength to do that. And she heard herself singing, though she still thought her own thoughts. For with every stroke of her needle she told herself that neither she nor her needlework would ever see Nezuke. She never forgot this for an instant. Only, thus working and thus singing, it seemed to her that it was a long way from Velje Lug to Nezuke and that a month was a long time. At night it was the same. At night when, with the excuse that she had some work to finish, she remained alone there opened before her a world rich and full of light, of joyful and unlimited change.

At Velje Lug the nights were warm and fresh. The stars seemed low and dancing, as though bound together by a white shimmering radiance. Standing before her window, Fata looked out at the night. Through all her body she felt a calm strength, overflowing and sweet, and every part of her body seemed a special source of strength and joy, her legs, her hips, her arms, her neck and above all her breasts. Her breasts, full and large but firm, touched the frame of the window with their nipples. And in that place she felt the whole hillside with all that was on it, houses, outbuildings, fields, breathing warmly, deeply, rising and falling with the shining heavens and the expanse of the night. With that breathing the wooden frame of the window rose and fell, touching the tips of her breasts, leaving them once more for some vast distance and then returning once again to touch them, then rising and falling again and again.

Yes, the world was great, the world was limitless even by day when the valley of Višegrad quivered in the heat and one could almost hear the wheat ripening and when the white town was strung out along the green river, framed by the straight lines of the bridge and the dark mountains. But at night, only at night, the skies grew alive and burst open into infinity and the power of that world where a living being is lost, and has no longer the sense of what he is, where he is going or what he wishes or what he must do. Only there one lived truly, serenely and for long; in that space there were no longer words that bound one tragically for one's whole life, no longer fateful promises or situations from which one could not escape, with the brief time that flows and flows onward inexorably, with death or shame as the only out-come. Yes, in that space it was not as it is in everyday life, where what has once been said remains irrevocable and what has been promised inescapable. There everything was free, endless, nameless and mute.

Then, from somewhere below her, as from afar, could be heard a heavy, deep and stifled sound:

'A-a-a-aah, kkkh . . . A-a-a-aaah . . . kkkkh!'

Down on the ground floor Avdaga was struggling with his nightly attack of coughing.

She heard the sound and could see her father clearly, almost as if he were there before her, as he sat and smoked, sleepless and tormented by his cough. She could see his big brown eyes, as well known as a dear landscape, eyes which were just like her own, save that they were shadowed by old age and bathed in a tearful yet laughing shimmer, eyes in which for the first time she had seen the inevitability of her fate on that day she was told that she had been promised to Hamzić and that she must finish her preparations within a month.

'Kkha, kkha, kkha, Aaaaah!'

That ecstasy of a moment before at the beauty of the night and the greatness of the world was suddenly extinguished. That perfumed breath of the earth ceased. The girl's breasts tightened in a brief spasm. The stars and the expanse disap-peared. Only fate, her cruel and irrevocable fate on the eve of its realization was being completed and accomplished as the time passed in the stillness of that immobility and that void which remained beyond the world.

The sound of coughing echoed from the floor below.

Yes, she both saw and heard him as if he were standing beside her. That was her own dear, powerful, only father with whom she had felt herself to be one, indivisibly and sweetly, ever since she had been conscious of her own exist-ence. She felt that heavy shattering cough as if it had been in her own breast. In truth it had been that mouth that had said yes where her own had said no. But she was at one with

him in everything, even in this. That yes of his she felt as if
it were her own (even as she felt too her own no). Therefore
her fate was cruel, unusual, immediate, and therefore she
saw no escape from it and could see none, for none existed.
But one thing she knew. Because of her father's yes, which
bound her as much as her own no, she would have to appear
before the *kadi* with Mustajbeg's son, for it was inconceivable
to think that Avdaga Osmanagić did not keep his word. But
she knew too, equally well, that after the ceremony her feet
would never take her to Nezuke, for that would mean that
she had not kept her own word. That too was inconceivable, for that too was the word of an Osmanagić. There,
on that point of no return, between her no and her father's
yes, between Velje Lug and Nezuke, somewhere in that most
inescapable impasse, she must find a way out. That was all
she thought of now. No longer the expanses of the great rich
world, not even the whole route from Velje Lug to Nezuke,
but only that short and pitiful little scrap of road which led
from the courthouse in which the *kadi* would marry her to
Mustajbeg's son, as far as the end of the bridge where the stony
slope led down to the narrow track which led to Nezuke and
on which, she knew for a certainty, she would never set foot.
Her thoughts flew incessantly up and down that little scrap
of road, from one end to the other, like a shuttle through
the weave. They would fly from the courthouse, across the
market-place to the end of the bridge, to halt there as before
an impassable abyss, and then back across the bridge, across
the market-place to the courthouse. Always thus; back and
forward, forward and back! There her destiny was woven.

And those thoughts which could neither remain still nor
were able to find a way out, more and more often halted at
the *kapia*, on that lovely and shining *sofa*, where the townspeople sat in conversation and the young men sang, and
beneath which roared the deep swift green waters of the
river. Then, horrified at such a way of escape, they would fly
once again, as if under a curse, from one end of the journey
to the other and, without finding any other solution, would

stop there once again on the *kapia*. Every night her thoughts more and more often halted there and remained there longer. The very thought of that day, when in fact and not only in her thoughts she must go along that way and find her way out before she reached the end of the bridge, brought with it all the terror of death or the horror of a life of shame. It seemed to her, helpless and forsaken, that the very terror of that thought must remove or at least postpone that day.

But the days passed, neither fast nor slow, but regular and fateful and with them came at last the day of the wedding.

On that last Thursday in August (that was the fateful day) the Hamzićs came on horseback for the girl. Covered with a heavy new black veil, as if under a suit of armour, Fata was seated on a horse and led into the town. Meanwhile, in the courtyard, horses were loaded with the chests containing her trousseau. The marriage was announced in the courthouse before the *kadi*. So was kept the word by which Avdaga gave his daughter to Mustajbeg's son. Then the little procession set out on the way to Nezuke where the formal wedding ceremonies had been prepared.

They passed through the market-place, a part of that road without escape which Fata had covered so often in her thoughts. It was firm, real and everyday, almost easier to traverse than in her imagination. No stars, no expanse, no father's muffled cough, no desire for time to go more quickly or more slowly. When they reached the bridge, the girl felt once more, as in the summer nights before her window, every part of her body strongly and separately, and especially her breasts in a light constriction as if in a corselet. The party arrived on the *kapia*. As she had done so many times in her thoughts those last nights, the girl leant over and in a whisper begged the youngest brother who was riding beside her to shorten her stirrups a little, for they were coming to that steep passage from the bridge down to the stony track which led to Nezuke. They stopped, first those two and then, a little farther on, the other wedding guests. There was nothing un-usual in this. It was not the first nor would it be the last time that a wedding procession halted on the *kapia*. While the brother dismounted, went around the horse and threw the reins over his arm, the girl urged her horse to the very edge of the bridge, put her right foot on the stone parapet, sprang from the saddle as if she had wings, leapt over the parapet and threw herself into the roaring river below the bridge. The brother rushed after her and threw himself at full length on the parapet, managing to touch with his hand the flying veil but was unable to hold it. The rest of the wedding guests leapt from their horses with the most extraordinary cries and remained along the stone parapet in strange attitudes as if they too had been turned to stone.

That same day rain fell before evening, abundant and exceptionally cold for the time of year. The Drina rose and grew angry. Next day the yellowish flood waters threw Fata's corpse on to a shoal near Kalata. There it was seen by a fisherman who went at once to notify the police chief. A little later the police chief himself arrived with the *muktar*, the fisherman and Salko Ćorkan. For without Salko nothing of this sort could ever take place.

The corpse was lying in soft wet sand. The waves moved it to and fro and from time to time their cloudy waters washed over it. The new black veil which the waters had not succeeded in pulling off had been turned back and thrown over her head; mingled with her long thick hair it formed a strange black mass beside the white lovely body of the young girl from which the current had torn away the thin wedding garments. Frowning and with set jaws Salko and the fisherman waded out to the shoal, caught hold of the naked girl and, embarrassed and carefully, as if she were still alive, took her to the bank from the wet sand in which she had already begun to sink, and there at once covered her with the wet and mud-bespattered veil.

That same day the drowned girl was buried in the nearest Moslem graveyard, on the steep slope below the hill on which Velje Lug was built. And before evening the ne'er-do-wells of the town had collected in the inn around Salko and the fisherman with that unhealthy and prurient curiosity which is especially developed among those whose life is empty, deprived of every beauty and lacking in excitement and events. They toasted them in plum-brandy and offered them tobacco in order to hear some detail about the corpse and the burial. But nothing helped. Even Salko said nothing. He smoked continuously and with his one bright eye looked at the smoke which he blew as far away as possible from him with strong puffs. Only those two, Salko and the fisherman, looked at one another from time to time, lifted their little flasks in silence as if pledging something invisible and drained them at a gulp.

Thus it was that that unusual and unheard-of event took place on the *kapia*. Velje Lug did not go down to Nezuke and Avdaga's Fata never became the wife of a Hamzić.

Avdaga Osmanagić never again went down into the town. He died that same winter, suffocated by his cough, without speaking a word to anyone of the sorrow that had killed him.

The next spring Mustajbeg Hamzić married his son to another girl, from Brankovići.

For some time the townspeople talked about the incident and then began to forget it. All that remained was a song about a girl whose beauty and wisdom shone above the world as if it were immortal.

CHAPTER IX

SOME SEVENTY YEARS after the Karageorge insurrection war broke out again in Serbia and the frontier reacted by rebellion. Once more Turkish and Serbian houses flamed on the heights, at Žlijeba, Gostilje, Crniće and Veletovo. For the first time after so many years the heads of decapitated Serbs again appeared on the *kapia*. These were thin-faced short-haired peasant heads with bony faces and long moustaches, as though they were the same as those exposed seventy years before. But all this did not last long. As soon as the war between Serbia and Turkey ended, the people were again left in peace. It was, in truth, an uneasy peace which concealed many fearful and exciting rumours and anxious whisperings. More and more definitely and openly was there talk of the entry of the Austrian army into Bosnia. At the beginning of the summer of 1878 units of the regular Turkish army passed through the town on their way from Sarajevo to Priboj. The idea spread that the Sultan would cede Bosnia without a struggle. Some families made ready to move into the Sanjak, amongst them some of those who thirty years before, not wishing to live under Serbian rule, had fled from Užice and who were now once again preparing to flee from another and new Christian rule. But the majority stayed, awaiting what was to come in painful uncertainty and outward indifference.

At the beginning of July the *mufti* of Plevlje arrived with a small body of men, filled with a great resolve to organize resistance in Bosnia against the Austrians. A fair-haired serious man of calm appearance but fiery temperament, he sat on the *kapia* where, one lovely summer's day, he summoned the Turkish leaders of the town and began to incite them to fight against the Austrians. He assured them that the greater part of the regular army would remain in Bosnia despite its orders and would join with the people to oppose the new conqueror, and called on the young men to join him and the townspeople to send provisions to Sarajevo. The *mufti* knew that the people of Višegrad had never had the reputation of being enthusiastic fighters and that they preferred to live foolishly rather than to die foolishly, but he was none the less surprised at the lukewarm response that he encountered. Unable to control himself any longer he threatened them with the justice of the people and the anger of God, and then left his assistant Osman Effendi Karamanli to go on convincing the people of Višegrad of the need for their participation in a general insurrection.

During the discussions with the *mufti*, the greatest resistance had been shown by Alihodja Mutevelić. His family was one of the oldest and most respected in the town. They had never been noted for their fortune, but rather for their honesty and openness. They had always been reckoned obstinate men, but not susceptible to bribes, intimidation, flattery or any other consideration of lower type. For more than 200 years the oldest member of their family had been the *mutevelia*, the guardian and administrator of Mehmed Pasha's foundation in the town. He looked after the famous Stone Han near the bridge. We have seen how, after the loss of Hungary, the Stone Han lost the revenues on which it depended for its upkeep and by force of circumstances became a ruin. Of the Vezir's foundation there remained only the bridge, a public benefit which did not require special maintenance and brought in no revenue. So there remained for the Mutevelićs only their family name as a proud memorial of the calling which they had honourably carried out for so many years. That calling had in fact ceased at the time when Dauthodja had succumbed in his struggle to maintain the Stone Han, but the pride had remained and with it the traditional custom that the Mutevelić family was called upon above all others to look after the bridge and that it was in some way responsible for its fate, since the bridge was an integral part of the great religious foundation which the family had administered and which had so pitiably dried up. Also by long established custom one of the Mutevelić family went to school and belonged to the *ulema*, the learned body of the Moslem clergy. Now it was Alihodja. Otherwise the family had greatly diminished both in numbers and property. They now had only a few serfs and a shop, which they had kept for a long time past, in the best position in the market-place, quite close to the bridge. Two elder brothers of Alihodja had died in the wars, one in Russia and the other in Montenegro.

Alihodja himself was still a young man, lively, healthy and smiling. Like a real Mutevelić he held contrary opinions in everything, defending them tenaciously and sticking to them obstinately. Because of his outspoken nature and independence of his thought he was frequently at odds with the local *ulema* and the Moslem notables. He had the title and rank of *hodja* but neither carried out any of the duties of that office nor received any income from that calling. In order to be as independent as possible, he himself looked after the shop which had been left by his father.

Like the majority of the Višegrad Moslems, Alihodja too was opposed to any armed resistance. But in his case there could be no question of cowardice or religious lukewarmness. He loathed the foreign Christian power and all that it would bring with it as much as the *mufti* or any of the insurgents. But seeing that the Sultan had in fact left Bosnia at the mercy of the Schwabes (for so they called the Austrians) and knowing his fellow citizens, he was opposed to any disorganized popular resistance which could only end in disaster and make their misfortune the greater. When once this idea was firmly implanted in his mind, he preached it openly and defended it with spirit. On this occasion too he kept on asking awkward questions and made sarcastic comments which greatly disconcerted the *mufti*. Thus unintentionally he sustained among the people of Višegrad, who in any case would not have been so swift to battle or much inclined to make sacrifices, a spirit of open resistance against the *mufti*'s warlike intentions.

When Osman Effendi Karamanli remained in the town to continue his discussions with the people, he found himself faced with Alihodja. Those few begs and agas who swallowed their words and measured their phrases and who in fact were in complete agreement with Alihodja left it to the sincere and ebullient *hodja* to come into the open and enter into conflict with Karamanli.

Thus early one evening the leading Višegrad Turks were sitting on the *kapia*, cross-legged in a circle. In the centre was Osman Effendi, a tall thin pale man. Every muscle of his face was unnaturally set, his eyes were feverish and his forehead and cheeks marked all over with scars like an epileptic. Before him stood the *hodja*, reddish in face and small in stature, yet somehow impressive, asking more and more questions in his thin reedy voice. What forces had they? Where were they to go? With what means? How? What for? What will happen in case of failure? The cold and almost mischievous pedantry with which the *hodja* treated the matter only served to conceal his own anxiety and bitterness at the Christian superiority and the evident weakness and disorder of the Turks. But the hot-headed and sombre Osman Effendi was not the man to notice or understand such things. Of violent and uncontrolled temper, a fanatic with overstrung nerves, he quickly lost patience and control and attacked the *hodja* at every sign of doubt or wavering as if he were a Schwabe. This *hodja* irritated him and he replied to him only with generalities and big words. The main thing was not to allow the foe to enter the country without resistance, and whoever asked too many questions only hindered the good work and aided the enemy. In the end, completely beside himself, he replied with scarcely concealed disdain to every question of the *hodja*: 'The time has come to die', 'We will lay down our lives', 'We shall all die to the last man'.

'But,' broke in the *hodja*, 'I understood that you wanted to drive the Schwabes out of Bosnia and that was the reason why you were collecting us. If it is only a question of dying, then we too know how to die, Effendi, even without your assistance. There is nothing easier than to die.'

'*Ama*, I can see that you will not be one of those who die,' broke in Karamanli, harshly.

'I can see that you will be one,' answered the *hodja* sarcastically, 'only I do not see why you ask for our company in this senseless attempt.'

The conversation then degenerated into an open quarrel in which Osman Effendi referred to Alihodja as a renegade, one of those traitors whose heads, like the Serbs', should be exposed on the *kapia*, while the *hodja* imperturbably went on splitting hairs and demanding proofs and reasons, as if he had not even heard those threats and insults.

Indeed it would have been hard to find two worse negotiators or more unsuited contestants. Nothing more could have been expected of them than increasing general anxiety and the creation of one quarrel the more. That was to be regretted, but there was nothing to be done about it, for such moments of social upset and great inevitable change usually throw up just such men, unbalanced and incomplete, to turn things inside out or lead them astray. That is one of the signs of times of disorder.

None the less this barren quarrel was a boon to the begs and agas for the question of their participation in the insurrection remained unanswered and they themselves were not compelled to take sides at once. Quivering with rage and shouting insults at the top of his voice, Osman Effendi left the next day with a few of his men to follow the *mufti* to Sarajevo.

The news which arrived in the course of the month only served to confirm the agas and begs in their opportunist view that it would be better to preserve their town and their homes. By mid-August the Austrians entered Sarajevo. A little later there was a disastrous clash on Glasinac, which was also the end of all resistance. Remnants of the routed Turkish bands began to descend the steep road from Lijeska through Okolište. Amongst them were some regular soldiers who despite the Sultan's order had joined the resistance movement of the local insurgents on their own account. The soldiers only asked for bread and water and the way on to Uvac, but the insurgents were bitter and angry men whom the rout had not broken. Blackened, dusty and in rags, they replied curtly to the questions of the peaceable Višegrad Turks and made ready to dig trenches and defend the bridge.

Alihodja was again to the fore; he pointed out indefatigably and regardless of consequences that the town could not be defended and that resistance was senseless since the 'Schwabes had already swept through Bosnia from end to end'. The insurgents knew that well enough themselves but did not want to acknowledge it, for these well-fed and well-clothed men who had saved their houses and properties by keeping wisely and cravenly far from the revolt irritated and provoked them. With them came that same Osman Effendi Karamanli, as if out of his mind, paler and thinner than ever, even more frenzied and warlike. He was one of those men for whom failure has no meaning. He spoke of resistance in any place and at any price and continually of the need to die. Before his furious ardour everyone retreated or withdrew, save only Alihodja. He proved to the aggressive Osman Effendi, without the slightest malice, coldly and brutally, that what had happened to the revolt was exactly what he had foreseen a month ago on this very *kapia*. He recommended him to leave with his men as quickly as possible for Plevlje and not to make bad worse. The *hodja* was now less aggressive, even to a certain extent compassionate towards this Karamanli as towards a sick man. For within himself, beneath all his outward obstinacy the *hodja* was greatly shaken by the approaching misfortune. He was unhappy and embittered as only a true-believing Moslem could be who sees that a foreign force is approaching inexorably, before whose onslaught the ancient order of Islam could not long survive. That hidden rancour could be felt in his own words even against his will.

To all Karamanli's insults he replied almost sadly:

'Do you think, Effendi, that it is easy for me to be alive to await the coming of the Schwabes to our land? As if we did not know what is in store for us in the times to come? We know where it hurts us and what we are losing; we know it only too well. If you came here to tell us this, you should not have returned here. Indeed there was no need for you to come from Plevlje at all. For, as I see, you do not understand matters. Had you done so, you would not have done what you have done or said what you have said. This is a worse torment, Effendi, than you can think; nor do I know a remedy for it, but I know that what you suggest is not a remedy.'

But Osman Effendi was deaf to everything that did not accord with his deep and sincere passion for resistance and he hated this *hodja* as much as the Schwabes against whom he had revolted. So is it always when an overwhelming enemy is near and a great defeat certain. In every society appear fratricidal hatreds and mutual quarrels. Not finding anything fresh to say, he went on calling Alihodja a traitor, ironically recommending him to get baptized before the Schwabes came.

'My ancestors were not baptized, nor will I be. I, Effendi, have no wish either to be baptized with a Schwabe or to go to war with an idiot,' the *hodja* replied calmly.

All the leading Višegrad Turks were of the same opinion as Alihodja, but all did not think it discreet to say so, especially so harshly and uncompromisingly. They were afraid of the Austrians who were coming but they were also afraid of Karamanli who with his men had taken over control of the town. Therefore they shut themselves up in their houses or withdrew to their properties outside the town, and when they could not avoid meeting Karamanli and his men they looked away or replied with equivocal phrases looking for the most convenient pretext and the safest way of extricating themselves.

On the level space in front of the ruins of the caravanserai

Karamanli held open court from morning to evening. A motley crowd was always about him, his own men, chance passers-by, those who came to beg something from the new master of the town and travellers whom the insurgents brought more or less by force in front of their leader. And Karamanli talked incessantly. Even when he was talking to one man he shouted as if he were addressing hundreds. Still paler, he rolled his eyes, in which the whites had noticeably yellowed, and white foam gathered at the corners of his lips. One of the townsmen had told him of the Moslem tradition about Sheik Turhania who had died there long ago defending the passage of the Drina against an infidel army and now rested in his grave on the farther bank just above the bridge, but who without doubt would rise again the moment the first infidel soldier stepped on to the bridge. He seized on this legend, feverishly and passionately, expounding it to the people as a real and unexpected aid.

'Brothers, this bridge was a Vezir's bequest. It is written that an infidel force shall never cross it. It is not we alone who are to defend it but also this "holy one" whom rifles cannot hit nor swords cut. Should the foe come, he will rise from his grave and will stand in the centre of the bridge with outstretched arms; and when the Schwabes see him their knees will tremble, and their hearts fail so that they will not even be able to run away. Turkish brothers, do not disperse but all follow me to the bridge.'

So Karamanli shouted to the crowd. Standing stiffly in his black shabby cloak, stretching out his arms and showing how the 'holy one' would stand, he looked exactly like a tall thin black cross with a turban on top.

This the Višegrad Turks knew even better than Karamanli, for every one of them had heard and told this legend countless times in his childhood, but they none the less showed not the least desire to mingle fact with legend or reckon on the help of the dead since nothing could be expected of the living. Alihodja, who had not moved far from his shop, but to whom the people told all that was said or done before the Stone Han, only waved his arms sorrowfully and compassionately.

'I knew that that idiot would not leave either the living or the dead in peace. *Allah selamet olsun!* May God help us!'

But Karamanli, helpless before the real enemy, turned all his fury against Alihodja. He threatened, he shouted and swore that before he was forced to leave the town he would nail the obstinate *hodja* to the *kapia* like a badger to await the Schwabes in that way, since he did not want to fight or to allow others to do so.

All this bickering was cut short by the appearance of the Austrians on the Lijeska slopes. Then it was seen that the town really could not be defended. Karamanli was the last to leave the town, abandoning on the raised level space before the caravanserai both the iron cannons that he had dragged there. But before he left he carried out his threat. He ordered his servant, a smith by profession, a man of giant size but with the brain of a bird, to bind Alihodja and to nail him by the right ear to that oak beam wedged between two stone steps on the *kapia*, which was all that remained of the former blockhouse.

In the general crush and confusion which reigned in the market-place and around the bridge, all heard that order given in a loud voice but no one even dreamed that it would be carried out in the form in which it was given. In such circumstances all sorts of things, brave words and loud curses, can be heard. So too it was in this case. At first sight the thing seemed inconceivable. It was to be considered a threat or an insult or something of the sort. Nor did Alihodja himself take the matter very seriously. Even the smith himself who had been ordered to carry it out and who was busy spiking the guns hesitated and seemed to think it over. But the thought that the *hodja* must be nailed to the *kapia* was in the air and the suspicious and embittered townsmen turned over in their minds the prospects and probabilities of such a crime being carried out or not carried out. Would it be, or would it not be? At first the majority of them thought the affair to be, as indeed it was, senseless, ugly and impossible. But in moments of general excitement, something has to be done, something big and unusual, and that was the only thing to be done. Would it be – or would it not be? The possibility seemed stronger and became every moment and with every movement more probable and more natural. Why not? Two men already held the *hodja* who did not defend himself overmuch. They bound his hands behind his back. But all this was still far from so mad and terrible a reality. But it was coming nearer and nearer. The smith, as if suddenly ashamed of his weakness and indecision, produced from somewhere or other the hammer with which a short time before he had been spiking the guns. The thought that the Schwabes were so to speak already here, half an hour's march from the town, gave him the resolution to bring the matter to a head. And with this same painful thought the *hodja* obstinately maintained his indifference to everything, even towards that mad, undeserved and shameful punishment to which they had condemned him.

So in a few moments there took place what in any one of those moments would have seemed impossible and incredible. There was no one who would have considered that this deed was good or possible, yet everyone to some extent played his part in the fact that the *hodja* found himself on the bridge nailed by his right ear to a wooden beam which was on the *kapia*; and when everyone fled in all directions before the Schwabes who were coming down the slopes into the town, the *hodja* remained in this strange but comic position, forced to kneel motionless since every movement, even the slightest, was exceedingly painful and threatened to tear off his ear, which seemed to him as heavy and as large as a mountain. He cried out, but there was no one to hear him or release him from his painful situation for everything living had hidden in the houses or scattered into the villages for fear, partly of the Schwabes who were coming and partly of the insurgents who were leaving. The town seemed dead and the bridge as empty as if death had swept it clean. There was neither living nor dead to defend it, only on the *kapia* the motionless Alihodja crouched down with his head stuck to the beam, groaning with pain but even in this position thinking up fresh proofs against Karamanli.

The Austrians approached slowly; from the farther bank their patrols had seen the two cannons in front of the caravanserai and they at once halted to await the arrival of their mountain guns. About midday they fired a few shells from the shelter of a little wood at the deserted caravanserai. They damaged the already ruined *han* and destroyed those exceptionally fine window grilles, each cut from a single piece of soft stone. Only after they had got the range and overturned the two Turkish cannons and seen that they were abandoned and that no one replied did the Schwabes cease their fire and begin to approach the bridge and the town with every precaution. Some Magyar *honveds* approached the *kapia* slowly with their rifles at the ready. They halted in uncertainty before the huddled *hodja* who in fear of the shells, which had whistled and grumbled above his head, had for a moment forgotten the pain from his nailed ear. When he saw the hated soldiers with their rifles trained on him, he began to utter piteous and prolonged sobs, since that was a language that everyone understood. This prevented him from being shot. Some of them continued their slow advance step by step across the bridge while others remained by him looking at him more closely and unable to understand his position. Only when a hospital orderly arrived did they find a pair of pliers, carefully extracted the nail, one of those used for shoeing horses, and released Alihodja. So stiff and exhausted was he that he collapsed on the stone step, groaning and sobbing. The orderly dressed his ear with some sort of liquid which stung. Through his tears the *hodja* as if in a strange dream looked at the broad white band on the soldier's left arm and on it a large regular cross in red material. Only in fever could such repulsive and terrible sights be seen. This cross swam and danced before his eyes and filled his whole horizon like a nightmare. Then the soldier bound up his wound and fixed his turban over the bandage. His head thus bandaged, and as if broken in his loins, the *hodja* dragged himself to his feet and remained so for some moments leaning on the stone parapet of the bridge. With difficulty he collected himself and regained his calm.

Opposite him, on the far side of the *kapia*, beneath the Turkish inscription in the stone, a soldier had affixed a large white paper. Though his head was throbbing with pain the *hodja* could not restrain his curiosity and looked at that white placard. It was a proclamation by General Filipović, in Serbian and Turkish, addressed to the population of Bosnia and Herzegovina on the occasion of the entry of the Austrian army into Bosnia. Screwing up his right eye, Alihodja spelt out the Turkish text, but only those sentences printed in large letters:

'People of Bosnia and Herzegovina!

'The Army of the Emperor of Austria and King of Hungary has crossed the frontier of your country. It does not come as an enemy to take the land by force. It comes as a friend to put an end to the disorders which for years past have disturbed not only Bosnia and Herzegovina but also the frontier districts of Austria–Hungary.

*   *   *

'The King-Emperor could no longer see how violence and disorder ruled in the neighbourhood of his dominions and how misery and misfortune knocked at the frontiers of his lands.

'He has drawn the attention of the European States to your position and at a Council of the Nations it has been unanimously decided that Austria-Hungary shall restore to you the peace and prosperity that you have so long lost.

'His Majesty the Sultan who has your good at heart has felt it necessary to confide you to the protection of his powerful friend the King-Emperor.

*   *   *

'The King-Emperor decrees that all sons of this land shall enjoy the same rights before the law and that the lives, faith and property of all shall be protected.

* * *

'People of Bosnia and Herzegovina! Put yourselves with confidence under the protection of the glorious standards of Austria-Hungary. Welcome our soldiers as friends, submit yourselves to the authorities and return to your occupations. The fruits of your toil will be protected.'

The *hodja* read haltingly, sentence by sentence. He did not understand every word, yet every word caused him pain, a special sort of pain completely distinct from those pains which he felt in his wounded ear, in his head and in his loins. Only now, from these words, these 'imperial words', was it at once clear to him that everything was ended for them, all that was his and theirs, ended in some strange fashion once and for all; eyes go on seeing, lips speaking, man goes on living but life, real life, exists no more. A foreign tsar had put his hand on them and a foreign faith ruled. That emerged clearly from those big words and obscure commands, and still more clearly from that leaden pain in his breast which was fiercer and harder to bear than any human pain that could be imagined. It was not thousands of fools like that Osman Karamanli who could do anything or change anything (thus the *hodja* continued to argue within himself). 'We shall all die', 'We must die'. What was the use of all that hullabaloo when, here and now, there had come for a man a time of disaster in which he could neither live nor die, but rotted like a stake in the earth and belonged to whomever you wished but not himself. That was the great misery which the Kara-manlis of all sorts did not see and could not understand and which by their lack of understanding they made even heavier and more shameful.

Deep in his thoughts Alihodja slowly left the bridge. He did not even notice that the Austrian red-cross man was accompanying him. His ear did not pain him as much as that leaden and bitter pain which had risen in his breast after reading 'the imperial words'. He walked slowly and it seemed to him that never again would he cross to the farther bank, that this bridge which was the pride of the town and ever since its creation had been so closely linked with it, on which he had grown up and beside which he had spent his life, was now suddenly broken in the middle, right there at the *kapia*; that this white paper of the proclamation had cut it in half like a silent explosion and that there was now a great abyss; that individual piers still stood to right and to left of this break but that there was no way across, for the bridge no longer linked the two banks and every man had to remain on that side where he happened to be at this moment.

Alihodja walked slowly, immersed in these feverish visions. He seemed like a seriously wounded man and his eyes continually filled with tears. He walked hesitantly as if he were a beggar who, ill, was crossing the bridge for the first time and entering a strange unknown town. Voices aroused him. Beside him walked some soldiers. Amongst them he saw that fat, good-natured, mocking face of the man with a red cross on his arm who had taken out the nail. Still smiling, the soldier pointed to his bandage and asked him something in an incomprehensible language. The *hodja* thought that he was offering to help him and at once stiffened and said sullenly:

'I can myself. . . . I need no one's help.'

And with a livelier and more determined step he made his way home.

CHAPTER X

THE FORMAL AND official entry of the Austrian troops took place the following day.

No one could remember such a silence as then fell on the town. The shops did not even open. The doors and windows of the houses remained shuttered though it was a warm sunny day towards the end of August. The streets were empty, the courtyards and gardens as if dead. In the Turkish houses depression and confusion reigned, in the Christian houses caution and distrust. But everywhere and for everyone there was fear. The entering Austrians feared an ambush. The Turks feared the Austrians. The Serbs feared both Austrians and Turks. The Jews feared everything and everyone since, especially in times of war, everyone was stronger than they. The rumbling of the previous day's guns was in everyone's ears. But even if men were now only listening to their own fear, no one living that day would have dared to poke his nose out of doors. But man has other masters. The Austrian detachment which had entered the town the day before had routed out the police chief and gendarmes. The officer in command of the detachment had returned his sword to the police chief and ordered him to continue his duties and maintain order in the town. He told him that at one hour before noon next day the commandant, a colonel, would arrive and that the leading men of the town, that was to say the representatives of the three faiths, were to be there to meet him when he entered the town. Grey and resigned, the police chief at once summoned Mula Ibrahim, Husseinaga the schoolmaster, Pop Nikola, and the rabbi David Levi and informed them that as 'recognized notables' they must await the Austrian commandant next day at noon on the *kapia*, must welcome him in the name of the citizens and accompany him to the market-place.

Long before the appointed time the four 'recognized notables' met on the deserted square and walked with slow steps to the *kapia*. Already the assistant chief of police, Salko Hedo, with the aid of a gendarme, had spread out a long Turkish carpet in bright colours to cover the steps and the middle of the stone seat on which the Austrian commandant was to sit. They stood there together for some time, solemn and silent, then seeing that there was no trace of the commandant along the white road from Okolište, they looked at one another and as if by common consent sat down on the uncovered part of the stone bench. Pop Nikola drew out a huge leather tobacco pouch and offered it to the others.

So they sat on the *kapia* as they had once done when they were young and carefree and like the rest of the young people wasted their time there. Only now they were all advanced in years. Pop Nikola and Mula Ibrahim were old, and the schoolmaster and the rabbi in the prime of life. They were all in their best clothes, filled with anxiety both for themselves and for their flocks. They looked at one another closely and long in the fierce summer sun, and each seemed to the others grown old for his years and worn out. Each of them remembered the others as they had been in youth or childhood, when they had grown up on this bridge, each in his own generation, green wood of which no one could tell what would be.

They smoked and talked of one thing while turning another over in their minds, glancing every moment towards Okolište whence the commandant upon whom everything depended was to come and who could bring them, their people and the whole town, either good or evil, either peace or fresh dangers.

Pop Nikola was undoubtedly the most calm and collected of the four, or at least seemed so. He had passed his seventieth year but was still fresh and strong. Son of the celebrated Pop Mihailo whom the Turks had beheaded on this very spot, Pop Nikola had passed a stormy youth. He had several times fled into Serbia to take refuge there from the hatred and revenge of certain Turks. His indomitable nature and his conduct had often given occasion both for hatred and revenge. But when the troublous years had passed, Pop Mihailo's son had settled down in his old parish, married, and calmed down. Those times were long ago and now forgotten. ('My character has changed long ago and our Turks have become peaceable,' Pop Nikola would say in jest.) For fifty years now Pop Nikola had administered his widespread, scattered and difficult frontier parish calmly and wisely, without other major upheavals and misfortunes than those which life brings normally in its train, with the devotion of a slave and the dignity of a prince, always just and equitable with Turks, people and leaders.

Neither before him nor after him in any class of men or in any faith was there a man who enjoyed such general respect and such a reputation amongst all the townspeople without distinction of faith, sex or years, as this priest whom everyone called 'grandad'. He represented for the whole town the Serbian church and all that the people called or regarded as Christianity. The people looked on him as the perfect type of priest and leader so far as this town in these conditions could imagine one.

He was a man of great stature and exceptional physical strength, not over literate but of great heart, sound common sense and a serene and open spirit. His smile disarmed, calmed and encouraged. It was the indescribable smile of a man who lives at peace with himself and with everything around him; his big green eyes contracted into narrow slits whence flashed golden sparks. And so he remained in old age. In his long overcoat of fox-fur, with his great red beard just beginning to turn grey with the years and which covered his whole chest, with his enormous hood beneath which his flowing hair was plaited into a pigtail, he walked through the market-place as if he had indeed been the priest of this town beside the bridge and all this mountainous district, not for fifty years only and not for his church only, but from time immemorial, from those times when the people were not divided into their present faiths and churches. From the shops on both sides of the market-place the merchants greeted him, whatever their faith. Women stood to one side and waited with bowed head for 'grandad' to pass. The children (even the Jewish ones) left off their play and stopped shouting and the oldest among them, solemnly and timidly, would come up to the enormous hand of 'grandad' to feel it for a moment on their shaven heads and faces heated by play, and hear his merry and powerful voice fall upon them like a good and pleasant dew:

'God grant you life! God grant you life, my son!'

This token of respect towards 'grandad' had become a part of the ancient and universally recognized ceremonial in which generations of the townsfolk had grown up.

But even in Pop Nikola's life there was one shadow. His marriage had remained childless. That was, without doubt, a heavy blow but no one could recall having heard a bitter word or seen a regretful glance either from him or from his wife. In their house they always maintained at their own expense at least two children belonging to some of their relatives in the villages. These they would look after until they married, and then find others.

Next to Pop Nikola sat Mula Ibrahim, a tall, thin, dried-up man with a sparse beard and pendulant moustaches. He was not much younger than Pop Nikola, had a large family and a fine property left him by his father, but he was so slipshod, thin and timid, that he seemed with his clear blue childlike eyes more like some hermit or some poor and pious pilgrim than the *hodja* of Višegrad, descendant of many *hodjas*. Mula Ibrahim had one affliction: he stuttered in his speech, long and painfully ('A man must have nothing to do before he can talk with Mula Ibrahim,' the townsmen used to say in jest). But Mula Ibrahim was known for far around for his goodness and generosity. Mildness and serenity breathed out of him and at the first meeting men forgot his outward appearance and his stutter. He attracted all who were overburdened by illness, poverty or any other misfortune. From the most

distant villages men came to ask advice of Mula Ibrahim.
Before his house there was always a crowd to see him, and
men and women often stopped him in the street to seek
his advice. He never refused anyone and never handed out
expensive charms or amulets as other *hodjas* did. He would sit
down at once in the first patch of shade or on the first stone,
a little to the side; the man would then tell all his troubles in
a whisper. Mula Ibrahim would listen attentively and sympa-
thetically, then say a few good words to him, always finding
the best possible solution for his troubles, or would thrust his
thin hand into the deep pocket of his cloak, taking care not
to be overseen by anyone, and slip a few coins into his hand.
Nothing was difficult or repugnant or impossible to him
if it were a question of helping some Moslem. For that he
could always find time and money. Nor did his stutter hinder
him in this, for when whispering with his co-religionist in
misfortune he forgot to stutter. Everyone went away from
him if not completely consoled, then at least momentarily
relieved, for it could be seen that he felt their misfortunes as
if they were his own. Continually surrounded with every
sort of trouble and need and never thinking of himself, he
none the less, or so it seemed, passed his whole life healthy,
happy and rich.

The Višegrad schoolmaster, Hussein Effendi, was a
smallish plump man, well dressed and well cared for. He
had a short black beard carefully trimmed in a regular oval
about his pink and white face with round black eyes. He had
been well educated and knew a good deal, but pretended to
know much more and deceived himself that he knew even
more. He loved to talk and to have an audience. He was
convinced that he spoke well and that led him to speak a lot.
He expressed himself carefully and affectedly with studied
gestures, holding his arms up a little, both at the same height,
with white soft hands with pinkish nails, shadowed by short
black hairs. When speaking he behaved as if he were in front
of a mirror. He had the largest library in the town, a bound
chest full of books kept carefully locked, which had been

bequeathed him by his teacher, the celebrated Arap-hodja, and which he not only conscientiously preserved from dust and moth but even on rare occasions read. But the mere knowledge that he had so great a number of such valuable books gave him repute amongst men who did not know what a book was, and raised his value in his own eyes. It was known that he was writing a chronicle of the most important events in the history of the town. Among the citizens this gave him the fame of a learned and exceptional man, for it was considered that by this he held in some way the fate of the town and of every individual in it in his hands. In actual fact that chronicle was neither extensive nor dangerous. In the last five or six years, since the schoolmaster had first begun this work, only four pages of a small exercise book had been filled. For the greater number of the town's events were not considered by the schoolmaster as of sufficient importance to warrant entry into his chronicle and for that reason it remained as unfruitful, dry and empty as a proud old maid.

The fourth of the 'notables' was David Levi, the Višegrad rabbi, grandson of that famous old rabbi Hadji Liacho who had left him as inheritance his name, position and property but nothing of his spirit and his serenity.

He was pale and puny, with dark velvety eyes and melancholy expression. He was inconceivably timid and silent. He had only recently become rabbi and had married not long before. In order to seem bigger and more important he wore a wide rich suit of heavy cloth and his face was overgrown with beard and whiskers, but beneath all this one could discern a weak sickly body and the childish oval of his face peered out fearfully from the black sparse beard. He suffered terribly whenever he had to appear in public and take his part in discussions and decisions, always feeling himself to be weak and undeveloped.

Now all four of them sat in the sun and sweated under their formal clothes, more moved and anxious than they wished to show.

'Let's light another one. We've time, by the soul of my grandmother! He's no bird to fly down to the bridge,' said Pop Nikola, like a man who has long learnt how to conceal with a jest his own and others' thoughts and fears.

All looked at the Okolište road and then went on smoking.

The conversation flowed slowly and carefully, forever coming back to the imminent welcome to the commandant. All were agreed that it was Pop Nikola who should greet him and bid him welcome. With half-closed eyes and brows furrowed so that his eyes became those two golden-studded slits that formed his smile, Pop Nikola looked at the three others long, silently and intently.

The rabbi was quivering with fright. He had hardly strength to puff the smoke away from him but let it linger in his moustaches and beard. The schoolmaster was no less scared. All his eloquence and his dignity as a man of learning had vanished suddenly the day before. He was very far from realizing how disconsolate he looked and how greatly he was scared, for the high opinion which he had of himself did not allow him to believe anything of the sort. He tried to deliver one of his literary addresses with his studied gestures that explained everything, but his fine hands only fell into his lap and his words became mixed up and halting. Even he himself wondered where his customary dignity had vanished, and vainly tormented himself trying to recover it, as something to which he had long been accustomed and which now, when he needed it most, had somehow deserted him.

Mula Ibrahim was somewhat paler than usual but otherwise calm and collected. He and Pop Nikola looked at one another from time to time as if they understood one another by their eyes alone. They had been close acquaintances since youth and good friends, insofar as one could speak of friendship between a Turk and a Serb in times as they then were. When Pop Nikola in his youthful years had had his 'troubles' with the Višegrad Turks and had had to fly for refuge, Mula Ibrahim, whose father had been very influential in the town, had been of some service to him. Later, when more peaceful times had come and relations between the two faiths had become more bearable and the two of them were already grown men, they had made friends and called one another 'neighbour' in jest, for their houses were at opposite ends of the town. On occasions of drought, flood, epidemic or other misfortune they found themselves working together, each among men of their own faith. Otherwise, whenever they met at Mejdan or Okolište, they greeted one another and asked after one another's health, as priest and *hodja* never did elsewhere. Then Pop Nikola would often point with his pipestem at the town beside the river and say half in jest:

'All that breathes or creeps or speaks with human voice down there is either your or my responsibility.'

'It is so, neighbour,' Mula Ibrahim would stutter in reply, 'indeed they are.'

(And so the townsmen who could always find time to mock at everyone and everything would say of men who lived in friendship: 'They are as close as the priest and the *hodja*'; and this saying became a proverb with them.)

These two now understood one another perfectly though they did not exchange a word. Pop Nikola knew how hard it was for Mula Ibrahim and Mula Ibrahim knew that it was not easy for the priest. They looked at one another as they had done so many times before in their lives and on so many different occasions, as two men who had on their souls that double burden of the town, the one for those who crossed themselves, the other for those who bowed down in the mosque.

At that moment the sound of trotting was heard and a Turkish gendarme hurried up on a scraggy pony. Scared and out of breath, he shouted at them from a distance like a town-crier.

'Here he is; the one on the white horse!'

The police chief too arrived, always calm, always amiable, always silent.

Dust rose from along the Okolište road.

These men, born and brought up in this remote district of Turkey, the rotten-ripe Turkey of the nineteenth century, had naturally never had the chance of seeing the real, powerful and well-organized army of a great power. All that they had been able to see till then had been the incomplete, badly fed, badly clothed and badly paid units of the Sultan's *askers* or, which was even worse, the Bosnian irregulars, the *bashibazouks*, recruited by force, undisciplined and fanatic. Now for the first time there appeared before them the real 'power and force' of an Empire, victorious, glistening and sure of itself. Such an army dazzled them and checked the words in their throats. At the first sight of the saddlery and the tunic-buttons another world could be sensed behind these hussars and *jaegers* in parade kit. Their astonishment was great and the impression profound.

First rode two trumpeters on two fat bays, then a detachment of hussars on black horses. The horses were well groomed and moved like girls with short tidy steps. The hussars, all young and fresh, with waxed moustaches, in red shakos and yellow frogged tunics, seemed rested and vigorous as if they had just come out of barracks. Behind them rode a group of six officers led by a colonel. All eyes were fixed on him. His horse was larger than the others, a flea-bitten grey with a very long and curved neck. A little behind the officers came the infantry detachment, *jaegers*, in green uniforms, with a panache of feathers on their leather caps and white bands across their chests. They shut out everything save themselves and seemed like a moving forest.

The trumpeters and hussars rode past the priest and the police chief, halted on the market-place, and drew up along the sides.

The men on the *kapia*, pale and shaken, stood in the centre of the bridge facing the officers. One of the younger officers spurred his horse up to the colonel and said something to him. All slowed down. A few paces in front of the 'notables' the colonel suddenly halted and dismounted, as did the officers behind him as if by order. The soldiers whose duty it was to hold the horses hurried up and led them a few paces back.

As soon as his foot touched the ground, the colonel seemed another man. He was a small, undistinguished, overtired, unpleasant and aggressive man, behaving as if he alone had fought for all of them. Only now could it be seen that he was simply dressed, dishevelled and ungroomed, in contrast to his pale-faced smartly-uniformed officers. He was the image of a man who drives himself mercilessly, who continually overtaxes himself. His face was flushed, his beard untrimmed, his eyes troubled and anxious, his tall helmet a little on one side and his crumpled uniform seemingly too big for his body. He was wearing cavalry boots of soft unpolished leather. Walking with legs apart like a horseman he came closer, swinging his riding-crop. One of the officers spoke to him, pointing out the men ranged before him. The colonel looked at them shortly and sharply, the angry glance of a man continually occupied with difficult duties and great dangers. It was at once evident that he did not know how to look in any other way.

At that moment Pop Nikola began to speak in a calm deep voice. The colonel looked up and fixed his gaze on the face of the big man in the black cloak. That broad serene mask of a biblical patriarch held his attention for a moment. It may be that he did not understand, or that he pretended not to listen to, what the old man was saying, but that face could not go unnoticed. Pop Nikola spoke fluently and naturally, addressing himself more to the young officer who was to translate his words than to the colonel himself. In the name of all the faiths here present, he assured the colonel that they, and their people, were willing to submit themselves to the coming authorities and would do all that was in their power to maintain peace and order as the new authorities demanded. They asked the army to protect them and their families and make a peaceful life and honest toil possible for them.

Pop Nikola spoke shortly and ended abruptly. The

nervous colonel did not have any excuse to lose patience. But all the same he did not wait for the end of the young officer's translation. Brandishing his riding-crop, he interrupted him in a harsh and uneven voice:

'Good, good! All those who behave themselves will be protected. Peace and order must be maintained everywhere. It must be, whether they like it or not.'

Then, shaking his head, he moved onward without a glance or a greeting. The 'notables' moved aside. The colonel passed them, followed by the officers and the orderlies with the horses. None of them paid the least attention to the 'notables' who remained alone on the *kapia*.

All of them were disillusioned. For the day before, and all through the previous night, in which not one of them had slept much, each had asked himself a hundred times what that moment would be like when they had to welcome the commandant of the Imperial Army on the *kapia*. They had imagined him in every sort of way, each according to his nature and intelligence, and had been ready for the worst. Some of them had already seen themselves carried away immediately to exile in faraway Austria, never again to see their homes or their town. Others remembered the stories about Hairuddin who at one time used to cut off heads on this very *kapia*. They had imagined in every possible way, save that in which it had actually happened, the meeting with that small but curt and bad-tempered officer to whom war was life, who did not think of himself or pay any heed to others, but saw all men and all lands only as a subject or an occasion for war and conflict, and who behaved as if he were waging war on his own account and in his own name.

So they stood, looking at one another in uncertainty. Each of their looks seemed to say dumbly: 'We have got out of this alive. Have we really gone through the worst? What is still in store for us and what must be done?'

The police chief and Pop Nikola were the first to come to themselves. They came to the conclusion that the 'notables' had done their duty and that nothing more was left for them

to do but to go home and tell the people not to be frightened and run away, but to take good care what they did.
The others, without blood in their faces or thoughts in their
heads, accepted this conclusion as they would have accepted
any other, since they themselves were in no state to come to
any conclusion.

The police chief, whom nothing could ruffle, went about
his duties. The gendarme rolled up the long multicoloured
carpet which had not been fated to receive the visit of the
commandant, with Salko Hedo standing beside him as cold
and unfeeling as Fate. Meanwhile the 'notables' dispersed
each in his own way and each in his own direction. The
rabbi hurried off with tiny steps in order to get home as
soon as possible and feel again the warmth and protection
of the family circle in which his mother and his wife lived.
The schoolmaster left more slowly, deep in thought. Now
that everything had passed so unexpectedly well and easily,
though harshly and unpleasantly enough, it seemed to him
quite clear that there had never been any real reason for panic
and it seemed to him that he had never in fact been afraid of
anyone. He thought only what importance this event should
have in his chronicle and how much space should be devoted
to it. A score of lines should be enough. Perhaps even fifteen, or maybe less. The nearer he got to his house the more
he reduced the number. With every line spared it seemed
to him that he saw all around him diminished in importance while he, the schoolmaster, became greater and more
important in his own eyes.

Mula Ibrahim and Pop Nikola walked together as far as
the slope leading to Mejdan. They both remained silent,
astonished and discouraged at the appearance and bearing
of the Imperial colonel. Both were hastening to get home
as soon as possible and foregather with their families. At the
point where their paths diverged, they stood and looked at
one another for a moment in silence. Mula Ibrahim rolled his
eyes and moved his lips as if continually chewing over some
word that he was unable to utter. Pop Nikola, who had once

more recovered his smile of golden sparks which encouraged both himself and the *hodja*, uttered his own and the *hodja*'s thought:

'A bloody business, this army, Mula Ibrahim!'

'You are right, a b-b-b-bloody business,' stuttered Mula Ibrahim raising his arms and saying farewell with a movement of his head.

Pop Nikola went back to his house by the church, slowly and heavily. His wife who was waiting for him asked no questions. She at once took off his boots, took his cloak and removed the hood from the thick sweaty mass of red and grey hair. He sat down on a low divan. On its wooden arm a glass of water and a lump of sugar were ready waiting. After refreshing himself and lighting a cigar he closed his eyes wearily. But in his inmost thoughts still flashed the image of that colonel, like a flash of lightning that dazzles a man and fills his whole field of vision so that nothing else may be seen and yet it is impossible to look away from it. The priest puffed his smoke far away from him with a sigh and then spoke quietly as if to himself:

'A strange sort of bastard, on my grandmother's soul!'

From the town could be heard a drum and then a bugle of the *jaeger* detachment, gay and penetrating, a new and unusual melody.

CHAPTER XI

THUS THE GREAT change in the life of the town beside the bridge took place without sacrifices other than the martyrdom of Alihodja. After a few days life went on again as before and seemed essentially unchanged. Even Alihodja himself plucked up his courage and opened his shop near the bridge like all the other traders, save that now he wore his turban slightly tipped to the right so that the scar on his wounded ear could not be seen. That 'leaden weight' which he had felt in his chest after seeing the red cross on the arm of the Austrian orderly and reading the 'Imperial words' had not actually vanished, but it had become quite small like the bead of a rosary, so that it was possible to live with it. Nor was he the only one who felt such a weight.

So began the new era under the occupation which the people, unable to prevent, considered in their hearts to be temporary. What did not pass across the bridge in those first few years after the occupation! Yellow military vehicles rumbled across it in long convoys bringing food, clothing and furniture, instruments and fittings hitherto unheard of.

At first only the army was to be seen. Soldiers sprang up, like water from the earth, behind every corner and every bush. The market-place was full of them, but they were also in every part of the town. Every minute of the day some frightened woman would scream, having unexpectedly come across a soldier in her courtyard or in the plum-orchard behind her house. In dark blue uniforms, tanned by two months of marching and fighting, glad that they were alive and eager for rest and enjoyment, they sauntered through the town and the country around. Few of the citizens went to the *kapia* for now it was always full of soldiers. They would sit there, singing in various languages and buying fruit in their blue leather-peaked caps with a yellow metal cockade on which was cut the imperial initials FJI.

But when autumn came the soldiers began to move away. Slowly and imperceptibly there seemed fewer and fewer of them. There remained only the gendarme detachments. These requisitioned houses and prepared for a long stay. At the same time officials began to arrive, civil servants with their families and, after them, artisans and craftsmen for all those trades which up till then had not existed in the town. Among them were Czechs, Poles, Croats, Hungarians and Austrians.

At first it seemed that they had come by chance, as if driven by the wind, and as if they were coming for a short stay to live more or less the same life as had always been lived here, as though the civil authorities were to prolong for a short time the occupation begun by the army. But with every month that passed the number of newcomers increased. However, what most astonished the people of the town and filled them with wonder and distrust was not so much their numbers as their immense and incomprehensible plans, their untiring industry and the perseverance with which they proceeded to the realization of those plans. The newcomers were never at peace; and they allowed no one else to live in peace. It seemed that they were resolved with their impalpable yet ever more noticeable web of laws, regulations and orders to embrace all forms of life, men, beasts and things, and to change and alter everything, both the outward appearance of the town and the customs and habits of men from the cradle to the grave. All this they did quietly without many words, without force or provocation, so that a man had nothing to protest about. If they encountered resistance or lack of understanding, they at once stopped, discussed the matter somewhere out of sight and then changed only the manner and direction of their work, still carrying out whatever was in their minds. Every task that they began seemed useless and even silly. They measured out the waste land, numbered the trees in the forest, inspected lavatories and drains, looked at the teeth of horses and cows, asked about the illnesses of the people, noted the number and types of fruit trees and of different kinds of sheep and poultry. (It seemed that they were playing games, so incomprehensible, unreal and futile all these tasks of theirs appeared to the people.) Then all that they had carried out with so much care and zeal vanished somewhere or other as if it had been lost without trace or sound. But a few months later, sometimes even a year later, when the whole thing had been completely forgotten by the people, the real sense of these measures which had seemed so senseless was suddenly revealed. The *mukhtars* of the individual quarters would be summoned to the *konak* (the administrative centre) and told of a new regulation against forest felling, or of the fight against typhus, or the manner of sale of fruit and sweetmeats, or of permits for the movement of cattle. Every day a fresh regulation. With each regulation men saw their individual liberties curtailed or their obligations increased, but the life of the town and the villages, and of all their inhabitants as a mass, became wider and fuller.

But in the homes, not only of the Turks but also of the Serbs, nothing was changed. They lived, worked and amused themselves in the old way. Bread was still mixed in kneading troughs, coffee roasted on the hearth, clothes steamed in coppers and washed with soda which hurt the women's fingers; they still span and wove on tambours and hand-looms. Old customs of *slavas* (patronal feasts), holidays and weddings were kept up in every detail and as for the new customs which the newcomers had brought with them there were only whispers here and there as of something far off and incredible. In short, they lived and worked as they had always done and as in most of the houses they would continue to work and live for another fifteen or twenty years after the occupation.

But on the other hand the outward aspect of the town altered visibly and rapidly. Those same people, who in their own homes maintained the old order in every detail and did not even dream of changing anything, became for the most part easily reconciled to the changes in the town and after a longer or shorter period of wonder and grumbling accepted them. Naturally here, as always and everywhere in similar circumstances, the new life meant in actual fact a mingling of the old and the new. Old ideas and old values clashed with the new ones, merged with them or existed side by side, as if waiting to see which would outlive which. People reckoned in florins and kreutzers but also in grosh and para, measured by arshin and oka and drams but also by metres and kilos and grams, confirmed terms of payment and orders by the new calendar but even more often by the old custom of payment on St. George's or St. Dimitri's day. By a natural law the people resisted every innovation but did not go to extremes, for to most of them life was always more important and more urgent than the forms by which they lived. Only in exceptional individuals was there played out a deeper, truer drama of the struggle between the old and the new. For them the forms of life were indivisibly and unconditionally linked with life itself.

Such a man was Shemsibeg Branković of Crnče, one of the richest and most respected begs in the town. He had six sons, of whom four were already married. Their houses comprised a whole small quarter surrounded by fields, plum-orchards and shrubberies. Shemsibeg was the undisputed chief, the strict and silent master of this community. Tall, bent with years, with a huge white gold-embroidered turban on his head, he only came down to the market to pray in the mosque on Fridays. From the first day of the occupation he stopped nowhere in the town, spoke to no one and would not look about him. Not the smallest piece of new clothing or costume, not a new tool or a new word was allowed to enter the Branković house. Not one of his sons had any connection with the new authorities and his grandchildren were not allowed to go to school. All the Branković community suffered from this; amongst his sons there was dissatisfaction at the old man's obstinacy but none of them dared to oppose him by a single word or a single glance. Those Turks from the market-place, who worked and mingled with the newcomers, greeted Shemsibeg when he passed through the market with a dumb respect in which was mingled fear and admiration and an uneasy conscience. The oldest and most respected Turks of the town often went to Crnče as if on a pilgrimage to sit and talk with Shemsibeg. Those were meetings of men who were determined to persevere in their resistance to the end and were unwilling to yield in any way to reality. These were, in fact, long sessions without many words and without real conclusions.

Shemsibeg sat and smoked on a red rug, cloaked and buttoned up in summer as in winter, with his guests around him. Their conversation was usually about some new incomprehensible and sinister measure of the occupation authorities, or of those Turks who were more and more accommodating themselves to the new order. Before this harsh and dignified man, they all felt the need to give vent to their bitterness, their fears and their uncertainties. Every conversation ended with the questions: where is all this leading and where will it stop? Who and what were these strangers who, it seemed, did not know the meaning of rest and respite, knew neither measure nor limits? What did they want? With what plans had they come? What was this restlessness which continually drove them on, like some curse, to new works and enterprises of which no one could see the end?

Shemsibeg only looked at them and for the most part remained silent. His face was darkened, not by the sun, but by his inner thoughts. His glance was hard, but absent and as if lost. His eyes were clouded and there were whitish-grey circles around the black pupils as in an ageing eagle. His big mouth, with scarcely perceptible lips, was firmly set but moved slowly as if he were always turning over in his mind some word which he did not pronounce.

None the less, men left him with a feeling of comfort, neither calmed nor consoled, but touched and exalted by his firm and hopeless intransigence.

Whenever Shemsibeg went down to the market-place on

Fridays, he was met with some fresh change in men or buildings which had not been there the Friday before. In order not to have to look at it, he kept his eyes fixed on the ground but there, in the drying mud of the streets, he saw the marks of horses' hooves and noticed how alongside the broad rounded Turkish shoes the sharp-pointed bent Austrian horseshoes were becoming more and more common. So that even there in the mud his gaze read the same merciless judgement that he read everywhere in men's faces and in the things about him, a judgement of time which would not be halted.

Seeing that there was nowhere to rest his eyes, Shemsibeg ceased altogether to come down into the market. He withdrew completely to his Crnče and sat there, a silent but strict and implacable master, severe towards all but most of all towards himself. The oldest and most respected Turks of the town continued to visit him there, regarding him as a sort of living saint (amongst them, in particular, Alihodja). At last, in the third year of the occupation, Shemsibeg died without ever having been ill. He passed away without ever pronouncing that bitter word which was for ever on the tip of his old lips and never again setting foot in the market-place, where all men had set out on the new ways.

Indeed the town changed rapidly in appearance, for the newcomers cut down trees, planted new ones in other places, repaired the streets, cut new ones, dug drainage canals, built public buildings. In the first few years they pulled down in the market-place those old and dilapidated shops which were out of line and which, to tell the truth, had up till then inconvenienced no one. In place of those old-fashioned shops with their wooden drop-counters, new ones were built, well sited, with tiled roofs and metal rollers on the doors. (Alihodja's shop too was destined to be a victim of these measures, but the *hodja* opposed it resolutely, took the affair to law, contested it and dragged it on in every possible way until at last he succeeded, and his shop remained just as it was and just where it was.) The market-place was levelled and widened. A new *konak* was erected, a great building intended to house the law courts and the local administration. The army, too, was working on its own account, even more rapidly and inconsiderately than the civil authorities. They put up barracks, cleared waste land, planted and changed the appearance of whole hills.

The older inhabitants could not understand, and wondered; just when they thought that all this incomprehensible energy had come to an end, the newcomers started some fresh and even more incomprehensible task. The townsmen stopped and looked at all this work, but not like children who love to watch the work of adults but as adults who stop for a moment to watch children's games. This continual need of the newcomers to build and rebuild, to dig and to put back again, to put up and modify, this eternal desire of theirs to foresee the action of natural forces, to avoid or surmount them, no one either understood or appreciated. On the other hand all the townsmen, especially the older men, saw this unhealthy activity as a bad omen. Had it been left to them the town would have gone on looking as any other little oriental town. What burst would be patched up, what leant would be shored up, but beyond that no one would needlessly create work or make plans or interfere in the foundations of buildings or change the aspect which God had given to the town.

But the newcomers went on with their tasks, one after the other, quickly and logically, according to unknown and well prepared plans, to the even greater wonder and astonishment of the townsfolk. Thus unexpectedly and quickly came the turn of the dilapidated and abandoned caravanserai, which was always regarded as an integral part of the bridge, even as it had been 300 years before. In fact what had been known as the Stone Han had long ago become completely ruined. The doors had rotted, those lace-like grilles of soft stone on the windows broken, the roof had fallen into the interior of the building and from it grew a great acacia and a welter of nameless shrubs and weeds, but the outer walls were still whole, a true and harmonious rectangle of stone still standing upright. In the eyes of the townspeople, from birth to death, this was no ordinary ruin but the completion of the bridge, as much an integral part of the town as their own houses, and no one would ever have dreamt that the old *han* could be touched or that it was necessary to change anything about it that time and nature had not already changed.

But one day its turn came too. First engineers who spent a long time measuring the ruins, then workmen and labourers who began to take it down stone by stone, frightening and driving away all sorts of birds and small beasts which had their nests there. Rapidly the level space above the market-place by the bridge became bald and empty and all that was left of the *han* was a heap of good stone carefully piled.

A little more than a year later, instead of the former caravanserai of white stone, there rose a high, massive two-storeyed barracks, washed in pale-blue, roofed with grey corrugated iron and with loopholes at the corners. Soldiers drilled all day on the open space and stretched their limbs or fell head first in the dust like suppliants to the loud shouts of the corporals. In the evening the sound of incomprehensible soldiers' songs accompanied by an accordion could be heard from the many windows of the ugly building. This went on until the penetrating sound of the bugle with its melancholy melody, which set all the dogs of the town howling, extinguished all these sounds together with the last lights in the windows. So disappeared the lovely bequest of the Vezir and so the barracks, which the people true to ancient custom went on calling the Stone Han, commenced its life on the level by the bridge in complete lack of harmony with all that surrounded it.

The bridge now remained completely isolated.

To tell the truth, things were happening on the bridge too, where the old unchanging customs of the people clashed with the innovations which the newcomers and their way of life brought with them, and in these clashes all that was old and local was always forced to give way and adapt itself.

As far as the local people were concerned, life on the *kapia* went its way as of old. Only it was noticed that now Serbs and Jews came more freely and in greater numbers to the *kapia* and at all times of day, paying no heed as they once had done to the habits and privileges of the Turks. Otherwise all went on as before. In the daytime merchants sat there waiting for the peasant woman and buying from them wool, poultry and eggs, and beside them the lazy and idle who moved from one part of the town to another in keeping with the movements of the sun. Towards evening other citizens began to arrive and the merchants and workers gathered there to talk a little or to remain silent for a time looking at the great green river bordered by dwarf willows and sandbanks. The night was for the young. They had never known, nor did they know now, any limits for the time that they stayed on the bridge nor for what they did there.

In that night-time life of the *kapia* there were, at least at first, changes and misunderstandings. The new authorities had introduced permanent lighting in the town. In the first years of the occupation they put lanterns on green stand-ards, in which petrol lamps burned, in the main streets and at the crossroads. The lanterns were cleaned, filled and lit by big Ferhat, a poor devil with a house full of children, who until then had been a servant in the municipality. He discharged the petards announcing Ramazan and carried out similar jobs, without any fixed or certain wages. The bridge too was lighted at several points, including the *kapia*. The standard for this lantern was fixed to that oak beam which was all that remained of the former blockhouse. This lantern on the *kapia* had to endure a long struggle with the local jokers, with those who loved to sing in the darkness or to smoke and chat on the *kapia* as also with the destructive impulses of the young men in whom love-yearning, solitude and plum-brandy mingled and clashed. That flickering light irritated them and so countless times both the lantern and the lamp inside were smashed to pieces. There were many fines and sentences because of that lantern. At one time a special police agent was told to keep an eye on the light.

So the nightly visitors now had a living witness, even more unpleasant than the lantern. But time exercised its influence and the new generation grew accustomed to it and so reconciled to its existence that they gave free vent to their night feelings under the weak light of the municipal lantern, and no longer threw at it whatever came to hand, sticks, stones or anything else. This reconciliation was made so much the easier because on moonlit nights, when the *kapia* was most visited, the lantern was generally not lit.

Only once a year the bridge had to experience a great illumination. On the eve of August 18th every year, the Emperor's birthday, the authorities decorated the bridge with garlands and lines of young pine trees and, as darkness fell, lit strings of lanterns and fairy-lights; hundreds of army ration tins, filled with lard and fat, flamed in long rows along the parapet of the bridge. They lit up the centre of the bridge, leaving the ends and the piers lost in the darkness, so that the illuminated part seemed as if floating in space. But every light quickly burns out and every feast comes to an end. By the next day the bridge was once again what it had always been. Only in the eyes of some of the children there remained a new and unusual picture of the bridge under the short-lived play of light, a bright and striking vision, but short and transient as a dream.

Besides permanent lighting, the new authorities also introduced cleanliness on the *kapia*, or more exactly that special sort of cleanliness that accorded with their ideas. The fruit peelings, melon seeds and nutshells no longer remained for days on the flagstones until the rain or the wind carried them away. Now a municipal sweeper brushed them up every morning. But that irritated no one, for men quickly become accustomed to cleanliness even when it forms no part of their needs or habits; naturally on condition that they personally do not have to observe it.

There was still one more novelty which the occupation and the newcomers brought with them; women began to come to the *kapia* for the first time in its existence. The wives and daughters of the officials, their nursemaids and servants would stop there to chat or come to sit there on holidays with their military or civil escorts. This did not happen very often, but none the less it was enough to disturb the older men who came there to smoke their pipes in peace and quiet over the water, and disconcerted and confused the younger ones.

There had, naturally, always been a link between the *kapia* and the women in the town, but only in so far as the menfolk gathered there to pass compliments to the girls crossing the bridge or to express their joys, pains and quarrels over women and find relief from them on the *kapia*. Many a lonely man would sit for hours or even days singing softly to himself 'for my soul only', or wreathed in tobacco smoke, or simply watching the swift waters in silence, paying tribute to that exaltation to which we must all pay due and from which few escape. Many a contest between rivals was settled there, many love intrigues imagined. Much was said or thought about women and about love, many passions were born and many extinguished. All this there was, but women had never stopped or sat on the *kapia*, neither Christian nor, still less, Moslem. Now all that was changed.

Now on Sundays and holidays on the *kapia* could be seen cooks tightly laced and red in the face, with rolls of fat overflowing above and below their corsets in which they could scarcely breathe. With them were their sergeants in well brushed uniforms, with shining metal buttons and riflemen's pompoms on their chests. And on working days at dusk, officers and civil servants strolled there with their wives, halted on the *kapia*, chatted in their incomprehensible language, strolled about at their ease and laughed loudly.

These idle, laughing women were a cause of scandal to all, some more some less. The people wondered and felt insulted for a time and then began to grow accustomed to them, as they had grown accustomed to so many other innovations, even though they did not approve them.

In fact it could be said that all these changes on the bridge were insignificant, fleeting and superficial. The many and important changes which had taken place in the spirits and habits of the citizens and in the outward appearance of the town seemed as though they had passed by the bridge without affecting it. It seemed that the white and ancient bridge, across which men had passed for three centuries, remained unchanged without trace or mark even under the 'new Emperor' and that it would triumph over this flood of change and innovation even as it had always triumphed over the greatest floods, arising once more, white and untouched, from the furious mass of troubled waters which had wanted to flow over it.

CHAPTER XII

NOW LIFE ON the *kapia* became even livelier and more varied. A large and variegated crowd, locals and newcomers, old and young, came and went on the *kapia* all day long until a late hour of the night. They thought only of themselves, each one wrapped up in the thoughts, moods and emotions which had brought him to the *kapia*. Therefore they paid no heed to the passers-by who, impelled by other thoughts and by their own cares, crossed the bridge with lowered heads or absent glances, looking neither to right nor left and paying no attention to those seated on the *kapia*.

Among such passers-by one was certainly Milan Glasičanin of Okolište. He was tall, thin, pale and bowed. His whole body seemed transparent and without weight, yet attached to leaden feet, so that he swayed and bent in his walk like a church banner held in a child's hands during the procession. His hair and moustaches were grey, like those of an old man, and his eyes were always lowered. He did not notice that anything had changed on the *kapia* or among the people gathered there, and passed among them almost unnoticed by those who came there to sit, to dream, to sing, to trade, to chat or simply to waste time. The older men had forgotten him, the younger men did not recall him and the newcomers had never known him. But none the less his fate had been closely bound up with the *kapia*, at least judging from what was said about him or whispered in the town ten or twelve years before.

Milan's father, Nikola Glasičanin, had settled in the town about the time when the insurrection in Serbia was at its height. He had bought a fine property at Okolište. It was generally believed that he had fled from somewhere or other with a large but ill-gotten fortune. No one had any proof of this and everyone only half believed it. But no one ever definitely denied it. He had married twice but none the less had few children. He had brought up one child only, his son Milan, and left him all that he possessed, whether open or hidden. Milan, too, had only a single son, Peter. His property would have been sufficient and he would have left that to his son after his death had he not had one vice, only one, but that an overwhelming passion – gambling.

The real townsmen were not gamblers by nature. As we have seen, their passions were other and different; an immoderate love of women, an inclination to alcohol, song, lounging and idle dreamings beside their native river. But man's capacities are limited, even in such matters. Therefore their vices often clashed with one another, contradicted one another and often completely cancelled one another out. This did not mean that in the town there were not men addicted to this vice, but the actual number of gamblers was always few in comparison with other towns, and for the most part they were strangers or newcomers. Anyhow, Milan Glasičanin was one of them. From his earliest youth he had been entirely given over to gambling. When he could not find the company he needed in the town, he would go to nearby districts whence he would return, either weighed down with money like a merchant from a fair or with empty pockets, without watch or chain, tobacco pouch or rings, but always pale and washed out like a sick man.

His habitual place was in Ustamujić's inn at the far end of the Višegrad market. There, in a narrow windowless room where a candle burned day and night, could always be found three or four men to whom gambling was dearer than anything else on earth. In that room, shut off from the world, they would crouch in the tobacco smoke and stale air, with bloodshot eyes, dry mouths and quivering hands. They met there frequently, day or night, slaves to their passion like martyrs. In that little room Milan passed a great part of his youth and there left a good part of his strength and property.

He had not been much more than thirty when that

sudden and to most people inexplicable change took place in him, which cured him for ever of his driving passion but at the same time altered his whole way of life and completely transfigured him.

One autumn, some fourteen years before, a stranger had come to the inn. He was neither young nor old, neither ugly nor handsome, a man of middle age and medium height, silent and smiling only with his eyes. He was a man of business, entirely wrapped up in the affairs for which he had come. He passed the night there and at dusk entered that little room in which the gamblers had been shut up since early afternoon. They greeted him with distrust but he behaved so quietly and meekly that they did not even notice when he too began to put small stakes on the cards. He lost more than he won, frowned uncertainly and with an unsure hand took some silver money from an inner pocket. After he had lost a considerable sum, they had to give him the deal. At first he dealt slowly and carefully, then more swiftly and freely. He played without showing his feelings but was prepared to stake the limit. The pile of silver coins before him grew. One by one, the players began to drop out. One offered to stake a gold chain on a card, but the newcomer refused coldly, saying that he played for money only.

About the time of the last prayer the game broke up, for no one had any ready money left. Milan Glasičanin was the last, but in the end he too had to withdraw. The newcomer politely took his leave and retired to his own room.

Next day they played again. Again the stranger alternately lost and won, but always won more than he lost, so that once again the townsmen were left without ready money. They looked at his hands and his sleeves, watched him from every angle, brought fresh cards and changed places at the table, but all to no purpose. They were playing that simple but ill-famed game called *otuz bir* (thirty-one) which they had all known from childhood, but none the less they were not able to follow the newcomer's mode of play. Sometimes he drew twenty-nine and sometimes thirty, and sometimes he stood pat at twenty-five. He accepted every stake, the smallest as well as the greatest, overlooked the petty irregularities of individual players as if he had not noticed them, but denounced more serious ones curtly and coldly.

The presence of this newcomer at the inn tormented and irritated Milan Glasičanin. He was in any case at that time feverish and washed out. He swore to himself that he would play no more, but came again, and again lost his last coin, returning home filled with gall and shame. The fourth and fifth evenings he managed to control himself and remained at home. He had dressed and prepared his ready money but none the less stood by his resolution. His head felt heavy and his breath came in fits and starts. He ate his supper in haste, scarcely knowing what he was eating. Finally he went out, smoked, walked up and down in front of his house several times, and looked at the silent town in the clear autumn night. After he had walked thus for some time, he suddenly saw a vague figure going along the road who turned and stopped before his house.

'Good evening, neighbour!' shouted the unknown. Milan knew the voice. It was the stranger from the inn. Clearly the man had come to see him and wanted to talk to him. Milan came up to the fence.

'Why didn't you come to the inn tonight?' the stranger asked casually, calm and indifferent.

'I was not in the mood today. Are the others there?'

'There is no one left. They all left earlier than usual. Come along and let's have a hand together.'

'It is too late, and there's nowhere to go.'

'Let us go down and sit on the *kapia*. The moon will soon be rising.'

'But it is not the right time,' Milan objected. His lips were dry and his words seemed as if another had spoken them.

The stranger went on waiting, certain that his suggestion would be accepted.

And, in fact, Milan unlatched his gate and followed the man, as though his words and thoughts and efforts had all given way before that calm power which drew him on and from which he could not free himself, however much he felt humiliated by this stranger who roused in him resistance and revulsion.

They descended the slope from Okolište quickly. A large and waxing moon was rising behind Staniševac. The bridge seemed endless and unreal, for its ends were lost in a milky mist and the piers merged into the darkness; one side of each pier and of each arch was brightly lit while the other remained in the deepest shadow. These moonlit and darkened surfaces were broken and cut into sharp outlines, so that the whole bridge seemed like a strange arabesque created by a momentary play of light and darkness.

On the *kapia* there was not a living soul. They sat down. The stranger took out a pack of cards. Milan started to say how unsuitable this was, that they could not see the cards well and could not distinguish the money, but the stranger paid no attention to him. They began to play.

At first they still exchanged an occasional word, but as the game grew faster they fell silent. They only rolled cigarettes and lit them one after the other. The cards changed hands several times, only to remain finally in the hands of the stranger. The money fell soundlessly on the stones which were covered by a fine dew. The time had come, which Milan knew so well, when the stranger drew a two to twenty-nine or an ace to thirty. His throat contracted and his gaze clouded. But the face of the stranger, bathed in moonlight, seemed calmer than usual. In not quite an hour Milan no longer had any ready money. The stranger proposed that he should go home and get some more and said that he would accompany him. They went there and returned and went on with the game. Milan played as if dumb and blind, guessing at the cards and showing by signs what he wanted. It almost seemed as if the cards between them had become incidental, a pretext in this desperate and unrelenting duel. When he again ran out of money, the stranger ordered him to go home and bring some more, while he himself remained on the *kapia* smoking. He no longer thought it necessary to accompany him, for he could no longer imagine that Milan would not obey, or play a trick on him and remain at home. Milan obeyed, went without argument and returned humbly. Then the luck suddenly changed. Milan won back all that he had lost. The knot in his throat tightened more and more under the stress of emotion. The stranger began to double the stakes and then to treble them. The game grew more and more swift, more and more intense. The cards flew between them weaving a web of gold and silver. Both were silent. Only Milan breathed excitedly, sweating and feeling chilled alternately in the mild moonlit night. He played, dealt and covered his cards, not from the pleasure of the game but because he had to. It seemed to him that this stranger wanted to draw out of him not only all his money, ducat by ducat, but also the marrow from his bones and the blood from his veins, drop by drop, and that his strength and his will-power were leaving him with every new loss in the game. From time to time he stole a glance at his opponent. He expected to see a satanic face with bared teeth and eyes like red hot coals, but on the contrary he still saw before him the stranger's ordinary face with the intent expression of a man working at an everyday task, hastening to finish the work in hand which was neither easy nor pleasant.

Once more Milan rapidly lost all his ready money. Then the stranger proposed staking cattle, land and property.

'I wager four good Hungarian ducats against your bay with its saddle. Is it a deal?'

'I agree.'

So the bay went, and after it two packhorses, then cows and calves. Like a careful and meticulous merchant, the stranger numbered all the beasts in Milan's stables by name and set down accurately the value of each head, as if he had been born and reared in the house.

'Here are thirteen ducats for that field of yours you call *salkusha*. Have I your word?'

'You have.'

The stranger dealt. Milan's five cards totalled twenty-eight.

'More?' asked the stranger calmly.

'One,' muttered Milan in a scarcely audible voice and all his blood rushed to his heart.

The stranger slowly turned a card. It was a two, a lucky draw. Milan muttered indifferently through closed teeth.

'Enough.'

He closed his cards, concealing them feverishly. He tried to make his voice and expression indifferent, to prevent his opponent from guessing how he stood.

Then the stranger began to draw for himself, with open cards. When he got to twenty-seven he stopped and looked Milan in the eyes, but Milan looked away. The stranger turned another card. It was a two. He sighed quickly, scarcely audibly. It seemed that he would stand pat at twenty-nine and the blood began to flow back to Milan's head in a joyful presentiment of victory. Then the stranger started, expanded his chest and threw back his head so that his eyes and fore-head shone in the moonlight and turned up another card. Another two. It seemed impossible that three twos should turn up one after the other, but so it was. On the turned-up card Milan seemed to see his field, ploughed and harrowed as it was in spring when it was at its best. The furrows whirled about him as in delirium, but the calm voice of the stranger recalled him to himself.

'*Otuz bir!* The field is mine!'

Then came the turn of the other fields, then both houses and then the oak grove at Osojnica. They invariably agreed on the values. Sometimes Milan would win and would snatch up the ducats. Hope shone before him like gold but after two or three unlucky hands he was again without money and again began staking his property.

When the game had swept away everything like a tor-rent both players stopped for a moment, not to take breath for both of them it seemed feared to do so, but to consider what else they could wager. The stranger was calm like a conscientious worker who has finished the first part of his task and wants to hasten on with the second. Milan remained tense as if turned to ice; his blood was beating in his ears and the stone seat beneath him rose and fell. Then the stranger suggested in that monotonous, even, somewhat nasal voice:

'Do you know what, friend? Let us have one more turn at the cards, but all for all. I will wager all that I have gained tonight and you your life. If you win, everything will be yours again just as it was, money, cattle and lands. If you lose, you will leap from the *kapia* into the Drina.'

He said this in the same dry and business-like voice as he had said everything else, as if it were a question of the most ordinary wager between two gamblers absorbed by their play.

So it has come to losing my soul or saving it, thought Milan and made an effort to rise, to extricate himself from that incomprehensible whirlpool that had taken everything from him and even now drew him on with irresistible force, but the stranger sent him back to his place with a glance. As if they had been playing at the inn for a stake of three or four grosh he lowered his head and held out his hand. They both cut. The stranger cut a four and Milan a ten. It was his turn to deal and that filled him with hope. He dealt and the stranger asked for a complete new hand.

'More! More! More!'

The man took five cards and only then said: 'Enough!' Now it was Milan's turn. When he reached twenty-eight he stopped for a second, looked at the cards in the stranger's hand and at his enigmatic face. He was unable to get any idea at how many the stranger had stopped, but it was exceedingly likely that he had more than twenty-eight; firstly, because all evening he had never stopped at low scores and secondly, because he had five cards. Summoning the last of his strength Milan turned over one more card. It was a four; that meant thirty-two. He had lost.

He looked at the card but was unable to believe his eyes. It seemed to him impossible that he should have lost everything so quickly. Something fiery and noisy seemed to course through him, from his feet to his head. Suddenly everything became clear; the value of life, what it meant to be a man and the meaning of his curse, that inexplicable passion to gamble with friends or strangers, with himself and with all around him. All was clear and light as if the day had dawned and he had only been dreaming that he had gambled and lost, but everything was at the same time true, irrevocable and irreparable. He wanted to make some sound, to groan, to cry out for help, even were it only a sigh, but he could not summon up enough strength.

Before him the stranger stood waiting.

Then, all of a sudden, a cock crowed somewhere on the bank, high and clear, and immediately after, a second. It was so near that he could hear the beating of its wings. At the same time the scattered cards flew away as if carried off by a storm, the money was scattered and the whole *kapia* rocked to its foundations. Milan closed his eyes in fear and thought that his last hour had come. When he opened them again he saw that he was alone. His opponent had vanished like a soap bubble and with him the cards and the money from the stone flags.

An orange-coloured moon swam on the horizon. A fresh breeze began to blow. The roar of waters in the depths became louder. Milan tentatively fingered the stone on which he was sitting, trying to collect himself, to remember where he was and what had happened; then he rose heavily and as if on someone else's legs moved slowly homeward to Okolište.

Groaning and staggering he scarcely reached the door of his house before he fell like a wounded man, striking the door heavily with his body. Those in the house, wakened by the noise, carried him to bed.

For two months he lay in fever and delirium. It was thought that he would not survive. Pop Nikola came and consecrated the holy oils. None the less he recovered and got up again, but as a different man. He was now a man old before his time, an eccentric who lived in a world apart,

who spoke little and associated with other men as little as
possible. On his face, which never smiled, was an expression
of painful and concentrated attention. He concerned himself
only with his own house and went about his own business,
as if he had never heard of company or of cards.

During his illness he had told Pop Nikola all that had
happened that night on the *kapia*, and later he told it all to
two good friends of his, for he felt that he could not go
on living with that secret on his mind. The people heard
the rumours of what had happened but, as if what had actually happened had been a small matter, they added further
details and elaborated the whole story, and then, as is usually
the case, turned their attention elsewhere and forgot all
about Milan and his experience. So what was left of the one-
time Milan Glasičanin lived, worked and moved among the
townsfolk. The younger generation only knew him as he
was in their time and never suspected that he had been different. And he himself seemed to have forgotten everything.
When, descending from his house to the town, he crossed
the bridge with his heavy slow sleepwalker's step, he passed
by the *kapia* without the least emotion, even without any
memory of it. It never even crossed his mind that that *sofa*
with its white stone seats and carefree crowd could have any
connection with that terrible place, somewhere at the ends
of the earth, where he had one night played his last game,
staking on a deceiving card all that he possessed, even his
own life in this world and the next.

Often Milan asked himself if all that night episode on the
kapia had been only a dream which he had dreamt as he lay
unconscious before the door of his house, the consequence
and not the cause of his illness. To tell the truth, both Pop
Nikola and those two friends in whom he had confided were
more inclined to regard the whole of Milan's tale as a hallu-
cination, a fantasy which had appeared to him in a fever. For
none of them believed that the devil played *otuz bir* or that
he would take anyone he wished to destroy to the *kapia*. But
our experiences are often so heavy and clouded that it is no

wonder that men justify themselves by the intervention of Satan himself, considering that this explains them or at least makes them more bearable.

But whether true or not, with the devil's help or without it, in dream or in fact, it was sure that Milan Glasičanin, since he had lost his health and his youth and a large sum of money overnight, had by a miracle been finally liberated for ever from his vice. And not only that. To the story of Milan Glasičanin was added yet another tale of yet another destiny, whose thread started also from the *kapia*.

The day after the night when Milan Glasičanin (in dream or in waking) had played his terrible final game on the *kapia* dawned a sunny autumn day. It was a Saturday. As always on Saturdays, the Višegrad Jews, merchants with their male children, were gathered on the *kapia*. At leisure and in formal dress, with satin trousers and woollen waistcoats, with dull red shallow fezzes on their heads, they strictly observed the Sabbath Day, walking beside the river as if looking for someone in it. But for the most part they sat on the *kapia*, carrying on loud and lively conversations in Spanish, only using Serbian when they wanted to swear.

Among the first to arrive on the *kapia* that morning was Bukus Gaon, the eldest son of the pious, poor and honest barber, Avram Gaon. He was sixteen and still had not found permanent work or a regular occupation. The young man, unlike all the other Gaons, was somewhat scatter-brained and this had prevented him from behaving reasonably and settling down to a trade, and drove him to look for something higher and better for himself. When he wanted to sit down, he looked to see if the seat was clean. It was while doing this that he saw, in a crack between two stones, a thin line of shining yellow. That was the shine of gold, so dear to men's eyes. He looked more closely. There could be no doubt; a ducat had somehow fallen there. The young man looked around him, to see if anyone was watching, and searched for something to pry loose the ducat which laughed at him from its hiding place. Then suddenly he remembered that it was

a Saturday and that it would be a shame and a sin to do any
kind of work. Excited and embarrassed, he went on sitting
on that spot and did not move until noon. When it was time
for lunch and all the Jews, old and young, had gone home,
he found a thick barley stalk and, forgetting the sin and the
holy day, carefully pried the ducat loose from between the
stones. It was a real Hungarian ducat, thin and weighing no
more than a dead leaf. He was late for lunch. When he sat
down at the sparse table around which all thirteen of them
(eleven children, father and mother) were sitting, he did not
hear how his father scolded him and called him a lazy wastrel
who could not even be in time for lunch. His ears hummed
and his eyes were dazzled. Before him opened those days
of unheard-of luxury of which he had often dreamed. It
seemed to him that he was carrying the sun in his pocket.

Next day, without much reflection, Bukus went to
Ustamujić's inn and edged his way into that little room
where at almost any time of the day or night the cards were
in play. He had always dreamed of doing this, but had never
had enough money to dare to go in and try his luck. Now he
was able to realize that dream.

There he passed several hours filled with anguish and
emotion. At first they had all greeted him with disdain and
mistrust. When they saw him change the Hungarian ducat
they at once thought that he had stolen it from someone
but they agreed to accept him and his stake (for if gamblers
questioned the origin of every stake, the game would never
begin). But then fresh miseries commenced for the beginner.
Whenever he won, the blood rushed to his head and his eyes
clouded with sweat and heat. When he made a rather greater
loss it seemed to him that he stopped breathing and his heart
died. But despite all his torments, each of which seemed
insoluble, he none the less left the inn that evening with four
ducats in his pocket. Though he was broken and feverish
with emotion as if he had been beaten with fiery rods, he
walked proud and erect. Before his glowing imagination
opened far and glorious prospects which threw a glittering

sheen over his poverty and swept away the whole town down to its foundations. He walked with a solemn pace as though drunk. For the first time in his life he was able to feel not only the shimmer and the sound of gold but also its weight.

That same autumn, though still young and green, Bukus became a gambler and a vagabond and left the family home. Old Gaon shrivelled up from shame and grief for his eldest son, and the whole Jewish community felt the misfortune as if it had been its own. Later he left the town and went out into the world with his evil gambler's destiny. And nothing more was ever heard of him for all those fourteen years. The cause of all that, they said, was that 'devil's ducat' which he had found on the *kapia* and had pried loose on the Sabbath Day.

CHAPTER XIII

IT WAS THE fourth year of the occupation. It seemed as if everything had somehow or other calmed down and 'was working'. Even if the sweet peace of Turkish times had not been restored, at least order had been established according to the new ideas. But then there were once more troubles in the land, fresh troops arrived unexpectedly and a guard was once again mounted on the *kapia*. This was the way of it.

The new authorities that year began recruiting in Bosnia and Herzegovina. This provoked great agitation among the people, especially the Turks. Fifty years before, when the Sultan had introduced the *nizam* (the first Turkish regular army), clothed, drilled and equipped in the European manner, they had revolted and waged a series of small but bloody wars, for they would not wear the infidel clothing and put on belts which crossed over the chest and so created the hated symbol of the cross. Now they had to put on that same odious 'tight clothing' and that, furthermore, in the service of a foreign ruler of another faith.

In the first years after the occupation, when the authorities had begun numbering houses and taking a census of the population, these measures had already excited mistrust among the Turks and stirred up undefined but deeply felt misgivings.

As always in such cases, the most learned and respected of the Višegrad Turks met stealthily to discuss the significance of these measures and the attitude they should adopt towards them.

One May morning these leaders gathered on the *kapia* as if by chance and occupied all the seats on the *sofa*. Peacefully drinking their coffee and looking straight in front of them, they talked in whispers of the new and suspicious measures of the authorities. They were all ill at ease about the new ideas, the very nature of which was contrary to their ideas and habits, for each of them considered this interference by the authorities in his personal affairs and his family life as an unnecessary and incomprehensible humiliation. But no one knew how to interpret the real sense of this numbering, nor could suggest how it could best be resisted. Amongst them was Alihodja who otherwise rarely came to the *kapia*, for his right ear always throbbed painfully when he happened to look at those stone steps leading up to the *sofa*.

The Višegrad schoolmaster, Husseinaga, a learned and loquacious man, interpreted, as the most competent amongst them to do so, what this noting down of houses by number and this counting of men and children might mean.

'This has, it seems, always been an infidel custom; thirty years ago, if not more, there was a Vezir in Travnik, a certain Tahirpasha Stambolija. He was one of the converted, but false and insincere. He remained a Christian in his soul, as he had once been. He kept, it is said, a bell beside him and when he wanted to call one of his servants he would ring this bell like a Christian priest until someone answered. It was this Tahirpasha who began to number the houses in Travnik and on each house he nailed a tablet with the number (it was for this reason that he was known as "the nailer"). But the people rebelled and collected all those tablets from the houses, made a pile of them and set fire to it. Blood was about to flow for this, but luckily a report of this reached Stambul and he was recalled from Bosnia. May all trace of him be abolished! Now this is something of the same sort. The Schwabes want to have registers of everything, even our heads.'

They all stared straight in front of them and listened to the schoolmaster who was well known to prefer recounting long and detailed stories of the past to giving his own opinion shortly and clearly on what was taking place in the present.

As always, Alihodja was the first to lose patience.

'This does not concern the Schwabes' faith, Muderis Effendi; it concerns their interests. They are not playing and do not waste their time even when they are sleeping but look well to their own affairs. We cannot see today what all this means, but we shall see it in a month or two, or perhaps a year. For, as the late lamented Shemsibeg Branković used to say: "The Schwabes' mines have long fuses!" This numbering of houses and men, or so I see it, is necessary for them because of some new tax, or else they are thinking of getting men for forced labour or for their army, or perhaps both. If you ask me what we should do, this is my opinion. We have not got the army to rise at once in revolt. That God sees and all men know. But we do not have to obey all that we are commanded. No one need remember his number nor tell his age. Let them guess when each one of us was born. If they go too far and interfere with our children and our honour, then we shall not give way but will defend ourselves, and then let it be as God wills!'

They went on discussing the unpalatable measures of the authorities for a long time, but in the main they were in agreement with what Alihodja had recommended: passive resistance. Men concealed their ages or gave false information, making the excuse that they were illiterate. And as for women no one even dared to ask about them, for that would have been considered a deadly insult. Despite all the instructions and threats of the authorities the tablets with the house numbers were nailed upside down or hidden away in places where they were invisible. Or else they immediately whitewashed their houses and, as if by chance, the house number was whitewashed too.

Seeing that the resistance was deep-seated and sincere, though concealed, the authorities turned a blind eye, avoiding any strict application of the laws with all the consequences and disputes which would inevitably have ensued.

Two years passed. The agitation about the census had been forgotten when the recruitment of young men, irrespective of faith and class, was actually put into force. Open rebellion broke out in Eastern Herzegovina, in which not only Turks but also Serbs took part. The leaders of the rebels tried to establish ties with foreign countries, especially with Turkey, and claimed that the occupation authorities had gone beyond the powers granted them at the Berlin Congress and that they had no right to recruit in the occupied districts which still remained under nominal Turkish suzerainty. In Bosnia there was no organized resistance, but the revolt spread by way of Foča and Goražda to the borders of the Višegrad district. Individual insurgents or the remnants of routed bands tried to seek refuge in the Sanjak or in Serbia, crossing the bridge at Višegrad. As always in such circumstances, in addition to the rebellion, banditry began to flourish.

So once more, after so many years, a guard was mounted on the *kapia*. Though it was winter and heavy snow had fallen, two gendarmes kept watch on the *kapia* day and night. They stopped all unknown or suspected persons crossing the bridge, interrogated them and inspected their belongings.

A fortnight later a detachment of *streifkorps* appeared in the town and relieved the gendarmes on the *kapia*. The *streifkorps* had been organized when the rebellion in Herzegovina had begun to assume serious proportions. They were mobile storm troops, picked men equipped for action in difficult terrain, and made up of well paid volunteers. Amongst them were men who had responded to the first call-up with the occupation troops and did not want to return to their homes, but remained to serve in the *streifkorps*. Others had been seconded from the gendarmerie to the new mobile units. Finally, there were also a certain number of local inhabitants who served as informers and guides.

Throughout that winter, which was neither short nor mild, a guard of two *streifkorps* men kept watch on the bridge. Usually the guard consisted of one stranger and one local man. They did not build a blockhouse, as the Turks had done during the Karageorge insurrection in Serbia. There was no killing or cutting off of heads. But none the less this time, as always when the *kapia* was closed, there were unusual events which left their trace on the town. For hard times cannot pass without misfortune for someone.

Among the *streifkorps* men who mounted guard on the *kapia* was a young man, Gregor Fedun, a Ruthenian from Eastern Galicia. This young man was then in his twenty-third year, of gigantic stature but childlike mind, strong as a bear but modest as a girl. He had almost completed his military service when his regiment was sent to Bosnia. He had taken part in fighting at Maglaj and on the Glasinac Mountains and had then spent eighteen months on garrison duty in Eastern Bosnia. When his time was up, he had not wanted to go back to his Galician town of Kolomea and to his father's house which was rich in children but in little else. He was in Pest with his group when the call for volunteers to enrol in the *streifkorps* was made. As a soldier who knew Bosnia through several months of fighting, Fedun was accepted at once. He was sincerely glad at the thought that he was again to see the Bosnian townships and hamlets where he had spent both hard and pleasant days, of which his memory recalled the days of hardship as more beautiful and lively even than the pleasant ones. He melted with joy and was filled with pride, imagining the faces of his parents, brothers and sisters when they received the first silver florins which he would send them from his ample *streifkorps* pay. Above all he had the good fortune not to be sent into Eastern Herzegovina where the fighting with the insurgents was tiring and often very dangerous, but to the town on the Drina where his duties consisted of patrolling and guard-keeping.

There he spent the winter, stamping his feet and blowing on his fingers on the *kapia* in the clear frosty nights, when the stones cracked in the frost and the sky paled above the town so that the large autumn stars became tiny, wicked little candles. There he awaited the spring and watched its first signs on the *kapia*: that dull, heavy booming of the ice on the Drina which a man feels deep down in his entrails, and that sullen soughing of some new wind which has howled all night through the naked forests on the mountains close pressed above the bridge.

The young man mounted guard in his turn and felt how the spring, with all its signs on the earth and on the waters, was slowly entering into him also, flooding his whole being and troubling his senses and his thoughts. He kept watch and hummed all the Ruthenian songs which were sung in his own country. As he sang it seemed to him, more and more every spring day, as if he were waiting for someone on that exposed and windy spot.

At the beginning of March, headquarters sent an order to the detachment guarding the bridge to double their precautions since, according to reliable information, the notorious brigand Jakov Čekrlija had crossed from Herzegovina into Bosnia and was now hiding somewhere near Višegrad whence, in all likelihood, he would try to reach either the Serbian or the Turkish frontier. The *streifkorps* men on guard were given a personal description of him, with the comment that the brigand, though physically small and insignificant, was very strong, daring and exceptionally cunning, and had already several times succeeded in escaping and outwitting the patrols that had surrounded him.

Fedun had listened to this warning when making his report, and had taken it seriously as he did all official communications. But he had considered it to be unnecessarily exaggerated, since he could not imagine how anyone could cross unperceived that ten paces which constituted the width of the bridge. Calm and unworried he passed several hours, by day and by night, on the *kapia*. His attention was indeed doubled, but it was not taken up with the appearance of Jakov, of whom there was neither sight nor sound, but with those countless signs and portents by which spring announced its arrival on the *kapia*.

It is not easy to concentrate all one's attention on a single object when one is twenty-three years old, when one's body is quivering with strength and life and when around one, on all sides, spring is burgeoning, shining and filling the air with perfume. The snow was melting in the ravines, the river ran swift and grey as smoked glass, the wind which blew from the north-east brought the breath of snow from the mountains and the first buds to the valleys. All this intoxicated and distracted Fedun as he paced out the space from one terrace to the other or, when on night duty, leant against the parapet and hummed his Ruthenian songs to the accompaniment of the wind. By day or by night the feeling that he was waiting for someone never left him, a feeling tormenting and yet sweet, and which seemed to find confirmation in all that was taking place around him, in the waters, the earth and the sky.

One day about lunchtime a Turkish girl passed the guard. She was of the age when Turkish girls, not yet veiled in the heavy *feridjah*, no longer go with uncovered faces but wrap themselves in a large thin shawl which conceals the whole body, the hair and the hands, chin and forehead, but still leaves uncovered a part of the face: eyes, nose, mouth and cheeks. She was in that short phase between childhood and womanhood when the Moslem girls show innocently and gaily their still childish and yet womanly features which, perhaps even the next day, will be covered forever by the *feridjah*.

There was not a living soul on the *kapia*. Fedun's fellow guard was a certain Stevan of Prača, one of the peasants attached to the *streifkorps*. He was a man of a certain age, by no means averse to plum-brandy, who sat drowsing, contrary to regulations, on the stone *sofa*.

Fedun looked at the girl timidly and cautiously. Around her floated her gaily-coloured shawl, waving and shimmering in the sunlight as if alive, moving with the gusts of wind and in rhythm with the girl's pace. Her calm lovely face was closely and tightly framed by the stretched weave of the shawl. Her eyes were downcast but flickering. So she passed before him and disappeared across the bridge into the market.

The young man paced more briskly from one terrace to

the other and kept an eye fixed on the market-place. Now it seemed to him that he really had someone for whom to wait. After half an hour — the noonday lull was still unbroken on the bridge — the Turkish girl returned from the market and again crossed before the troubled youth. This time he looked at her a little longer and more boldly, and what was even more wonderful she too looked at him, a short but candid glance, with a sort of half-smile, almost cunningly but with that innocent cunning with which children get the better of one another at their games. Then she swayed away again, moving slowly but none the less vanishing quickly from his sight, with a thousand bends and movements of the wide shawl wrapped about her young but sturdy figure. The oriental design and lively colours of that shawl could long be seen between the houses on the farther bank.

Only then did the young man wake from his reverie. He stood in the same place and in the same position as he had been at the moment when she had passed before him. With a start he fingered his rifle and looked around him with the sensation of a man who has let slip his opportunity. Stevan was still dozing in the deceptive March sun. It seemed to the young man that both of them had in some way failed in their duty and that a whole army platoon could have passed by them without him being able to say how many of them there were, or what significance they might have had for himself or for others. Ashamed of himself, he woke Stevan in exaggerated zeal and they both remained on guard until their relief arrived.

All that day, both when he was off duty and while he was mounting guard, the picture of the young Turkish girl passed like a vision countless times through his mind. Next day, once again about noon when there were very few people on the bridge, she again crossed. Fedun again saw that face framed in the brightly-coloured shawl. All was as it had been the day before. Only their glances were longer, livelier and bolder, almost as if they were playing a game together. Stevan was again drowsing on the stone bench and later, as he always did, swore that he had not been asleep and that even when he was at home in bed he could not close an eye. On the way back the girl seemed almost ready to stop, looked the *streifkorps* boy straight in the eyes while he muttered a couple of vague and unimportant words, feeling as he did so that his legs failed him through emotion and forgetting completely where he was.

Only in dreams do we dare so much. When the girl was once more lost to sight on the farther bank the young man shivered with fright. It was incredible that a young Turkish girl should think of looking at an Austrian soldier. Such an unheard-of and unprecedented thing could only happen in dreams, in dreams or in spring on the *kapia*. He knew very well that nothing in this land or in his position was as scandalous and as dangerous as to touch a Moslem woman. They had told him that when he had been in the army and again in the *streifkorps*. The punishment for such daring was a heavy one. There had been some who had paid with their lives at the hands of the insulted and infuriated Turks. All that he knew, and most sincerely desired to keep the orders and regulations, but none the less he acted contrary to them. The misfortune of unlucky men lies in just this, that those things which for them are impossible and forbidden become in a moment easy and attainable, or at least appear so. Yet when once such things are firmly fixed in their desires they seem once again as they were, unattainable and forbidden, with all the consequences that they have for those who, despite everything, still attempt them.

On the third day too, about noon, the Turkish girl appeared. And as it is in dreams all took place as he would have wished, like a unique reality to which all else was subordinate. Stevan was again drowsing, convinced and always ready to convince others that he had not closed an eye; there were no passers-by on the *kapia*. The young man spoke again, muttering a few words, and the girl slowed her pace and replied, equally timidly and vaguely.

The dangerous and incredible game went on. On the

fourth day the girl in passing, choosing a moment when there was no one on the *kapia*, asked in a whisper when he would next be on guard. He told her that he would be on duty on the *kapia* again at dusk.

'I will bring my old grandmother to the market-place, where she is to spend the night, and I will return alone,' whispered the girl without stopping or turning her head, but darting a provocative and eloquent glance at him. And in each of those very ordinary words was the hidden joy that she would soon see him again.

Six hours later Fedun was once more on the *kapia* with his sleepy comrade. After the rain a chill twilight had fallen which seemed to him full of promise. Passers-by became fewer and fewer. Then on the road from Osojnica the Turkish girl appeared, wrapped in her shawl, its colours dimmed by the twilight. Beside her walked an old, bowed Turkish woman bundled up in a thick black *feridjah*. She walked almost on all fours, supporting herself by a staff in her right hand and holding on to the girl with her left.

They passed by Fedun. The girl walked slowly, accommodating her pace to the slow walk of the old crone whom she was leading. Her eyes, made larger by the shadows of early dusk, now gazed boldly and openly into the young man's as if they could not look away from him. When they disappeared into the market-place, a shiver passed through the youth and he began to pace with more rapid steps from one terrace to the other as if he wanted to make up for what he had lost. With an excitement that was almost fear he waited for the girl's return. Stevan was dozing.

'What will she say to me when she passes?' thought the youth. 'What shall I say to her? Will she perhaps suggest meeting somewhere at night in a quiet spot?' He quivered with delight and the excitement of danger lay in that thought.

A whole hour passed thus, waiting, and the half of another, and still the girl did not return. But even in that waiting there was delight. His eagerness rose with the falling darkness. At last, instead of the girl, his relief came. But this

time not only the two *streifkorps* men who were to remain
there on guard but also the sergeant-major Draženović in
person. A strict man with a short black beard, he ordered
Fedun and Stevan in a sharp and strident voice to go to the
dormitory as soon as they reached barracks and not to leave
it until further orders. The blood rushed to Fedun's face at
the idea that he was in some way to blame.

The huge chill dormitory with twelve regularly spaced out
beds was empty. The men were all at supper or in the town.
Fedun and Stevan waited, troubled and impatient, thinking
things over and making vain guesses why the sergeant-major
had been so stern and had so unexpectedly confined them to
barracks. After an hour, when the first of the soldiers began
to come in to sleep, a corporal burst in and ordered them
loudly and harshly to follow him. From everything about
him, the two felt that the severity against them was increasing and that all this presaged no good. As soon as they left
the dormitory they were separated and questioned.

The night wore on. Even the last lights in the town were
extinguished, but the windows of the barracks still blazed
with light. From time to time there was a ring at the main
gates, the clink of keys and the thud of heavy doors. Orderlies came and went, hurrying through the dark and sleeping
town between the barracks and the *konak*, where lamps also
burned on the first floor. It could be seen from all these signs
that something unusual was afoot.

When, about eleven o'clock at night, they brought Fedun
into the sergeant-major's office, it seemed to him that days
and weeks had passed from those moments on the *kapia*. On
the table burned a metal oil-lamp with a shade of green porcelain. By it was seated the major, Krčmar. The light fell on
his arms up to the elbows, but the upper half of his body and
his head were in shadow cast by the green shade. The young
man knew that pale, full, almost womanly face, clean-shaven,
with fine moustaches and dark rings around the eyes. The
soldiers feared the slow heavy words of this big placid officer.
There were few of them who could endure for long the gaze

of those large grey eyes, and who did not stammer when replying to his questions, in which each word was softly yet separately, distinctly and clearly enunciated from the first to the last syllable as at school or in the theatre. A little away from the table stood the sergeant-major Draženović. The whole upper part of his body also was in shadow and only his hands were strongly illuminated, hanging limply at his side; on one finger glistened a heavy gold ring.

Draženović opened the interrogation:

'Tell us how you passed the time between five and seven o'clock while you were with assistant *streifkorps* private Stevan Kalacan on guard duty on the *kapia*?'

The blood rushed to Fedun's head. Every man passed his time as best he could, but no one had ever thought that he would later have to answer for it before some strict judge and give account of everything that had taken place, to the minutest detail, to the most hidden thoughts and the last minute. No one, least of all when one is twenty-three years old and that time has been spent on the *kapia* in spring. What was he to answer? Those two hours on guard had passed as they had always done, as they had done the day before and the day before that. But at that moment he could not remember anything everyday and usual which he could report. Only incidental, forbidden things rose in his memory, things that happen to everyone but which are not told to one's superiors; that Stevan had dozed as usual; that he, Fedun, had exchanged a few words with an unknown Turkish girl, that then, as dusk was falling, he had sung softly and fervently all the songs of his own country awaiting the girl's return and with it something exciting and unusual. How hard it was to reply, impossible to tell everything but embarrassing to remain silent. And he must hurry, for time was passing and that only increased his confusion and embarrassment. How long had his silence lasted already?

'Well?' said the major. Everyone knew that 'well' of his, clear, smooth and forceful like the sound of some strong, complex and well oiled machine.

Fedun began to stammer and get confused as though he felt himself guilty from the very start.

The night wore on, but the lamps were not extinguished either in the barracks or in the *konak*. Interrogations, evidence and the confrontation of witnesses followed one another. Others who had mounted guard on the *kapia* that day were also interrogated. But it was clear that the net was closing around Fedun and Stevan and, in their interrogation, about the old Turkish woman whom a young girl had taken across the bridge.

It seemed to the young man as if all the magical and inextricable responsibilities that he had felt in his dreams were falling on his shoulders. Before dawn he was confronted with Stevan. The peasant closed his eyes cunningly and spoke in a forced voice, continually harking back to the fact that he was an illiterate man, a peasant, and sheltering himself from all responsibility by always referring to 'that Mr Fedun' as he insisted on calling his companion on guard.

That's the way to answer, the young man thought to himself. His entrails were crying out from hunger and he himself was trembling all over from emotion though it was still not clear to him what this was all about and where exactly lay the question of his guilt or innocence. But morning brought complete explanation.

All through that night a fantastic round-dance whirled about him; in its centre was the major, cold and implacable. Himself dumb and unmoving, he allowed no one else to be silent or at peace. In bearing and appearance he no longer seemed like a man, but like duty embodied, the terrible ministrant of justice inaccessible to weakness or sentiment, gifted with supernatural strength and immune from the ordinary human needs of food, rest or sleep. When dawn broke, Fedun was once again brought before the major. There was now in the office, besides the major and Draženović, an armed gendarme and a woman who, at first sight, seemed unreal to the young man. The lamp had been extinguished. The room, facing north, was cold and in semi-darkness. The young man felt as if this were a continuation of his dream of the night before which refused to pale and vanish even in the light of day.

'Is that the man who was on guard?' Draženović asked the woman.

With a great effort which caused him pain Fedun only then looked full at her. She was the Moslem girl of the day before, only bareheaded without her shawl and with her heavy chestnut plaits wrapped around her head. She was wearing brightly coloured Turkish trousers, but the rest of her dress, blouse, sash and bolero, was that of the Serbian girls from the villages on the high plateau above the town. Without her shawl, she seemed older and sturdier. Her face seemed different, her mouth large and bad-tempered, her eyelids reddened and her eyes clear and flashing as if the shadows of the day before had fled from them.

'It is,' the woman replied indifferently in a hard voice which was as new and unusual to Fedun as her present appearance.

Draženović went on asking her how many times in all she had crossed the bridge, what she had said to Fedun and he to her. She replied for the most part precisely, but proudly and indifferently.

'Good, Jelenka, and what did he say to you the last time you crossed?'

'He said something but I don't know exactly what, for I was not listening but only thinking how I could get Jakov across.'

'You were thinking of that?'

'Of that,' answered the woman unwillingly. She clearly worn out and did not want to say more than she must. But the sergeant-major was inexorable. In a threatening voice which betrayed his conviction that he must be answered without argument he forced the woman to repeat all that she had said at her first interrogation at the *konak*.

She defended herself, shortened and skipped various bits of her earlier evidence, but he always checked her and by sharp and skilful questioning made her go back over it all again.

Little by little the whole truth was laid bare. Her name was Jelenka and she came from the village of Tasić in Upper Lijeska. Last autumn the *haiduk* Jakov Čekrlija had come into her district to pass the winter hidden in a stable above her village. They had brought him food and clothing from her house. For the most part it had been she who had brought it. They had liked the look of each other and had become lovers. When the snow began to melt and the *streifkorps* squads came more frequently, Jakov had decided to cross into Serbia at all costs. At that time of year the Drina was hard to cross even if it had not been patrolled and there had not been a permanent guard on the bridge. She had gone with him, determined to help him even at the risk of her life. They had first descended to Lijeska and then to a cave above Okolište. Earlier, on Glasinac, Jakov had obtained some Turkish women's clothes from some gipsies; a *feridjah*, Turkish trousers and a shawl. Then she, on his instructions, began to cross the bridge at a time when there were not many Turks about, since one of them might ask whose was that unknown girl, and in order that the guard might grow accustomed to her. Thus she crossed three days running, and then decided to take Jakov with her.

'And why did you take him across when this particular soldier was on guard?'

'Because he seemed to me the softest of them.'

'So?'

'So.'

At the sergeant-major's insistence the woman continued. When everything had been prepared, Jakov had wrapped himself in the *feridjah* and just as it was beginning to get dark she took him disguised as her old grandmother across the bridge past the guard. The guard had noticed nothing, for this young man was looking at her and not at the old woman, while the other, older guard was sitting on the *sofa* dozing.

When they got to the market-place, they had taken the

precaution of not going right across it, but had used the side-streets. It was this had proved their undoing. They had lost their way in the town, which neither of them knew, and instead of coming out at the bridge across the Rzav and thus joining the road which led from the town towards both frontiers, they had found themselves in front of a Turkish café, just as some people were coming out. One of them was a Turkish gendarme, born in the town. This closely wrapped up old woman and the girl whom he had never seen before seemed suspect to him, and he followed them. He kept them in sight as far as the Rzav. Then he came nearer to ask them who they were and where they were going. Jakov, who had been watching him attentively through his face-veil, considered that the moment had come to flee. He threw off his *feridjah*, and pushed Jelenka at the gendarme so violently that they both lost their footing ('for he is small and insignificant to look at, but as strong as the earth and courageous above all other men'). She, as she calmly and clearly confessed, tangled herself with the legs of the gendarme. By the time that the gendarme had freed himself of her, Jakov had already rushed across the Rzav as if it had been a stream, though the water was above his knees, and was lost in the willow clumps on the farther side. Then they had taken her to the *konak*, beaten and threatened her, but she had nothing more to say and would say nothing more.

In vain the sergeant-major tried evasive questions, flatteries and threats to get something more out of the girl, to learn from her about others who helped or sheltered bandits, or about Jakov's further intentions. All this had not the slightest effect on her. She had spoken freely enough of what she wanted to tell but despite all Draženović's efforts they could not get a word out of her about what she did not want to tell.

'It would be better for you to tell us all you know than for us to question and torture Jakov who has surely by now been caught on the frontier.'

'Caught who? Him? Ha, ha!'

The girl looked at the sergeant-major with pity, as at a

man who does not know what he is talking about, and the right corner of her upper lip rose disdainfully. In fact the movement of this upper lip, which looked like a writhing leech, expressed her feelings of anger, disdain or pride, whenever those feelings grew more than she could express in words. That writhing movement gave for a moment to her otherwise beautiful and regular face a troubled and unpleasant expression. Then with some quite childlike and fervent expression completely in contrast to that ugly writhing she looked out of the window as a peasant looks at a field when he wants to gauge the influence of the weather on the harvest.

'God help you! It's dawn now. From last night till now he has had time to get across all Bosnia, not merely to cross a frontier only an hour or two's march away. I know that much. You can beat me and kill me, I came with him for that, but him you will never see again. Don't even dream of it! Ha!'

Her upper lip writhed and lifted and her whole face seemed suddenly older, more experienced, bold and ugly. And when that lip suddenly ceased to writhe, her face again took on that childlike expression of bold and innocent daring.

Not knowing what more to do, Draženović looked at the major, who gave a sign to send the girl away. Then he resumed the interrogation of Fedun. This could no longer be either long or hard. The young man admitted everything and had nothing to put forward in his own defence, not even what Draženović himself had hinted at in his questions. Not even the major's words which contained a merciless and implacable judgement, but in which none the less there was restrained pain because of their own severity, could wake the youth from his torpor.

'I had always considered you, Fedun,' Krčmar said in German, 'a serious young man, conscious of your duties and of your aim in life, and I had thought that one day you would become a perfect soldier, a credit to our unit. But you have been blinded by the first female animal to run in front of your nose. You have behaved like a weakling, like one to whom serious work cannot be entrusted. I am forced to hand you over to court-martial. But whatever its sentence may be, your greatest punishment will be to know that you have not shown yourself worthy of the confidence placed in you and that at the right moment you were unable to behave at your post like a man and a soldier. Now go!'

Not even these words, heavy, curt, carefully enunciated, could bring anything fresh to the young man's mind. He felt all that already. The appearance and speech of that woman, the bandit's mistress, the behaviour of Stevan and the whole course of that short enquiry had suddenly revealed to him in its true light his thoughtless, naïve and unpardonable spring fever on the *kapia*. The major's words only seemed to him to place the official seal on all that; they were more necessary to the major himself, in order to satisfy some unwritten but eternal demand for law and order, than to Fedun. As before a prospect of unsuspected grandeur, the young man found himself faced with a knowledge that he could not grasp; the meaning of a few moments of forgetfulness in an evil hour and in a dangerous place. Had they been lived through and remained unknown, there on the *kapia*, they would have meant nothing at all; one of those youthful pranks later told to friends during dull patrol duties at night. But thus, reduced to a question of definite responsibility, they meant everything. They meant more than death, they meant the end of everything, an unwanted and unworthy end. There would be no more full and frank explanations either to himself or to comrades. There would be no more letters from Kolomea, no more family photographs, no money orders such as he had sent home with pride. It was the end of one who has deceived himself and allowed others to deceive him.

Therefore he found not a word to reply to the major.

The supervision over Fedun was not particularly strict. They gave him breakfast, which he ate as though with someone else's mouth, and ordered him to pack up his personal effects, hand in his arms and all government property and be ready to leave at ten o'clock accompanied by a gendarme by the postal courier for Sarajevo, where he would be handed over to the garrison court.

While the young man was taking down his things from the shelf above his bed, those of his comrades who were still in the dormitory tiptoed out, closing the door carefully and silently behind them. Around him grew that circle of loneliness and deep silence which is always formed around a man whom ill fortune has struck, as around a sick animal. First he took off its hooks the black tablet on which his name, rank, detachment number and unit were written in oil colours in German and placed it on his knees, with the writing down. On the black back of the tablet the young man scribbled hastily with a scrap of chalk: 'All that I leave please send to my father at Kolomea. I send greetings to all my comrades and beg my superiors to pardon me. G. Fedun.' Then he looked once more through the window, relishing that little piece of the outside world that he was able to see through its narrow frame. Then he took down his rifle, loaded it with a single charge of ball still sticky with grease. Then he took off his shoes and with a penknife cut his stocking over his big toe, lay down on the bed, wrapped his arms and legs around the rifle so that the top of the barrel was pressed firmly beneath his chin, shifted his right leg so that the hole in his stocking fitted over the trigger and pressed. The sound of the shot rang through the barracks.

After a great decision, everything becomes simple and easy. The doctor came. A Commission of Enquiry was held and attached to its findings a record in duplicate of Fedun's interrogation.

Then arose the question of Fedun's burial. Draženović was ordered to go to Pop Nikola and discuss the matter with him; could Fedun be buried in the graveyard even though he had taken his own life, and would the priest agree to conduct the service, for the deceased was by faith a Uniate.

In the last year Pop Nikola had suddenly grown old and weak in his legs, so he had taken as assistant for his great parish Pop Joso, a taciturn and nervous sort of man, thin and black as a spent match. In the previous few months, he had carried out almost all the duties of the priest and the services in the town and villages, while Pop Nikola, who could only move with difficulty, dealt mainly with what he could do at home or in the church next to his house.

By the major's order, Draženović went to Pop Nikola. The old man received him lying on a divan; by him stood Pop Joso. After Draženović had explained the circumstances of Fedun's death and the question of his burial, both priests remained silent for a moment. Seeing that Pop Nikola did not speak, Pop Joso began first, timidly and uncertainly; the matter was exceptional and unusual, there were difficulties both in the canons of the church and in established custom, but if it could be shown that the suicide had not been of sound mind then something might be done. But then Pop Nikola sat up on his hard and narrow couch, covered with an old and faded rug. His body once again assumed that monumental form which it had once had when he walked through the market-place and was greeted on all sides. The first word that he said illuminated his broad and still ruddy face, with his huge moustaches which tangled in his beard and his heavy almost white eyebrows, thick and bushy, the face of a man who has learnt from birth how to think independently, to give his opinion sincerely and to defend it well.

Without hesitation and without big words he answered both priest and sergeant-major directly:

'Now that the misfortune has happened, there is nothing more to be done about it. Who with a sound mind would ever raise his hand against himself? And who would dare to take it on his soul to bury him as if he were without faith, somewhere behind a fence and without a priest? But you, sir, go and give orders that the dead man be prepared and we shall bury him as soon as we can. In the graveyard, most certainly! I will sing his requiem. Later, if ever some priest of his law should happen to pass this way, let him add or alter as he wishes, should he not find everything to his liking.'

When Draženović had left, he turned once more to Pop Joso, who was astonished and humiliated.

'How could we forbid a Christian to be buried in the graveyard? And why should I not sing his requiem? Isn't it enough that he had bad luck when he was alive? There, on the other side, let those ask about his sins who will ask all the rest of us about ours.'

Thus the young man who had made his mistake on the *kapia* remained for ever in the town. He was buried the following morning. Pop Nikola sang the requiem, assisted by the sacristan Dimitrije.

One by one his comrades of the *streifkorps* filed past the grave and each threw on it a handful of earth. While two sextons worked rapidly, they stood there a few seconds longer as if waiting for orders, looking across to the far side of the river where, close to their own barracks, rose a straight white column of smoke. There, on the level patch of grass above the barracks, they were burning the bloodstained straw from Fedun's mattress.

The cruel fate of the young *streifkorps* boy, whose name no one ever remembered and who had paid with his life for a few spring moments of inattention and emotion on the *kapia*, was one of those incidents for which the townspeople had much understanding and long remembered and repeated. The memory of that sensitive and unlucky youth lasted far longer than the guard on the *kapia*.

By next autumn the insurrection in Herzegovina had fizzled out. A few of the more important leaders, Moslems and Serbs, fled to Montenegro or Turkey. There remained only a few *haiduks* who in fact never had much real connection with the insurrection about conscription but had worked for themselves. Then those too were either captured or driven away. Herzegovina was pacified. Bosnia gave recruits without resistance. But the departure of the first recruits was neither simple nor easy.

Not more than 100 young men were taken from the entire district, but on the day they were mustered before the *konak*, peasants with their bags and a few townsmen with their wooden chests, it seemed as if there were plague and uproar in the town. Many of the recruits had been drinking steadily from early morning and mixing their drinks. The peasants were in clean white shirts. There were few who had not been drinking and these sat near their belongings, drowsing behind a wall. The majority were excited, flushed with drink and sweating in the heat of the day. Four or five boys from the same village would embrace, and then put their heads close together and swaying like a living forest begin a harsh and long-drawn chanting as if they were the only people in the world.

'Oy my mai-ai-ai-ai-den! O-o-o-y!'

A far greater commotion than that made by the recruits themselves was made by the women, mothers, sisters and other relatives of the young men, who had come from distant villages to say farewell, to see them for the last time, to weep, to wail and to give them some last gift or final sign of love. The square near the bridge was packed with women. They sat there as if turned to stone, talked among themselves and from time to time wiped away their tears with the fringes of their kerchiefs. In vain it had been earlier explained to them in their villages that the young men were going neither to war nor to slavery, but that they would serve the Emperor in Vienna, and be well fed, well clothed and well shod; that after a term of two years they would return home, and that young men from all the other parts of the Empire served in the army, and that they served for a three-year term. All that passed over their heads like the wind, foreign and completely incomprehensible. They listened only to their instincts and would only be guided by them. These ancient and inherited instincts brought tears to their eyes and a wail to their throats, forced them persistently to follow as long as they could and try to get a last glance at him whom they loved more than life and whom an unknown Emperor was carrying off into an unknown land, to unknown trials and tasks. In vain even now the gendarmes and officials from the *konak* went among them and assured them that there was no reason for such exaggerated grief, and advised them not to block the way nor rush after the recruits and create trouble and disorder, for they would all return hale and hearty. But it was all in vain. The women listened to them, agreed to all they said dully and humbly and then returned once more to their tears and wailing. It seemed as if they loved their tears and their wailing as much as they loved those for whom they wept.

When the time came to move and the young men were drawn up in four ranks in the correct manner and moved across the bridge, a crowding and rushing began in which even the most equable of gendarmes could hardly retain his composure. The women ran and tore themselves from the hands of the gendarmes in order to be beside someone of their own, pushing and overturning one another. Their wails were mingled with cries, entreaties and last moment recommendations. Some of them even ran in front of the line of recruits whom four gendarmes were keeping in file and fell under their feet, clutching at their bare breasts and shouting:

'Over my body! Over my body!'

The men lifted them up with difficulty, carefully disentangling boots and spurs from dishevelled hair and disordered skirts.

Some of the recruits, ashamed, tried by angry gestures to make the women return home. But most of the young men sang or shouted, increasing the general disorder. The few townsmen among them, pale with emotion, sang together in the town manner:

> 'In Sarajevo and Bosnia
> Every mother mourns
> Who has sent her son
> As a recruit for the Emperor. . . .'

This song created even greater weeping.

When, somehow or other, they crossed the bridge towards

which the whole convoy was headed and took the Sarajevo road, all the townspeople were awaiting them, drawn up on each side of the road, in order to see the recruits and to weep for them as if they were being taken away to be shot. There were many women there too who wept for every one of them although none of their own relations was amongst those who were going. For every woman has some reason to weep and weeping is sweetest when it is for another's sorrow.

But little by little the ranks along the road became sparser. Even some of the peasant women gave up. The most persistent were the mothers who ran around the convoy as though they were fifteen years old, leapt the ditch at the side of the road from one side to the other and tried to outwit the gendarmes and stay as long as possible close to their sons. When they saw that, the young men themselves, pale with emotion and a sort of embarrassment, turned and shouted:

'Get along home when I tell you!'

But the mothers went on for long, blind to all save the sons that were being taken from them and listening to nothing save their own weeping.

But even these troublous days passed. The people dispersed to their villages and the town again grew calm. When letters and the first photographs from the recruits in Vienna began to arrive, everything became easier and more tolerable. The women wept for long over those letters and photographs, but more gently and more calmly.

The *streifkorps* was disbanded and left the barracks. For a long time there had been no guard on the *kapia* and the townsfolk went on sitting there as they had done before.

Two years quickly pass. That autumn the first recruits returned from Vienna, clean, close-cropped and well-fed. The people clustered around them as they told tales of army life and of the greatness of the cities they had seen, their talk interlarded with strange names and unfamiliar expressions. At the next call-up there was less weeping and agitation.

Generally speaking, everything became easier and more normal. Young men grew up who no longer had any clear or lively memory of Turkish times and who had to a great extent accepted the new ways. But on the *kapia* they still lived according to the ancient custom of the town. Without regard for the new fashions of dress, new professions and new trades, the townspeople still went on meeting there as they had done for centuries past, in those conversations which had always been and still were a real need of their hearts and their imaginations. The recruits went to their service without uproar and without commotion. The *haiduks* were mentioned only in old men's tales. The *streifkorps* was forgotten as completely as that earlier Turkish guard when there had been a blockhouse on the *kapia*.

CHAPTER XIV

LIFE IN THE town beside the bridge became more and more animated, seemed more and more orderly and fuller, assuming an even pace and a hitherto unknown balance, that balance towards which all life tends, everywhere and at all times, and which is only rarely, partially and temporarily achieved.

In the far-off cities unknown to the townsmen whence at that time the power and administration over these districts originated, there was – in the last quarter of the nineteenth century – one of those short and rare lulls in human relationships and social events. Something of that lull could be felt even in these remote districts, just as a great calm at sea may be felt even in the most distant creeks.

Such were those three decades of relative prosperity and apparent peace in the Franz Joseph manner, when many Europeans thought that there was some infallible formula for the realization of a centuries-old dream of full and happy development of individuality in freedom and in progress, when the nineteenth century spread out before the eyes of millions of men its many-sided and deceptive prosperity and created its *fata morgana* of comfort, security and happiness for all and everyone at reasonable prices and even on credit terms. But to this remote Bosnian township only broken echoes penetrated of all this life of the nineteenth century, and those only to the extent and in the form in which this backward oriental society could receive them and in its own manner understand and accept them.

After the first years of distrust, misunderstanding and hesitation, when the first feeling of transience had passed, the town began to find its place in the new order of things. The people found order, work and security. That was enough to ensure that here too life, outward life at least, set out 'on the road of perfection and progress'. Everything else was flushed away into that dark background of consciousness where live and ferment the basic feelings and indestructible beliefs of individual races, faiths and castes, which, to all appearances dead and buried, are preparing for later far-off times unsuspected changes and catastrophes without which, it seems, peoples cannot exist and above all the peoples of this land.

The new authorities, after the first misunderstandings and clashes, left among the townspeople a definite impression of firmness and of permanence (they were themselves impregnated with this belief without which there can be no strong and permanent authority). They were impersonal and indirect and for that reason more easily bearable than the former Turkish rulers. All that was cruel and grasping was concealed by the dignity and glitter of traditional forms. The people still feared the authorities but in much the same way as they feared sickness and death and not as one fears malice, misery and oppression. The representatives of the new authority, military as well as civil, were for the most part newcomers to the land and unskilful in their dealings with the people and were themselves of little importance, but with every step they made they felt themselves to be part of a greater mechanism and that behind each one of them stood more powerful men and greater organizations in long rows and countless gradations. That gave them a standing which far surpassed their own personality and a magic influence to which it was easier to submit. By their titles which appeared to be great, by their calm and their European customs, they aroused among the people, from whom they so greatly differed, feelings of confidence and respect and did not excite envy or real criticism, even though they were neither pleasant nor loved.

On the other hand, after a certain time, even these newcomers were unable to avoid completely the influence of the unusual oriental milieu in which they had to live. Their children introduced the children of the townspeople to strange phrases and foreign names, brought with them new games and toys, but equally they easily picked up from the local children the old songs, ways of speech, oaths and the traditional games of knucklebones, leap-frog and the like. It was the same with the grown-ups; they too brought a new order, with unfamiliar words and habits, but at the same time they too accepted every day something of the speech and manner of life of the older inhabitants. It is true that the local people, especially the Christians and Jews, began to look more and more like the newcomers in dress and behaviour, but the newcomers themselves did not remain unchanged or untouched by the milieu in which they had to live. Many of these officials, the fiery Magyar or the haughty Pole, crossed the bridge with reluctance and entered the town with disgust and, at first, were a world apart, like drops of oil in water. Yet a year or so later they could be found sitting for hours on the *kapia*, smoking through thick amber cigarette-holders and, as if they had been born in the town, watching the smoke expand and vanish under the clear sky in the motionless air of dusk; or they would sit and wait for supper with the local notables on some green hillock, with plum-brandy and snacks and a little bouquet of basil before them, conversing leisurely about trivialities or drinking slowly and occasionally munching a snack as the townsmen knew how to do so well. There were some among these newcomers, officials or artisans, who married in the town and had decided never to leave it.

But for none of the townspeople did the new life mean the realization of what they felt deep down within themselves and had always desired; on the contrary all of them, Moslems and Christians alike, had taken their place in it with many and definite reservations, but these reservations were secret and concealed, whereas life was open and powerful with new and apparently great possibilities. After a longer or shorter period of wavering, most of them fell in with the new ideas, did their business, made fresh acquisitions, and lived according to the new ideas and customs which offered greater scope and, it seemed, gave greater chances to every individual.

Not that the new existence was in any way less subject to conditions or less restricted than in Turkish times, but it was easier and more humane, and those conditions and restrictions were now far away and skilfully enforced, so that the individual did not feel them directly. Therefore it seemed to everyone as if the life around him had suddenly grown wider and clearer, more varied and fuller.

The new state, with its good administrative apparatus, had succeeded in a painless manner, without brutality or commotion, to extract taxes and contributions from the local people which the Turkish authorities had extracted by crude and irrational methods or by simple plunder; and, moreover, it got as much or more, even more swiftly and surely.

Even as the gendarmes, in their own time, had replaced the soldiers and after the soldiers had come the officials, so now, after the officials, came the merchants. Felling began in the forests and brought with it foreign contractors, engineers and workers, and provided varied sources of gain for the ordinary people and traders, with changes in dress and speech. The first hotel was built, of which we shall have much to say later. Canteens and workshops sprang up which had not been known hitherto. Besides the Spanish-speaking Jews, the Sephardi, who had been living in the town for hundreds of years, for they had first settled there about the time when the bridge had been built, there now came the Galician Jews, the Ashkenazi.

Like fresh blood, money began to circulate in hitherto unknown quantities and, which was the main thing, publicly, boldly and openly. In that exciting circulation of gold, silver and negotiable paper, every man could warm his hands or at least 'gladden his eyes', for it created even for the poorest of men the illusion that his own bad luck was only temporary and therefore the more bearable.

Earlier too there had been money and rich people, but these last had been rare and had concealed their money like a snake its legs and had revealed their superiority only as a form of power and protection, difficult both for themselves and for those about them. Now wealth, or what passed as such and was so named, was openly displayed in the form of pleasure and personal satisfaction, therefore the mass of the people could see something of its glitter and its gleanings.

So it was with all else. Pleasures which up till then had been stolen and concealed, could now be purchased and openly displayed, which increased their attraction and the number of those who sought them. What had earlier been unattainable, far-off and expensive (forbidden by law or all-powerful custom) now became, in many cases, possible and attainable to all who had or who knew. Many passions, appetites and demands which till then had been hidden in remote places or left completely unsatisfied could now be boldly and openly sought and fully or at least partially satisfied. In fact even in that there was greater restriction, order and legal hindrance; vices were punished and enjoyments paid for even more heavily and dearly than before, but the laws and methods were different and allowed the people, in this as in all else, the illusion that life had suddenly become wider, more luxurious and freer.

There were not many more real pleasures nor, certainly, more happiness but it was undoubtedly easier to come by such pleasures and it seemed that there was room for everyone's happiness. The old inborn partiality of the people of Višegrad for a carefree life of enjoyment found both support and possibilities of realization in the new customs and the new forms of trading and profit brought by the newcomers. Immigrant Polish Jews with their numerous families based all their business on that. Schreiber opened what he called a 'general store', Gutenplan a canteen for the soldiers, Zahler ran a hotel, the Sperling brothers set up a soda-water factory and a photographer's 'atelier' and Zveker a jeweller's and watchmaker's shop.

After the barracks which had replaced the Stone Han, Municipal Offices were built of the stone that remained, with local administrative offices and courts. After these, the largest building in the town was the Zahler hotel. It was built on the river bank just beside the bridge. That right bank had been supported by an ancient retaining wall which shored up the bank on both sides of the bridge and had been built at the same time. So it happened that both to left and right of the bridge stretched two level spaces, like two terraces above the water. On these open spaces, which were called racecourses by the people of the town, children had played from generation to generation. Now the local authorities took over the left-hand 'racecourse', put a fence round it and made a sort of municipal botanical garden. On the right-hand one the hotel was built. Until then the first building at the entry to the market-place had been Zarije's inn. It was 'in the right place', for the tired and thirsty traveller on entering the town from across the bridge must first light on it. Now it was overshadowed by the great building of the new hotel; the low old inn seemed every day lower and more humiliated as if it had sunk into the earth.

Officially the new hotel had been given the name of the bridge beside which it had been built. But the townspeople named everything according to their own special logic and according to the real significance it had for them. Over the entrance of the Zahler Hotel the inscription 'Hotel zur Brücke', which a soldier skilled in the trade had painted in large letters, quickly faded. The people called it 'Lotte's Hotel' and the name stuck. For the hotel was run by the fat and phlegmatic Jew, Zahler, who had a sickly wife, Deborah, and two little girls, Mina and Irene, but the real proprietress was Zahler's sister-in-law Lotte, a young and very pretty widow with a free tongue and a masculine energy.

On the top floor of the hotel were six clean and well furnished guest-rooms and on the ground floor two public rooms, one large and one small. The large one was patronized by the humbler clients, ordinary citizens, non-commissioned officers and artisans. The smaller one was separated from the larger by large frosted-glass doors on one of which was

written EXTRA and on the other ZIMMER. That was
the social centre for officials, officers and the richer townspeople. One drank and played cards, sang, danced, held
serious conversations and closed business deals, ate well
and slept well in clean sheets at Lotte's. It often happened
that the same group of begs, merchants and officials would
sit from dusk until dawn and still go on until they collapsed
from drink and lack of sleep or grew so tired over their cards
that they could no longer distinguish them (they no longer
played hidden away secretly in that dark stuffy cubby-hole at
Ustamujić's inn). Those who had drunk too much or had lost
all they had Lotte would see off the premises and then turn to
welcome fresh and sober guests eager for drink and play. No
one knew and no one ever asked when that woman rested,
when she slept or ate and when she found time to dress and
freshen herself up. For she was always there (or at least so it
seemed) at everyone's beck and call, always amiable, always
the same and always bold and discreet. Well built, plump,
with ivory-white skin, black hair and smouldering eyes,
she had a perfectly assured manner of dealing with guests,
who would spend freely but were often aggressive and crude
when overcome by drink. She would talk sweetly, boldly,
wittily, sharply, flatteringly with all of them, smoothing
them down. Her voice was hoarse and uneven but could at
moments become a sort of deep and soothing cooing. She
spoke incorrectly, for she never learnt Serbian well, in her
own piquant and picturesque language in which the cases
were never right and the genders uncertain, but which in
tone and meaning was entirely in keeping with the local way
of expression. Every client had her at his disposal to listen to
all his troubles and desires in recompense for the money he
spent and the time he wasted. But these two things, spending money and wasting time, were all he could be sure of;
everyone thought there would be more to it, whereas in fact
there was not. For two generations of the rich spendthrifts
of the town Lotte was a glittering, expensive and cold *fata
morgana* who played with their senses. Those rare individuals

who had supposedly got something out of her, but who were quite unable to say what or how much, were the subject of local stories.

It was no simple matter to know how to deal with the rich and drunk townsmen in whom unsuspected and coarse desires were often roused. But Lotte, that untiring and cold woman of chilled passions, quick intelligence and masculine heart tamed every fury, silenced every demand of uncontrolled men by the inexplicable play of her perfect body, her great cunning and her no less great daring, and always succeeded in maintaining the necessary distance between herself and them, which only served to inflame their desires and increase her own value. She played with these uncontrolled men in their coarsest and most dangerous moments of drunkenness and rage, like a torero with a bull, for she quickly got to know the people with whom she had to deal and easily found the key to their apparently complex demands and all the weak points of those cruel and sensual sentimentalists. She offered them everything, promised much and gave little, or rather nothing at all. For their desires were, of their very nature, such as never could be satisfied and in the end they had to content themselves with little. With most of her guests she behaved as if they were sick men who from time to time had passing crises and hallucinations. In fact it could be said that despite her trade, which of its nature was neither pleasant nor particularly chaste, she was an understanding woman of kind nature and compassionate heart who could help and console whoever had spent more than he should on drinks or had lost more than he should at cards. She sent them all mad, for they were naturally mad, deceived them for they wanted to be deceived and, finally, took from them only what they had already been determined to throw away and lose. In fact she earned very much, took good care of her money and in the first few years had already managed to accumulate a considerable fortune, but she also knew how to 'write off' a debt magnanimously and to forget a loss without a word. She gave to beggars and the sick and with much tact and care helped rich families who had fallen into destitution, orphans and widows from better houses, all those 'ashamed poor' who did not know how to beg and were embarrassed at accepting alms. All this she did with the same skill as she showed in running the hotel and controlling the drunken, lustful and aggressive guests, taking from them all that she could, giving them nothing and yet never refusing them finally or completely.

Men who knew the world and its history often thought that it was a pity that fate had given this woman so narrow and undistinguished a part to play. Had her fate not been what or where it was, who knows what this wise and humane woman, who did not think only of herself and who, predatory yet unselfish, beautiful and seductive but also chaste and cold, ran a small town hotel and emptied the pockets of petty Casanovas, could have been or could have given to the world. Perhaps she would have been one of those famous women of whom history tells and who have controlled the destinies of great families, of courts or states, always turning everything to good.

At that time, about 1885, when Lotte was at the height of her powers, there were rich men's sons who spent days and nights in the hotel, in that special room with doors of milky frosted glass. In the early evening they would drowse there, beside the stove, forgetting in dreams or fatigue where they were or why they were sitting there or what they were waiting for. Profiting by this lull, Lotte would withdraw into a little room on the first floor intended for the potboys, which she had converted into her 'office' where she allowed no one to enter. That tiny room was heaped up with every kind of furniture, with photographs and objects of gold, silver and crystal. There too, hidden behind a curtain, was Lotte's green steel safe and her little desk which was quite invisible beneath a pile of papers, bills, receipts, accounts, Austrian newspapers, cuttings about the money market and lottery lists.

In that tiny overcrowded and stuffy room, whose only window, smaller than any other in the building, looked directly and at short range on to the smallest arch of the bridge, Lotte spent her spare moments and lived that second, hidden part of her life which belonged to her alone.

In it Lotte, in those hours of stolen freedom, read money market reports and studied prospectuses, wrote up accounts, answered letters from banks, made decisions, gave instructions, dealt with bank deposits and made fresh payments. To all those downstairs and to the world in general this was an unknown side of Lotte's work, the true and invisible part of her life. There she cast aside the smiling mask and her face grew hard and her glance sharp and sombre. From this room she corresponded with her very numerous relatives, the Apfelmaiers of Tarnovo, her married sisters and brothers, various nephews and nieces and all the hordes of Jewish poor from Eastern Galicia, now scattered throughout Galicia, Austria and Hungary. She controlled the destinies of a whole dozen Jewish families, entered into the minutest details of their lives, arranged their marrying and giving in marriage, sent healing to the sick, warned and admonished the workshy and spendthrift and praised the thrifty and industrious. She resolved their family quarrels, gave counsel in cases of misunderstanding and doubt, and incited all of them to a more understanding, better and more dignified way of life and at the same time made this more possible and easier for them. For with each of her letters she sent a money order for a sum sufficient to ensure that her counsels were listened to and her advice followed and that certain spiritual or bodily needs be satisfied or shortages avoided. In this raising of the standard of the whole family and the setting of each individual member on his feet, she found her sole real satisfaction and a reward for all the burdens and renunciations of her life. With each member of the Apfelmaier family who rose even a single step in the social scale, Lotte felt that she too rose and in that found her reward for her hard work and the force to struggle onward.

Sometimes it happened that when she came up from the *Extrazimmer* so exhausted or disgusted that she had not even the strength to write or to read letters and accounts she simply went to the little window to breathe the fresh air from the river. Then her gaze would fall on that strong and graceful arch of stone, which filled the entire view, and the swift waters beneath. At dusk or dawn, in sunshine, winter moonlight or the soft light of the stars, that arch was always the same. Its two sides swept upwards, met at the sharp apex and supported one another in perfect and unwavering balance. As the years rolled on that became her only and familiar view, the dumb witness to whom this Jewess with the two faces turned in the moments when she demanded rest and freshness and when in her trade and her family trials, which she always solved for herself, she came to a dead centre and a point where there was no way out.

But such restful moments never lasted long for it always happened that they were interrupted by some cry from the café below; or new clients demanding her presence or some drunkard, awakened and ready for renewed onslaughts, shouting for more drinks, for the lamps to be lighted, for the orchestra to come, and always calling for Lotte. Then she would leave her lair and, carefully locking the door with a special key, go down to welcome the guests, or by her smile and her special vocabulary to smooth down the drunkard like a newly awakened child and to help him to a chair where he could recommence his nightly session of drinking, conversation, song and spending.

Down below everything went wrong when she was not there. The guests squabbled among themselves. A beg from Crnče, young, pale and haggard, spilled every drink brought to him, retorted to everything said to him and insisted on picking quarrels with the staff or the guests. Save for a few short intervals, he had been drinking in the hotel for days past, and lusting after Lotte, but he had drunk so much and longed so greatly that it was clear that some deeper, much greater misery unknown even to himself was driving him on, something greater than his unrequited love for, and unreasonable jealousy of, the lovely Jewess from Tarnovo.

Lotte went up to him fearlessly, easily and naturally.

'What is it, Eyub? What are you making such a noise about?'

'Where have you been? I want to know where you have been . . .' stammered the drunkard in a voice already appeased and looking at her as if she were a vision. 'They are giving me some sort of poison to drink. They are poisoning me, but they do not know that I . . . if I . . .'

'Sit down, sit down quietly,' the woman consoled him, with her white perfumed hands playing just in front of the young beg's face. 'Sit down. I will get you bird's milk to drink if you want it. I will get it for you myself.'

She called the waiter and gave an order in German.

'Don't talk that lingo which I don't understand in front of me; all this *firtzen-fürtzen*, for I . . . well you know me. . . .'

'I know, I know, Eyub: I know no one better than you, Eyub, but you I know. . . .'

'Hm! Who have you been with? Tell me!'

The conversation between the drunk man and the sober woman maundered on without end or meaning, without sense or conclusion, beside bottles of some expensive wine and two glasses; one, Lotte's, always full and the other, Eyub's, continually filled and emptied.

While the young spendthrift stuttered and muttered on in his thick drunkard's voice about love, death, hopeless yearning and similar matters which Lotte knew by heart, for they were the stock in trade of every local drunkard, she rose, went over to the other tables at which sat the other guests who met regularly every evening in the hotel.

At one table was a group of young worthies who had only just begun to frequent the cafés and drink, town snobs for whom Zarije's inn was too boring and too ordinary and who were still intimidated by the hotel. At the others were officials, strangers, with an officer or two who had abandoned the officers' mess for that day and come down to the civilian hotel with the aim of touching Lotte for a quick loan. At a third were the engineers who were building the first forest railway for the export of timber.

In a corner reckoning something sat Pavle Ranković, one of the young but richer merchants and some Austrian or other, a contractor for the railway. Pavle was in Turkish-style dress with a red fez which he did not take off in the café. His small eyes looked like two lighted slits, black and thin in his pale face, but which could widen and become un-usually large and diabolically merry in exceptional moments of joy or triumph. The contractor was in a grey sports suit with high yellow laced boots which reached to his knees. The contractor was writing with a gold pencil attached to a silver chain, and Pavle with a short stub which some wood dealer, a military contractor, had left behind in his shop five years before when buying nails and hinges. They were concluding an agreement for the feeding of the workers on the line. Completely wrapped up in their tasks, they multi-plied, divided and added; they ranged rows of figures, one set visible, on paper, by which each hoped to convince and deceive the other, and another, invisible and in their heads, closely and quickly reckoned, in which each for himself sought for hidden possibilities and profits.

For each of these guests Lotte found the right words, a full smile or even a silent glance full of understanding. Then she returned once more to the young beg who was again beginning to become uneasy and aggressive.

In the course of that night, throughout the whole drink-ing bout, with all its noisy, yearning, lachrymose or coarse phases, which she knew so well, Lotte would find a few moments in which she could go back once again to her room and in the milky light of the porcelain lamp continue her rest or her correspondence, until downstairs some scene would begin again or until they called her down.

Tomorrow was another day, just such another with the same scene of drunken spending, and for Lotte the same anxieties which she must meet with a smiling face and the same task which always seemed an easy yet desperate game.

It seemed incomprehensible and inexplicable how Lotte could manage the quantity and variety of tasks which she carried out day after day and which demanded of her more cunning than a woman has and more strength than any man could muster. But none the less she was able to finish everything, never complaining, never explaining anything to anyone, never speaking about any task which she had just finished or which still awaited her. Despite all that she always managed to find an hour or two every day for Alibeg Pašić. He was the only man whom the town believed had won Lotte's sympathy, genuinely and independently of any source of profit. But he was also the most reserved and taciturn man in the town. The eldest of the four Pašić brothers, he had never married (in the town it was believed that this was be-cause of Lotte), never took part in business or public life. He never drank to excess or went into cafés with men of his own age. He was always of the same mood, universally amiable and restrained towards all, without distinction. Quiet and reserved, he did not avoid society or conversation, yet no one ever remembered any opinion expressed by him or ever repeated anything that he had said. He was sufficient unto himself and completely satisfied with what he was and what he seemed in the eyes of others. He himself had no need to be or to seem in any way different from what he was and no one expected him or asked him to be anything else. He was one of those men who bear their social position as some heavy and noble calling which completely fills their lives; an inborn, great and dignified position justified by itself alone and which cannot be explained, nor denied nor imitated.

With the guests in the large hall Lotte had little contact. That was the job of the waitress Malčika and the 'zahlkelner' Gustav. Malčika was a shrewd Hungarian girl well known to the whole town who looked like the wife of some lion tamer, and Gustav, a small, reddish Czech-German of irascible nature, bloodshot eyes, bow legs and flat feet. They knew all the guests and all the townspeople; they knew who were or were not good payers, their habits when drunk, whom to receive coldly and whom to welcome cordially and whom not to allow to enter at all for 'he was not for this hotel'. They took care that the guests should drink a lot and should pay regularly, but that everything should end smoothly and well since it was Lotte's motto: 'Nur kein Skandal!' If sometimes, exceptionally, it so happened that someone went unexpectedly berserk in his cups or, after already getting drunk at some less reputable café, should force his way into the room, then Milan the servant appeared, a tall broad-shouldered and hairy man from Lika, of gigantic strength, a man who spoke little and did all the odd jobs. He was always correctly dressed as a hotel servant (Lotte saw to that). He was always in his shirt-sleeves, with a brown waistcoat and white shirt, with a long apron of green cloth, with sleeves rolled back summer and winter to show his huge forearms as hairy as two brushes, and with finely waxed moustaches and black hair stiff with perfumed military pomade. Milan was the man who extinguished every scandal at its very conception.

There was a long-established and consecrated tactic for this disagreeable and undesired operation. Gustav kept the furious and drunken guest in conversation until Milan came up behind him; then the *zahlkelner* suddenly moved out of the way and Milan seized the drunkard from behind, one arm round his waist and the other round his neck, so swiftly and skilfully that no one was ever able to see what 'Milan's grip' really was. Then even the strongest of the town ne'er-do-wells flew like a rag-doll through the doors which Malčika held open at just the right moment, and through them into the street. At the same moment Gustav threw his hat, stick and anything else he had with him after him and Milan put the whole weight of his body and clanged down the metal shutter over the door. All this was over in the twinkling of an eye, in close co-operation and smoothly, and almost before the other guests could turn to look, the unwelcome visitor was already in the street and could, if he were really maddened, beat a few times with knife or stone on the roller-blinds as the marks on it showed. But that was not a scandal in the hotel but in the street, a matter for the police who in any case always had a man on patrol in front of the hotel. It had never happened to Milan, as had been the case in other cafés, that the guest knocked anyone down or rushed through the rooms breaking tables and chairs or clung with arms and legs to the door so that afterwards not even a yoke of oxen could drag him away. Milan never brought any excessive zeal or bad humour to his task, no love of fighting or personal prejudice; therefore he finished the matter swiftly and perfectly. A minute after the expulsion he was back at his work in the kitchen or pantry as if nothing had happened. Gustav only went, as if by chance, through the *Extrazimmer* and looking at Lotte, who sat at some table with the better guests, suddenly closed both eyes which meant that something had happened but that everything was now settled. Then Lotte, without stopping her conversation or ceasing to smile, also blinked quickly and imperceptibly, which meant:

'All right, thank you; keep an eye on it!'

There remained only the question of what the expelled guest had drunk or broken. That sum Lotte wrote off in Gustav's accounts when they made up the accounts for the day, which they did late at night behind a red screen.

CHAPTER XV

THERE WERE MANY ways by which the turbulent and skilfully expelled guest, if he were not immediately taken to prison from outside the hotel, could recover his spirits and his strength after the unpleasantness that had befallen him. He could totter to the *kapia* and refresh himself there in the cool breeze from the waters and the surrounding hills; or he could go to Zarije's inn which was only a little farther on, in the main square, and there freely and without hindrance grind his teeth, threaten and curse the invisible hand that had so painfully and definitely thrown him out of the hotel. There, after the solid citizens and artisans who had only come to drink their 'evening nip' or chat with their fellows had dispersed, there was no scandal, nor could there be, for everyone drank as much as he liked or as much as he could pay for, and everyone did and said what he liked. There was no question of asking a guest to spend money and drink up and at the same time behave as if he was sober. Though if anyone went beyond due measure there was always the solid and taciturn Zarije himself whose scowling and bad-tempered face discouraged even the most rabid drunkards and brawlers. He quietened them with a slow movement of his heavy hand and a few words in his gruff voice:

'Hey you there! Drop it! Enough of your fun and games!'

But even in that old-fashioned inn where there were no separate rooms or waiters, for there was always some fellow or other from the Sanjak to serve the drinks, new habits mingled wondrously with the old.

Withdrawn into the farthest corners the notorious addicts of plum-brandy sat silent. They were lovers of shadow and silence, sitting over their plum-brandy as if it were something sacred, hating movement and commotion. With burnt-out stomachs, inflamed livers and disordered nerves, unshaven and uncared for, indifferent to everything else in the world and a burden even to themselves, they sat there and drank and, while drinking, waited until that magical light which shines for those completely given over to drink should at last burst upon them, that joy for which it is sweet to suffer, to decay and finally to die, but which unfortunately appears more and more rarely and shines more and more weakly.

The most noisy and talkative were the beginners, for the most part sons of local worthies, young men in those dangerous years which mark the first steps on the road to ruin, paying that tribute which all must pay to the vices of drink and idleness, some for shorter, others for longer periods. Most of them did not remain long on this road but turned away from it, founded families and devoted themselves to thrift and labour, to the daily life of a citizen with vices suppressed and passions moderated. Only an insignificant minority, accursed and preordained, continued on that road forever, choosing alcohol instead of life, that shortest and most deceptive illusion in this short and deceptive life; they lived for alcohol and were consumed by it, until they became sullen, dull and puffy like those who sat in the corners in the shadows.

Since the new ways of life began, without discipline or consideration, with more lively trade and better wages, as well as Sumbo the Gipsy who had accompanied all the townsmen's orgies for the past thirteen years with his *zurla*, or peasant clarinet, there now came often to the inn Franz Furlan with his accordion. He was a thin reddish man with a gold earring in his right ear, a woodcarver by profession, but too great a lover of wine and music. The soldiers and foreign workmen loved to listen to him.

It often happened that a *guslar* (a player on the one-stringed fiddle) could also be found there, usually some Montenegrin, thin as a hermit, poorly dressed but proud in bearing, famished but ashamed, proud but forced to accept alms. He would sit for some time in a corner, noticeably withdrawn, ordering nothing and looking straight in front of him, pretending to notice nothing and to be indifferent to everything. None the less it could be seen that he had other thoughts and intentions than his appearance revealed. Within him wrestled invisibly many contrary and irreconcilable feelings, especially the contrast between the greatness that he felt in his soul and the misery and weakness of what he was able to express and reveal before others. Therefore he was always a little confused and embarrassed. Proudly and patiently he waited for someone to ask for a song from him and then hesitantly took his *gusle* out of his bag, breathed on it, looked to see if his bow had been slackened by damp, and tuned up, all the while quite clearly wanting to attract as little attention as possible to these technical preliminaries. When he first passed the bow across the string it was still a wavering sound, uneven as a rutted road. But just as somehow or other one passes such a road, so he too through his nose with closed mouth began softly to accompany the sound and complete and harmonize it with his voice. When at last the two sounds merged into a single melancholy even note which wove an accompaniment for his song, the miserable singer changed as if by magic and all his troubled hesitation disappeared, his inner contradictions calmed and all his outer cares forgotten. The *guslar* suddenly raised his head, like a man who throws off the mask of humility, no longer having need to conceal who and what he was, and began unexpectedly in a strong voice his introductory verses:

> 'The sprig of basil began to weep,
> O gentle dew, why fall you not upon me?'

The guests, who until then had pretended not to notice and had been chatting together, all fell silent. At these first verses all of them, Turks and Christians alike, felt the same shiver of undefined desire, of thirst for that dew which lived in themselves as in the song, without distinction or difference. But when immediately afterwards the *guslar* continued softly:

> 'But it was not the sprig of basil . . .'

and lifting the veil from his metaphor began to enumerate the real desires of Turks and Serbs concealed behind these words of dew and basil, there arose divided feelings among the listeners which led them along opposing paths according to what each felt within himself and what each desired or believed. But none the less, by some unwritten rule, they all quietly listened to the end of the song and, patient and enduring, did not reveal their mood, but only looked into the glasses before them where, on the shining surface of the plum-brandy, they seemed to see the victories so desired, the fights, the heroes, the glory and the glitter, such as existed nowhere in the world.

It was liveliest in the inn when the younger men, sons of rich local worthies, sat down to drink. Then there was work for Sumbo and Franz Furlan and Ćorkan the One-Eyed and Šaha the Gipsy.

Šaha was a squinting gipsy woman, a bold virago who drank with anyone who could pay, but never got drunk. No orgy could be imagined without Šaha and her meaty jokes.

The men who made merry with them changed, but Ćorkan, Sumbo and Šaha were always the same. They lived on music, jokes and plum-brandy. Their work lay in the time-wasting of others and their reward in others' spendings. Their true life was at night, especially in those unusual hours when healthy and happy men are asleep, when plum-brandy and hitherto restrained instincts create a noisy and glittering mood and unexpected enthusiasms which are always the same yet seem always new and unimaginably beautiful. They were close-mouthed paid witnesses before whom everyone dared to show himself as he really was, or in the local expression 'to show the blood beneath the skin', without having afterwards either to repent or be ashamed; with them and in their presence everything was permitted which would be considered scandalous by the rest of the world and at home would be sinful and impossible. All these rich, respected fathers and sons of good families could, in their name and to their account, be for a moment what they did not dare show themselves, at least at certain times and at least in a part of their being. The cruel could mock at them or beat them, the cowards could shout insults at them, the prodigal could reward them generously; the vain bought their flattery, the melancholic and moody their jokes and pleasantries, the debauched their boldness or their services. They were an eternal but unrecognized need of the townsmen whose spiritual lives were stunted and deformed. They were rather in the position of artists in a milieu where art is unknown. There are always such people in a town, singers, jesters, buffoons, eccentrics. When one of them grew threadbare or died, another replaced him, for besides the notorious and well known there developed fresh ones to shorten the hours and make gay the lives of new generations. But much time would have to pass before such another appeared as Salko Ćorkan the One-Eyed.

When, after the Austrian occupation, the first circus had come to the town Ćorkan had fallen in love with the tight-rope walker and because of her had behaved so madly and eccentrically that he had been beaten and sent to prison, and the local worthies who had heedlessly led him astray and encouraged him to lose his head had had to pay heavy fines.

Some years had passed since then, the people had grown accustomed to many things and the arrival of strange players, clowns and conjurers no longer excited such universal and contagious sensation as had the first circus, but Ćorkan's love for the dancer was still remembered.

For a long time he had wasted his strength in doing odd jobs by day and by night helping the local begs and rich men to forget their cares in drinking and brawling. So it went from generation to generation. As some sowed their wild oats and withdrew, got married and settled down, other and younger ones who wanted to sow theirs took their places. Now Ćorkan was washed out and old before his time; he was far more often in the inn than at work and lived not so much from what he earned as from free drinks and snacks given him by the customers.

On rainy autumn nights the guests in Zarije's inn were overcome by boredom. Their thoughts came slowly and were all concerned with melancholy and unpleasant matters; speech came with difficulty and sounded empty and irritating, faces were cold, absent or mistrustful. Not even plum-brandy could enliven and improve their mood. On a bench in a corner of the inn Ćorkan drowsed overcome by fatigue, the moist heat and the first glasses of plum-brandy; it was raining cats and dogs.

Then one of the sullen guests at the main table mentioned, as if by chance, the dancer from the circus and Ćorkan's unhappy love. They all glanced at the corner but Ćorkan did not budge and pretended to go on dozing. Let them say what they liked; he had firmly decided that very morning, after a heavy night's drinking, not to reply to their jeering and mocking and not to let them play crude jokes on him as some of them had done the night before in that very inn.

'I believe that they still write to each other,' said one.

'So you see, the bastard writes love-letters to one while another is on her knees to him here!' retorted another.

Ćorkan forced himself to remain indifferent but the conversation irritated and excited him as if the sun were burning his face; his only eye seemed as if it forced itself to open and all the muscles of his face stretched into a happy laugh. He was no longer able to maintain his motionless silence. At first he waved his hand in a casual and indifferent gesture and then said:

'All that is over, over long ago.'

'All over, is it? What a wretch this fellow Ćorkan is! One girl is pining away for him somewhere far away while another is going mad for him here. One is all over, this one here will soon be the same and then it will be the turn of a third. What sort of a fellow are you, you wretch, to turn their heads one after the other?'

Ćorkan leapt to his feet and approached the table. He had forgotten his drowsiness and fatigue and his decision not to be drawn into conversation. With hand on heart he assured the guests that it had not been his fault and that he was not so great a lover and seducer as they made out. His clothes were still damp and his face streaked and dirty, for the colour of his cheap red fez ran, but it was lighted up with a smile of alcoholic bliss. He sat down near the table.

'Rum for Ćorkan!' shouted Santo Papo, a fat and greasy Jew, son of Mente and grandson of Morde Papo, leading hardware merchants.

Ćorkan had recently begun to drink rum instead of plum-brandy whenever he could get hold of it. The new drink was as if made for such as he; it was stronger, quicker in effect and pleasantly different from plum-brandy. It came in small flasks of two *decis* each, with a label showing a young mulatto girl with luscious lips and fiery eyes with a wide straw hat on her head, great golden earrings and the inscription beneath: Jamaica. (That was something exotic for a Bosnian in the last stages of alcoholism bordering on delirium. It was made in Slavonski Brod by the firm of Eisler, Sirowatka and Co.) When he looked at the picture of the young mulatto girl, Ćorkan also felt the fire and aroma of the new drink and at once thought that he would never have been able to know this earthly treasure had he died even a year before. 'And how many such wonderful things there are in this world!' He felt deeply moved at this thought and therefore always waited for a few pensive moments before he opened a bottle of rum. And after the satisfaction of that thought came the delight of the drink itself.

This time too he held the bottle before his face as if conversing with it unheard. But he who had first managed to draw him into conversation asked him sharply:

'Why are you dreaming about that girl, you wretch; are

you going to take her as your wife or play about with her as you did with all the others?'

The girl in question was a certain Paša from Dušče. She was the prettiest girl in the town, poor and fatherless, a seamstress as was also her mother.

During the countless picnics and drinking bouts of the past year the young bachelors had talked and sung much about Paša and her inaccessible beauty. Listening to them Ćorkan had gradually and imperceptibly become enthusiastic too, he himself did not know how or why. So they began to tease him about her.

One Friday they took Ćorkan with them for *ašikovanje* (to flirt with the town girls in the Turkish manner) when from behind the courtyard gates or the window lattices muffled giggles could be heard and the whispering of the unseen girls within. From one courtyard where Paša and her friends lived a sprig of tansy was thrown over the wall and fell at Ćorkan's feet. He hesitated in confusion, not wanting to tread on the flower and undecided whether to pick it up. The youths who had brought him clapped him on the back and congratulated him that Paša had chosen him from so many and had shown him greater attention than anyone else had ever obtained from her.

That night they had gone drinking beside the river under the walnut trees at Mezalin and continued until dawn. Ćorkan sat beside the fire, solemn and withdrawn, now joyous, now pensive. That night they would not let him serve the drinks or busy himself preparing coffee and snacks.

'Don't you know, fellow, the meaning of a sprig of tansy thrown by a girl?' said one of them. 'It means that Paša is telling you: I am pining away for you like this plucked flower; but you neither ask for my hand nor allow me to go to another. That is what it means.'

They all began to talk to him about Paša, so lovely, so chaste, alone in the world, waiting for the hand that should pluck her, and that the hand for which she was waiting was Ćorkan's and his alone.

They pretended to get angry and shouted loudly; how did she come to cast her eye on Ćorkan? Others defended him. As Ćorkan went on drinking he came almost to believe in this marvel, only to reject it at once as an impossibility. In conversation he insisted that she was not the girl for him, and defended himself against their jeers by saying that he was a poor man, that he was growing old and not very attractive, but in his moments of silence he let his thoughts dwell on Paša, her beauty and the joy that she would bring, heedless whether such joy were possible for him or not. In that wonderful summer night which with the plum-brandy and the songs and the fire burning on the grass seemed endless, everything was possible or at least not completely impossible. That the guests were mocking and ridiculing him he knew; gentlemen could not live without laughter, someone had to be their buffoon, it always had been and always would be. But if all this were only a joke, his dream of a marvellous woman and an unattainable love, of which he had always dreamed and still dreamed today, was no joke. There was no joke in those songs in which love was both real and unreal and woman both near and unattainable as in his dream. For the guests all that too was a joke, but for him it was a true and sacred thing which he had always borne within himself and which had become real and indubitable, independent of the guests' pleasure, of wine and of song, of everything, even of Paša herself.

All this he knew well and yet easily forgot. For his soul would melt and his mind flow like water.

So Ćorkan, three years after his great love and the scandal about the pretty German tight-rope walker, fell into a new and enchanted love and all the rich and idle guests found a fresh game, cruel and exciting enough to give them cause for laughter for months and years to come.

That was in midsummer. But autumn and winter passed and the game about Ćorkan's love for the beautiful Paša filled the evenings and shortened the days for the merchants from the market-place. They always referred to Ćorkan as the bridegroom or the lover. By day, overcome by the night's drinking and lack of sleep, when Ćorkan did odd jobs in the shops, fetching and carrying, he was surprised and angered that they should call him so, but only shrugged his shoulders. But as soon as night came and the lamps were lit in Zarije's inn, someone would shout 'Rum for Ćorkan!' and another sing softly as if by chance:

> 'Evening comes and the sun goes down:
> On thy face it shines no longer. . . .'

then suddenly everything changed. No more burdens, no more shrugging of shoulders, no more town or inn or even Ćorkan himself as he was in reality, snuffling, unshaven, clothed in rags and cast-off clothing of other men. There existed a high balcony lit by the setting sun and wreathed in vines, with a young girl who looked for him and waited for the man to whom she had thrown a sprig of tansy. There was still, to be true, the coarse laughter around him and the crude jests, but they were all far away, as in a fog, and he who sang was near him, close by his ear:

> 'If I could grow warm again
> In the sunlight that you bring me. . . .'

and he warmed himself in that sun, which had set, as he had never been warmed by the real sun which rose and set daily over the town.

'Rum for Ćorkan!'

So the winter nights passed. Towards the end of that winter Paša got married. The poor seamstress from Dušče, in all her beauty of not quite nineteen years, married Hadji Omer who lived behind the fortress, a rich and respected man of fifty-five – as his second wife.

Hadji Omer had alread been married more than thirty years. His wife came from a famous family and was renowned for her cleverness and good sense. Their property behind the fortress was a whole settlement in itself, progressive and rich in everything. His shops in the town were solidly built and his income assured and large. All this was not so much due to the peaceable and indolent Hadji Omer, who did little more than walk twice a day to the town and back, as to his able and energetic, always smiling wife. Her opinion was the last word on many questions for all the Turkish women of the town.

His family was in every way among the best and most respected in the town, but the already ageing couple had no children. For long they had hoped. Hadji Omer had even made the pilgrimage to Mecca and his wife had made bequests to religious houses and given alms to the poor. The years had passed, everything had increased and prospered, but in this one most important matter they had received no blessing. Hadji Omer and his good wife had borne their evil fortune wisely and well but there could be no longer any hope of children. His wife was in her forty-fifth year.

The great inheritance which Hadji Omer was to leave behind him was in question. Not only his and his wife's numerous relations had concerned themselves in this matter, but to some extent the whole town also. Some had wanted the marriage to remain childless to the end, while others had thought it a pity that such a man should die without heirs and that his goods should be dispersed among the many relations, and had therefore urged him to take a second, younger wife while there was still a chance of heirs. The local Turks were divided into two camps on the question. But the matter was settled by the barren wife herself. Openly, resolutely and sincerely, as in everything she did, she told her undecided husband:

'The good God has given us everything, all thanks and praise to Him, concord and health and riches, but He has not given us what he gives to every poor man; to see our children and to know to whom to leave what shall remain after us. That has been my bad fortune. But even if I, by the will of God, must bear this, there is no reason why you should do so. I see that the whole market-place is concerning itself with our troubles and urging you to marry again. Well, since they are trying to marry you off, then it is I who want to arrange your marriage for you, for no one is a greater friend to you than I.'

She then told him her plan; as there was no longer any likelihood that they two could ever have children, then he must bring to their home, beside her, a second wife, a younger one, by whom he might still be able to have children. The law gave him that right. She, naturally, would go on living in the house as 'the old *hadjinica*' and see that everything was done properly.

Hadji Omer long resisted and swore that he asked no better companion than she, that he did not need a second wife, but she stuck to her opinion and even informed him which girl she had chosen. Since he must marry in order to have children, then it were best that he take a young, healthy and pretty girl of poor family who would give him healthy heirs and, while she was alive, would be grateful for her good fortune. Her choice fell on pretty Paša, daughter of the seamstress from Dušče.

So it was done. At the wish of his older wife and with her assistance, Hadji Omer married the lovely Paša and eleven months later Paša gave birth to a healthy boy. So the question of Hadji Omer's inheritance was settled, the hopes of many relations were extinguished and the mouths of the market-place sealed. Paša was happy and 'the old *hadjinica*' satisfied, and the two lived in Hadji Omer's house in concord like mother and daughter.

That fortunate conclusion of the question of Hadji Omer's heir was the beginning of Ćorkan's great sufferings. That winter the principal amusement of the idle guests in Zarije's inn was Ćorkan's sorrow at Paša's marriage. The unfortunate lover was drunk as he had never been before; the guests laughed till they cried. They all toasted him and each one of them got good value for his money. They mocked him with imaginary messages from Paša, assuring him that she

wept night and day, that she was pining for him, not telling anyone the real reason for her sorrow. Ćorkan was in
a frenzy, sang, wept, answered all questions seriously and
in detail and bewailed the fate which had created him so
unprepossessing and poor.

'Very well, Ćorkan, but how many years younger are
you than Hadji Omer?' one of the guests would begin the
conversation.

'How do I know? And what good would it do me even if
I were younger?' Ćorkan answered bitterly.

'Eh, if I were to judge by heart and youth, then Hadji
Omer would not have what he has, nor would our Ćorkan
be sitting where he is,' broke in another guest.

It did not need much to make Ćorkan tender and sentimental. They poured him rum after rum and assured him
that not only was he younger and handsomer and more
suitable for Paša but that, after all, he was not so poor as
he thought or as he seemed. In the long nights these idle
men over their plum-brandy thought up a whole history;
how Ćorkan's father, an unknown Turkish officer, whom
no one had ever seen, had left a great property somewhere
in Anatolia to his illegitimate son in Višegrad as sole heir,
but that some relations down there had stayed the execution
of the will; that now it would only be necessary for Ćorkan
to appear in the rich and distant city of Brusa to counter the
intrigues and lies of these false heirs and recover what rightly
belonged to him. Then he would be able to buy up Hadji
Omer and all his wealth.

Ćorkan listened, went on drinking and only sighed. All
that pained him but at the same time did not stop him from
sometimes thinking of himself so, and behaving as a man
who has been cheated and robbed both in this town and over
there somewhere in a distant and beautiful land, the homeland of his supposed father. Those around him pretended
to make preparations for his journey to Brusa. Their jokes
were long, cruel and worked out to the smallest detail. One
night they brought him a supposedly complete passport, and

with coarse jokes and roars of laughter pulled Ćorkan into
the centre of the inn and turned him round and examined
him, in order to inscribe his personal characteristics on it.
Another time they calculated how much money he would
need for his trip to Brusa, how he would travel and where he
would spend his nights. That too passed a good part of the
long night.

When he was sober Ćorkan protested; he both believed
and disbelieved all he was told, but he disbelieved more than
he believed. When he was sober he believed, in fact, nothing
at all but as soon as he was drunk he behaved as though he
believed it all. For when alcohol got a grip on him he no
longer asked himself what was true and what was a lie. The
truth was that, after the second little bottle of rum, he already
seemed to feel the scented air from distant and unattainable
Brusa and saw, a lovely sight, its green gardens and white
houses. He had been deceived, unfortunate in everything
from birth, in his family, his property and his love; wrong
had been done to him, so great a wrong that God and men
were alike his debtors. It was clear that he was not what he
appeared to be or as men saw him. The need to tell all those
around him tormented him more with every glass, though
he himself felt how hard it was to prove a truth that was to
him clear and evident, but against which cried out all that
was in him and about him. After the first glass of rum, he
explained this to everyone, all night long, in broken sentences
and with grotesque gestures and drunkard's tears. The more
he explained the more those around him joked and laughed.
They laughed so long and heartily that their ribs and their
jaws ached from that laughter, contagious, irresistible and
sweeter than any food or drink. They laughed and forgot
the boredom of the winter night, and like Ćorkan drank
themselves silly.

'Kill yourself!' shouted Mehaga Sarač who by his cold
and apparently serious manner best knew how to provoke
and excite Ćorkan. 'Since you have not been man enough
to seize Paša from that weakling of a Hadji Omer, then you

oughtn't to live any longer. Kill yourself, Ćorkan; that is my advice.'

'Kill yourself, kill yourself!' wailed Ćorkan. 'Do you think I haven't thought of that? A hundred times I have gone to throw myself into the Drina from the *kapia* and a hundred times something held me back.'

'What held you back? Fear held you back, full breeches, Ćorkan!'

'No, no. It was not fear, may God hear me, not fear!'

In the general uproar and laughter Ćorkan leapt up, beat his breast and tore a piece of bread from the loaf before him and thrust it under the cold and immobile face of Mehaga.

'Do you see this? By my bread and my blessing, it was not fear, but . . .'

Suddenly someone began to hum in a low voice:

'On thy face it shines no longer. . . .'

Everyone picked up the song and drowned Mehaga's voice shouting at Ćorkan.

'Kill . . . kill . . . your – self . . .!'

Thus singing they themselves fell into that state of exaltation into which they had tried to drive Ćorkan. The evening developed into a mad orgy.

One February night they had thus awaited dawn, driving themselves mad with their victim Ćorkan, and themselves victims of his folly. It was already day when they came out of the inn. Heated with drink, with veins swollen and crackling, they went to the bridge which at the time was coated with a fine layer of ice.

With shouts and gusts of laughter, paying no heed to the few early passers-by, they bet among themselves; who dares to cross the bridge, but along the narrow stone parapet shining under the thin coating of ice.

'Ćorkan dares!' shouted one of the drunkards.

'Ćorkan? Not on your life!'

'Who daren't? I? I dare to do what no living man dares,' shouted Ćorkan beating his breast noisily.

'You haven't the guts! Do it if you dare!'

'I dare, by God!'

'Ćorkan dares!'

'Liar!'

These drunkards and boasters shouted each other down, even though they could scarcely keep their feet on the broad bridge, staggering, teetering and holding on to one another for support.

They did not even notice when Ćorkan climbed on to the stone parapet. Then, suddenly, they saw him floating above them and, drunk and dishevelled as he was, begin to stand upright and walk along the flagstones on the parapet.

The stone parapet was about two feet wide. Ćorkan walked along it swaying now left now right. On the left was the bridge and on the bridge, there beneath his feet, the crowd of drunken men who followed his every step and shouted words at him which he scarcely understood and heard only as an incomprehensible murmur; and on the right a void, and in that void somewhere far below, the unseen river; a thick mist floated upwards from it and rose, like white smoke, in the chill morning air.

The few passers-by halted, terrified, and with wide-open eyes watched the drunken man who was walking along the narrow and slippery parapet, poised above the void, waving his arms frantically to retain his balance. In that company of drunkards a few of the more sober who still had some commonsense watched the dangerous game. Others, not realizing the danger, walked along beside the parapet and accompanied with their cries the drunken man who balanced and swayed and danced above the abyss.

All at once, in his dangerous position, Ćorkan felt himself separated from his companions. He was now like some gigantic monster far above them. His first steps were slow and hesitating. His heavy clogs kept slipping on the stones covered with ice. It seemed to him that his legs were failing him, that the depths below attracted him irresistibly, that he must slip and fall, that he was already falling. But his unusual position and the nearness of great danger gave him strength and hitherto unknown powers. Struggling to maintain his balance, he made more and more little jumps and bent more and more from his waist and knees. Instead of walking he began to dance, he himself did not know how, as free of care as if he had been on a wide green field and not on that narrow and icy edge. All of a sudden he felt himself light and skilful as a man sometimes is in dreams. His heavy and exhausted body felt without weight. The drunken Ćorkan danced and floated above the depths as if on wings. He felt as if a gay strength flowed through his body which danced to an unheard music and that gave him security and balance. His dance bore him onward where his walk would never have borne him. No longer thinking of the danger or the possibility of a fall, he leapt from one leg to the other and sang with outstretched arms as if accompanying himself on a drum.

'Tiridam, tiridam, tiritiritiritiridam, tiridam, tiridam . . .'

Ćorkan sang and himself beat out the rhythm to which dancing surefootedly he made his dangerous crossing. His legs bent at the knees and he moved his head to left and right.

'Tiridam, tiridam . . . hai hai . . .'

In that unusual and dangerous position, exalted above all the others, he was no longer Ćorkan the One-Eyed, the butt of the town and the inn. Below him there was no longer that narrow and slippery stone parapet of that familiar bridge on which he had countless times munched his bread and, thinking of the sweetness of death in the waves beneath, had gone to sleep in the shade of the *kapia*.

No, this was that distant and unattainable voyage of which they had spoken every night at the inn with coarse jokes and mockery and on which now, at last, he had set out. This was that glorious long-desired path of great achievements and that in the distance at the end of it was the imperial city of Brusa with its real riches and his legitimate heritage, the setting sun and the lovely Paša with his son; his wife and his child.

So, dancing in a sort of ecstasy, he passed the parapet around the *sofa* and then the second half of the bridge. When he came to the end he leapt down and looked confusedly about him, in wonder that he had once again landed on the hard and familiar Višegrad road. The crowd which till then had accompanied him with encouragement and jokes welcomed him. Those who had halted in fear rushed up. They began to embrace him, to clap him on the back and on his faded fez. All of them shouted together:

'*Aferim*, bravo, Ćorkan, our falcon!'

'Bravo, hero!'

'Rum for Ćorkan!' yelled Santo Papo in a raucous voice with a Spanish accent, thinking that he was in the inn.

In this general uproar and commotion someone proposed that they stay together and not go home, but go on drinking in honour of Ćorkan's exploit.

Those children who were then in their eighth and ninth years and were that morning hurrying across the frozen bridge to their distant school stopped and stared at the unusual sight. They opened their mouths in astonishment and little clouds of steam rose from them. Tiny, muffled up, with slates and schoolbooks under their arms, they could not understand this game of the grown-ups, but for the rest of their lives they would remember, together with the lines of their own bridge, the picture of Ćorkan the One-Eyed, that man so well known to them who now, transfigured and light, dancing daringly and joyously as if transported by magic, walked where it was forbidden to walk and where no one ever dared to go.

CHAPTER XVI

A SCORE OF years had passed since the first yellow Austrian military vehicles had crossed the bridge. Twenty years of occupation – that is a long sequence of days and months. Each such day and month, taken by itself, seemed uncertain and temporary, but all of them taken together constituted the longest period of peace and material progress that the town ever remembered, the main part of the life of that generation which at the moment of the occupation had just come to years of discretion.

These were years of apparent prosperity and safe gains, even though small, when mothers speaking of their sons said: 'May he live and be healthy and may God grant him easy bread!', and when even the wife of tall Ferhat, the eternal poor man, who lit the municipal street lamps and received for his work the wage of twelve florins a month, said with pride: 'Thanks be to God, even my Ferhat has become an official.'

The last years of the nineteenth century, years without upheavals or important events, flowed past like a broad calm river before reaching its unknown mouth. Judging from them, it seemed as if tragic moments had ceased to disturb the life of the European peoples or that of the town beside the bridge. In so far as they took place now and again in the world outside, they did not penetrate to Višegrad and were far-off and incomprehensible to its townspeople.

Thus, one summer day after so many years, there once more appeared on the *kapia* a white official notice. It was short and this time framed in a heavy black border, and announced that Her Majesty the Empress Elizabeth had died in Geneva, the victim of a dastardly assassination by an Italian anarchist, Lucchieni. The announcement went on to express the disgust and profound sorrow of all the peoples of the great Austro-Hungarian Monarchy and called on them to rally still more closely around the throne in loyal devotion and thereby afford the greatest consolation to the ruler whom fate had so heavily bereaved.

The announcement was pasted up below the white plaque with the Turkish inscription, as had at one time been the proclamation of General Filipović about the occupation, and all the people read it with emotion since it concerned an Empress, a woman, but without any real understanding or deep sympathy.

For a few evenings there were no songs or noisy gatherings on the *kapia* by order of the authorities.

There was only one man in the town whom this news deeply affected. He was Pietro Sola, the only Italian in the town, a contractor and builder, stone-mason and artist, in short a man of all tasks and the specialist of the town. Maistor-Pero, as the whole town called him, had come at the time of the occupation and had remained in the town, marrying a certain Stana, a poor girl of not too savoury a reputation. She was reddish, powerful, twice as big as Maistor-Pero and was considered a woman of sharp tongue and heavy hand with whom it was better not to quarrel. Maistor-Pero himself was a small, bent, good-natured man with mild blue eyes and pendent moustaches. He worked well and earned much. In time he had become a real townsman only, like Lotte, he was never able to master the language and the pronunciation. Because of his skilful hands and gentle nature he was loved by the whole town and his athletically powerful wife led him through life strictly and maternally, like a child.

When, returning home from work grey with stone-dust and streaked with paint, Maistor-Pero read the announcement on the *kapia*, he pulled his hat down over his eyes and feverishly bit on the thin pipe which was always between his teeth. He explained to the more serious and respected citizens whom he met that he, although an Italian, had nothing in common with this Lucchieni and his dastardly crime.

The people listened to him, consoled him and assured him that they believed him and that, furthermore, they had never even thought anything of the sort about him. None the less, he went on explaining to everyone that he was ashamed to be alive, that he had never even killed a chicken in his life how much less a human being, and that a woman and so great a personage. In the end his timidity became a real mania. The townspeople began to laugh at Maistor-Pero's worries, his zeal and his superfluous assurances that he had nothing in common with anarchists and murderers. The urchins of the town at once made up a cruel game. Hidden behind some fence they would shout at Maistor-Pero: 'Lucchieni!' The poor devil defended himself from these shouts as from a swarm of wasps, pulled his hat down over his eyes and fled home to bewail his fate and weep on the broad lap of his Stana.

'I am ashamed, I am ashamed,' sobbed the little man, 'I can't look anyone in the face.'

'Get along, you old fool, what have you to be ashamed of? That an Italian has murdered the Empress? Let the Italian king be ashamed of that! But who are you and what have you done to be ashamed of?'

'I am ashamed to be alive,' wailed Maistor-Pero to the woman, who shook him and tried to instil a little strength and resolution into him and to teach him to walk through the market-place with head held high, not lowering his gaze before anyone.

Meanwhile the older men sat on the *kapia* with stony faces and downcast looks and listened to the most recent news, with details of the murder of the Austrian Empress. The news was no more than an excuse for a discussion on the fate of crowned heads and great men. Surrounded by a group of respectable, inquisitive and unlettered Turkish merchants, the Višegrad schoolmaster Hussein Effendi was holding forth on who and what were anarchists.

The schoolmaster was just as stiff and solemn, clean and neat, as he had been twenty years before when awaiting the arrival of the first Schwabes with Mula Ibrahim and Pop Nikola, both of whom had long been lying in their respective graveyards. His beard was already grey but just as carefully trimmed and rounded, his whole smooth face calm and peaceful, for men with a rigid understanding and hard heart age slowly. The high opinion which he had always had of himself had grown even greater in these last twenty years. It may be said in passing that the case of books on which his reputation as a learned man rested to a great extent was still largely unread, and his chronicle of the town had grown in these twenty years by four pages only, for the older the schoolmaster grew he esteemed himself and his chronicle more and more and the events around him less and less.

Now he spoke in a low voice, slowly as if reading from some obscure manuscript and in a dignified manner, solemnly and severely, using the fate of the infidel Empress only as a pretext which did not in any way enter into the real sense of his interpretation. According to this interpretation (and that too was not his own, for he had found it in the good old books inherited from his one-time teacher, the famous Arap-hodja) those now known as anarchists had always existed and would always exist while the world lasted. Human life was so ordered – and God, the One, the Merciful and Compassionate, had so ordained – that for every dram of good there were two drams of evil and there could be no goodness on this earth without hatred and no greatness without envy, even as there was not even the smallest object without its shadow. That was particularly true of famous people. Beside each one of them, alongside their glory, was also their executioner waiting for his chance and who seized it, sometimes earlier, sometimes later.

'Take for example our countryman Mehmed Pasha who has long been in Paradise,' said the schoolmaster and pointed to the stone plaque above the proclamation, 'who served three Sultans and was wiser than Asaf and who by his power and piety erected even this stone on which we are sitting and who too died by the knife. Despite all his power and wisdom he was unable to escape his appointed hour. Those whom the Grand Vezir hindered in their plans, and they were a great and powerful party, found a way to arm and suborn a mad dervish to kill him, and that just at the moment when he was entering the mosque to pray. With his shabby dervish cloak on his back and a rosary in his hand the dervish barred the way of the Vezir's suite and humbly and hypocritically asked for alms, and when the Vezir was about to put his hand in his pocket to give them to him, the dervish stabbed him. And so Mehmed Pasha died as a martyr to the faith.'

The men listened and blowing the smoke of their cigarettes far from them looked now at the stone plaque with the inscription, now at the white placard bordered by a black line. They listened attentively, though not one of them fully understood every word of the schoolmaster's interpretation. But, looking through their cigarette smoke into the distance, beyond the inscription and the placard, they seemed to see somewhere in the world another and different life, a life of great ascents and sudden falls, in which greatness mingled with tragedy and which in some manner maintained a balance with this peaceful and monotonous existence of theirs on the *kapia*.

But those days passed too. The old order returned to the *kapia* with its usual loud conversations, jokes and songs. Discussions about anarchists ceased; the announcement of the death of that foreign and little-known Empress changed under the influence of sun, rain and dust until at last the wind tore it away and it floated in fragments down river into the void.

For a little longer the ragamuffins of the town shouted 'Lucchieni' after Maistor-Pero without knowing themselves what they meant nor why they did so, but solely from that childish need to tease and torment weak and sensitive creatures. They shouted, and then ceased to shout having found some other amusement. Stana of Mejdan contributed not a little to this result by mercilessly beating two of the most obstreperous of the urchins.

After a couple of months no one mentioned the Empress's death or anarchists any longer. That life at the end of the century, which seemed tamed and domesticated for ever, concealed everything beneath its wide and monotonous course and left among men the feeling that a century was opening of peaceful industry leading into some distant and unattainable future.

That unceasing and irresistible activity to which the foreign administrators seemed condemned and with which the townspeople were with difficulty reconciled, though they had just this to thank for their livelihood and their prosperity, changed many things in the course of those twenty years, in the outward appearance of the town and in the costume and habits of its citizens. It was natural that it would not stop short of the ancient bridge which looked eternally the same.

It was in 1900, the close of that happy century and the beginning of the new, which in the feelings and opinions of many was to be even happier, that engineers came to examine the bridge. The people were already accustomed to such things; even the children knew what it meant when these men in leather overcoats, with breast-pockets stuffed with varicoloured pencils, began to prowl about some hill or some building. It meant that something would be demolished, built, dug up or changed. Only no one was able to imagine what they could be doing with the bridge which to every living soul in the town meant a thing as eternal and unalterable as the earth on which they trod or the skies above them. But the engineers inspected it, measured it and took notes; then they went away and the matter was forgotten. But about midsummer, when the river was at its lowest, contractors and workmen suddenly began to arrive and erect temporary lean-tos to store their tools near the bridge. Already the rumour spread that the bridge was to be repaired, and complicated scaffolding was erected near the piers and on the bridge itself windlass lifts were set up; by their help the workers moved up and down the piers as on some narrow wooden balcony and stopped at places where there was a hole or where tufts of grass had grown out of the stonework.

Every hole was plugged, the grasses plucked out and the birds' nests removed. When they had finished this task, work began on the waterlogged foundations of the bridge. The current was checked and its course altered so that the blackened and corroded stone could be seen, together with an occasional oak beam, worn away but petrified by the waters in which it had been placed 330 years before. The indefatigable lifts lowered cement and gravel, load after load, and the three central piers which were the most exposed to the strong current and the most corroded were filled in at the bases as a rotten tooth is filled at its root.

That summer there were no sessions on the *kapia* and the customary life around the bridge was suspended. The bridge was crowded with horses and carts bringing sand and cement. The shouts of the workmen and the orders of the foremen echoed from all sides. On the *kapia* itself a wooden toolshed was erected.

The townsmen watched the work on the great bridge, astonished and perplexed. Some made a jest of it, others only waved their arms and went their way, and to all of them it seemed that the foreigners were doing this work, as they did all other work, only because they must work at something. Work for them was a necessity and they could not do otherwise. No one said this, but everybody thought it.

All those who had been accustomed to pass their time on the *kapia* now sat outside Lotte's hotel, Zarije's inn or in front of the wooden door-shutters of the shops near the bridge. There they drank coffee and told stories, waiting until the *kapia* should be free again and that attack on the bridge should pass, as a man waits for the end of a shower or some other inconvenience.

In front of Alihodja's shop which was sandwiched between the Stone Han and Zarije's inn, where the bridge could be seen from an angle, two Turks sat from early morning, two hangers-on in the market-place, chatting about everything and more especially about the bridge.

Alihodja listened to them in ill-humoured silence, pensively watching the bridge which was swarming with workmen like ants.

In those twenty years the *hodja* had married three times. Now he had a wife much younger than himself and malicious tongues said that that was the reason he was always ill-humoured until noon. By these three wives he had fourteen children. His house was filled with a noisy crowd all day long and in the market-place they said in jest that the *hodja* did not know all his own children by name. They even told a story of how one of his numerous brood met the *hodja* in a side-street and took his hand to kiss it, but the *hodja* only stroked his head and asked: 'God give you good health, son! And whose may you be?'

To the eye the *hodja* had not changed greatly; only he was now plumper and redder in the face. He no longer moved so briskly and went home up that steep slope to Mejdan more slowly than before, for his heart had been troubling him for some time, even when he was asleep. He had therefore gone to the district doctor, Dr Marovski, the only one of the newcomers whom he recognized and respected. The doctor gave him some drops which did not cure his ills, but helped him to bear them, and from him Alihodja learnt the Latin name for his complaint: *angina pectoris*.

Alihodja was one of the few local Turks who had accepted none of the novelties and changes which the newcomers had brought, either in dress, in customs, in speech or in methods of trade and business. With that same bitter obstinacy with which he had at one time stood out against useless resistance, he had for years stood out against everything that was Austrian and foreign and against everything that was gathering impetus around him. For that reason he sometimes came into conflict with others and had had to pay fines to the police. Now he was a little tired and disillusioned, but he was essentially just the same as he had been when he had argued with Karamanli on the *kapia*, obstinate in everything and at all times; save that his proverbial freedom of speech had turned to sharpness and his fighting spirit into a sullen bitterness which even the most daring words could not express and which was calmed and extinguished only in silence and in solitude.

With time the *hodja* had fallen more and more into a sort of calm meditation in which he had no need of anyone else and found all men hard to endure. Everyone, the idle merchants of the market-place, his customers, his young wife and all that horde of urchins which filled his house with noise, irritated him. Before the sun rose he fled from his house to his shop which he opened before any of the other merchants. There he carried out his morning devotions. There his lunch was brought to him. And when, during the day, conversation, visitors and business bored him, he put up the wooden shutters and withdrew into a tiny closet behind the shop which he called his coffin. That was a secret place, narrow, low and dark; the *hodja* almost filled it when he crawled in. He had there a small stool covered with a rug on which he could sit with crossed legs, a few shelves with empty boxes, old scales and all sorts of rubbish for which there was no room in the shop. In that narrow dark hole the *hodja* could hear through the thin walls of his shop the hum of life in the market-place, the sound of horses' hooves and the cries of the sellers. All that came to him as from another world. He could hear too some of the passers-by who stopped before his closed shop and made malicious jokes and comments about him. But he listened to them calmly, for to him these men were dead and had not realized it; he knew and forgot them in the same moment. Hidden behind those few planks, he felt himself completely protected from all that this life could bring him, this life which in his opinion had long become rotten and proceeded along evil ways. There the *hodja* shut himself in with his thoughts on the destiny of the world and the course of human affairs, and forgot all else, the market-place, his worries about debts and bad tenants, his too young wife whose youth and beauty had suddenly turned into a stupid and malicious ill-humour, and that brood of children which would have been a heavy burden on an Emperor's treasury and about which he thought only with horror.

After he had recovered his spirits and rested there, the *hodja* would again take down his shutters as if he had just come back from somewhere.

So now he listened to the empty chatter of his two neighbours.

'You see now how the times are and the gifts of God; time eats away even stone like the sole of a shoe. But the Schwabes will not have it so and at once mend what is damaged,' philosophized one of them, a well-known lazybones from the market-place, as he sipped Alihodja's coffee.

'While the Drina is the Drina the bridge will be the bridge. Even if they had not touched it, it would last its appointed time. All this expense and all this trouble will serve them nothing,' said the other guest, of the same occupation as the first.

They would have dragged on their idle chatter indefinitely had not Alihodja interrupted.

'And I tell you that no good will come of their interfering with the bridge. You will see, nothing good will come of all this restoration. What they repair today they will tear down again tomorrow. The late lamented Mula Ibrahim used to tell me that he had learnt from ancient books that it is a great sin to meddle with living water, to turn its course aside or change it, were it even for a day or an hour. But the Schwabes do not feel themselves alive unless they are hammering or chiselling something or other. They would turn the whole world upside down if they could!'

The first of the idlers tried to show that, when all was said and done, it was not so bad that the Schwabes should repair the bridge. If it did not prolong its life it would at any rate do it no harm.

'And how do you know that they will do it no harm?' the *hodja* broke in angrily. 'Who told you? Don't you know that a single word can destroy whole cities; how much more then such a babel! All this earth of God's was built upon a word. If you were literate and educated, as you are not, then you would know that this is not a building like any other, but one of those erected by God's will and for God's love; a certain time and certain men built it, and another time and other men will destroy it. You know what the old men say about the Stone Han; there was none other like it in the Empire. Yet who destroyed it? Had it been a question of its solidity and the skill of its construction it would have lasted a thousand years; yet it has melted away as if it had been made of wax and now on the place where it was the pigs grunt and the Schwabes' trumpet sounds.'

'But, as I think, I believe . . .' the idler replied.

'You believe wrongly,' interrupted the *hodja*. 'According to your ideas nothing would ever have been built and nothing destroyed. That has never occurred to you. But I tell you that all this is not good, it foretells evil, for the bridge and for the town and for all of us who are looking at it with our own eyes.'

'He is right. The *hodja* knows best what the bridge is,' broke in the other idler, maliciously recalling Alihodja's one-time martyrdom on the *kapia*.

'You needn't think that I don't know,' said the *hodja* with conviction and at once began, quite calmly to tell one of his stories at which the townsfolk used to mock, but to which they loved to listen time and time again.

'At one time my late lamented father heard from Sheik Dedije and told me as a child how bridges first came to this world and how the first bridge was built. When Allah the Merciful and Compassionate first created this world, the earth was smooth and even as a finely engraved plate. That displeased the devil who envied man this gift of God. And while the earth was still just as it had come from God's hands, damp and soft as unbaked clay, he stole up and scratched the face of God's earth with his nails as much and as deeply as he could. Therefore, the story says, deep rivers and ravines were formed which divided one district from another and kept men apart, preventing them from travelling on that earth that God had given them as a garden for their food and their support. And Allah felt pity when he saw what the Accursed One had done, but was not able to return to the task which the devil had spoiled with his nails, so he sent his angels to help men and make things easier for them. When the angels saw how unfortunate men could not pass those abysses and ravines to finish the work they had to do, but tormented themselves and looked in vain and shouted from one side to the other, they spread their wings above those places and men were able to cross. So men learned from the angels of God how to build bridges, and therefore, after fountains, the greatest blessing is to build a bridge and the greatest sin to interfere with it, for every bridge, from a tree trunk crossing a mountain stream to this great erection of Mehmed Pasha, has its guardian angel who cares for it and maintains it as long as God has ordained that it should stand.'

'So it is, so it is, by God's will!' the two idlers marvelled humbly.

So they passed their time in conversation, as the days passed and the work went on there on the bridge, whence they could hear the squeaking of carts and the pounding of machines mixing sand and cement.

As always, in this discussion too, the *hodja* had the last word. No one wanted to press an argument with him to the end, least of all those two idle and empty-headed fellows who drank their coffee there and knew well that the next day also they would have to pass a good part of their long day in front of his shop.

So Alihodja talked to everyone who stopped before the shutters of his shop, whether on business or just making a call. They all listened to him with mocking curiosity and apparent attention, but no one in the town shared his opinions or had any understanding of his pessimism or his forebodings of evil, which he himself was unable to explain or to support by proof. Furthermore they had for long been accustomed to look on the *hodja* as an eccentric and an obstinate man who now, under the influence of ripening years, difficult circumstances and a young wife, saw the black side of everything and gave everything a special and ill-omened significance.

The townspeople were, for the most part, indifferent to the work on the bridge, as they were towards everything which the newcomers had been doing for years in and about the town. Only the children were disappointed when they saw that the workmen with their wooden ladders went in through that black opening in the central pier, that 'room' in which by universal childish belief the Arab lived. From this place the workmen brought out and tipped into the river countless baskets of birds' droppings. And that was all. The Arab never appeared. The children made themselves late for school, waiting vainly for hours for the black man to emerge from his darkness and strike the first workman in his path, strike him so strongly that he would fly from his moving scaffolding in a great curve into the river. They were furious that this had not happened, and some of the urchins tried to say that it had happened already, but they did not sound convincing and all their 'words of honour' were to no purpose.

As soon as the repair work on the bridge was finished, work began on a water supply. Till then the town had had wooden fountains of which only two on Mejdan gave pure spring water; all the others, down on the level, were connected with water from the Drina or the Rzav and ran cloudy whenever the water of those two rivers was cloudy, and dried up altogether during the summer heats when the river level fell. Now engineers found that this water was unhealthy. The new water was brought right from the mountains on the other side of the Drina, so that the pipes had to be taken across the bridge into the town.

Once again there was noise and commotion on the bridge. Flagstones were raised and a channel dug for the conduits. Fires burnt on which pitch was boiled and lead melted. Hemp was plaited into ropes. The townspeople watched the work with distrust and curiosity as they had always done before. Alihodja was irritated by the smoke which drifted across the square to his shop, and spoke disdainfully of the 'new' unclean water which passed through iron pipes so that it was not fit to drink or for ablutions before prayer and which not even horses would drink if they were still of the good old breed that they once were. He laughed at Lotte who brought the water into her hotel. To everyone willing to listen he proved that the waterworks were only one of the signs of the approaching evil which sooner or later would fall upon the town.

However, next summer, the water supply was installed, even as so many earlier works had been introduced and completed. Clean and abundant water, which was no longer dependent either on drought or flood, flowed into the new iron fountains. Many brought the water into their courtyards and some even into their houses.

That same autumn the building of the railway began. That was a much longer and more important task. At first it did not seem to have any connection with the bridge. But that was only apparent.

This was the narrow gauge railway described in newspaper articles and official papers as the 'eastern railway'. It was to link Sarajevo with the Serbian frontier at Vardište and the boundary of the Turkish-held Sanjak of Novi Pazar at Uvce. The line ran right through the town which was the most important station on it.

Much was said and written about the political and strategic significance of this line, of the impending annexation of Bosnia and Herzegovina, of the further aims of Austro-Hungary through the Sanjak to Salonica and all the complicated problems connected with them. But in the town all these things still seemed completely innocent and even attractive. There were new contractors, fresh hordes of workmen and new sources of gain for many.

This time everything was on a grand scale. The building of the new line, 166 kilometres long, on which were about 100 bridges and viaducts and about 130 tunnels, cost the state seventy-four million crowns. The people spoke of this great number of millions and then looked vaguely into the far distance as if trying in vain to see there this great mountain of money which went far beyond any calculation or imagining. 'Seventy-four millions!' repeated many of them knowingly as if they could count them on the palm of their hand. For even in this remote little town where life in two-thirds of its forms was still completely oriental, men began to become enslaved by figures and to believe in statistics. 'Something less than half a million, or to be accurate 445,782.12 crowns per kilometre.' So the people filled their mouths with big figures but thereby neither became richer nor wiser.

During the building of the railway, the people for the first time felt that the easy, carefree gains of the first years after the occupation existed no longer. For some years past the prices of goods and everyday necessities had been leaping upward. They leapt upward but never fell back and then, after a shorter or a longer period, leapt up again. It was true there was still money to be made and wages were high, but they were always at least twenty per cent less than real needs. This was some mad and artful game which more and more embittered the lives of more and more people, but in which they could do nothing for it depended on something far away, on those same unattainable and unknown sources whence had come also the prosperity of the first years. Many men who had grown rich immediately after the occupation, some fifteen or twenty years before, were now poor and their sons had to work for others. True, there were new men who had made money, but even in their hands the money played like quick-silver, like some spell by which a man might easily find himself with empty hands and tarnished reputation. It became more and more evident that the good profits and easier life which they had brought had their counterpart and were only pieces in some great and mysterious game of which no one knew all the rules and none could foresee the outcome. And yet everyone played his part in this game, some with a smaller some with a greater role, but all with permanent risk.

In the summer of the fourth year the first train, decorated with green branches and flags, passed through the town. It was a moment of great popular rejoicing. The workmen were served with a free luncheon with great barrels of beer. The engineers had their pictures taken around the first loco-motive. All that day travel on the railway was free ('One day free and a whole century for money,' mocked Alihodja at those who took advantage of this first train).

Only now, when the railway had been completed and was working, could it be seen what it meant for the bridge and its role in the life of the town. The line went down to the Drina by that slope below Mejdan, cut into the hillside, cir-cumvented the town itself and then went down to the level ground by the farthest houses near the banks of the Rzav, where the station was. All traffic, both passengers and goods, with Sarajevo and beyond Sarajevo to the rest of the western world, now remained on the right bank of the Drina. The left bank, and with it the bridge, was completely paralysed. Only those from the villages on the left bank now went across the bridge, peasants with their little overburdened horses and bullock carts or wagons dragging timber from distant forests to the station.

The road which led upwards from the bridge across Lijeska to Semeć and thence across the Glasinac and Romania ranges to Sarajevo, and which had at one time echoed to the songs of the drovers and the clatter of packhorses, began to be overgrown with grass and that fine green moss which gradually accompanies the decline of roads and buildings. The bridge was no longer used for travelling, farewells were no longer said on the *kapia* and men no longer dismounted there to drink the stirrup-cups of plum-brandy 'for the road'.

The packhorse owners, their horses, the covered carts and little old-fashioned fiacres by which men at one time travelled to Sarajevo remained without work. The journey no longer lasted two whole days with a halt for the night at

Rogatica, as up till now, but a mere four hours. That was one of those figures which made men stop and think, but they still spoke of them without understanding and with emotion, reckoning up all the gains and savings given them by speed. They looked with wonder at the first townsmen who went one day to Sarajevo, finished their business, and returned home again the same evening.

Alihodja, always mistrustful, pig-headed, plain-spoken and apart in that as in all else, was the exception. To those who boasted of the speed with which they could now finish their business and reckoned how much time, money and effort they had saved, he replied ill-humouredly that it was not important how much time a man saved, but what he did with it when he had saved it. If he used it for evil purposes then it had been better he had never had it. He tried to prove that the main thing was not that a man went swiftly but where he went and for what purpose and that, therefore, speed was not always an advantage.

'If you are going to hell, then it is better that you should go slowly,' he said curtly to a young merchant. 'You are an imbecile if you think that the Schwabes have spent their money and brought their machine here only for you to travel quickly and finish your business more conveniently. All you see is that you can ride, but you do not ask what the machine brings here and takes away other than you yourself and others like you. That you can't get into your head. Ride then, my fine fellow, ride as much as you like, but I greatly fear that all your riding will lead only to a fall one of these fine days. The time will come when the Schwabes will make you ride where you don't want to go and where you never even dreamt of going.'

Whenever he heard the engine whistle as it rounded the bends on the slope behind the Stone Han, Alihodja would frown and his lips would move in incomprehensible murmurs and, looking out slantwise from his shop at the unchanging bridge, he would go on elaborating his former idea; that the greatest buildings are founded by a word and that the peace and existence of whole towns and their inhabitants might depend upon a whistle. Or so at least it seemed to this weakened man who remembered much and had grown suddenly old.

But in that as in all else Alihodja was alone in his opinions like an eccentric and a dreamer. In truth the peasants too found it hard to grow accustomed to the railway. They made use of it, but could not feel at ease with it and could not understand its ways and habits. They would come down from the mountains at the first crack of dawn, reaching the town about sunrise, and by the time they reached the first shops would begin asking everyone they met:

'Has the machine gone?'

'By your life and health, neighbour, it has gone long ago,' the idle shopkeepers lied heartlessly.

'Really gone?'

'No matter. There'll be another tomorrow.'

They asked everyone without stopping for a moment, hurrying onwards and shouting at their wives and children who lagged behind.

They arrived at the station running. One of the railwaymen reassured them and told them that they had been misinformed and that there were still three good hours before the departure of the train. Then they recovered their breath and sat down along the walls of the station buildings, took out their breakfasts, ate them, and chatted or dozed, but remained continually alert. Whenever they heard the whistle of some goods engine they would leap to their feet and bundle their things together, shouting:

'Get up! Here comes the machine!'

The station official on the platform cursed them and drove them out again:

'Didn't I just tell you that it was more than three hours before the train comes? What are you rushing for? Have you taken leave of your senses?'

They went back to their old places and sat down once more, but still suspicious and distrustful. At the first whistle or even only at some uncertain noise they once more leaped to their feet and crowded on to the platform, only to be repulsed once more to wait patiently and listen attentively. For however much the officials told them and explained to them, they could not get it into their heads that the 'machine' was not some sort of swift, mysterious and deceitful contraption invented by the Schwabes which slipped away from anyone inattentive enough to wink an eye and which had only one idea in its mind: how to cheat the peasant and leave without him.

But all these things, the peasants' stupidity and Alihodja's bad-tempered grumbling, were things of no importance. The people laughed at them and at the same time soon grew accustomed to the railway as they had to everything else that was new, easy and pleasant. They still went out to the bridge and sat on the *kapia* as they had always done, and crossed it on their everyday affairs, but they travelled in the direction and manner imposed on them by the new times. Quickly and easily they grew reconciled to the idea that the road across the bridge no longer led to the outside world and that the bridge was no longer what it once had been: the link between East and West. Better to say, most of them never thought about it.

But the bridge still stood, the same as it had always been, with the eternal youth of a perfect conception, one of the great and good works of man, which do not know what it means to change and grow old and which, or so it seemed, do not share the fate of the transient things of this world.

CHAPTER XVII

BUT THERE, BESIDE the bridge, in the town bound to it by fate, the fruits of the new times were ripening. The year 1908 brought with it great uneasiness and a sort of obscure threat which thenceforward never ceased to weigh upon the town.

In fact this had begun much earlier, about the time of the building of the railway line and the first years of the new century. With the rise in prices and the incomprehensible but always perceptible fluctuations of government paper, dividends and exchanges, there was more and more talk of politics.

Till then the townspeople had concerned themselves exclusively with what was near to them and well known, with their gains, their pastimes and, in the main, only with questions of their family and their homes, their town or their religious community, but always directly and within definite limits, without looking much ahead or too far into the past. Now, however, more and more frequently in conversation questions arose which lay farther away, outside this narrow circle. In Sarajevo religious and national organizations and parties were founded, Serbian and Moslem, which immediately set up their sub-committees in Višegrad. New papers were started in Sarajevo and began to arrive in the town. Reading rooms and choral societies were founded; first Serbian, then Moslem and finally Jewish. Students from the secondary schools and the universities at Vienna and Prague returned to their homes in the vacations and brought with them new books, pamphlets and a new manner of expression. By their example they showed to the younger townsfolk that they did not always have to keep their mouths shut and keep their thoughts to themselves as their elders had constantly believed and affirmed. Names of new organizations began to come into the conversation, religious and national, on wide bases and with bold aims, and finally workers' organizations also. Then the word 'strike' was heard in the town for the first time. The young apprentices became more serious. In the evenings on the *kapia* they carried on conversations incomprehensible to others and exchanged little paper-backed pamphlets with such titles as: 'What is socialism?', 'Eight hours of work, eight hours of rest, eight hours of self-improvement' and 'Aims and ways of the world proletariat'.

There was talk to the peasants on the agrarian problem, the relations between serfs and landowners, of Turkish feudal landholding. The peasants listened, looking a little aside with imperceptible movements of their moustaches and little frowns, as if trying to remember all that was said in order to think it over later, either alone or in discussion with their fellows.

There were plenty of citizens who continued to keep a discreet silence and who rejected such novelties and such boldness of thought and language. But there were many more, especially among the younger ones, the poor and the idle, who accepted all this as a joyful confirmation which corresponded to their inner needs long kept silent, and brought into their lives that something great and exciting which had up till then been lacking. When reading speeches and articles, protests and memoranda issued by party or religious organizations, each one of them had the feeling that he was casting off chains, that his horizon was widening, his thoughts freed and his forces linked with those of men more distant and with other forces never thought of until then.

Now they began to look at one another from a point of view they had never before taken. In short, it seemed to them, in this matter also, that their life had become more expansive and richer, that the frontiers of the impermissible and the impossible had moved back and that there opened before them prospects and possibilities such as had never before existed, even for him who until then had never possessed them.

In actual fact, even now they had nothing new nor were they able to see anything better, but they were able to look beyond the everyday life of the town, and that gave them the exciting illusion of space and power. Their habits had not changed, their ways of life and the forms of mutual relations remained the same, only that in the time-honoured ritual of sitting idly over coffee, tobacco and plum-brandy, bold words and new methods of conversation had been introduced. Men began to leave their old associates and form new groups, to be repelled or attracted according to new criteria and new ideas, but under the stress of old passions and ancestral instincts.

Now too, external events began to find their echo in the town. First there were the dynastic changes of 1903 in Serbia and then the change of régime in Turkey. The town which was right on the Serbian frontier and not far from the Turkish boundaries, linked by deep and invisible bonds to one or other of these two lands, felt these changes, lived them and interpreted them, although nothing of all that was thought and felt about them was ever said publicly or talked of openly.

The activities and pressure of the authorities began to be felt more openly in the town, first the civil authorities and then the military as well. And that in quite a new form; at first they had paid attention to who did what and how he behaved, and now they inquired about who thought what and how he expressed his opinions. The number of gendarmes in the surrounding villages along the frontier was gradually increased. A special Information Officer, a man from the Lika, arrived at the local headquarters. The police arrested and fined youths for imprudent declarations or for singing prohibited Serbian songs. Suspected foreigners were deported; and differences of opinion led to arguments and quarrels among the citizens themselves.

With the introduction of the railway travelling became quicker and the transport of goods easier, and somehow at about the same time events too quickened their pace. The townspeople did not notice this, for the quickening was gradual and all of them were involved in it. They became accustomed to sensations; exciting news was no longer something rare and unusual but an everyday food and a real need. The whole of life seemed to be hastening somewhere, suddenly speeded up, as a freshet quickens its pace before it breaks into rapids, rushes over steep rocks and becomes a cascade.

Only four years had passed since the arrival of the first train in the town when, one October morning, a huge white proclamation was posted on the *kapia*, beneath the plaque with the Turkish inscription. It was put up by the municipal official Drago. At first only the idlers and children gathered round it and then, later, the rest of the citizens. Those who knew how to read deciphered the proclamation, spelling it out and halting at the foreign expressions and unfamiliar phrasing. The others listened in silence and with downcast eyes and after listening for a while dispersed without looking up, stroking their beards and moustaches as if to brush away words which had never been spoken.

After the noon prayer Alihodja too came, placing a bar across his shop front as a sign that the shop was closed. This time the proclamation was not written in Turkish also, so that the *hodja* could not read it. A boy was reading the proclamation aloud, quite mechanically, as if at school.

'PROCLAMATION
to the People of Bosnia and Herzegovina.

'We, Franz Joseph, Emperor of Austria, King of Bohemia etc. and Apo-apo-apo-stolic King of Hungary, to the inhabitants of Bosnia and Herzegovina: When a gen-gener-generation ago Our Armies crossed the frontiers of Your lands . . .'

Alihodja felt his right ear tingling beneath his white turban and, as if it had been the day before, his quarrel with Karamanli flashed before his eyes, the outrage then committed on him, the red cross which swam before his eyes filled with tears, while the Austrian soldier carefully extracted the nail, and the white placard with the proclamation then addressed to the people.

The youth went on:

'An ass-ass-assurance was then given You that they had not come as enemies but as Your friends with the avowed intention of rooting out all the evils which had for years op-op-oppressed You.

'That word given to You in that crit-critical moment . . .'

Everyone shouted at the inexpert reader who, blushing and embarrassed, slipped away into the crowd. In his place came some unknown man in a leather jacket, who seemed as if he were only waiting for his chance, who began to read quickly and fluently as if it were a prayer that he already knew by heart.

'That word given to You in that critical moment has been honestly kept. Our Government has always seriously concerned itself and worked to maintain peace and order, to lead Your Fatherland towards a happier future.

'And We, to Our great joy, dare freely to say: the seed which has been sown in the furrows of the soil so prepared has produced a rich harvest. You too must feel those facts as a blessing; that in place of violence and tyranny have come order and security, that work and life have developed continuously, that the ennobling influence of its work has multiplied opportunities for culture and that under the protection of a regular administration every man may enjoy the fruits of his labours.

'It is the solemn duty of all of Us to continue along this way.

'Having this aim constantly before Our eyes, We hold that the time has come to give the inhabitants of these two lands a fresh proof of Our faith in their political maturity. In order to raise Bosnia and Herzegovina to a higher level of political life, We have decided to grant constitutional institutions – such as will answer to their present conditions and their common interests – to both these lands and to give in this manner a legal basis for the representation of their wishes and interests.

'Let Your voices also be heard when in the future decisions will be made touching the affairs of Your country which will have, as it has had up till now, its separate administration.

'But the first necessary condition for the introduction of this national constitution is the clear and indubitable definition of the legal position of both these lands. Starting from this principle and bearing in mind those bonds which in olden times existed between Our glorious predecessors on the Throne of Hungary and these lands, We extend Our rights of sovereignty over Bosnia and Herzegovina and We desire that these lands accept the order of succession which is valid for Our House.

'Thus the inhabitants of both lands will become participators in all these benefits which will assure them the lasting consolidation of those bonds which, up to the present, have linked them to Us. The new state of affairs will be the guarantee that culture and prosperity will continue to find a sure home in Your country.

'Bosnians and Herzegovinians!

'Among the countless cares which surround Our Throne, that which We shall have for Your material and moral prosperity will not be the least. The supreme conception of the equality of all before the law, the participation in the making of laws and the administration of the country, an equal protection afforded to all faiths, languages and national characteristics – all these supreme benefits You will enjoy in full measure.

'The freedom of the individual and the good of the community will be the guiding star of Our Government for both these lands . . .'

With mouth half open and head lowered, Alihodja listened to these words, for the most part unfamiliar or unknown to him, and even those words which were not of themselves unfamiliar became in that context in some manner queer and incomprehensible. 'Seed . . . sown in the

furrows of the soil so prepared . . . first and necessary condition for the introduction of this local constitution; clear
and indubitable definition of legal position . . . guiding star
of Our Government!' Yes, those were the 'Imperial words'
once again! Each one of them opened before the *hodja*'s inner
vision now some distant, extraordinary and dangerous horizon, now some sort of curtain which fell, black and leaden,
just before his eyes. So, first one thing and then the other;
either he saw nothing or he saw something that he did not
understand and which presaged no good. In this life nothing is impossible and every wonder possible. It could even
happen that a man might listen carefully and yet understand
nothing in detail while at the same time, when all those
details were taken together, he could realize completely and
understand perfectly! That seed, that star, those cares about
the throne; all those things might just as well have been in
some foreign language, yet none the less the *hodja*, or so it
seemed to him, could understand what they were intended
to mean and what they wished to convey. These Emperors
had for the past thirty years shouted across the lands and
cities and over the heads of the peoples; yet every word in
every proclamation of every Emperor was pregnant with
meaning. For these countries were broken into fragments
and in these countries heads rolled because of these words.
So they spoke of 'seed . . . stars . . . cares of the throne' lest
they call things by their real names and speak what was the
fact; that lands and provinces and, with them, living men
and their habitations passed from hand to hand like small
change; that a well-intentioned true-believing man could no
longer find peace on this earth, no more than he could find
the little he needed for this short life; that his position and his
goods changed independently of himself and contrary to his
wishes and his best intentions.

Alihodja listened and he had continually the impression
that these words were the same words of thirty years ago; he
felt the same leaden heaviness in his breast, the same message
that the Turkish times were ended and that 'the Turkish

candle was burned out', but that it was necessary to repeat them for they would not understand or realize them, but deceived themselves and pretended to know nothing of them.

'You will therefore show Yourselves worthy of the confidence placed in You, so that the noble harmony existing between ruler and people, that most precious gage of all state progress, will always accompany Our common labours.

'Given in our Royal and Capital City of Budapest.

Franz Joseph.'

The man in the leather jacket suddenly ceased reading and shouted unexpectedly:

'Long live His Majesty the Emperor!'

'Long life,' shouted tall Ferhat, the municipal lamplighter, as if by order.

All the others dispersed at the same moment in silence.

Before dark that day the great white proclamation was torn down and thrown into the Drina. The next day some Serbian youths were arrested on suspicion and a fresh copy of the white proclamation was put up on the *kapia* and a local gendarme posted there to guard it.

Whenever a government feels the need of promising peace and prosperity to its citizens by means of a proclamation, it is time to be on guard and expect the opposite. Towards the end of October, the army began to arrive, not only by train but also along the old deserted road. As it had done thirty years before, it came down the steep slope from Sarajevo and crossed the bridge into the town, with arms and commissariat. There were units of all kinds except cavalry. All the barracks were full. They camped under canvas. Fresh units were continually arriving, stayed a few days in the town and were then posted to the villages along the Serbian frontier. The soldiers were mainly reservists, of various nationalities, with plenty of money. They made their minor personal purchases in the shops and bought fruit and sweetmeats at the street-corners. Prices leapt. Hay and oats completely

disappeared. Fortifications began to be built on the hills surrounding the town. And on the bridge itself a very strange
task began. In the middle of the bridge, just beyond the *kapia*
as one came from the town to go to the left bank of the
Drina, workmen specially brought for the job began to drill
a hole about a yard square in one of the piers. The spot where
they worked was concealed under a green tent, from beneath
which continual hammering could be heard as they went
deeper and deeper. The stone excavated was at once thrown
over the parapet into the river. But however much the work
was concealed, it was soon known in the town that the bridge
was being mined, that is to say that a deep opening was being
dug through one of the piers, right to the foundations, and
that explosives would be placed in it in case war broke out
and it was found necessary to destroy the bridge. Long iron
ladders led down into the opening and when everything was
finished an iron manhole cover was placed over it. Within
a few days this cover could no longer be distinguished from
the stones and dust. Carts passed over it, horses trotted by,
and the townsmen hurried on their business without giving
a thought to the mine and the explosives beneath. Only
the children on their way to school halted for a moment at
this spot, tapped inquisitively at that iron cover, trying to
guess what was beneath it. They made up tales of some Arab
hidden in the bridge, and argued among themselves about
what an explosive was, what it did and whether it could ever
destroy so great a building.

Among the grown-ups, only Alihodja prowled around
and gazed sombrely and suspiciously both at the green tent
while the work was going on and at the iron cover which
remained on the bridge after it had been finished. He listened to all that was said or whispered; that a hole as deep
as a well had been made in that pier and explosives placed
in it, and that it was connected by an electrical lead to the
bank so that the commandant could at any time of the day
or night destroy the bridge right in the middle as though
it were made of sugar and not of stone. The *hodja* listened,

shook his head, thought it over by day when he retired to his 'coffin' and by night in bed when he should have been asleep; now he believed, now he rejected such an idea as mad and godless, but he worried about it continually so that even in his sleep the one-time *mutevelis* of Mehmed Pasha's *vakuf* appeared before him and asked him severely what all this was and what were they doing to the bridge. He turned his troubles over and over in his mind. He did not want to ask anyone in the market, considering that for a long time past there had been no one with whom a sensible man could consult or converse reasonably, since all the people had either lost their senses and their reputations or were just as embittered and confused as he himself was.

None the less, he soon found an opportunity to learn more about it. One of the Branković begs from Crnće, Muhamed, who had done his army service in Vienna, had stayed there as a long-service man and been promoted to sergeant-major (he was the grandson of that Shemsibeg who after the occupation had shut himself up in Crnće and died of sorrow, and who was still quoted by the older Turks as an unattainable example of moral grandeur and logic). Muhamed-beg had that year come home on leave. He was a big tall man of reddish complexion, dressed in an impeccable dark-blue uniform with yellow rank-badges, red piping and little silver stars on his lapel, with white kid-gloves on his hands and red fez on his head. Courteous, smiling, irreproachably clean and neat, he walked in the market-place, his long sword tapping gently on the cobbles, greeting everyone amiably and confidently like a man who has eaten the bread of the Emperor, who has no doubt of his own importance or any reason to be afraid of others.

When this Muhamed-beg came to his shop, asked about his health and sat down to drink a cup of coffee, Alihodja took the opportunity of asking him, as an 'imperial man' who lived far from the town, for an explanation of the cares that oppressed him. He told him what the trouble was, what had been done on the bridge and what they were saying in

the town, and asked him if such a thing were possible and
whether they could plan the destruction of a bequest of such
universal benefit as this one.

As soon as he had heard what was in question, the sergeant-
major suddenly became serious. His broad smile disappeared
and his ruddy clean-shaven face took on a wooden expression as if he were on parade at the moment of the command:
attention. He was silent for a moment as if in indecision and
then replied in a sort of hushed voice.

'There is something in all you say. But if you really want
my advice, then it is best not to inquire about this or speak
of it, for it comes under the head of military preparedness,
official secrets and so forth and so on.'

The *hodja* hated all the new expressions and especially that
'and so forth and so on'. It was not only that the words grated
on his ears, but he felt clearly that, in the speech of these
strangers, it took the place of an unspoken truth and that all
that had been said before meant nothing at all.

'In the Name of God, don't stuff me up with their . . .
"and so forth and so on", but tell me and explain, if you can,
what they are doing to the bridge. There can be no secret
about that. In any case what sort of a secret is that, if even the
schoolchildren talk about it?' the *hodja* interrupted angrily.
'What has the bridge to do with their war?'

'It has, Alihodja; it has very much to do with it,' said
Branković, once again smiling.

And he explained to Alihodja amiably but a little con-
descendingly, as if speaking to a child, that all this was provided for in the rules of the service, that this was the duty
of engineers and bridge-builders, and that in the Imperial
Army everyone knew only his own job and did not concern
himself in the affairs of some other branch.

The *hodja* listened to him, listened and watched, but did
not understand very much. Finally, he could no longer hold
himself in.

'All that is very fine, my fine fellow, but do they know
that this is a Vezir's bequest, built for the good of his soul

and the glory of God and that it is a sin to take even a stone from it?'

The sergeant-major only waved his hands, shrugged his shoulders, pursed his lips and closed his eyes, so that his whole face assumed a crafty and obsequious expression, unmoving, blind, deaf, such as men can only achieve by long years of practice in old-fashioned and decaying administrations in which discretion has long degenerated into insensibility and obedience into cowardice. A page of white unsullied paper is eloquent compared with the dumb caution of such a face. A moment later, the Emperor's man opened his eyes, let fall his hands, composed his face and once again resumed his usual appearance of confidence and serenity in which Viennese good-humour and Turkish courtesy met and mingled like two waters. Changing the subject and praising with well-chosen words the *hodja*'s health and youthful appearance, he took his leave with the same inexhaustible amiability with which he had come. The *hodja* remained confused and un-certain in himself but in no way less troubled than he had been before. Lost in his thoughts he looked out from his shop at the shining loveliness of that first day of March. Opposite him, a little to the side, stood the eternal bridge, everlast-ingly the same; through its white arches could be seen the green, sparkling, tumultuous waters of the Drina, so that they seemed like some strange diadem in two colours which sparkled in the sun.

CHAPTER XVIII

THE TENSION KNOWN to the outside world as 'the annexation crisis', which had thrown its ill-omened shadow over the bridge and the town beside it, rapidly subsided. Somewhere out there, by diplomacy and discussions between the interested parties, a peaceful solution had been found.

The frontier, always so inflammable, for once did not flare up. The army which had filled the town and the frontier villages in the first days of spring began to withdraw. But as always the changes which the crisis had brought remained after it had passed. The permanent garrison in the town was much larger than it had been before. The bridge remained mined. But no one gave it a thought except Alihodja Mutevelić. The piece of land on the left flank of the bridge above the ancient retaining wall, which had been the town park, was taken over by the military authorities. The fruit trees in the centre of the park were cut down and a fine building erected. That was the new officers' mess, for the former mess, a small one-storeyed building up at Bikavac, was now too small for the increased number of officers. So that now, on the right of the bridge was Lotte's hotel and on the left the officers' mess, two white almost identical buildings and between them the square, surrounded by shops and, on a small rise above the square, the great barracks which the people still called the Stone Han in memory of Mehmed Pasha's caravanserai which had once been there but had now disappeared without trace.

Prices, which had leapt up the previous autumn because of the large number of soldiers, remained unchanged, with much greater likelihood of further rises than of returning to their former level. That year a Serbian and a Moslem bank were opened. The people made use of money-orders like medicines. Now everybody incurred debts more freely. But the more money a man had the more he needed. Only to those who spent more than they gained did life seem easy and good. But the merchants and business men were worried. Terms of payment become shorter than ever. Good and reliable customers were fewer and fewer. The number of articles whose price was higher than the people could afford to pay was ever greater. Business was on a small scale, and cheaper and cheaper types of goods were in demand. Only bad payers bought freely. The only sure and safe business was army contracting or work for some government institution, but not everyone could get it. State taxes and municipal dues became larger and more numerous; the strictness of the collectors increased. One could feel from afar the unhealthy fluctuations of the exchanges. The profits which arose from them went into unseen hands, while the losses reached even the most remote corners of the monarchy and struck the retail traders, both as sellers and consumers.

The general feeling in the town was neither more serene nor more calm. That sudden slackening of tension did not result in a real appeasement either among the Serbs or the Moslems; it left to the first a concealed disillusionment, to the second distrust and fear of the future. The expectation of great events began to grow once more, without visible reason or direct cause. The people hoped for something or were afraid of something (in actual fact some hoped while others feared) and looked on everything in the light of those hopes and fears. In a word, men's hearts were disturbed, even among the simple and illiterate, especially among the younger people, and no one was any longer satisfied with the monotonous sort of life which had dragged on for years. Everyone wanted more, asked for better or trembled in fear of worse. The older people still regretted that 'sweet tranquillity' which in Turkish times had been regarded as the main aim of existence and the most perfect expression of public and private life, and which had still existed in the first decades of the Austrian administration. But there were few of these. All the others demanded an animated, noisy and exciting life. They wanted sensations or the echo of sensations or at least variety, noise and excitement which would give the illusion of sensation. That desire changed not only the state of men's minds but even the external appearance of the town. Even that time-honoured and established life on the *kapia*, that life of quiet conversation and peaceful meditations, simple jokes and lovesick songs between the waters, the sky and the mountains, began to change.

The coffee merchant obtained a gramophone, a clumsy wooden box with a big tin trumpet in the shape of a bright blue flower. His son changed the records and the needles and was continually winding this raucous contraption which echoed from both banks and made the *kapia* quiver. He had been forced to get it in order not to be left behind by his competitors, for now gramophones could be heard not only at meetings and in the reading rooms but even in the humblest cafés where the guests sat under a lime tree, on the grass or on brightly-lit balconies, and talked with few words and in low voices. Everywhere the gramophone ground and churned out Turkish marches, Serbian patriotic songs or arias from Viennese operettas, according to the tastes of the guests for whom it played. For men would no longer go where there was neither noise, glitter nor movement.

Newspapers were read avidly, but superficially and hastily; everyone looked only for the sensational news printed in large type on the front page. There were few who read the articles or the news in small type. All that took place was accompanied by clamour and the brilliance of big words. The younger people did not think that they had lived that day if by the evening their ears were not singing or their eyes had not been dazzled by what they had heard or seen in the course of the day.

The *agas* and *effendis* of the town came to the *kapia*, serious and outwardly indifferent, to listen to the latest news about the Turco-Italian war in Tripoli. They listened avidly to all that was written in the papers about the heroic young Turkish major, Enver Bey, who beat the Italians and defended the Sultan's lands like a descendant of the Sokollis or the Kuprulus. They frowned at the raucous music of the gramophone, which prevented their thinking, and, without showing it, trembled deeply and sincerely for the fate of the distant Turkish province in Africa.

It chanced that just then Pietro the Italian, Maistor-Pero, returning from work clothed in his linen overall, white with stone-dust and stained with paint and turpentine, crossed the bridge. He had grown old and bent and even more humble and timid. As at the time when Lucchieni assassinated the Empress, it seemed, by some logic incomprehensible to him, that he was again guilty of something which his Italian fellow countrymen, with whom for many years he had had no contact, had done somewhere in the outer world. One of the Turkish youths shouted:

'So you want Tripoli, you bastard! You there, I mean!' and made obscene gestures at him.

But Maistor-Pero, bent and tired, with his tools under his arm, only pulled his hat further over his eyes, feverishly bit on his pipestem and hurried home to Mejdan.

There his Stana was waiting for him. She too had grown older and had lost some of her physical strength, but she was still a formidable and outspoken woman. He complained bitterly to her about the young Turks who said things they should not have said and had asked him about Tripoli, which until a few days ago he had not even known existed. But Stana, as always, would not understand him or console him, but went on saying that it was he himself who was at fault and even deserved to have insults shouted at him.

'If you were a real man, which you are not, you would have hit their ugly phizzes with your chisel or your hammer. Then those ragamuffins would not even think of jeering at you but would get to their feet when you cross the bridge.'

'Eh, Stana, Stana,' said Maistor-Pero good-humouredly and a little sadly, 'how could a man hit another in the face with a hammer?'

So those years passed in a succession of greater or lesser sensations, or in the constant need of them. So it came to the autumn of 1912; then 1913 with the Balkan wars and the Serbian victories. By a strange exception, just these things which were of such great importance to the fate of the bridge and the town and all who lived in it came silently and almost unnoticed.

Flushed with red at sunrise and sunset, golden at midday, the October days passed over the town, which was waiting for the maize crop and the new season's plum-brandy. It was still pleasant to sit on the *kapia* in the noonday sun. Time, it seemed, was holding its breath over the town. It was just then that it happened.

Even before the literates in the town could find their way through the contradictory newspaper reports, the war between Turkey and the four Balkan States had already broken out and followed the well-worn paths across the Balkans. Before the people had fully grasped the sense and import of this war it was practically over as a result of the victories of the Serbian and Christian armies; all was ended far from Višegrad, without fires on the frontiers, without the grumble of the guns and without heads on the *kapia*. As it had been with trade and money, so it was with those more important things also; everything happened far away and unbelievably quickly. Somewhere far away in the world the dice had been thrown, the battles fought, and it was there that the fate of each one of the townsfolk was decided.

But if the outward appearance of the town remained peaceful and unchanged, these events stirred up in the minds of men whole tempests of the greatest enthusiasm and the deepest depression. As in the case of everything else that had happened in the world in recent years, they were looked on in the town with diametrically opposed feelings by the Serbs and the Moslems; only in their intensity and depth were they perhaps equal. These events surpassed all the hopes of the one; all the fears of the others appeared justified. Those desires which for hundreds of years had flown before the slow pace of history could now no longer keep pace with it but outdistanced it by some fantastic flight along the road to the most daring realization.

Everything that the town could see or feel directly of that fateful war took place incredibly simply and with the swiftness of an arrow.

At Uvce where the frontier between Austro-Hungary and Turkey followed the little river Uvac, and where a wooden bridge separated the Austrian gendarmerie barracks from the Turkish blockhouse, the Turkish officer with his small guard crossed to the Austrian side. There, he broke his sword with a theatrical gesture on the parapet of the bridge and surrendered to the Austrian gendarmes. At that moment the grey-clad Serbian infantry came down from the hills. They replaced the old-fashioned *askers* along the whole frontier between Bosnia and the Sanjak. The triangle between Austria, Turkey and Serbia disappeared. The Turkish frontier which only the day before had been about nine miles from the town was suddenly withdrawn more than 600 miles, somewhere far beyond Jedrene (Adrianople).

So many and such important changes, carried out in so short a time, shook the town to its foundations.

For the bridge on the Drina this change was fateful. The railway link with Sarajevo had, as we have seen, reduced its connection with the West and now, in a moment, its connection with the East also ceased. In fact the East, which had created it and which had up to the day before still been there, greatly shaken and weakened no doubt, but still as permanent and real as sky and land, had now vanished like an apparition. Now the bridge in reality no longer linked anything save the two parts of the town and those dozen or so villages on one or the other side of the Drina.

The great stone bridge which, according to the ideas and the pious intentions of the Grand Vezir from Sokolović, was meant to link the two parts of the Empire, and 'for the love of God' make easier the passage from West to East and from East to West, was now in fact cut off from both East and

West and abandoned like a stranded ship or a deserted shrine. For three whole centuries it had endured and experienced everything and, unchanging, had truly served its purpose, but human needs had altered and world conditions changed; now its task had betrayed it. By its size, its solidity and its beauty, armies might pass across it and caravans follow one another for centuries to come, but thus, by the eternal and unforeseen play of human relations, the Vezir's bequest suddenly found itself abandoned and, as if by some magic spell, outside the main stream of life. The present role of the bridge in no way corresponded to its eternally young appearance and its gigantic but harmonious proportions. But it still stood the same as when the Grand Vezir had seen it in his inward vision behind closed eyes and as when his masons had built it; powerful, beautiful and enduring, beyond all possibility of change.

It needed time, it needed effort, before the townspeople understood all that has been said here in a few lines and what had in fact taken place in a few months. Not even in dreams did frontiers change so quickly or go so far away.

All that had lain quiescent in men, as ancient as that bridge and equally dumb and motionless, now suddenly came alive and began to influence their everyday life, their general mood and the personal fate of every individual.

The first summer days of 1913 were rainy and oppressive. On the *kapia* by day sat the Moslems of the town, morose and disconsolate, about a dozen elderly men grouped around a younger one who read to them from the newspapers, interpreting foreign expressions and unusual names and explaining the geography. All smoked peacefully and gazed unwaveringly in front of them but could not completely conceal that they were anxious and shaken. Hiding their emotion, they bent over the map which showed the future partition of the Balkan Peninsula. They looked at the paper and saw nothing in those curving lines, but they knew and understood everything, for their geography was in their blood and they felt biologically their picture of the world.

'Who will get Uskub (Skoplje)?' asked one old man, apparently indifferently, to the youth who was reading.

'Serbia.'

'Uh!'

'And who will get Salonica?'

'Greece.'

'Uh! Uh!'

'And Jedrene?' asked another in a low voice.

'Bulgaria, probably.'

'Uh! Uh! Uh!'

These were not loud and mournful wailings, like women or weaklings, but deep and stifled sighs which were lost with the tobacco smoke which drifted through their moustaches into the summer air. Many of these old men had passed their seventieth year. In their childhood, the Turkish power had stretched from the Lika and the Kordun right to Stambul and from Stambul to the uncertain desert frontiers of far-off and illimitable Arabia (that Turkish power had been the great, indivisible and indestructible unity of the Moslem faith, all that part of the terrestrial globe where the muezzin called the faithful to prayer). They remembered that well, but they also remembered how, later on, in the course of their lives, that Turkish power had withdrawn from Serbia into Bosnia and then from Bosnia into the Sanjak. And now, now they lived to see that power like some fantastic ocean tide suddenly withdraw and pass away somewhere far out of sight, while they remained here, deceived and menaced, like seaweed on dry land, left to their own devices and their own evil fate. All this came from God and was, without doubt, envisaged in the ordinances of God, but it was hard for men to understand; their breath came short, their consciousness was troubled, they felt as if the solid earth was being drawn irresistibly away from under their feet as if it were a carpet, and how frontiers which should have been firm and lasting had become fluid and shifting, moving away and lost in the distance like the capricious rivulets of spring.

With such thoughts and feelings the old men sat on the

kapia and listened vaguely to all that the newspapers wrote. They listened silently though the words in which the papers spoke of kingdoms and states seemed to them mad, impudent and out of place, and their whole manner of writing as something godless, contrary to the eternal laws and the logic of life, something which would 'get no better' and with which no decent or honourable man could become reconciled. Above their heads floated clouds of tobacco smoke, and in the skies cruised white, fleecy clouds of a rainy summer, casting quick broad shadows on the earth.

At night on the *kapia* youths from the Serbian houses sat till the small hours, singing loudly and provocatively the song about the Serbian gun and no one came to fine or punish them. Amongst them could often be noticed students from the universities or secondary schools. They were mostly thin, pale youths with long hair and black shallow hats with wide brims. That autumn they came very often, though the school year had already commenced. They came by train from Sarajevo with instructions and recommendations, passed the night here on the *kapia*, but were no longer in the town at dawn next day for the young men of Višegrad sent them on by underground routes to Serbia.

With the summer months, at the time of the school holidays, the town and the *kapia* became lively with schoolboys and students, born in the town and returning to their homes. They influenced the whole life of the town.

At the end of June a group of students from the Sarajevo secondary school arrived in the town and in the first half of July students of law, medicine and philosophy from the Universities of Vienna, Prague, Graz and Zagreb, began to arrive one by one. With their arrival even the outward aspect of the town began to change. Their young faces could be seen in the market-place and on the *kapia* and they were easily distinguishable by their bearing, their speech and their clothes from the established customs and unchanging clothing of the townspeople. They wore clothes of dull colours and the latest cut. This was the 'Glöckenfaçon' then considered the height of fashion and the best of taste in all Central Europe. On their heads they wore soft Panama hats with turned-down brims and ribbons of six different but discreet colours; on their feet wide American shoes with sharply turned-up toes. Most of them carried very thick bamboo canes and in the lapels of their coats they wore metal Sokol badges or those of some student organization.

The students brought with them new words and jokes, new dances from the balls of the previous winter, and especially new books and pamphlets, Serbian, Czech and German.

It had happened earlier too, in the first years of the Austrian occupation, that young men from the town had gone away to study, but not in such large numbers nor inspired by this sort of spirit. In those first few decades a few of them had finished at the Teachers' Training College at Sarajevo, and two or three had even read philosophy at Vienna, but these had been rare exceptions, modest youths who had passed their examinations quietly and without advertisement and once their studies had been completed had been lost in the grey and countless ranks of the state bureaucracy. But for some time past the number of students from the town had suddenly increased. By the help of national cultural institutions even peasants' sons and the children of petty artisans went to the university. The spirit and character of the students themselves changed.

These were no longer those one-time students of the first years after the occupation, mild and timid youths devoted to their studies in the closest sense of the word. But neither were they the ordinary town dandies and goodfellows of an earlier time, future landowners and shopkeepers who at a certain period in their lives wasted their excess of youth and strength on the *kapia* till their families said of them: 'Marry him off and stop his squalling!' These were a new sort of young men, educated in various cities and states and under various influences. From the great cities, from the universities and schools which they attended, these young men came back intoxicated with that feeling of proud audacity with which his first and incomplete knowledge fills a young man, and carried away by ideas about the rights of peoples to freedom and of individuals to enjoyment and dignity. With every summer vacation they brought back with them free-thinking views on social and religious questions and an enthusiastically revived nationalism which recently, especially after the Serbian victories in the Balkan wars, had grown to a universal conviction and, in many of these youths, to a fanatical desire for action and personal sacrifice.

The *kapia* was the main scene of their meetings. They would meet there after supper. In the darkness, under the stars or in the moonlight, above the boisterous river, echoed their songs, jests, noisy conversation and endless arguments, new, bold, naïve, sincere and unself-conscious.

With the students were also their childhood friends who had studied with them in the local elementary school, but had remained in the town as apprentices, shop assistants or clerks in the municipal offices. There were two types. Some were satisfied with their destiny and the life of the town in which they would pass their days. They looked with curiosity and sympathy at their educated comrades, admired them and never thought of comparing themselves with them, and, without the slightest jealousy, followed their development and their career. There were others who were dissatisfied with life in the town to which they were condemned by force of circumstances and who longed for something that they considered higher and better and which had escaped them, becoming every day farther away and more inaccessible. Though they used to meet together with their student comrades, these youths usually kept apart from their educated fellows either by some crude form of irony or by their unfriendly silence. They could not take part as equals in their conversations. Therefore, constantly tormented by their feeling of inferiority, they now exaggerated and stressed in conversation their crudeness and ignorance by comparison with their more fortunate comrades or, from the height of their ignorance, mocked at all that they could not understand. In either case, envy breathed out of them as an almost visible and tangible force. But youth easily bears with even the worst instincts, and lives and moves freely and easily amongst them.

There had been and there would be again starlight nights on the *kapia* and rich constellations and moonlight, but there had never been, and God alone knows whether there would be again, such young men who in such conversations and with such feelings and ideas would keep vigil on the *kapia*. That was a generation of rebel angels, in that short moment while they still had all the power and all the rights of angels and also the flaming pride of rebels. These sons of peasants, traders or artisans from a remote Bosnian township had obtained from fate, without any special effort of their own, a free entry into the world and the great illusion of freedom. With their inborn small-town characteristics, they went out into the world, chose more or less for themselves and according to their own inclinations, momentary moods or the whims of chance, the subject of their studies, the nature of their entertainments and the circle of their friends and acquaintances. For the most part they were unable, or did not know how, to seize and make use of what they succeeded in seeing, but there was not one of them who did not have the feeling that he could take what he wished and that all that he took was his. Life (that word came up very often in their conversations, as it did in the literature and politics of the time, when it was always written with a capital letter), Life stood before them as an object, as a field of action for their liberated senses, for their intellectual curiosity and their sentimental exploits, which knew no limits. All roads were open to them, onward to infinity; on most of those roads they would never even set foot, but none the less the intoxicating lust for life lay in the fact that they could (in theory at least) be free to choose which they would and dare to cross from one to the other. All that other men, other races, in other times and lands, had achieved and attained in the course of generations, through centuries of effort, at the cost of lives, of renunciations and of sacrifices greater and dearer than life, now lay before them as a chance inheritance and a dangerous gift of fate. It seemed fantastic and improbable but was none the less true; they could do with their youth what they liked, and give their judgements freely and without restriction; they dared to say what they liked and for many of them those words were the same as deeds, satisfying their atavistic need for heroism and glory, violence and destruction, yet they did not entail any obligation to act nor any visible responsibility for what had been said. The most gifted amongst them despised all that they should have learnt and underestimated all that they were able to do, but they boasted of what they did not know and waxed enthusiastic at what was beyond their powers to achieve. It is hard to imagine a more dangerous manner of entering into life or a surer way towards exceptional deeds or total disaster. Only the best and strongest amongst them threw themselves into action with the fanaticism of fakirs and were there burnt up like flies, to be immediately hailed by their fellows as martyrs and saints (for there is no generation without its saints) and placed on pedestals as inaccessible examples.

Every human generation has its own illusions with regard to civilization; some believe that they are taking part in its upsurge, others that they are witnesses of its extinction. In fact, it always both flames up and smoulders and is extinguished, according to the place and the angle of view. This generation which was now discussing philosophy, social and political questions on the *kapia* under the stars, above the waters, was richer only in illusions; in every other way it was similar to any other. It had the feeling both of lighting the first fires of one new civilization and extinguishing the last flickers of another which was burning out. What could especially be said of them was that there had not been for a long time past a generation which with greater boldness had dreamed and spoken about life, enjoyment and freedom and which had received less of life, suffered worse, laboured more hardly and died more often than had this one. But in those summer days of 1913 all was still undetermined, unsure. Everything appeared as an exciting new game on that ancient bridge, which shone in the moonlight of those July nights, clean, young and unalterable, strong and lovely in its perfection, stronger than all that time might bring and men imagine or do.

CHAPTER XIX

JUST AS ONE warm summer night in August is like another, so the discussions of these schoolboys and students on the *kapia* were always the same or similar.

Immediately after a good supper hurriedly eaten (for the day had passed in bathing and basking in the sun) they arrived one by one on the *kapia*. There was Janko Stiković, son of a tailor from Mejdan, who had already been studying natural science at Graz for two years. He was a thin young man with sharp features and smooth black hair, vain, sensitive, dissatisfied with himself but even more with everyone about him. He read much and wrote articles under a pen-name which was already well known in revolutionary youth papers published in Prague and Zagreb. He also wrote poems and published them under another pen-name. He was preparing a book of them which was to be published by *Zora*, the Nationalist Edition. He was also a good speaker and a fiery debater at students' meetings. Velimir Stevanović was a healthy, well-built youth, an adopted child of uncertain parentage; he was ironic, down to earth, thrifty and industrious; he had completed his medical studies at Prague. There was Jacov Herak, son of the good-natured and popular Višegrad postman, a small, dark law student, of piercing eyes and swift words, a socialist of polemical spirit, who was ashamed of his kind heart and concealed every trace of emotion. Ranko Mihailović was a taciturn and good-natured youth who was studying law at Zagreb and was already thinking of a career as a civil servant. He took little part and that half-heartedly in his comrades' arguments and discussions on love, politics, views on life and social conditions. On his mother's side he was the great grandson of that Pop Mihailo whose head, with a cigar stuck between its lips, had been put on a stake and exposed on that very *kapia*.

There were also a few Sarajevo secondary school students who listened avidly to their older colleagues and their tales of life in the great cities, and with the imagination that whips up the vanity and hidden desires of children thought of everything as even greater and more beautiful than it really was or ever could be. Among them was Nikola Glasičanin, a pale stiff youth who because of poverty, poor health and lack of success had had to leave the secondary school after the fourth class and return to the town and accept a post as clerk to a German timber exporting firm. He came from a decayed landowning family at Okolište. His grandfather, Milan Glasičanin, had died a short time after the occupation, in the Sarajevo lunatic asylum, after gambling away in his youth the greater part of his property. His father, Peter, a sickly creature without will, force or reputation had died some time ago. Now Nikola spent all day long on the river bank with the workmen who poled the heavy pine logs and made them into rafts. He measured the cubic meterage of the wood and afterwards, in the office, entered it in the books. This monotonous task among such people, without ideals and without wider views, he felt as a torture and a humiliation, and the absence of any likelihood of being able to change his social status or get on in the world had created of the sensitive youth a man old before his time, bilious and taciturn. He read much in his spare time, but that spiritual food did nothing to give him force or exalt him, for everything in him took a sour turn. His bad luck, his loneliness and his suffering opened his eyes and sharpened his senses to many things, but even the most beautiful thoughts and most precious knowledge could only discourage and embitter him the more, for they threw an even stronger light on his lack of success and his lack of prospects in the town.

There was also Vlado Marić, a locksmith by trade, a merry and good-humoured man whom his colleagues from the higher schools loved and invited, as much for his strong and lovely baritone as for his simple-heartedness and goodness.

This vigorous young man with his locksmith's cap on his head was one of those humble men who are always sufficient to themselves and do not think of comparing themselves with others, but calmly and thankfully accept whatever life offers to them and give simply and naturally all they can.

There were also the two local schoolmistresses, Zorka and Zagorka, both born in the town. All the youths competed for their favours and around them played that naïve, complicated, brilliant and tormenting game of love. In their presence the discussions raged like a court of love in earlier centuries; because of them young men would later sit on the *kapia* smoking in the darkness and solitude or singing with others after an evening spent drinking somewhere else; because of them there were hidden enmities between comrades, badly concealed jealousies and open quarrels. About ten o'clock the girls would go home; but the young men remained for long, though the mood on the *kapia* slackened and the rival eloquence diminished.

Stiković, who usually took the lead in these discussions, that evening sat silent, smoking. He was troubled and out of humour with himself, but he concealed it as he always concealed all his true feelings, though he never succeeded in concealing them completely. That afternoon he had had his first rendezvous with the schoolmistress Zorka, an attractive girl with a full figure, pale face and fiery eyes. On Stiković's insistence, they had been able to do the most difficult of all things in a small town; that is for a youth and a girl to meet in a hidden place where no one could see them or know anything about it. They had met in her school which was deserted at that time because of the holidays. He had gone in from one street, through the garden, and she from another by the main entrance. They had met in a dimly-lit, dusty room piled almost to the ceiling with benches. It is thus that the passion of love is often compelled to look for remote and ugly places. They could neither sit nor lie down. Both of them were embarrassed and awkward. Too full of desire, too impatient, they embraced and mingled on one of those benches which she knew so well, without looking at or noticing anything around them. He was the first to recover. Abruptly, without transition, as young men do, he stood up to arrange his clothing and go away. The girl burst into tears. Their disillusion was mutual. When he had more or less calmed down he went out, almost as if escaping, by a side door.

At home he met the postman who had brought the youth-paper with his article 'The Balkans, Serbia and Bosnia-Herzegovina'. Reading the article again turned his thoughts away from the incident of a few moments before. But even in that he found reason for dissatisfaction. There were printers' errors in the article and some of the sentences sounded silly to him; now, when it was no longer possible to make alterations, it seemed to him that many things could have been better expressed, more clearly and more concisely.

The same evening they sat on the *kapia* discussing his article in the presence of Zorka herself. His principal adversary was the talkative and aggressive Herak who looked at everything and criticized everything from an orthodox socialist viewpoint. The others only intervened in the discussion from time to time. The two schoolmistresses remained silent, preparing an unseen wreath for the victor. Stiković defended himself weakly, firstly because he himself now saw many weaknesses and illogicalities in his own article, though he would never admit this before his colleagues; and secondly because he was troubled by the memory of the afternoon in the dusty and stuffy classroom, a scene which now seemed to him both comic and ugly but which had long been the aim of his most intense desires and his most ardent feelings towards the pretty schoolmistress. She herself was sitting there in the summer darkness looking at him with shining eyes. He felt like a debtor and a criminal and would have given much not to have been in the school that day and not to be here with her now. In such a mood, Herak seemed to him like an aggressive gadfly from whose attacks he could only defend himself with difficulty. It seemed to him that he must answer not only for his article but also for all that had happened that day in the school. Above all he wanted to be alone, somewhere far away, so that he could think calmly of something other than the article or the girl. But self-love drove him on to defend himself. Stiković quoted Cvijić and Štrosmajer, Herak Kautsky and Babel.

'You are putting the cart before the horse,' shouted Herak, analysing Stiković's article. 'It is not possible for the Balkan peasant, plunged in poverty and every sort of misery, to found a good and lasting state organization. Only the preliminary economic liberation of the exploited classes, the peasants and the workers, that is to say the greater number of the people, can create real conditions for the formation of independent states. That is a natural process and the road we all must take, and in no way the other way round. Therefore both national liberation and unification must be carried out in the spirit of socialist liberation and renascence. Otherwise it will happen that the peasant, worker and ordinary citizen will introduce their pauperism and their slavish mentality, like a mortal contagion, into the new state formations and the small number of exploiters will instil into them their parasitical, reactionary mentality and their anti-social instincts. Therefore enduring states or a healthy society cannot exist.'

'All that is foreign book-learning, my good fellow,' answered Stiković, 'which vanishes before the living impetus of awakened nationalist forces among the Serbs and then among the Croats and Slovenes also, though tending to one aim. Things do not come to pass according to the forecasts of German theoreticians but advance in complete accord with the deep sense of our history and our racial destiny. From Karageorge's words: "Let each kill his Turkish chief" the social problem in the Balkans has always solved itself by the way of national liberation movements and wars. It all moves beautifully logically, from the less to the great, from the regional and tribal to the national and the formation of the State. Were not our victories at Kumanovo and on the

Bregalnica also the greatest victories of progressive thought and social justice?'

'That remains to be seen,' broke in Herak.

'Who does not see it now, will never see it. We believe . . .'

'You believe, but we believe nothing, but want to be convinced by actual proofs and facts,' answered Herak.

'Surely the disappearance of the Turks and the weakening of Austro-Hungary as the first step towards her annihilation are really the victories of small, democratic peoples and enslaved classes in their aspiration to find a place in the sun?' Stiković developed his idea.

'If the realization of nationalist aims brings with it the creation of social justice, then in the Western European states which have for the most part achieved all their nationalist ideals and are in that matter satisfied, there should no longer be any major social problems, or movements, or conflicts. Yet we see that that is not so. On the contrary.'

'And I keep telling you,' Stiković answered weariedly, 'that without the creation of independent states on the basis of national unity and modern conceptions of personal and social liberty, there can be no talk of "social liberation". For, as some Frenchman once said, politics come first. . . .'

'The stomach comes first,' interrupted Herak.

The others too became heated and the naïve students' discussion became a youthful squabble with everyone talking at once and interrupting one another and which, at the first quips, degenerated into laughter and shouting.

That was a welcome excuse for Stiković to break off the argument and remain silent, without having to give the impression of a withdrawal or a defeat.

After Zorka and Zagorka who went home about ten o'clock, escorted by Velimir and Ranko, the others too began to disperse. At last only Stiković and Nikola Glasičanin were left.

These two were about the same age. At one time they had gone to school together and had shared the same lodgings in Sarajevo. They knew one another down to the last detail and just for that reason they could neither of them make up their mind whether they really liked one another. With the years the distance between them naturally became wider and harder to bridge. Every vacation they met again here in the town and each took the other's measure and looked on the other as an inseparable enemy. Now the beautiful and way-ward schoolmistress Zorka had also come between them. In the long months of the previous winter she had gone about with Glasičanin who had never concealed, or been able to conceal, that he was in love. He had plunged head over heels in love with all the fire that embittered and dissatisfied persons can put into such an emotion. But as soon as the summer months came and the students began to appear, the sensitive Glasičanin was unable to avoid seeing the interest that the schoolmistress showed in Stiković. For that reason the old tension between them, which had always been kept hidden from others, had greatly increased. All this vacation they had not once been alone together as they were now.

Now that chance had so arranged it, the first thought of each of them was to separate as soon as possible without con-versation which could only be unpleasant for both. But some ridiculous consideration, known only to youth, prevented them from doing as they wished. But in this embarrassment chance again helped them and lessened at least for a moment the heavy silence that oppressed them.

In the darkness could be heard the voices of two youths who were walking on the bridge. They were moving slowly and just then halted by the *kapia* behind the angle of the para-pet, so that Stiković and Glasičanin could not see them, or be seen by them, from their seat on the *sofa*. But they could hear every word and the voices were well known to them. They were two of their younger comrades, Toma Galus and Fehim Bahtijarević. These two kept themselves a little apart from the group which comprised most of the other students and which gathered every evening on the *kapia* around Stiković and Herak, for, although younger, Galus was a rival of Stiković both as a poet and as a nationalist speaker. He did not like Stiković nor admire him, while Bahtijarević was exceptionally silent, proud and reserved as befitted a true grandchild of a family of begs.

Toma Galus was a tall youth with red cheeks and blue eyes. His father, Alban von Galus, the last descendant of an ancient family of the Burgenland, had come to the town as a civil servant immediately after the occupation. He had been for twelve years a forestry inspector and now lived in the town on pension. At the very beginning, he had married the daughter of one of the local landowners, Hadji Toma Stanković, a robust and full-blown young woman of dark skin and strong will. They had had three children, two daughters and one son, all of whom had been christened into the Serbian Orthodox Church and had grown up like real townsmen's children and grandchildren of Hadji Toma.

Old Galus, a tall and formerly a very handsome man, with a pleasant smile and masses of thick white hair, had long become a real townsman, 'Mr Albo', whom the younger generation could not think of as a foreigner and a newcomer. He had two passions which harmed no one; hunting and his pipe, and had made many old and true friends, both among the Serbs and among the Moslems, throughout the whole district who shared his passion for the chase. He had completely assimilated many of their customs as if he had been born and bred amongst them, especially their habit of cheerful silence and calm conversation, so characteristic of men who are passionate smokers and who love hunting, the forests and life in the open.

Young Galus had matriculated that year at Sarajevo and that autumn was due to go on to Vienna to study. But in the matter of these studies there was a division of opinion in the family. The father wanted his son to study technical sciences or forestry and the son wanted to study philosophy. For Toma Galus only resembled his father in appearance and all his desires led him in a completely opposite direction. He was one of those good scholars, modest and exemplary in everything, who pass all their examinations with ease as if playing at them, but whose real and sincere interests are taken up with satisfying their somewhat confused and disordered spiritual aspirations outside school and outside the official curriculum. These are students of serene and simple heart but of uneasy and inquisitive spirit. Those difficult and dangerous crises of the life of the senses and emotions through which so many other young men of their age pass, are almost unknown to them, therefore they find difficulty in stilling their spiritual anxieties and very often remain all their lives dilettantes, interesting eccentrics without stable occupation or definite interests. As every young man must not only fulfil the eternal and natural demands of youth and maturity and also pay tribute to the current spiritual moods and fashions of his time, which for the moment reign amongst youth, Galus too had written verses and was an active member of the revolutionary nationalist student organizations. He had also studied French for five years as an optional subject, taken an interest in literature and, more especially, philosophy. He read passionately and indefatigably. The main body of reading of the young men at school in Sarajevo at that time consisted of works from the well-known and enormous German publishing list *Reclams Universal-Bibliotek*. These small, cheap booklets with yellow covers and exceptionally small print were the main spiritual food available to the students of that time; from them they could become acquainted not only with German literature, but with all the more important works in world literature in German translation. From them Galus drew his knowledge of modern German philosophers, especially Nietzsche and Stirner, and in his walks in Sarajevo along the banks of the Miljačka held endless discussions about them with a sort of cold passion, in no way linking his reading with his personal life, as so many youths often do. This type of young scholar just through his examinations, ripened too early and overloaded with all kinds of varied, chaotic and unco-ordinated knowledge, was not rare among the students of that time. A modest youth and a good student, Galus knew the freedom and the unrestraint of youth only in the daring of his thoughts and the exaggerations of his reading.

Fehim Bahtijarević was a townsman on his mother's side only. His father had been born in Rogatica and was now *kadi* (Moslem judge) there, but his mother was from the great local family of Osmanagić. From his earliest childhood he had passed a part of the summer vacation in the town with his mother and her relatives. He was a slender youth, graceful and well formed, fine-boned but strong. Everything about him was measured, restrained, controlled. The fine oval of his face was sunburnt, his skin browned with light touches of a dark bluish shade, his movements few and abrupt; his eyes were black with blue shadings in the whites and his glance burning but without sparkle. He had thick eyebrows which met, and a fine black down on his upper lip. Such faces are reminiscent of Persian miniatures.

That summer he too had matriculated and he was now waiting to get a state grant to study oriental languages in Vienna.

The two young men were continuing some conversation begun earlier. The subject was Bahtijarević's choice of studies. Galus was proving to him that he would be making a mistake in taking up oriental studies. In general Galus spoke much more, and more animatedly, than his companion for he was accustomed to be listened to and to lay down the law, while Bahtijarević spoke shortly, like a man who has his own fixed ideas and feels no need to convince anyone else. Like most young men who have read much, Galus spoke with a naïve satisfaction in words, picturesque expressions and comparisons, and with a tendency to generalize, whereas Bahtijarević spoke dryly, curtly, almost indifferently.

Hidden in the shadows and reclining on the stone seats, Stiković and Glasičanin remained silent as if they had tacitly agreed to listen to the conversation of their two comrades on the bridge.

Finishing the conversation about studies, Galus said belligerently:

'In that you Moslems, you begs' sons, often make a mistake. Disconcerted by the new times, you no longer know your exact and rightful place in the world. Your love for everything oriental is only a contemporary expression of your "will to power"; for you the eastern way of life and thought is very closely bound up with a social and legal order which was the basis of your centuries of lordship. That is understandable. But it in no way means that you have any sense for orientalism as a study. You are orientals but you are making a mistake when you think that you are thereby called upon to be orientalists. In general you have not got the calling or the true inclination for science.'

'Really!'

'No, you haven't. And when I say that, I am not saying anything insulting or offensive. On the contrary. You are the only nobles in this country, or at least you were; for centuries you have enlarged, confirmed and defended your privileges by sword and pen, legally, religiously and by force of arms; that has made of you typical warriors, administrators and landowners, and that class of men nowhere in the world worries about abstract sciences but leaves them to those who have nothing else and can do nothing else. The true studies for you are law and economics, for you are men of practical knowledge. Such are men from the ruling classes, always and everywhere.'

'You mean that we should remain uneducated?'

'No, it does not mean that, but it means that you must remain what you are or, if you like, what you have been; you must, for no one can be at the same time what he is and the contrary of what he is.'

'But we are no longer a ruling class today. Today we are all equal,' Bahtijarević broke in once more with a touch of irony, in which was both bitterness and pride.

'You are not, naturally you are not. The conditions which at one time made you what you were have changed long ago, but that does not mean that you can change with the same speed. This is not the first, nor will it be the last, instance of a social caste losing its reason for existence and yet remaining the same. Conditions of life change but a class remains what it is, for only so can it exist and as such it will die.'

The conversation of the two unseen youths broke off for a moment, stifled by Bahtijarević's silence.

In the clear June sky, above the dark mountains on the horizon, the moon appeared. The white plaque with the Turkish inscription suddenly shone in the moonlight, like a dimly lit window in the blue-black darkness.

Bahtijarević then said something, but in so low a voice that only disjointed and incomprehensible words reached Stiković and Glasičanin. As so often in young men's discussions, in which changes of subject are rapid and bold, the conversation was now about another matter. From the study of oriental languages, they had now passed on to the content of the inscription on the white plaque before them and to the bridge and he who had built it.

Galus's voice was the louder and more expressive. While agreeing with Bahtijarević's praises of Mehmed Pasha Sokolović and the Turkish administration of his times, which had made possible the building of such a bridge, he now developed his nationalist views on the past and present of the people, their culture and civilization (for in such student discussions each follows his own train of thought).

'You are right,' said Galus. 'He must have been a man of genius. He was not the first nor the last man of our blood who distinguished himself in the service of a foreign empire. We have given hundreds of such men, statesmen, generals and artists, to Stambul, Rome and Vienna. The sense of our national unification in a single, great and powerful modern state lies just in that. Our own forces should remain in our own country and develop there and make their contribution to general culture in our name and not from foreign centres.'

'Do you really think that those "centres" arose by chance and that it is possible to create new ones at will whenever and wherever one likes?'

'Chance or not, that is no longer the question; it is not important how they arose, but it is important that today they are disappearing, that they have flowered and decayed, that they must make way for new and different centres, through which young and free nations, appearing for the first time on the stage of history, can express themselves directly.'

'Do you think that Mehmed Pasha Sokolović, had he remained a peasant's child up there yonder at Sokolovići, would have become what he became and would, among other things, have built this bridge on which we are now talking?'

'In those times, certainly, he would not. But, when you come to think of it, it was not hard for Stambul to put up such buildings, when it took from us, and from so many other subject peoples, not only property and money, but also our best men and our purest blood. If you stop to think what we are and how much has been stolen from us through the centuries, then all these buildings are merely crumbs. But when we finally achieve our national freedom and our independence, then our money and our blood will be ours alone, and will stay ours. Everything will be solely and uniquely for the improvement of our own national culture, which will bear our mark and our name and which will be mindful of the happiness and prosperity of all our people.'

Bahtijarević remained silent, and that silence, like the most lively and eloquent speech, provoked Galus. He raised his voice and continued in a sharper tone. With all his natural vivacity and all the vocabulary then prevalent in nationalist literature, he set out the plans and aims of the revolutionary youth movement. All the living forces of the race must be awakened and set in action. Under their blows the Austro-Hungarian monarchy, that prison of the peoples, would disintegrate as the Turkish Empire had disintegrated. All the anti-national and reactionary forces which today hinder, divide and lull to sleep our national forces will be routed and trampled underfoot. All this can be done, for the spirit of the times in which we live is our strongest ally, for all the efforts of all the other small and oppressed nations support us. Modern nationalism will triumph over religious diversities and outmoded prejudice, will liberate our people from foreign influence and exploitation. Then will the national state be born.

Galus then described all the advantages and beauties of the new national state which was to rally all the Southern Slavs around Serbia as a sort of Piedmont on the basis of complete national unity, religious tolerance and civil equality. His speech mixed up bold words of uncertain meaning and expressions that accurately expressed the needs of modern life, the deepest desires of a race, most of which were destined to remain only desires, and the justified and attainable demands of everyday reality. It mingled the great truths which had ripened through the generations but which only youth could perceive in advance and dare to express, with the eternal illusions which are never extinguished but never attain realization, for one generation of youth hands them on to the next like that mythological torch. In the young man's speech there were, naturally, many assertions which could not have stood up to the criticism of reality and many suppositions which could not, perhaps, have borne the proof of experience, but in it too was that freshness, that precious essence which maintains and rejuvenates the tree of humanity.

Bahtijarević remained silent.

'You will see, Fehim,' Galus enthusiastically assured his friend as if it were a matter of the same night or the next morning, 'you will see. We shall create a state which will make the most precious contribution to the progress of humanity, in which every effort will be blessed, every sacrifice holy, every thought original and expressed in our own words, and every deed marked with the stamp of our name. Then we will carry out work which will be the result of our free labour and the expression of our racial genius, put up buildings in comparison with which all that has been done in the centuries of foreign administration will appear like silly toys. We will bridge greater rivers and deeper abysses. We will build new, greater and better bridges, not to link foreign centres with conquered lands but to link our own lands with the rest of the world. There cannot be any doubt any longer. We are destined to realize all that the generations before us have aspired to; a state, born in freedom and founded on justice, like a part of God's thought realized here on earth.'

Bahtijarević remained silent. Even Galus's voice lowered in tone. As his ideas became more exalted, his voice became lower and lower, hoarser and hoarser, till it became a strong and passionate whisper and was finally lost in the great silence of the night. At last both young men were silent. But none the less Bahtijarević's silence seemed a thing apart, heavy and obstinate in the night. It seemed like an impassable wall in the darkness which by the very weight of its existence resolutely rejected all that the other had said, and expressed its dumb, clear and unalterable opinion.

'The foundations of the world and the bases of life and human relationships in it have been fixed for centuries. That does not mean that they do not change, but measured by the length of human existence they appear eternal. The relation between their endurance and the length of human existence is the same as the relation between the uneasy, moving and swift surface of a river and its stable and solid bed whose changes are slow and imperceptible. The very idea of the change of these "centres" is unhealthy and unacceptable. That would be as if someone wished to change and measure the sources of great rivers or the sites of mountains. The desire for sudden changes and the thought of their realization by force often appears among men like a disease and gains ground mainly in young brains; only these brains do not think as they should, do not amount to anything in the end and the heads that think thus do not remain long on their shoulders. For it is not human desires that dispose and administer the things of the world. Desire is like a wind; it shifts the dust from one place to another, sometimes darkens the whole horizon, but in the end calms down and falls and leaves the old and eternal picture of the world. Lasting deeds are realized on this earth only by God's will, and man is only His blind and humble tool. A deed which is born of desire, human desire, either does not live till realization or is not lasting; in no case is that good. All these tumultuous desires and daring words under the night sky on the *kapia* will not change anything basically; they will pass, beneath the great and permanent realities of the world and will be lost where all desires and winds are stilled. In truth great men and great buildings rise and will rise only where they are appointed to arise in God's thought, in their right place independent of empty transient desires and human vanity.'

But Bahtijarević did not utter a single one of these words. Those who, like this Moslem youth of noble family, carry their philosophy in their blood, live and die according to it, do not know how to express it in words, or feel the need to do so. After this long silence Stiković and Glasičanin only saw one or other of the pair of unseen comrades throw a cigarette stub over the parapet and watched it fall like a shooting star in a great curve from the bridge into the Drina. At the same time they heard the two friends slowly and softly moving away towards the market-place. The sound of their footsteps was soon lost.

Alone once more, Stiković and Glasičanin started and looked at one another as though they had only just met.

In the pale moonlight their faces showed in bright and dark surfaces sharply defined, so that they seemed much older than in fact they were. The glow from their cigarettes had a sort of phosphorescence. Both were depressed. Their reasons were quite different, but the depression was mutual. Both had the same wish; to get up and go home. But both seemed as if nailed to the stone seats still warm from the day's sunlight. The conversation of that pair of young comrades which they by chance overheard had been welcome to them as a postponement of their own conversation and mutual explanation. But now it could no longer be avoided.

'Did you hear Herak and his arguments?' Stiković spoke first, referring to the evening's discussion, and at once felt the weakness of his position.

Glasičanin, who for his part felt the momentary advantage of his position as arbiter, did not reply at once.

'I ask you,' went on Stiković impatiently, 'in these days to speak of class struggle and recommend small measures, when it is clear to every last man amongst us that national unity and liberation carried out by revolutionary methods is the most pressing aim of our community! Why, that is downright silly!'

His voice held both a question and an appeal. But again Glasičanin did not reply. In the hush of that revengeful and vindictive silence, the sound of music came to them from the officers' mess on the river bank. The ground-floor windows were wide open and brightly lit. A violin was playing with a piano accompanying it. It was the military doctor, Regimentsarzt Balas, who was playing, accompanied by the wife of the commander of the garrison, Colonel Bauer. They were practising the second movement of Schubert's Sonatina for violin and piano. They played well together but before they were halfway through the piano was ahead and the violinist stopped playing. After a short silence, during which they were doubtless arguing about the disputed passage, they began again. They practised together almost every evening and played until late at night, while the Colonel sat in another room playing endless games of *preference* or simply dozing over Mostar wine and tobacco while the younger officers joked among themselves at the expense of the enamoured musicians.

Between Madame Bauer and the young doctor a complicated and difficult story had in fact been building up for months. Not even the keenest-eyed among the officers had been able to decide on the real nature of the relationship. Some said that the tie between them was wholly spiritual (and naturally laughed at it), while others said that the body had its due share in the matter also. The two were, however, inseparable, with the full fatherly approval of the Colonel who was a good-natured man, already blunted by long service, the weight of years, wine and tobacco.

The whole town looked on these two as a couple. Otherwise, the whole officers' mess lived a completely isolated life, without any connection with the local people and citizens or even the foreign officials. At the entrance to their parks, filled with beds of rare flowers laid out in circles and stars, a notice announced impartially that it was forbidden to bring dogs into the parks and that civilians were not allowed to enter. Their pleasures and their duties were alike inaccessible to all who were not in uniform. Their whole life was in fact that of a huge and completely exclusive caste, which cherished its exclusiveness as the most important aspect of its power and which beneath a brilliant and stiff exterior concealed all that life gave to other men of greatness and poverty, sweetness and bitterness.

But there are things which by their very nature cannot remain hidden, which break down every barrier however strong and cross even the most strictly guarded frontier. 'There are three things which cannot be hidden,' say the Osmanlis, 'and these are: love, a cough and poverty.' This was the case with this pair of lovers. There was not an old man or a child, man or woman, in the town who had not come across them on one of their walks on unfrequented paths around the town, lost in conversation and completely blind and deaf to everything about them. The shepherds were as used to them as to those pairs of beetles that can be seen in May on the leaves by the wayside, always two by two in loving embrace. They were to be seen everywhere; along the Drina and the Rzav, by the ruins of the old fortress, on the road leading from the town, or around Stražište, and that at any time of the day. For time is always short to lovers and no path long enough. They sometimes rode or drove in a light carriage, but for the most part walked, and walked at that pace usual to two persons who exist only one for the other, and with that characteristic gait which shows that they are indifferent to everything in the world save what each has to say to the other.

He was a Hungarianized Slovak, son of a civil servant and educated at state expense, young and genuinely musical. He was ambitious but over-sensitive about his origins which prevented him from feeling at ease with the Austrian or Hungarian officers from rich and famous families. She was a woman in her forties, eight years older than he. She was tall and blonde, already a little faded but her skin was still a clear pink and white. With her large shining dark-blue eyes, in appearance and bearing she looked like one of those portraits of queens which so enchant young girls.

Each of them had personal, real or imagined but deep, reasons for dissatisfaction with life. Furthermore they had one great reason in common; both felt themselves to be unhappy and like outcasts in this town and this society of officers, for the most part frivolous and empty-headed. So they clung to one another feverishly like two survivors of a shipwreck. They lost themselves in one another and forgot themselves in long conversations or, as now, in music.

Such was the invisible pair whose music filled the troubled silence between the two youths.

A few moments later the music which had been pouring into the peaceful night again ran into difficulties and stopped for a time. In the silence that followed, Glasičanin began to speak in a wooden sort of voice, picking up Stiković's last words.

'Silly? There was much that was silly in that whole discussion, if we look at it fairly.'

Stiković suddenly took the cigarette from his lips, but Glasičanin went on slowly but resolutely to express views which were clearly not based on that night only but which had long troubled him.

'I listen carefully to all these discussions, both those between you two and other educated people in this town; also I read the newspapers and reviews. But the more I listen to you, the more I am convinced that the greater part of

these spoken or written discussions have no connection with
life at all and its real demands and problems. For life, real life,
I look at from very close indeed; I see its influence on others
and I feel it on myself. It may be that I am mistaken and that
I do not know how to express myself well, but I often think
that technical progress and the relative peace there is now in
the world have created a sort of lull, a special atmosphere,
artificial and unreal, in which a single class of men, the so-
called intellectuals, can freely devote themselves to idleness
and to the interesting game of ideas and "views on life and
the world". It is a sort of conservatory of the spirit, with an
artificial climate and exotic flowers but without any real connection with the earth, the real hard soil on which the mass
of human beings move. You think that you are discussing
the fate of these masses and their use in the struggle for the
realization of higher aims which you have fixed for them but
in fact the wheels which you turn in your heads have no connection with the life of the masses, nor with life in general.
That game of yours becomes dangerous, or at least might
become dangerous, both for others and for you yourselves.'

Glasičanin paused. Stiković was so astonished by this long
and considered exposition that he had not even thought of
interrupting him or answering him. Only when he heard
the word 'dangerous' he made an ironical gesture with his
hand. That irritated Glasičanin who continued even more
animatedly.

'For heaven's sake! Listening to you, one would think
that all questions were settled happily, all dangers for ever
removed, all roads made smooth and open so all we have
to do is to walk along them. But in life there is nothing
solved, or which can easily be solved, or even has any chance
of being solved at all. Everything is hard and complicated,
expensive and accompanied by disproportionately high risk;
there is no trace either of Herak's bold hopes or of your wide
horizons. Man is tormented all his life and never has what he
needs, let alone what he wants. Theories such as yours only
satisfy the eternal need for games, flatter your own vanity,

deceive yourself and others. That is the truth, or at least that is how it appears to me.'

'It is not so. You have only to compare various historical periods and you will see the progress and meaning of man's struggle and therefore also the "theory" that gives sense and direction to that struggle.'

Glasičanin at once took this to be an allusion to his interrupted schooling and as always in such a case quivered inwardly.

'I have not studied history. . . .' he began.

'You see. If you had studied it, you would see. . . .'

'But neither have you.'

'What? That is . . . well, yes of course I have studied. . . .'

'As well as natural sciences?'

His voice quivered vindictively. Stiković was embarrassed for a moment and then said in a dead sort of voice:

'Oh well, if you really want to know, there it is; besides natural sciences, I have been taking an interest in political, historical and social problems.'

'You are lucky to have had the chance. For as far as I know, you are an orator and an agitator also, as well as being a poet and a lover.'

Stiković smiled unnaturally. That afternoon in the deserted schoolroom passed through his mind as a distant but irritating thing. Only then he realized that Glasičanin and Zorka had been close friends until his arrival in the town. A man who does not love is incapable of feeling the greatness of another's love or the force of jealousy or the danger concealed in it.

The conversation of the two young men changed without transition into that bitter personal quarrel that had from the very beginning been hovering in the air between them. Young people do not try to avoid quarrels, even as young animals easily take part in rough and violent games among themselves.

'What I am and what I do is none of your business. I don't ask you about your cubes and your tree trunks.'

That spasm of anger which always gripped Glasičanin at any mention of his position made him suffer.

'You leave my cubes alone. I live from them, but I don't trick people with them. I deceive no one. I seduce no one.'

'Whom do I seduce?' broke in Stiković.

'Anyone who will let you.'

'That is not true.'

'It is true. And you know it is true. Since you force me to speak, then I will tell you.'

'I am not inquisitive.'

'But I will tell you, for even leaping about tree trunks all day long a man may still see something and learn how to think and feel. I want to tell you what I think about your countless occupations and interests and your daring theories and your verses and your loves.'

Stiković made a movement as if to rise but none the less remained where he was. The piano and violin from the officers' mess had resumed their duet some time ago (the third movement of the Sonatina, gay and lively) and their music was lost in the night and the roar of the river.

'Thank you. I have heard all that from others more intelligent than you are.'

'Oh no! Others either do not know you or lie to you or think as I do but keep silent. All your theories, all your many spiritual occupations, like your loves and your friendships, all these derive from your ambition, and that ambition is false and unhealthy for it derives from your vanity, only and exclusively from your vanity.'

'Ha, ha!'

'Yes, even that nationalist idea which you preach so ardently is only a special form of vanity. For you are incapable of loving your mother or your sister or your own blood brother, so how much less an idea. Only from vanity could you be good, generous, self-sacrificing. For your vanity is the main force that moves you, the only thing you revere, the one and only thing that you love more than yourself. One who doesn't know you might easily be mistaken, seeing

your force and your industry, your devotion to the nationalist
ideal, to science, to poetry or to any other great aim which is
above personal feelings. But you cannot in any case serve it
for long or remain with it for long, for your vanity will not
let you. The moment your vanity is no longer in question,
everything becomes meaningless to you. You do not want
anything and would not even move a finger to obtain it.
Because of it you will betray yourself, for you are yourself
the slave of your own vanity. You do not know yourself how
vain you are. I know your very soul and I know that you are
a monster of vanity.'

Stiković did not reply. At first he had been surprised at the
considered and passionate outburst of his comrade who now
suddenly appeared to him in a new light and an unexpected
role. Therefore that caustic, even speech which at first irritated and insulted him, now seemed interesting and almost
pleasant. Individual phrases had, it is true, hit home and
hurt, but on the whole all that sharp and profound exposure
of his character had flattered and pleased him in a special sort
of way. For to tell a young man that he is a monster merely
means to tickle his pride and his self-love. In fact he wanted
Glasičanin to continue this cruel probing into his inner self,
that clear projection of his hidden personality, for in it he
found only one more proof of his exceptional superiority.
His eyes fell on the white plaque opposite him which shone
in the moonlight. He looked straight at the incomprehensible Turkish inscription as if he were reading it and trying to
decipher the deeper sense of what his friend beside him had
been saying penetratingly and consideredly.

'Nothing is really important to you and, in fact, you
neither love nor hate, for to do either you must at least for a
moment stand outside yourself, express yourself, forget yourself, go beyond yourself and your vanity. But that you cannot
do; nor is there anything for which you would do so even
were you able. Someone else's sorrow cannot move you,
how much less hurt you; not even your own sorrow unless it
flatters your vanity. You desire nothing and you find joy in

nothing. You are not even envious, not from goodness but from boundless egoism, for you do not notice the happiness or unhappiness of others. Nothing can move you or turn you from your purpose. You do not stop at anything, not because you are brave, but because all the healthy impulses in you are shrivelled up, because save for your vanity nothing exists for you, neither blood ties nor inward considerations, neither God nor the world, neither kin nor friend. You do not esteem even your own natural capacities. Instead of conscience it is only your own wounded vanity that can sting you, for it alone, always and in everything, speaks with your mouth and dictates your actions.'

'Is this an allusion to Zorka?' Stiković suddenly asked.

'Yes, if you like, let us talk of that too. Yes, because of Zorka also. You do not care a jot for her. It is only your inability to stop and restrain yourself before anything which momentarily and by chance is offered you and which flatters your vanity. Yes, that is so. You seduce a poor, muddled and inexperienced schoolmistress just as you write articles and poems, deliver speeches and lectures. And even before you have completely conquered them you are already tired of them, for your vanity becomes bored and looks for something beyond. But that is your own curse too, that you can stop nowhere, that you can never be sated and satisfied. You submit everything to your vanity but you are yourself the first of its slaves and its greatest martyr. It may well be that you will have still greater glory and success, a greater success than the weakness of some love-crazed girl, but you will find no satisfaction in any one thing, for your vanity will whip you onwards, for it swallows everything, even the greatest successes and then forgets them immediately, but the slightest failure or insult it will remember forever. And when everything is withered, broken, soiled, humiliated, disintegrated and destroyed about you, then you will remain alone in the wilderness you have yourself created, face to face with your vanity and you will have nothing to offer it. Then you will devour yourself, but that will not help you, for your vanity accustomed to richer food will despise and reject you. That is what you are, though you may seem different in the eyes of most men and though you think differently of yourself. But I know.'

Glasičanin ceased suddenly.

The freshness of the night could already be felt on the *kapia* and the silence spread, accompanied by the eternal roar of the waters. They had not even noticed when the music from the bank had ceased. Both youths had completely forgotten where they were and what they were doing. Each had been carried away by his own thoughts as only youth can be. The jealous and unhappy 'cube-measurer' had spoken only of what he had so many times thought over passionately, deeply and intensely, but for which he had never before been able to find suitable words and expressions and which that night had come easily and eloquently, bitterly and exaltedly. Stikovič had listened, motionlessly looking at the white plaque with the inscription as if it had been a cinema screen. Every word had hit home. He felt every harsh comment but he no longer found in all that this scarcely visible friend beside him had said any insult or any danger. On the other hand, it seemed to him that with every word of Glasičanin he grew, and that he flew on invisible wings, swift and unheard, exulting and daring, high above all men on this earth and their ties, laws and feelings, alone, proud and great, and happy or with some feeling akin to happiness. He flew above everything. That voice, those words of his rival, were only the sound of the waters and the roar of an invisible, lesser world far below him: it mattered little to him what it was, what it thought and what it said, for he flew above it as a bird.

The momentary silence of Glasičanin seemed to bring them both to their senses. They did not dare to look at one another. God alone knows in what form the quarrel would have continued had there not appeared on the bridge a crowd of drunkards coming from the market-place, shouting loudly and singing snatches of songs. Loudest among them was a tenor who sang in falsetto an ancient song:

'Thou art wise as thou art lovely,
Lovely Fata Avdagina! . . .'

They recognized the voices of a number of young merchants' and landowners' sons. Some were walking slowly and sedately, others wavered and tottered. From their noisy jests it could be concluded that they had come from 'Under the Poplars'.

More than fifteen years earlier, even before the building of the railway had begun, a certain Hungarian and his wife had settled in the town. He was called Terdik and his wife Julka. She spoke Serbian for she had been born in Novi Sad. It soon became known that they had come with the intention of opening a business in the town for which the local people had no name. They opened it on the outskirts of the town, under the tall poplars which grew on the Stražište slopes, in an old Turkish house which they completely rebuilt.

This was the town's house of shame. All day long the windows remained shuttered. As dusk fell a white acetylene lamp was lit in the doorway which burned there all night. Songs and the tinkle of an automatic piano echoed from the ground floor. Young men and dissolute idlers bandied about among themselves the names of the girls whom Terdik had brought and kept there. At first there were four of them: Irma, Ilona, Frieda and Aranka.

Every Friday 'Julka's girls' could be seen going in two cabs up to the hospital for their weekly inspection. They were heavily rouged and powdered, with flowers in their hats and with long-handled sunshades with streamers of floating lace. When these cabs went by, the women of the town hustled their daughters out of sight and averted their eyes with mixed feelings of shame, disgust and pity.

When work began on the railway and there was an influx of money and workers, the number of girls was increased. Besides the old Turkish house, Terdik built a new 'planned' one with a red-tiled roof which could be seen from afar.

There were three rooms; the general room, the *extra-zimmer* and the officers' salon. In each of them were different prices and different guests. At 'Under the Poplars', as it was known in the town, the sons and grandsons of those who had once drunk at Zarije's inn, or later at Lotte's, could leave their inherited or hard-won money. The grossest practical jokes, the most notorious quarrels, wild drinking parties and sentimental dramas took place there. Many personal and family misfortunes had their origins in that house.

The centre of that group of drunkards who had spent the first part of the night 'Under the Poplars' and had now come to cool off on the *kapia* was a certain Nikola Pecikoza, a silly good-natured youth whom they made drunk and on whom they played their jokes.

Before the drunkards reached the *kapia* they halted by the parapet. A loud and drunken argument could be heard. Nikola Pecikoza bet two litres of wine that he would walk along the stone parapet to the end of the bridge. The bet was taken and the young man climbed on to the parapet and set out with arms outspread, placing one foot carefully before the other like a sleepwalker. When he reached the *kapia* he noticed the two late visitors; he said nothing to them but humming some song and wavering in his drunkenness continued on his dangerous way, while the merry party accompanied him. His great shadow in the weak moonlight danced on the bridge and broke into fragments on the opposite parapet.

The drunkards passed by in a frenzy of disconnected shouts and stupid comments. The two young men rose and, without saying goodnight, each went his own way to his own house.

Glasičanin disappeared into the darkness towards the left bank where was the path which led to his house up at Okolište. Stiković made his way with slow steps in the opposite direction towards the market-place. He walked slowly and irresolutely. He did not want to leave that place which was lighter and fresher than in the town. He halted by the parapet. He felt the need to catch hold of something, to lean on something.

The moon had set behind the Vidova Gora. Leaning on the stone parapet at the end of the bridge the young man looked long at the huge shadows and few lights of his native town as if he now saw it for the first time. Only two windows were still lighted in the officers' mess. The music could no longer be heard. Probably the unhappy lovers were there, the doctor and the Colonel's lady, holding their discussions on music and on love or about their personal fates which would not permit them to be at peace with themselves or with one another.

From the spot where Stiković was now standing he could see that one window was still lighted in Lotte's hotel. The young man looked at those lighted windows on each side of the bridge as if he expected something from them. He was tired out and melancholy. The vertiginous walk of that idiot Pecikoza suddenly reminded him of his earliest childhood, when on his way to school he had seen in the mist of a winter's morning the squat figure of Ćorkan dancing on that same parapet. Every memory of his childhood aroused sorrow and uneasiness in him. That sentiment of fateful and exalted greatness and universal flight above everyone and everything which Glasičanin's bitter and fiery words had excited in him was now lost. It seemed to him that he had suddenly fallen from the heights and that he was crawling on the darkened earth with everyone else. The memory of what had happened with the schoolmistress, and should not have happened, tormented him as if someone else had done it in his name; so too did the article which now seemed to him weak and full of faults, as if another had written it and had published it in his name and against his will. He thought of the long conversation with Glasičanin which now all of a sudden seemed to him full of malice and hate, of bitter insults and real perils.

He shivered inwardly and from the chill which arose from the river. As if suddenly awakened he noticed that the two windows in the officers' mess were no longer lighted. The last guests were leaving the building. He could hear the clink of their swords as they crossed the darkened square and the sound of loud, artificial chatter. The young man regretfully left the parapet and, looking at the solitary window still alight in the hotel, the last light in the sleeping town, made his way slowly towards his simple house up there at Mejdan.

CHAPTER XX

THE ONLY LIGHTED window in the hotel, which remained as the last sign of life that night in the town, was that small window on the first floor where Lotte's room was. Even at night Lotte sat there at her overladen table. It was just as it had been earlier, more than twenty years before, when she had come to this little room to snatch a moment of respite from the bustle and noise of the hotel. Only now everything downstairs was dark and quiet.

At ten o'clock that night Lotte had withdrawn to her room to sleep. But before she lay down she went over to the window to breathe in the freshness from the river and to take a last glance at that arch of the bridge which was the only and eternally the same view from her window. Then she remembered some old account and sat down to look for it. Once she began looking through her accounts she became absorbed and remained for more than two hours at her table.

Midnight had long passed while Lotte, wakeful and absorbed, entered figure after figure and turned paper after paper.

Lotte was tired. In the daytime, in conversation and at work, she was still animated and talkative, but at night when she was alone she felt all the weight of her years and her fatigue. She had grown old. Of her onetime beauty only traces remained. She had grown thinner and yellow in the face; her hair was without lustre and was growing thin on her scalp, and her teeth, once shining and strong, were yellow and showed gaps. The glance of her black and still shining eyes was hard and at times sad.

Lotte was tired, but not with that blessed and sweet tiredness which follows heavy work and great gains, such as at one time had driven her to search for rest and respite in that room. Old age had come upon her and the times were no longer good.

She would not have been able to express in words, nor could she explain it to herself, but she felt at every step that the times were out of joint, at any rate for one who had always kept only her own good and that of her family before her eyes. When, thirty years before, she had come to Bosnia and begun work there, life had seemed all of a piece. Everyone was moving in the same direction as she was; work and family. Everyone was in his right place and there was a place for everyone. And over everyone reigned one order and one law, an established order and a strict law. So had the world then appeared to Lotte. Now everything had changed and was topsy-turvy. Men were divided and separated without, it seemed to her, rhyme or reason. The law of profit and loss, that divine law which had always controlled human activities, seemed as if it were no longer valid, for so many men worked, spoke or wrote about things of which she could not see the aim or the sense and which could only end in misfortune and damage. Life was bursting asunder, was crumbling, was disintegrating. It seemed to her that the present generation attached more importance to its views on life than to life itself. It seemed to her mad and completely incomprehensible, yet it was so. Therefore life was losing its value and wasting away in mere words. Lotte saw this clearly and felt it at every step.

Her business affairs, which at one time had seemed to gambol before her eyes like a flock of spring lambs, now lay inert and dead like the great tombstones in the Jewish cemetery. For the past ten years the hotel had done little business. The forests around the town had been cut down and felling was moving farther and farther away, and with it the best of the hotel's customers and the greater part of its profits. That shameless and insolent boor, Terdik, had opened his house 'Under the Poplars' and enticed away many of Lotte's guests, offering them easily and immediately all that they had never been able to get in her hotel however much they paid. Lotte had long revolted against this unfair and shameless competition and said that the last days had come, those days in which law and order existed no longer or the chance of making an honest living. At first she had bitterly referred to Terdik as 'the whoremaster'; but he had brought her before the courts and Lotte had been sentenced to pay a fine for defamation of character. But even now she never referred to him by any other term, though she took care before whom she was speaking. The new officers' mess had its own restaurant, a cellar of good wines and its own guest-rooms where distinguished visitors could be put up. Gustav, the sullen and bad-tempered but skilful and reliable Gustav, had left the hotel after many years of service and opened his own café in the most frequented part of the market-place, and so instead of a colleague he had become a competitor. The choral society and the various reading rooms which had been opened in the town in the past few years had their own cafés and attracted many guests.

There was no longer the former animation either in the main room or, still less, in the *extra-zimmer*. An occasional unmarried civil servant had his lunch there, read the newspapers and took coffee. Alibeg Pašić, the taciturn and impassioned friend of Lotte's youth, still went there every afternoon. Still as careful and discreet as ever, both in speech and actions, still correct and carefully dressed, he had grown grey and ponderous. His coffee was served with saccharine because of the severe diabetes from which he had been suffering for years. He smoked quietly and, silent as ever, listened to Lotte's chatter. When the time came he rose just as quietly and silently and went home to Crnče. There was also another daily visitor, Lotte's neighbour Pavle Ranković. He had long left off wearing national costume and now wore the 'tight' civilian dress, but he still stuck to his shallow red fez. He always wore a starched shirt with a stiff collar, and cuffs on which he noted down figures and accounts. He had long ago succeeded in taking over the leading place in the Višegrad trading community. His position was by now consolidated

and assured, but not even he was without his cares and difficulties. Like all the older men who had a certain amount
of property he was bewildered by the new times and the
clamorous onrush of new ideas and new ways of life, thought
and expression. All these things were embraced for him by
the single word 'politics'. It was those 'politics' that confused
and angered him and embittered those years which should
have been years of respite and satisfaction after so much work
and thrift and renunciation. He in no way wanted to stand
aside or withdraw himself from the majority of his fellow
countrymen, but at the same time he had no wish to come
into conflict with the authorities with whom he wished to
remain at peace and at least outwardly in agreement. But
that was difficult, almost impossible, to achieve. He could
not even understand his own sons as he should. Like all the
rest of the younger generation they were simply baffling
and incomprehensible to him; yet many older people either
from necessity or weakness followed their example. Their
bearing, behaviour and actions seemed to Pavle rebellious
as if they thought that to live and die in present conditions
was no better than to spend their lives like brigands in the
mountains. Young people did not think what they said, paid
no heed to what they did, did not count the cost and were
careless in their work; they ate their bread without stopping
to think whence it came and talked, talked, talked, 'baying
at the moon' as Pavle expressed it in his arguments with
his sons.

This way of thinking without limits, this speech without
consideration, and this life without calculation and hostile to
every calculation, drove Pavle, who had worked all his life
by and with calculation, to frenzy and desperation. He was
filled with fear whenever he heard or saw them; it seemed
to him that they imprudently and irresponsibly hacked away
at the very foundations of life, at all that was dearest and
most sacred to him. When he asked them for an explanation which would convince and reassure him they replied
disdainfully and haughtily with vague and high-sounding

words; freedom, future, history, science, glory, greatness. His skin crawled at all these abstract words. Therefore he liked to sit and drink coffee with Lotte, with whom he could talk about business and events, always based on a sure and admitted calculation, very different from the 'politics' and the big, dangerous words that questioned everything, explained nothing and affirmed nothing. During the conversation he often took out his pencil stub, not that of twenty-five years back but one just as shiny and almost equally invisible, and put all that was said to the infallible and irrefutable proof of figures. They often recalled in their talk some long ago happening, or some jest in which nearly all the participants were now dead, and then Pavle, bowed with cares, would go to his shop in the market-place and Lotte remained alone with her worries and her accounts.

Lotte's personal speculations were in no better shape than the hotel's business. In the first years after the occupation it had been enough to buy any share in any enterprise and one could be sure that the money was well invested and the only question that could arise was the amount of the profit. But at that time the hotel had only just started work and Lotte had neither the ready money at her disposal nor the credit which she later enjoyed. When she had achieved both money and credit the state of affairs on the exchanges had completely changed. One of the most serious of the cyclic crises had hit the Austro-Hungarian Monarchy at the end of the nine-teenth and the beginning of the twentieth century. Lotte's stocks and shares began to play like dust in a high wind. She would weep with rage when she read the most recent quota-tions each week in the Vienna *Merkur*. All the profits of the hotel, which at that time was still doing good business, were not enough to cover the losses caused by the general decline in values. At that time too she had had a severe nervous breakdown which lasted a full two years. She was almost mad with pain. She chatted to people without hearing what they said or thinking what she herself was saying. She looked them full in the face but did not see them but the small-print columns of the *Merkur* which were to bring her good or evil luck. Then she began to buy lottery tickets. Since everything was in any case only a game of chance, she might as well do it properly. She had lottery tickets from every country. She even succeeded in getting hold of a quarter share in a ticket of the great Spanish Christmas Lottery whose first prize amounted to fifteen million pesetas. She prayed God for a miracle and that her ticket should draw the first prize. But she never won anything.

Seven years before, Lotte's brother-in-law Zahler had gone into partnership with a couple of wealthy men on pension and founded the 'Modern Milk Co-operative' in the town. Lotte provided three-fifths of the capital. Business on a large scale was envisaged. It was reckoned that the initial successes, which could not fail to eventuate, would attract capital from outside the town and even outside Bosnia. But just at the moment when the enterprise was in its critical phase the annexation crisis took place. This destroyed every hope of attracting fresh capital. These frontier districts became so unsafe that capital already invested in them began to flee. The Co-operative went into liquidation after two years, with the total loss of all the invested capital. Lotte had to mortgage her best and safest shares, like those of the Sarajevo Brewery and the Solvaj Soda Factory at Tuzla, to cover the deficit.

Parallel with these financial misfortunes and allied to them were family troubles and disappointments. It was true that one of Zahler's daughters, Irene, had married unexpectedly well (Lotte had provided the dowry). But the elder daughter, Mina, remained. Embittered by the marriage of her younger sister and unfortunate in her suitors she had become before her time a vinegary and sharp-tongued old maid to whom life at home and work in the hotel seemed even heavier and more unbearable than in fact they were. Zahler who had never been lively or quick-witted grew even more ponderous and indecisive and lived at home like a dumb but good-natured guest from whom there was neither harm nor profit. Zahler's wife, Deborah, though sickly and in advanced years, had given birth to a son, but the boy was backward and rickety. He was now ten years old and still could not speak clearly or stand upright, but expressed himself in vague sounds and crawled about the house on his hands and knees. But this miserable creature was so pitiable and good and clung so desperately to his Aunt Lotte, whom he loved far more than his mother, that Lotte, despite all her worries and duties, looked after him, fed him, dressed him and sang him to sleep. With this cretin ever before her eyes, her heart contracted at the idea that business was now so bad that there was not enough money to send him to the famous doctors in Vienna or into some institution, and at the thought that the days of miracles were past and that such creatures could not grow healthy by God's will or by man's good works and prayers.

Lotte's Galician dependants, whom she had educated or given in marriage during the good years, also caused her no little worry and disappointment. Some amongst them had founded families, extended their business and acquired property. Lotte got regular news from them, letters filled with respect and gratitude and regular reports of the progress of their families. But the Apfelmaiers to whom Lotte had given a start in life, had educated or provided homes for, did not help her or take any responsibility for new relatives born and growing up in poverty in Galicia but, once settled in distant cities, only bothered about themselves and their own children. For them the greater part of their success lay in forgetting Tarnow and the cramped and wretched circumstances in which they had grown up and from which they had had the luck to liberate themselves, as quickly and as completely as possible; and Lotte herself was no longer able to set aside money as she had once done to give that black poverty of Tarnow its chance in life. She never went to sleep or woke now without the thought that someone of hers in Tarnow was forever sunk in the slough of hopeless poverty, condemned forever to ignorance and filth, in that shameful

poverty which she knew so well and which she had fought
against all her life.

Even amongst those whose lot she had already improved
there was reason enough for complaint and dissatisfaction.
Even the best among them had turned from the right
path and made mistakes after their first successes and most
shining hopes. One niece, a gifted pianist, who by Lotte's
help and encouragement had completed her studies at the
Vienna Conservatoire, had poisoned herself a few years
earlier at the time of her first and best successes; no one
knew why.

One of her nephews, Albert, Lotte's pride and the hope
of the family, had completed all his studies, both at secondary school and university, with outstanding success and
only because he was a Jew had not received his diploma '*sub
auspiciis regis*' or obtained the Imperial signet as Lotte had
secretly hoped. None the less, Lotte had imagined him at
least as a leading lawyer in Vienna or Lwow, since being a
Jew he could not become a senior civil servant which would
best have accorded with her ambitions. In such dreams she
reaped the reward for all her sacrifices for his education. But
there too she had had to suffer a painful disillusionment.
The young doctor of law went into journalism and became
a member of the Socialist Party, and of that extremist wing
which became notorious in the Vienna general strike of
1906. Lotte had to read with her own eyes in the Viennese
newspapers that 'during the cleaning up in Vienna of sub-
versive foreign elements, the well-known Jewish agitator Dr
Albert Apfelmaier has been expelled, after first purging a
sentence passed against him of twenty days' imprisonment'.
That, in the language of the town, meant the same as if
he had been a *haiduk*, a brigand. A few months later Lotte
received a letter from her dear Albert in which he told her
that he was emigrating to Buenos Aires.

In those days she could not find peace even in her own
room. With the letter in her hand she went to her sister
and brother-in-law and desperately, senselessly, flew into a

passion with her sister Deborah who could only weep. She shouted with rage:

'What is to become of us? I ask you, what is to become of us, when no one knows how to make his way and stand up for himself? Unless they are propped up they all fall. What is going to happen to us? We are accursed, that is all there is to it.'

'Gott, Gott, Gott,' wailed poor Deborah with tears flowing down her cheeks, naturally quite unable to answer Lotte's questions. Nor did Lotte herself find an answer but clasped her hands and lifted her eyes to heaven, not weeping and frightened like Deborah, but furious and despairing.

'He has become a Socialist! A Soc - ial - ist! Isn't it enough that we are Jews, but he must be that as well! O Great and Only God, how have I sinned that You must punish us thus? A Socialist!'

She wept for Albert as though he were dead and then never spoke of him again.

Three years later one of her nieces, sister of that same Albert, married well in Pest. Lotte took charge of the trousseau and took a leading part in the moral crisis that this marriage provoked in the great Apfelmaier family of Tarnow, rich only in children and an unsullied religious tradition. The man whom this niece was to marry was a rich speculator on the Bourse, but a Christian and a Calvinist, and he made it a condition that the girl should be converted to his faith. The relatives all opposed this but Lotte, with the interest of the whole family in mind, said that it was hard to keep afloat with so many persons in the boat and that it was sometimes necessary to throw something overboard for the salvation of all the rest. She supported the girl and her word was decisive. The girl was baptized and married. Lotte hoped that with the help of her new relative she would be able to introduce at least one of those cousins or nephews now of suitable age into the business world of Pest. But bad luck had it that the rich Pest speculator died in the first year of marriage. The young wife went almost mad with grief.

Months passed and her great grief did not lessen. The young widow had now been living in Pest for four years, given over to her unnatural grief which amounted to a mild form of madness. The great, richly furnished apartment was swathed in black cloth. She went every day to the cemetery, sat by her husband's grave and read softly and devotedly to him the list of market quotations for the day from beginning to end. To all suggestions made that she should awake from the lethargy into which she had fallen she answered softly that the dead man had loved that above all and that it had been the sweetest music he had ever known.

Thus many destinies of all kinds accumulated in that little room. There were many accounts, many doubtful bills, many others written off and expunged for ever in that great, many-sided book-keeping of Lotte's; but the great principle of work remained the same. Lotte was tired but she was not discouraged. After every loss or failure, she would call on her resources, set her teeth and go on with the struggle. In recent years she had been fighting a rearguard action but she went on struggling with the same aim before her eyes and with the same resolution as she had shown when she made money and went forward in the world. She was the 'man' of that household and 'Aunt Lotte' to the whole township. There were still many both in the town and in the outside world who waited for her aid, her advice or at least her encouragement, and who did not ask and could not imagine that Lotte was tired. But she was really tired, more than anyone suspected and more than she herself knew.

The little wooden clock on the wall struck one. Lotte rose with difficulty, her hands on her hips. She carefully extinguished the great green lamp on the wooden side-table and with the short steps of an old woman, steps she used only when she was in her own room and even then only when going to bed, she went to lie down.

There was complete and universal darkness over the sleeping town.

CHAPTER XXI

IT IS NOW 1914, the last year in the chronicle of the bridge on the Drina. It came as all earlier years had come, with the quiet pace of winter but with the sullen roar of ever new and ever more unusual events which piled upon one another like waves.

So many years had passed over the town and so many more would still pass over it. There had been, and there still would be, years of every sort, but the year 1914 will always remain unique. So at least it seemed to those who lived through it. To them it seemed that never would they be able to speak of all that they had seen then of the course of human destinies, however much, still concealed by time and events, might be said or written about it later. How could they explain and express those collective shudders which suddenly ran through all men and which from living beings were transmitted to inert objects, to districts and to buildings? How could they describe that swirling current among men which passed from dumb animal fear to suicidal enthusiasm, from the lowest impulses of bloodlust and pillage to the greatest and most noble of sacrifices, wherein man for a moment touches the sphere of greater worlds with other laws? Never can that be told, for those who saw and lived through it have lost the gift of words and those who are dead can tell no tales. Those were things which are not told, but forgotten. For were they not forgotten, how could they ever be repeated?

In that summer of 1914, when the rulers of human destinies drew European humanity from the playing fields of universal suffrage to the already prepared arena of universal military service, the town of Višegrad provided a small but eloquent example of the first symptoms of a contagion which would in time become European and then spread to the entire world. That was a time on the limits of two epochs in human history whence one could more easily see the end of that epoch which was closing than the beginning of that new one which was opening. Then one sought for a justification for violence and found some name borrowed from the spiritual treasury of the past century for savagery and bloodlust. All that took place still had the outer semblance of dignity and the attraction of novelty, a terrible, short-lived and inexpressible charm which later disappeared so completely that even those who then felt it so strongly could no longer evoke its memory.

But these are all things which we recall only in passing and which poets and scientists of coming ages will investigate, interpret and resurrect by methods and manners which we do not suspect and with a serenity, freedom and boldness of spirit which will be far above ours. Probably they will succeed in finding an explanation even for that strange year and will give it its true place in the history of the world and the development of humanity. But here it is unique for us, for above all that was the fatal year for the bridge on the Drina.

The summer of 1914 will remain in the memory of those who lived through it as the most beautiful summer they ever remembered, for in their consciousness it shone and flamed over a gigantic and dark horizon of suffering and misfortune which stretched into infinity.

That summer did in fact begin well, better than so many earlier summers. The plums ripened as they had not done for long before, and the wheat promised a good harvest. After ten years or so of troubles and commotions, the people hoped for at least a lull and a good year which would recompense in every way for the harms and misfortunes of earlier years. (The most deplorable and tragic of all human weaknesses is undoubtedly our total incapacity for seeing into the future, which is in sharp contrast to so many of our gifts, our skills and our knowledge.)

Sometimes there is such a year when the heat of the

sun and the moisture of the earth combine, and the whole Višegrad valley trembles from the superabundance of its force and the universal urge towards fecundity. The earth swells and everything in it bursts vigorously into buds and leaves and blossoms and brings forth fruit a hundredfold. That breath of fertility could easily be seen quivering like a warm blue cloud over every furrow and every heap of earth. The cows and goats walked with hindlegs astraddle and moved with difficulty because of swollen and brimming udders. The fish in the river which every year at the beginning of summer came in shoals down the Rzav to spawn at its mouth were in such numbers that the children scooped them out of the shallows in buckets and threw them on to the bank. The porous stone of the bridge became softer and as if it were alive swelled with the force and abundance which beat upwards from the soil and hovered over the whole town in the heat of the dog-days in which everything breathed more quickly and matured more vigorously.

Such summers were not frequent in the Višegrad valley. But when one occurred, men forgot all the bad days that had been and did not even think of the misfortunes which might still be in store, but lived with the threefold intensity of the life of the valley upon which the blessings of fertility had fallen, themselves only a part in that game of moisture and heat and ripening juices.

Even the peasants who always found occasion to complain of something had to agree that the year had fruited well, but to every word of praise they added the qualification: 'If this weather holds. . . .' The merchants of the market-place threw themselves headlong into business like bees into the cups of flowers. They scattered into the villages around the town to make deposit payments on wheat in the ear and plums still in blossom. The peasants, bewildered by this invasion of eager buyers, as well as by the large and exceptional yield, stood beside their fruit trees already bending under the weight of fruit or beside the fields which were like waves in the wind, and could not be sufficiently prudent and restrained to deal with the townsmen who had taken the trouble to come to visit them. That prudence and restraint gave their faces a shuttered and anxious expression, twin of that mask of woe worn by peasant faces in years of bad harvest.

When the merchants were rich and powerful, it was the peasants who came to them. On market days the shop of Pavle Ranković was always full of peasants in need of ready money. So too was the shop of Santo Papo who had for long been the leading figure among the Višegrad Jews, for even despite the fact that banks, mortgage banks and other credit facilities had long existed in the town, the peasants, especially the older ones, liked to commit themselves in the old-fashioned way with the merchants from whom they bought their goods and with whom their fathers before them had contracted obligations.

Santo Papo's shop was one of the highest and most solid in the Višegrad market. It was built of stone, with thick walls and a floor of stone flags. The heavy doors and window-shutters were of wrought iron and there were thick close grilles on the tall and narrow windows.

The front part of the building served as a shop. Along the walls were wooden shelves filled with enamel ware. From the ceiling, which was exceptionally high, so that it was lost in the gloom, hung lighter goods: lanterns of all sizes, coffee-pots, traps, mousetraps and other objects of twisted wire. All these hung in great bunches. Around the long counter were piled boxes of nails, sacks of cement, plaster and various paints; hoes, shovels and mattocks without handles were strung on wire in heavy garlands. In the corners were large tin containers with paraffin, turpentine and lamp-black. It was cool there even in the height of summer and even at noon was dark and gloomy.

But most of the stock was in the rooms behind the shop, through a low entry with iron doors. The heavy goods were kept there: iron stoves, crowbars, ploughshares, picks and other large tools. They were all piled up in great heaps so that one could only walk between the piled goods along the narrow paths as if between high walls. Perpetual darkness reigned there and no one entered save with a lantern.

A chill dank air of stone and metal, which nothing could warm or disperse, exuded from the thick walls, stone ceiling and piled-up iron. That air in a few years transformed the lively and red-cheeked apprentices into silent, pale and puffy assistants, but made them skilful and thrifty. It was undoubtedly harmful also to the generations of shopkeepers but it was at the same time sweet and dear to them since it meant the feeling of property, the thought of gain and the source of riches.

The man who now sat in the front part of the cool, half-lit shop at a small table beside a great green Wertheim safe in no way resembled that turbulent and vivacious Santo who had once, thirty years before, had his own special way of shouting 'Rum for Ćorkan!'. The passage of years and the work in the shop had changed him. Now he was heavy and ponderous and yellow in the face; dark rings about his eyes stretched half way down his cheeks; his eyes had grown weak, those black and protruding eyes which now peered out from behind spectacles with thick lenses and metal rims, with a severe and yet timid expression. He still wore his cherry-coloured fez as a last remnant of his one-time Turkish costume. His father, Mente Papo, a wizened and bald old man in his eighties, was still in reasonable health though his sight was failing. He would come to the shop on sunny days. With his watery eyes which seemed to be melting away behind thick spectacles he would look at his son seated by the safe and his grandson at the counter, breathe in that aroma of his shop and then return home at a slow pace, his right hand resting on the shoulder of his ten-year-old great grandson.

Santo had six daughters and five sons, most of them married. His eldest son, Rafo, already had grown-up children who helped his father in the shop. One of Rafo's sons, who bore his grandfather's name, was at the Sarajevo secondary school. He was a pale, short-sighted and slender youth who at the age of eight had known perfectly how to recite the poems of the patriotic poet Zmaj, but otherwise was not good at his studies, did not like to go to the synagogue or help in his grandfather's shop during the holidays and said that he was going to become an actor or something equally famous and unusual.

Santo sat bowed over the huge, worn and greasy counter with an alphabetical ledger, and in front of him, on an empty nailbox, squatted the peasant Ibro Ćemanović of Uzavnica. Santo was reckoning up how much Ibro already owed him and therefore how much and on what conditions he could obtain a fresh loan.

'Sinquenta, sinquenta i ocho . . . sinquenta i ocho, sesienta i tres . . .,' Santo whispered, reckoning in Ladino Spanish.

The peasant watched him with anxious anticipation as if watching an incantation and not listening to the account which he already knew to the last *para* and which ran through his head even when he was asleep. When Santo finished and announced the amount of the loan with interest, the peasant murmured slowly: 'Will that be so . . .?' merely to gain time enough to compare his own reckoning with Santo's.

'So it is, Ibraga, and in no way different,' replied Santo in the formula time-honoured in such cases.

After they had agreed on the state of present indebtedness, the peasant had to demand a fresh loan and Santo to make clear the likelihood and the conditions. But that was no rapid or easy task. A conversation developed between them, similar in the minutest detail to the conversations which, ten years ago or more, also before the harvest, had been held in this same spot between the father of Ibro from Uzavnica and Santo's father, Mente Papo. The main subject of the conversation would be broached in a torrent of words which meant nothing in themselves and which seemed entirely superfluous and almost senseless. Anyone uninitiated, looking at them and listening to them, might easily have thought that the talk had nothing to do with money or a loan, or at least so it often appeared.

'The plums are well forward and brought forth much fruit

amongst us, even more than in any other district,' said Santo. 'It has been years since there was such a crop.'

'Yes, thanks be, they have borne well enough; if Allah permits the weather to hold there will be fruit and bread. One cannot deny it. Only who knows what the price will be,' said the anxious peasant, rubbing his thumb along the seam of his heavy green cloth trousers and looking at Santo out of the corner of his eye.

'There is no way of telling that now, but we shall know by the time you bring them to Višegrad. You know the saying; the price is in the owner's hands.'

'Yes, that is so. If Allah allows them to ripen and mature,' the peasant again qualified.

'Without God's will, naturally, there is no gathering nor reaping; however much man looks to what he has sown, it will avail him nothing if he have not God's blessing,' broke in Santo, raising his hand to heaven to show whence that blessing should come, somewhere high above those heavy blackened rafters of the shop from which hung peasant lanterns of all sizes and bundles of other goods.

'It will avail nothing, you are right,' sighed Ibro. 'A man sows and plants but it is just as if, by the Great and Only God, he had thrown it all into the water; one digs, hoes, prunes and picks, but no! If it is not so written there will be no blessing on it. But if God decides to give us a good harvest then no one will lack and a man may clear himself of debt and then become indebted once more. Only let him keep his health!'

'Ah, yes. Health is the main thing. Nothing is as important as health. So is man's life; give him everything and take health from him and it is as if he were given nothing,' affirmed Santo, turning the conversation in that direction.

Then the peasant also expressed his views on health, which were just as general and commonplace as Santo's. For a moment it seemed as if the whole conversation would be lost in futilities and generalizations. But at a favourable moment, as if by some ancient ritual, he returned to the opening question. Then began the bargaining for a new loan, over the amount, the interest, the terms and the methods of payment. They discussed it for long, now vivaciously, now quietly and anxiously, but in the end they came to an agreement. Then Santo rose, took a bunch of keys on a chain from his pocket and without removing them from the chain, unlocked the safe which began by creaking, opened slowly and solemnly and then, like all large safes, closed with a fine metallic noise like a sigh. He counted out the money to the peasant, down to the copper *hellers*, all with the same care and attention, with a solemnity that seemed a little sad. Then in a changed and more animated voice:

'Well, is that all right by you, Ibraga? Are you satisfied?'

'Yes, by God,' the peasant replied quietly and pensively.

'May God send you blessing and profit! Till we meet again in good health and good friendship,' said Santo, now quite lively and gay; and he sent his grandson to the café across the way for two coffees, 'one bitter, one sweet'.

A second peasant was already awaiting his turn in front of the shop bound on the same errand and similar reckonings.

With these peasants and their reckoning about the coming harvest and the gathering of the plums, the warm and heavy breath of an exceptionally fruitful year penetrated into the twilit gloom of Santo's shop. The green steel safe sweated from it and Santo stretched the collar around his fat, soft, yellowish neck with his forefinger and wiped the steam off his spectacles with a handkerchief.

So did summer begin.

But none the less at the very beginning of that year of blessing there fell a tiny shadow of fear and sorrow. In the early spring, at Uvac, a small place on the former Turco-Austrian frontier and the new Serbo-Austrian border, a typhus epidemic broke out. As the place was on the frontier and two cases had occurred in the gendarmerie station, the Višegrad military doctor, Dr Balas, went there with one male nurse and the necessary medicines. The doctor skilfully and resolutely did all that was necessary to isolate the sick, and himself undertook their treatment. Of fifteen who had been taken ill only two died and the epidemic was limited to the village of Uvac and stamped out at its source. The last man to take ill was Dr Balas himself. The inexplicable manner in which he had caught the disease, the shortness of his illness, the unexpected complications and sudden death, all bore the stamp of genuine tragedy.

Because of the danger of infection the young doctor had to be buried at Uvac. Madame Bauer with her husband and a few other officers attended the funeral. She gave some money for a tombstone of roughly hewn granite to be erected over the doctor's grave. Immediately afterwards she left both the town and her husband and it was rumoured that she had gone to some sanatorium near Vienna. This was the story current among the girls in the town; the older people, as soon as the danger had passed and the measures against the epidemic ceased, forgot both the doctor and the Colonel's lady. Inexperienced and uneducated, the town girls did not know exactly what the word sanatorium meant, but they had known very well what it meant when two persons walked about the paths and foothills as the doctor and the Colonel's wife had done until lately. Pronouncing that strange word in their confidential discussions about the unhappy pair, they loved to imagine that sanatorium as some sort of mysterious, distant and melancholy place in which beautiful and sinful women expiated their forbidden loves.

That exceptionally lovely and fruitful summer grew and matured over the fields and summits around the town. In the evening the windows of the officers' mess, over the river and by the bridge, were lighted and wide open as in the previous year, only the sound of the piano and the violin no longer came from them. Colonel Bauer sat at his table with a few of his senior officers, good-humoured, smiling and sweating from the effects of the red wine and the heat of the summer.

The young men sat on the *kapia* on warm nights and sang. It was nearly the end of June and the students were shortly expected to arrive, as they did every year. On such nights on the *kapia* it seemed as if time had stopped, while life flowed on endless, rich and easy and one could not foresee how long it would continue thus.

At that time of the night the main streets were illuminated, for the town had had electric light since spring that year. About a year earlier an electrically driven sawmill had been built on the river bank about a mile from the town and beside it a factory for extracting turpentine from pine refuse; it also produced resin. This factory had made an agreement with the municipality to light the town streets from its private power station. So the green lamp-standards with their petroleum lights disappeared, and with them tall Ferhat who used to clean and light them. The main street which stretched the whole length of the town, from the bridge to the new quarter, was lit by powerful lamps of white milky glass, while the side-streets which branched off to right and left and meandered around Bikavac or climbed upwards to Mejdan and Okolište were lighted by ordinary bulbs. Between these lines of similar lights stretched long irregular patches of darkness. These were courtyards or large gardens on the slopes.

In one of these dark gardens Zorka the schoolmistress was sitting with Nikola Glasičanin.

The dissension which had arisen between these two last year, when Stiković had appeared at the time of the vacation, had lasted for long, right up to the beginning of the new year. Then, as every winter, preparations for the Festival of St Sava had been begun in the Srpski Dom. A concert and a play were being prepared. Both Zorka and Glasičanin took part and returning home after the rehearsals they had spoken together for the first time since the previous summer. At first their talks had been short, reserved and distant. But they did not stop seeing one another, for young people prefer even the most bitter and hopeless of lovers' quarrels to the boredom and loneliness of a life without the play and thoughts of love. Somewhere in the course of their endless arguments they had made peace, they themselves knew not how or when.

Now, on these warm summer nights, they met regularly. From time to time the figure of the absent Stiković rose between them and the whole pointless argument flamed up again, but it did not drive them apart, while every reconciliation drew them closer and closer together.

Now they sat in the warm darkness on the stump of an old walnut tree and wrapped in their own thoughts looked down at the big and little lights of the town along the river which roared monotonously. Glasičanin, who had been talking for a long time, was now silent for a moment. Zorka, who had been silent all evening, remained silent as only women know how when they are disentangling their love troubles in their minds, those troubles which are more intimate and more important to them than anything else in life.

About this time last year, when Stiković had first appeared on the scene, Zorka had thought that an endless paradise of happiness had opened before her, in which perfect affinity of feelings and unity of thought and desires had the sweetness of a kiss and the duration of a human existence. But that illusion had not lasted long. However inexperienced and enraptured she may have been, she could not fail to notice that this man quickly took fire but equally quickly burnt out, according to his own ideas, without any consideration for her and without any connection with those things which she considered greater and more important than either herself or him. He had left her almost without saying goodbye. She had been left a prey to indecision from which she suffered as from a hidden wound. The letter which had come from him had been perfectly phrased, a perfect example of literary skill, but as measured as a counsel's opinion and as clear and as transparent as an empty glass jar. In it he had spoken of his love, but as if the pair of them had already been a century in their graves, like persons famous and long dead. To her warm and vivid reply came his card: 'In the tasks and anxieties which harass and annoy me I think of you as of a peaceful Višegrad night, filled with the sound of the river and the perfume of unseen grasses.' And that was all. In vain she tried to remember when she had heard the sound of the river and sensed the perfume of those unseen grasses. They existed only on his postcard. Certainly she did not remember them, even as he, it seemed, did not remember anything that had taken place between them. Her mind darkened with the thought that she had been deceived and that he had deceived her, and then consoled herself with something that she herself did not understand and which was less likely than a miracle. 'It is not possible to understand him,' she thought to herself, 'he is strange and cold, selfish, moody and capricious, but perhaps all exceptional men are like that.' In any event what she felt was more like suffering than love. Her inner flinching and the break that she felt in the depths of her being made it seem to her that the whole burden of that love which he had provoked lay upon her alone, and that he was lost somewhere far in the fog and the distance which she dared not call by its real name. For a woman in love, even when she has lost all her illusions, cherishes her love like a child she has not been destined to bear. She hardened her heart and did not reply to his card. But after a silence of two months another card arrived. It was written from some high mountain in the Alps: 'At a height of 2,000 metres, surrounded by people of various tongues and nationalities, I look at the boundless horizon and think of you and last summer.' Even for her years and her little experience that was enough. Had he written: 'I did not love you, I do not love you now, nor will I ever be able to love you,' it could have been no clearer or more painful to her. For when all was said and done, it was love that was in question, not far-off memories or how many metres above sea-level a man was writing, nor what people were around him nor what languages they spoke. And there was nothing about love!

A poor girl and an orphan, Zorka had grown up in Višegrad with some relations. After she had finished her studies at the Teachers' Training College at Sarajevo, she had been posted to Višegrad and had returned to the house of the well-to-do but simple folk to whom she felt in no way attached.

Zorka had grown thin and pale and had withdrawn into herself, but she had confided in no one, and did not reply to his Christmas message of greetings, which was equally short, cold and faultless in style. She wanted to come to terms with her own grief and shame without anyone's help or consolation but, weak, discouraged, young, ignorant and inexperienced, she became more and more involved in that inextricable net of real events and great desires, of her own thoughts and his incomprehensible and inhuman behaviour. Had she been able to ask anyone or to take anyone's advice, it would certainly have been easier for her but shame held her back. Even so it often seemed to her that the whole town knew about her disappointment and that mocking and malicious glances seemed to burn into her as she walked through the market-place. Neither men nor books gave her any explanation; and she herself did not know how to explain anything. If he really did not love her why had there been all that comedy of passionate words and vows during the vacation last year? What had been the reason for that episode on the school bench, which could only be justified and defended by love, without which it fell into the mud of unbearable humiliation? Was it possible that there were men who respected themselves and others so little that they would enter lightheartedly into such a game? What drove them on if not love? What did his burning glances, his warm and halting breath, his passionate kisses mean? What could they mean, if not love? But it was not love! She saw that now, better and more clearly than she would have liked. But she could not resign herself truly and lastingly to such a thought (who has ever been able to resign themselves completely to it?). The natural conclusion of all these internal conflicts was the thought of death which always lurks on the frontiers of every dream of happiness. To die, thought Zorka, to slip from the *kapia* into the river as if by chance, without letters or farewells, without admissions or humiliations. 'To die' she thought to herself in the last moments before going to sleep and on recovering consciousness in the morning, in the midst of the most lively conversations and beneath the mask of every smile. Everything in her said and repeated those words – 'to die! to die!' – but one does not die, but lives with that insupportable thought within one.

Comfort came from the source she least of all expected. Some time about the Christmas vacation her hidden torment reached its height. Such thoughts and such unanswered questions destroy one even more than an illness. Everyone noticed changes for the worse in her and worried about her, her relatives, her headmaster, a merry man with many children, and her friends, advising her to see a doctor.

Good luck had it that just at this time were the rehearsals for the St Sava festivities and that, after so many months, she again talked with Glasičanin. Up till then he had avoided every meeting or conversation with her. But that goodwill that usually reigns at these naïve but sincere dramatic and musical shows in small places, and then the clear cold nights as they returned home, saw to it that these two young estranged persons should draw closer to one another. Her need to lessen her torment drove her on and his love, deep and sincere, drove him.

Their first words were naturally cold, defiant, double-edged, and their conversations long explanations without issue. But even those brought solace to the girl. For the first time she could talk with a living being about her inner, shameful wretchedness without having to confess its most shameful and painful details. Glasičanin spoke to her of it long and animatedly but with warmth and consideration, saving her pride. He did not express himself more harshly about Stiković than was inevitable. His explanation was such as we have already heard that night on the *kapia*. It was short, sure and unsparing. Stiković was a born egoist and a monster, a man who could love no one and who as long as he lived, himself tormented and unsatisfied, would torture all those whom he deceived and who were near to him. Glasičanin did not speak much of his own love, but it was evident in every word, every glance and every movement.

The girl listened to him, remaining silent for the most part. After every such conversation she felt more serene, more at peace with herself. For the first time after so many months she had moments of respite from her internal storms and for the first time succeeded in looking at herself as other than an unworthy being. For the young man's words, filled with love and respect, showed her that she was not irretrievably lost and that her despair was only an illusion even as her dream of love the previous summer had been only an illusion. They had taken her out of that gloomy world in which she had already begun to lose herself and sent her back to living human reality, where there was healing and aid for everyone, or nearly everyone.

Their talks continued even after the St Sava celebrations. The winter passed and after it the spring. They saw one another almost every day. In time the girl came to herself, grew stronger and healthier, and was transformed, quickly and naturally, as only youth can be. So too passed that fruitful and uneasy summer. People were already accustomed to regard Zorka and Glasičanin as a couple who were 'walking out'.

It was true that the long speeches of Glasičanin to which she had at first listened avidly, drinking them in like medicine, were now less interesting. At times this need for mutual confession and confidence weighed on her. She asked herself with genuine wonder how this closeness between them had come about, but then she remembered that last winter he had 'saved her soul' and, mastering her boredom, listened to him like a good debtor, as carefully as she could.

That summer night his hand was over hers (that was the ultimate limit of his modest daring). Through that contact the warm richness of the night penetrated him also. In such moments it was fully clear to him how much treasure was hidden in this woman and at the same time he felt how the bitterness and dissatisfaction of his life was being transformed into fruitful power sufficient to take two people to even the most distant goal, if love bound them and sustained them.

Filled with those feelings in the darkness he was no longer the everyday Glasičanin, a minor clerk of the great Višegrad enterprise, but quite another man, strong and self-confident, who controlled his own life freely and far-sightedly. For a man filled with a great, true and unselfish love, even if it be on one side only, there open horizons and possibilities and paths which are closed and unknown to so many clever, ambitious and selfish men.

He spoke to the woman beside him.

'I do not think I am mistaken; if for no other reason, then just because I should never be able to deceive you. While some talk and rave and others do business and make gains, I follow everything and watch everything and I see more and more clearly that there is no sort of life here. For a long time there will be neither peace nor order nor profitable work. Not even Stiković, not even Herak, can create them. On the other hand, everything will get worse. We must get away from here, as from a house that is falling down. These countless and uneasy saviours who pop up at every step are the best proof that we are heading for a catastrophe. Since we cannot help, we can at least save ourselves.'

The girl remained silent.

'I have never spoken to you about this, but I have thought often and much, and have even done a little. You know that Bogdan Djurović, my friend from Okolište, has now been in America for three years. I have been in correspondence with him since last year. I showed you the photograph he sent me. He has asked me to come over there and has promised me a safe job at a good wage. I know that it is not a simple matter to do all this, but I do not think it is impossible. I have thought everything over and calculated everything. I will sell the little property I have up there at Okolište. If you will say yes, we will get married as soon as possible and leave for Zagreb without saying anything to anyone. There is a company there which arranges for emigrants to get to America. We could wait there until Bogdan sends us an affidavit. In the interval we could learn English. If we are not successful, perhaps because of my military service, then we will cross over into Serbia and leave from there. I will arrange everything to make it as easy as possible for you. In America we will both work. There are Serbian schools there where you could teach. I would easily find work there, for over there all jobs are open and unrestricted. We will be free and happy. I will arrange everything, if only you would . . . if only you would agree.'

The young man stopped. By way of answer she put both her hands on his. In that he felt the expression of a great gratitude. But her answer was neither yes nor no. She thanked him for all his trouble and attention and for his boundless goodness and, in the name of that goodness, asked for a month before she gave him a definite answer; until the end of the school year.

'Thank you, Nikola, thank you! You are good to me!' she whispered, pressing his hands.

From the *kapia* below rose the sound of young men singing. They were Višegrad youths, perhaps also some students from Sarajevo. In a fortnight the university students were due to arrive. Until then she would not be able to come to any decision. Everything made her suffer, most of all the goodness of this man, but at that moment she would not have been able to say 'yes' even if she were to be cut to pieces. She no longer hoped for anything save to see once more 'that man who can love no one'. Once more, and then let be what would! Nikola would wait; that she knew.

They rose and, hand in hand, went slowly down the slope which led towards the bridge whence the singing came.

CHAPTER XXII

ON VIDOVDAN THE Serbs held their regular outing at Mezalin. Under the dense walnut trees, at the meeting of the two rivers Drina and Rzav, on the high green banks, tents were put up in which drinks were on sale and before which lambs were turning on spits over slow fires. Families who had brought their lunch with them sat in the shade. Below a canopy of fresh branches an orchestra was already playing. On the well beaten open space there had been a *kolo* since morning. Only the youngest and idlest were dancing, those who had come here directly after morning service, straight from the church. The real general outing only began in the afternoon. But the *kolo* was already lively and enthusiastic, better and more vigorous than it would be later on when the crowd came, and married women, unsatisfied widows and young children began to take part and when everything was transformed into a single long and gay, but haphazard and disconnected, garland. That shorter *kolo* in which more young men than girls were taking part was fast and furious, like a thrown lasso. Everything around it seemed to be moving, swaying to the rhythm of the music, the air, the thick crowns of the trees, the white summer clouds and the swift waters of the two rivers. The earth trembled under it and around it and seemed only to be trying to adapt its movement to the movements of the young bodies. Young men ran in from the main road to take their places in the *kolo*, but the girls restrained themselves and stood for a time watching the dancing as if counting the beats and waiting for some secret impulse in themselves; then they would suddenly leap in to the *kolo* with lowered heads and slightly bended knees as if eagerly leaping into cold water. The powerful current passed from the warm earth into the dancing feet and spread along the chain of warm hands; on that chain the *kolo* pulsed like a single living thing, warmed by the same blood and carried away by the same rhythm. The young men danced with heads thrown back, pale and with quivering nostrils, while the young girls danced with reddened cheeks and modestly downcast eyes, lest their glances betray the passion with which the dance had filled them.

At that moment, when the outing had only just begun, a number of gendarmes appeared at the edge of the meadow, their black uniforms and weapons shining in the afternoon light. There were more of them than was usual for the patrol which regularly visited fairs and outings. They went straight to the canopy where the musicians were playing. One after the other, irregularly, the players ceased. The *kolo* wavered and stopped. Young men's cries of protest could be heard. The dancers stood hand in hand. Some were so carried away and filled with the rhythm that they went on dancing where they were, waiting for the music to begin again. But the players rose in haste and wrapped up their trumpets and their violins. The gendarmes went on farther, to the tents and the families sitting on the grass. Everywhere the sergeant said his piece, in a low harsh voice, and like some magic charm the gaiety faded away, the dancing ceased and conversations were broken off. Whomever they approached left the place where he had been till then, forgot whatever he was doing, gathered up his things as quickly as possible and left. The last to disperse was the *kolo* of youths and girls. They did not want to abandon their dancing and could not get it into their heads that this was really the end of the gaiety and the outing. But when they saw the white face and bloodshot eyes of the sergeant of gendarmes even the most obstinate slunk away.

Disillusioned and perplexed, the people trailed back from Mezalin along the wide, white road; the farther they went into the town the more they heard vague and frightened whispers about the assassination that morning at Sarajevo and the death of the Archduke Franz Ferdinand and his wife and the persecution of the Serbs which was generally expected. In front of the Municipal Offices they came upon the first group of arrested men, amongst them the young priest Mihailo, being taken to prison.

So the second part of that summer day, which should have been a festival, was transformed into a bewildered, bitter and frightened expectation.

On the *kapia*, instead of a festival mood and the gaiety of men released from work, there was the silence of the dead. A guard had already been mounted. A soldier in a new uniform paced slowly from the *sofa* to the spot where the iron manhole covered the way down into the mined pier. He marched these five or six paces incessantly, and at each turn his bayonet glinted in the sun like a signal. The next day, beneath the plaque with the Turkish inscription, a white official notice appeared on the wall, printed in large letters and surrounded by a thick black border. It announced the news of the assassination and death in Sarajevo of the Crown Prince and expressed the indignation roused by this evil deed. None of the passers-by stopped to read it, but passed in front of the notice and the guard as quickly as possible with lowered heads.

From that time onward the guard remained on the bridge. The whole life of the town was suddenly interrupted, like the *kolo* at Mezalin and that July day which should have been a day of festivity.

The days to come were strange, filled with the avid reading of newspapers, of whispers, of fear and defiance, the arrests of Serbs and suspect travellers and the rapid reinforcement of military measures on the frontiers. The summer nights passed, but without song, without meetings of young men on the *kapia* and without the whispering of couples in the darkness. In the town mainly soldiers were to be seen. At nine o'clock at night when the buglers sounded the melancholy notes of the Austrian last-post in the cantonments at Bikavac and in the great barracks by the bridge, the streets were almost entirely deserted. Those were bad times for young lovers eager to meet and have private conversations. Every evening Glasičanin passed Zorka's house. She was sitting at an open window on the ground floor. There they talked, but only for a short time, since he was in haste to cross the bridge and return to Okolište before nightfall.

So it happened that evening also. Pale, hat in hand, he begged the girl to come out to the gate for he had something private to tell her. After some hesitation she came. Standing on the threshold of the courtyard she was now level with the youth who spoke excitedly in a scarcely audible whisper.

'We have decided to flee. This evening. Vlado Marić and two others. I think that we have foreseen everything and that we shall get across. But if not . . . if something should happen. Zorka!'

The young man's whisper ceased. In her wide-open eyes he saw fear and embarrassment. He was deeply moved as if he regretted that he had spoken to her and come to say goodbye.

'I thought it better to tell you.'

'Thank you! Then there is nothing of our . . . nothing of America!'

'No, not "nothing". Had you consented when I suggested a month ago that we should finish the matter at once, then perhaps we might already be far away from here. But perhaps it is better this way. Now you can see what the position is. I must go with my friends. The war is here already and there is need for all of us in Serbia. I must, Zorka, I must. It is my duty. If I come out of all this alive and if we become free, then it may no longer be necessary to go across the sea to America, for we shall have our own America here, a land in which a man may work hard and honestly and live well and freely. There will be a life in it for both of us, if only you will consent. It will depend on you. I will . . . I will think of you over there, and you, and you . . . sometimes . . .'

Words failed him and he suddenly put up his hand and quickly stroked her rich chestnut hair. That had always been his greatest desire and now, like a condemned man, he felt permitted to fulfil it. The girl withdrew in fright and he remained with his hand in the air. The gate shut silently and a moment later Zorka appeared at the window, pale, with wide-open eyes and feverishly twisting fingers. The young man came close up to the window, threw his head back and revealed his face, laughing, carefree, almost handsome. As if afraid to see what would happen next, the girl drew back into the room which was already dark. There she sat down on her bed, bent her head and began to weep.

At first she wept quietly and then more and more unrestrainedly with a feeling of heavy, universal hopelessness. The more she wept, the more reason she found to weep as everything around her seemed more and more hopeless. There was no way out, no solution; never would she be able to love, truly and as he deserved, that good and honest Nikola who was going away; never would she live to see the day when that other one, who could love no one, should love her. Never again would she see those lovely, happy days which she had passed only last year in this town. Not a single one of the Serbs would ever succeed in coming alive out of that dark circle of mountains, nor would see America, nor would create here a land where, so they said, a man could work hard and live freely. Never!

Next day the news spread that Vlado Marić, Glasičanin and a few other young men had fled to Serbia. All the other Serbs with their families, and all that they had, remained in that overheated valley as in a trap. Every day the atmosphere of danger and menace could be felt to be growing denser over the town. Then, in the last days of July, the storm burst over the frontier, a storm which would in time spread to the whole world and decide the fate of so many lands and cities, as well as that of the bridge on the Drina.

Only then began the real persecution of the Serbs and all those connected with them. The people were divided into the persecuted and those who persecuted them. That wild beast, which lives in man and does not dare to show itself until the barriers of law and custom have been removed, was now set free. The signal was given, the barriers were down. As has so often happened in the history of man, permission was tacitly granted for acts of violence and plunder, even for murder, if they were carried out in the name of higher interests, according to established rules, and against a limited number of men of a particular type and belief. A man who saw clearly and with open eyes and was then living could see how this miracle took place and how the whole of a society could, in a single day, be transformed. In a few minutes the business quarter, based on centuries of tradition, was wiped out. It is true that there had always been concealed enmities and jealousies and religious intolerance, coarseness and cruelty, but there had also been courage and fellowship and a feeling for measure and order, which restrained all these instincts within the limits of the supportable and, in the end, calmed them down and submitted them to the general interest of life in common. Men who had been leaders in the commercial quarter for forty years vanished overnight as if they had all died suddenly, together with the habits, customs and institutions which they represented.

The day after the declaration of war on Serbia a *schutzkorps* squad began to patrol the town. This squad, hastily armed and intended to assist the authorities in their hunt for Serbs, was made up of gipsies, drunkards and other persons of ill repute, mainly those who for long had been at odds with society and the law. A certain Huso Kokošar, a gipsy without honour or definite occupation, who had lost his nose in early youth as a result of a shameful disease, led the dozen or so ne'er-do-wells armed with old-fashioned Werndl rifles with long bayonets, and lorded it over the market-place.

Faced with this threat, Pavle Ranković, as President of the Serbian Church and School Community, went with a number of other leading members to the sub-prefect Sabljak. Sabljak was a pale, puffy man, completely bald, born in Croatia, who had only recently been appointed to Višegrad. Now he was excited and he had not slept well; his eyelids were reddened and his lips dry and bloodless. He was wearing high boots and in the lapel of his huntsman's coat wore some badge in two colours: black and yellow. He received them standing and did not offer them seats. Pavle, yellow in the face, his eyes like two thin black slits, spoke in a hoarse unfamiliar voice:

'Sir, you see what is going on and what is being prepared, and you know that we, Serbs and citizens of Višegrad, have not wanted this.'

'I know nothing, sir,' the Prefect curtly interrupted him in a voice harsh with vexation, 'and I want to know nothing. We have other, more important, things to do now than listen to speeches. That is all I have to say to you!'

'Sir,' Pavle began again calmly as if trying by his own calm to moderate even this irritable and angry man, 'we have come to offer you our services and to assure you. . . .'

'I have no need of your services and there is nothing for you to assure me about. You have shown at Sarajevo what you can do. . . .'

'Sir,' continued Pavle resolutely and with unchanged voice, 'we would have liked within the limits of the law . . .'

'So! Now you remember the law! To what laws have you the effrontery to appeal. . .?'

'The laws of the state, Sir, which apply to all.'

The Prefect suddenly became serious as if he had calmed down a little. Pavle at once took advantage of this moment of calm.

'Sir, permit us to ask you whether we may be sure that our lives and property and those of our families will be respected, and if not, what we should do?'

The Prefect spread out his hands, palms upward, shrugged his shoulders, closed his eyes and convulsively shut his thin, pale lips.

Pavle knew only too well this characteristic gesture, pitiless, blind-deaf-dumb, which state officials adopt in important moments and saw at once that it was no use going on talking. The Prefect, after lowering his hands, looked up and said more gently:

'The military authorities will advise everyone what they must do.'

Now it was Pavle's turn to spread out his hands, close his eyes and shrug his shoulders for a moment, and then say in a deep, changed voice:

'Thank you, Sir.'

The representatives bowed stiffly and clumsily. Then they filed out like condemned men.

The market-place was filled with aimless movement and secret consultations.

In Alihodja's shop were sitting a number of prominent Turks, Nailbeg Turković, Osmanaga Šabanović and Suljaga Mezildjić. They were pale and worried, with that heavy, fixed expression which can always be seen on the faces of those who have something to lose when faced with unexpected events and important changes. The authorities had called on them to place themselves at the head of the *schutzkorps*. Now they had, as if by chance, met here to discuss without being overheard, what they ought to do. Some were for accepting, others for holding back. Alihodja, red in the face, excited, with the old light in his eyes, resolutely opposed any idea of participation in the *schutzkorps*. He addressed himself especially to Nailbeg who was for taking up arms since they, as leading citizens, should place themselves at the head of the Moslem volunteer detachments instead of a bunch of gipsies.

'I will never mix myself up in their affairs as long as I am alive. And you, if you had any sense, would not do so either. Can't you see that these Vlachs are only making use of us and that, in the end, it will all come back on our own heads?'

With the same eloquence as he had once used in opposing Osman Effendi Karamanli on the *kapia* he showed them that there was nothing good 'for the Turkish ear' on either side and that every intervention on their part could only be harmful.

'For a long time past no one has asked us about anything or paid the least heed to our opinions. The Schwabes entered Bosnia and neither Sultan nor Kaiser asked: "By your leave,

begs and gentlemen". Then Serbia and Montenegro, until
yesterday our serfs, rose in revolt and took away half the
Turkish Empire and still no one ever thought about us.
Now the Kaiser attacks Serbia and once again no one asks
us anything, but only gives us rifles and trousers to make us
Schwabe decoy ducks and tells us to hunt the Serbs lest they
should tear their own trousers climbing Šargan. Can't you
get that into your heads? Since no one has ever asked us about
so many important things over so many years, this sudden
favour is enough to make one burst one's ribs laughing. I tell
you; there are big things at stake and it is best for him who
does not get himself mixed up in them more than he must.
Here on the frontier they have already come to grips and
who knows how far it will spread? There must be someone
behind this Serbia. It could not be otherwise. But you, up
at Nezuke, have a mountain in front of your windows and
can see no farther than its stones. Better give up what you
have begun; don't go into the *schutzkorps* and don't persuade
others to go. Better go on milking the dozen serfs you have
left while they still bring you in something.'

All were silent, serious and motionless. Nailbeg too was
silent. He was obviously offended, though he concealed it.
Pale as a corpse, he was turning over some decision in his
mind. Save for Nailbeg, Alihodja had undecided them and
cooled their ardour. They smoked and silently watched the
endless procession of military wagons and laden packhorses
crossing the bridge. Then, one by one, they rose and made
their farewells. Nailbeg was the last. To his sullen greeting,
Alihodja once more looked him in the eyes and said almost
sadly:

'I see that you have made up your mind to go. You too
want to die, and are afraid lest the gipsies get in first. But
remember that long ago old men said: "The time has not
come to die but to let it be seen of what stuff a man is made".
These are such times.'

The square between the *hodja*'s shop and the bridge was
crammed with carts, horses, soldiers of all kinds and reservists

coming to report. From time to time the gendarmes would lead a group of bound men across it; Serbs. The air was filled with dust. Everyone yelled at the top of his voice and moved about more quickly than the occasion demanded. Faces were flushed and running with sweat; curses could be heard in all languages. Eyes were shining with drink and from sleepless nights and that troubled anxiety which always reigns in the presence of danger and bloody events.

In the centre of the square, directly facing the bridge, Hungarian reservists in brand-new uniforms were hewing some beams. Hammers sounded and saws were busy cutting. Around them a group of children had gathered. From his shop window Alihodja watched two beams being set up-right. Then a mustachioed Hungarian reservist scrambled up them and placed a third horizontally across the top. The crowd pressed around them as if *halva* were being given away, forming a living circle around the gallows. Most of them were soldiers, but there were also some Turkish village wastrels and gipsies from the town. When all was ready a way was made through the crowd and a table was brought and two chairs for the officer and his clerk. Then the *schutzkorps* brought first two peasants and then a townsman. The peasants were village serfs from the frontier villages of Pozderčić and Kamenica and the townsman a certain Vajo, a man from the Lika, who had long ago come to the town as a contractor and had married there. All three were bound, haggard and covered with dust. A drummer was standing by, waiting to give a roll on his drums. In the general flurry and commotion the noise of the drum sounded like distant thunder. Silence fell on that circle around the gallows. The officer, a Hungarian reserve lieutenant, read in a harsh voice the sentences of death in German; they were then translated by a sergeant. All three had been sentenced to death by a summary court, for witnesses had declared on oath that they had seen them giving light-signals by night towards the Serbian frontier. The hanging was to be carried out publicly on the square facing the bridge. The peasants were silent, blinking as if in perplexity. Vajo, the man from Lika, wiped the sweat from his face and in a soft sad voice swore that he was innocent and with frenzied eyes looked around him for someone to whom he could still say it.

Just at that moment when the sentence was about to be carried out there burst through the crowd of onlookers a soldier, small and reddish, with legs bowed like an X. It was Gustav, the one-time *zahlkelner* in Lotte's hotel and now a café-owner in the lower market-place. He was in a new uniform with a corporal's stripes. His face was flushed and his eyes more bloodshot than usual. Explanations began. The sergeant began to hustle him away but the bellicose café-owner held his ground.

'I have been an intelligence agent here for fifteen years, in the confidence of the highest military circles,' he shouted in German in a drunken voice. 'Only the year before last in Vienna I was promised that I could hang two Serbs with my own hands when the time came. You don't know with whom you have to deal. I have earned my right to . . . and now you . . .'

There were murmurs and whispers in the crowd. The sergeant stood in perplexity not knowing what to do. Gustav became even more aggressive and demanded that two of the condemned men be handed over to him so that he could hang them personally. Then the lieutenant, a thin dark man with the manner of a gentleman, as despairing as if he were himself one of the condemned men, without a drop of blood in his face, rose. Gustav, even though drunk, stood to attention but his thin red moustaches quivered and his eyes rolled to left and right. The officer came close to him and thrust his head into that flushed face as if he would spit on it.

'If you don't get out of here at once, I will give orders for you to be bound and taken to prison. Tomorrow you will report to the officer of the day. Do you understand? Now get out! March!'

The lieutenant had spoken in German with a Hungarian accent, quite softly, but so sharply and exasperatedly that the drunken café-owner at once thought better of it and was lost in the crowd, incessantly repeating his military greeting and muttering vague words of excuse.

Only then did the attention of the crowd return to the condemned men. The two peasants, fathers of families, behaved exactly alike. They blinked and frowned from the sun and the heat of the crowd around them as if that were all that was troubling them. But Vajo in a weak and tearful voice asserted his innocence, that his competitor was responsible for the charge, that he had never done any military service and never in his life known that one could make signals with lights. He knew a little German and desperately linked word with word, trying to find some convincing expression to halt this mad torrent which had swept him away the day before and which now threatened to sweep him off this earth, innocent though he was.

'Herr Oberleutnant, Herr Oberleutnant, um Gottes willen. . . . Ich, unschuldiger Mensch . . . viele Kinder. . . . Unschuldig! Lüge! Alles Lüge! . . .' (Lieutenant, in God's name. . . . I am innocent . . . many children . . . innocent! Lies! . . . All lies!). Vajo chose his words as if searching for those which were right and could bring salvation.

The soldiers had already approached the first peasant. He quickly took off his cap, turned towards Mejdan where the church was and rapidly crossed himself twice. With a glance, the officer ordered them to finish with Vajo first. Then the desperate man from Lika, seeing it was now his turn, raised his hands to heaven imploringly and shouted at the top of his voice:

'Nein! Nein! Nicht, um Gottes willen! Herr Oberleutnant, Sie wissen . . . alles ist Lüge. . . . Gott! . . . Alles Lüge!' But the soldiers had already seized him by his legs and waist and lifted him on to the trestles under the rope.

Breathlessly the crowd followed all that happened as if it were some sort of game between the unlucky contractor and the lieutenant, burning with curiosity to know who would win and who lose.

Alihodja, who had up till then only heard meaningless voices and had no idea of what was happening in the centre of that circle of densely packed onlookers, suddenly saw the panic-stricken face of Vajo above their heads and at once leapt up to shut his shop though there was a specific order of the military authorities that all places of business must remain open.

Fresh troops kept arriving in the town and after them munitions, food and equipment, not only by the over-crowded railway line from Sarajevo but also by the old carriage road through Rogatica. Horses and carriages crossed the bridge day and night and the first thing to meet their eyes was the three hanged men on the square. As the head of the column usually became wedged in the overcrowded streets, this meant that the bulk of the column had to halt there on the bridge or in the square beside the gallows until those in front had extricated themselves. Covered with dust, red-faced and hoarse from furious shouting, the sergeants passed on horseback between the carts and laden packhorses, making desperate signals with their hands and swearing in all the languages of the Austro-Hungarian Monarchy and by all the sacred things of all recognized confessions.

On the fourth or fifth day, early in the morning, when the bridge was again crammed with supply vehicles which crawled slowly towards the crowded market-place, a sharp and unusual whistling was heard over the town and in the centre of the bridge, not far from the *kapia* itself, a shell burst on the stone parapet. Fragments of stone and iron struck horses and men. There was a rush of men, a rearing of horses and a general flight. Some fled forward into the market-place, others back along the road whence they had come. Immediately afterwards three more shells fell, two in the water and one more on the bridge among the press of men and horses. In a twinkling of an eye the bridge was deserted; in the emptiness so created could be seen, like black spots, dead horses and men. The Austrian field artillery from the Butkovo Rocks tried to get the range of that Serbian mountain battery which was spraying the scattered supply columns on both sides of the bridge with shrapnel.

From that day on, the mountain battery from Panos continually pounded the bridge and the nearby barracks. A few days later, again early in the morning, a new sound was heard from the east, from somewhere on Goleš. This sound was more distant but deeper, and incendiary shells fell even more frequently over the town. These were howitzers, two in all. The first shots fell in the Drina, then on the open space before the bridge where they damaged the houses around, Lotte's hotel and the officers' mess, and then regular salvos began to centre on the bridge and the barracks. Within an hour the barracks was on fire. The mountain battery from Panos sprinkled with shrapnel the soldiers trying to put out the fire. Finally, they left the barracks to its fate. In the heat of the day it burned as if made of wood, and shells fell from time to time into the burning mass and destroyed the interior of the building. So for the second time the Stone Han was destroyed and became once again a pile of stones.

After that the two howitzers from Goleš continually and regularly aimed at the bridge and especially the central pier. The shells fell sometimes in the river, right and left of the bridge, sometimes smashed to pieces against the massive stone piers and sometimes hit the bridge itself, but none of them hit the iron manhole over the opening which led into the interior of the central pier which held the explosive charge for mining the bridge.

In all that ten-days-long bombardment no major damage was done to the bridge. The shells struck against the smooth piers and rounded arches, ricocheted and exploded in the air without leaving other marks on the stone than light, white, scarcely perceptible scratches. The fragments of shrapnel bounced off the smooth firm stone like hail. Only those shells which actually hit the roadway left little holes in the gravel but these could hardly be seen save when one was on the bridge itself. Thus in all this fresh storm which had burst over the town, overturning and tearing up by the roots its ancient customs, sweeping away living men and inanimate things, the bridge remained white, solid and invulnerable as it had always been.

CHAPTER XXIII

BECAUSE OF THE continual bombardment all movement across the bridge ceased by day; civilians crossed freely and even individual soldiers scurried across, but as soon as a slightly larger group began to move they were sprayed by shrapnel from Panos. After a few days a certain regularity was established. The people took note of when the fire was strongest, when less and when it ceased altogether, and finished their more urgent tasks accordingly, so far as the Austrian patrols would let them.

The mountain battery from Panos fired only by day, but the howitzers from behind Goleš fired at night also and tried to hinder troop movements and the passage of supplies on both sides of the bridge.

Those citizens whose houses were in the centre of the town, near the bridge and the road, moved with their families to Mejdan or other sheltered and distant quarters, to stay with relatives or friends and take refuge from the bombardment. Their flight, with their children and their most necessary household goods, recalled those terrible nights when the 'great flood' came upon the town. Only this time men of different faiths were not mingled together or bound by the feeling of solidarity and common misfortune, and did not sit together to find help and consolation in talk as at those times. The Turks went to the Turkish houses and the Serbs, as if plague-stricken, only to Serbian homes. But even though thus divided and separated, they lived more or less similarly. Crushed into other people's houses, not knowing what to do, with time hanging on their hands and filled with anxious and uneasy thoughts, idle and empty-headed like refugees, in fear of their lives and in uncertainty about their property, they were tormented by differing hopes and fears which, naturally, they concealed.

As in earlier times during the 'great floods' the older people both among the Turks and the Serbs tried to cheer up those with them by jokes and stories, by an affected calm and an artificial serenity. But it seemed that in this sort of misfortune the old tricks and jokes no longer served, the old stories palled and the witticisms lost flavour and meaning, and it was a slow and painful process to make new ones.

At night they crowded together to sleep, though in fact no one was able to close an eye. They spoke in whispers, although they themselves did not know why they did so when every moment there was above their heads the thunder of the guns, now Serbian, now Austrian. They were filled with fear lest they should be 'making signals to the enemy' although no one knew how such signals could be made nor what they in fact meant. But their fear was such that no one even dared to strike a match. When the men wanted to smoke they shut themselves up in suffocating little rooms without windows, or covered their heads with counterpanes, and so smoked. The moist heat strangled and throttled them. Everyone was bathed in sweat, but all doors were fastened and all windows closed and shuttered. The town seemed like some wretch who covers his eyes with his hands and waits for blows from which he cannot defend himself. All the houses seemed like houses of mourning. For whoever wished to remain alive had to behave as though he were dead; nor did that always help.

In the Moslem houses there was a little more life. Much of the old warlike instincts remained but they had been awakened in an evil hour, embarrassed and pointless in face of that duel going on over their heads in which the artillery of the two sides, both Christian, were taking part. But there too were great and concealed anxieties; there too were misfortunes for which there seemed no solution.

Alihodja's house under the fortress had been turned into a Moslem religious school. To the crowd of his own children had been added the nine children of Mujaga Mutapdžić;

only three of these were grown up and all the rest small and weak ranged one after the other differing by an ear. In order not to have to watch them or to call them at every moment into the courtyard, they had been shut up with Alihodja's children in a large room and there their mothers and elder sisters dealt with them amid a continual flurry and fusillade of cries.

This Mujaga Mutapdžić, known as the 'man from Užice', was a recent comer to the town (we shall see a little later why and how). He was a tall man in his fifties, quite grey, with a great hooked nose and heavily lined face; his movements were abrupt and military. He seemed older than Alihodja although he was in fact ten years younger. He sat in the house with Alihodja, smoked incessantly, spoke little and seldom and was wrapped up in his own thoughts whose burden was expressed in his face and his every movement. He could not remain long in any one place. Every so often he would rise and go outside the house and from the garden watch the hills around the town, on both sides of the river. He stood thus with head raised, watching carefully as if for signs of bad weather. Alihodja, who never allowed him to remain alone, tried to keep him in conversation and followed him.

In the garden, which was on a steep slope but was large and beautiful, the peace and fecundity of the summer days reigned. The onions had already been cut and spread out to dry; the sunflowers were in full bloom and around their black and heavy centres the bees hummed. At the edges the small flowerets had already gone to seed. From that elevated place one could see the whole town spread out below on the sandy spit of land between the two rivers, Drina and Rzav, and the garland of mountains around, of unequal height and varied shapes. On the level space around the town and on the steep foothills scraps and belts of ripe barley alternated with areas of still green maize. The houses shone white and the forests that covered the mountains seemed black. The measured cannon fire from the two sides seemed like salutes, formal and harmless, so great was the extent of the earth and the sky above it in the serenity of the summer day which had only just begun.

The sight loosened the tongue even of the care-filled Mujaga. He thanked Alihodja for his kind words and told him the story of his own life, not that the *hodja* did not already know it, but Mujaga felt that here in the sunlight he could lessen the tension that gripped and strangled him. He felt that his fate was being decided here and now on this summer's day by every roar of the guns from one side or the other.

He had been not quite five years old when the Turks had had to leave the Serbian towns. The Osmanlis had left for Turkey but his father, Sulaga Mutapdžić, still a young man, but already respected as one of the leading Turks of Užice, had decided to cross into Bosnia whence his family had come in olden times. He had piled the children into baskets and with all the money which in such circumstances he had been able to get for his house and lands he had left Užice forever. With a few hundred other Užice refugees he had crossed into Bosnia where there was still Turkish rule, and settled with his family in Višegrad where a branch of the family had once lived. There he passed ten years and had just begun to consolidate his position in the market when the Austrian occupation had taken place. A harsh and uncompromising man, he had thought it not worth his while to fly from one Christian rule only to live under another one. So, a year after the arrival of the Austrians, he had left Bosnia with his whole family, together with a few other families who had not wished to pass their lives 'within the sound of the bell', and settled in Nova Varoš in the Sanjak. Mujaga had then been a young man of little over fifteen. There Suljaga had gone on with his trading and there the rest of the children had been born. But he was never able to forget all he had lost in Užice, nor could he get on with the new men and different manner of life in the Sanjak. That was the reason for his early death. His daughters, all pretty and of good reputation, had married well. His sons took over and extended the small inheritance left them by their father. But just when they had married and had begun to take deeper root in their new country came the Balkan Wars of 1912. Mujaga had taken part in the resistance put up by the Turkish army against the Serbs and Montenegrins. The resistance was short but it was neither weak nor unsuccessful in itself, but none the less, as if by some charm, his fate, like that of the war itself and of many thousands of men, was not decided there but somewhere far away, independent of any resistance, strong or weak. The Turkish army evacuated the Sanjak. Not willing to await an adversary from whom he had already fled as a child from Užice and whom he had now resisted without success, and having nowhere else to go, Mujaga decided to return to Bosnia under that same rule from which his father had fled. So now, for the third time a refugee, he had come with his whole family to the town in which he had passed his childhood.

With a little ready money and with the help of the Višegrad Turks, some of whom were his relatives, he had managed to build up a small business over the last two years. But it was not easy for, as we have seen, times were hard and insecure, and profits difficult to make even for those whose position was assured. He had been living on his capital while waiting for better and more peaceful times. Now, after only two years of the hard life of a refugee in the town, this storm had broken in which he could do nothing and could not even think of what to do next; the only thing left to him was to follow its course anxiously and await fearfully its outcome.

It was of this that the two men were now talking, softly, intermittently and disconnectedly, as one speaks of things already well-known and which can be looked at from the end, the beginning or any point in the middle. Alihodja, who liked and greatly respected Mujaga, tried to find some words of solace or consolation, not because he thought that anything would help, but because he felt it his duty in some way to partake in the misfortune of this honourable and unfortunate man and true Moslem. Mujaga sat and smoked, the very image of a man whom fate has loaded too heavily. Great beads of sweat broke out on his forehead and temples, stood there some time until they grew big and heavy, then shone in the sun and overflowed like a stream down his lined face. But Mujaga did not feel them nor brush them away. With dull eyes he looked at the grass in front of him and, wrapped up in his own thoughts, listened to what was happening within himself which was stronger and louder than any words of consolation or the most vigorous bombardment. From time to time he moved his hand a little and murmured something or other which was far more a part of his own inward conversation than any reply to what was being said to him or what was taking place around him.

'This has come upon us, my Alihodja, and there is no way out. The One God sees that we, my father (peace be to him) and myself, have done everything we could to remain in the pure faith and the true way of life. My grandfather left his bones in Užice and today we do not even know where he is buried. I myself buried my father in Nova Varoš and I do not know if by now the Vlachs are pasturing their cattle over his grave. I had thought that I at least would die here, where the muezzin still calls, but now it seems that it is written that our seed will be extinguished and that no one knows where his grave will be. Can it be that God's wishes are so? Only now I see that there is no way out. The time has come of which it is said that the only way left for the true faith is to die. For what can I do? Shall I go with Nailbeg and the *schutzkorps* and die with a Schwabe rifle in my hands, shamed both in this and in the next world? Or shall I wait and sit here until Serbia shall come, and wait once more for all that we fled from as refugees fifty years ago?'

Alihodja was about to utter some words of encouragement that might provide a little hope, but he was interrupted by a salvo from the Austrian battery on the Butkovo Rocks. It was immediately answered by the guns from Panos. Then those behind Goleš opened fire. They were firing low, directly over their heads, so that the shells wove a web of sound above them that catches at a man's entrails and tightens the blood-vessels until they hurt. Alihodja rose and suggested that they take refuge under the balcony, and Mujaga followed him like a sleepwalker.

In the Serbian houses huddled around the church at Mejdan there were, on the other hand, no regrets for the past or fears for the future; there was only the fear and burden of the present. There was a sort of special, dumb astonishment, that feeling which always remains among people after the first blows of a great terror, with arrests and killings without order or justice. But beneath this consternation everything was the same as it had been earlier, the same expectant waiting as before, more than a hundred years ago, when the insurgents' fires had burned on Panos, the same hope, the same caution and the same resolution to bear everything if it could not be otherwise, the same faith in a good result somewhere at the end of all ends.

The grandchildren and great grandchildren of those who from this same hillside, shut up in their houses, anxious and frightened but moved to the depths of their being, had listened intently trying to hear the feeble echo of Karageorge's gun on the hillside above Veletovo, now listened in the warm darkness to the thunder and rumble of the heavy howitzer shells passing above their heads, guessing from the sound which were Serbian and which Austrian, calling them endearing nick-names or cursing them. All this while the shells were flying high and falling on the outskirts of the town, but when they were aimed low at the bridge and the town itself everyone fell suddenly silent for then it seemed to them, and they would have sworn to it, that in that complete silence, in the midst of so much space around them, both sides were aiming only at them and the house in which they were. Only after the thunder and roar of a nearby explosion had died away, they would begin talking again, but in changed voices, assuring one another that the shell which had fallen quite close was of a particularly devilish kind, worse than any other.

The merchants from the market-place had for the most part taken refuge in the Ristić house. It was immediately above the priest's house, but larger and finer, sheltered from the artillery fire by the steep slopes of the plum-orchards. There were few men but many women, whose husbands had been arrested or taken as hostages, who had taken refuge here with their children.

In this rich and extensive house lived old Mihailo Ristić with his wife and daughter-in-law, a widow who had not wanted to marry again or return to her father's house after the death of her husband, but remained there with the two old people to bring up her children. Her eldest son had fled to Serbia two years before and been killed as a volunteer on the Bregalnica. He had been eighteen years old.

Old Mihailo, his wife and daughter-in-law served their unusual guests as if they were at a family feast, a *slava*. The old man especially was untiring. He was bareheaded, which was unusual, for as rule he never took off his red fez. His thick grey hair fell over his ears and forehead and his huge silvery moustaches, yellow at the roots from tobacco, surrounded his mouth like a perpetual smile. Whenever he noticed that anyone was frightened or more melancholy than the others, he would go up to him, talk to him and offer him plum-brandy, coffee and tobacco.

'I can't, *kum* Mihailo. I thank you like a father, but I can't; it hurts me here,' protested a young woman, pointing to her white and rounded throat.

She was the wife of Peter Gatal of Okolište. A few days before Peter had gone to Sarajevo on business. There he had been caught by the outbreak of war and from that time onward his wife had had no news of him. The army had driven them out of their house, and now she and her children had taken refuge with old Mihailo, to whom her husband's family had long been related. She was broken down with worry about her husband and her abandoned home. She wrung her hands, sobbing and sighing alternately.

Old Mihailo never took his eyes off her and kept near

her always. That morning it had been learnt that Peter, on his way back from Sarajevo by train, had been taken as a hostage to Vardište and there, after a false alarm of a revolt, had been shot in mistake. That was still being kept from her, and old Mihailo was doing his best to prevent anyone suddenly and inadvisedly telling her. Every few moments the woman would rise and try to go into the courtyard and look towards Okolište, but Mihailo prevented her and talked her out of it by every possible means, for he knew very well that the Gatal house in Okolište was already in flames and he wanted to spare the unfortunate woman this sight at least.

'Come, Stanojka, come, my lamb. Just a little glass. This is not plum-brandy, but a real balm and cure for all ills.'

The woman drank it meekly. Old Mihailo went on offering food and drink to everyone present and his untiring and irresistible hospitality forced them all to take heart. Then he went back to Peter's wife. The plum-brandy had in fact loosened the constriction in her throat. Now she was calmer and only gazed pensively in front of her. Mihailo would not leave her side, but went on talking to her as to a child, telling her how all this too would pass and her Peter come back from Sarajevo alive and well, and they would all go home again to their house at Okolište.

'I know Peter. I was at his christening. They talked about that christening for a long time. I remember it as if it had been today. I was a young man then, just ripe for marriage, when I went with my father, who was *kum* to Janko's children, to christen that Peter of yours.'

He told the tale of the christening of Peter Gatal which everyone already knew but which in these strange hours seemed as if new to them.

The men and women drew closer to listen, and in listening forgot their danger and paid no attention to the sound of the guns as old Mihailo told his tale.

In the good times of peace, when the famous Pop Nikola was priest in the town, Janko Gatal of Okolište, after many years of marriage and a whole succession of daughters, had a son. On the first Sunday after the birth, they brought the child to be christened and besides the joyous father and the *kum*, a number of relatives and neighbours came too. Even on the way down from Okolište they stopped often and had a nip from the *kum*'s big flat flask of plum-brandy. When on crossing the bridge they came to the *kapia*, they sat down for a short rest and another nip. It was a cold day in late autumn and there was no coffee-maker on the *kapia*, nor had the town Turks come there to sit and drink coffee. Therefore the people of Okolište sat down as if they were at home, opened their bags of food and began a fresh flask of plum-brandy. Toasting one another cordially and eloquently, they forgot all about the baby and the priest who was to christen it after the service. As in those days – the seventies of last century – there were still no bells, and dared not be, the merry party did not notice the passing of time and that the service had long been finished. In their conversations, wherein they boldly and at great length mingled the future of the baby with the past of its parents, time had no longer any importance or any measure. Several times the conscience of the *kum* smote him and he suggested that they should move on, but the others silenced him.

'Well, friends, let us go and finish what we have to do, by the law and the Christian faith,' muttered the *kum*.

'Why the hurry, in God's name; no one in this parish has ever stayed unchristened,' answered the others and each offered him a drink from his flask.

The father too at one time tried to hurry them on, but in the end the plum-brandy silenced and reconciled them all. His wife who up till then had been holding the baby in her arms which were blue from cold, now put it down on the stone seat and wrapped it in a coloured shawl. The baby was as quiet as if it were in its cradle, now sleeping, now opening its eyes inquisitively as if to take part in the general gaiety ('One can see that he is a true townsman,' said the *kum*. 'He loves good company and fun.').

'Your health, Janko,' shouted one of the neighbours. 'May your son be lucky and live long. God grant that he do you honour among the Serbs in all good and prosperity. God grant that. . . .'

'How would it be if we got on with the christening?' interrupted the father.

'Don't worry about the christening,' they all cried and once more passed round the flask of plum-brandy.

'Ragib Effendi Borovac has never been christened either, but you see what a fellow he is; his horse bends under him,' shouted one of the neighbours amid general laughter.

But if time had lost all meaning for the men on the *kapia*, it had not done so for Pop Nikola, who had till then been waiting in front of the church, but by this time had grown angry. He wrapped his fox-skin cape about him and marched down from Mejdan into the town. There someone told him that the men with the child were on the *kapia*. He went there to give them a good browbeating, as he well knew how, but they welcomed him with so much heartfelt and sincere respect, with such solemn excuses and warm wishes and good words that even Pop Nikola, who was a hard and severe man, but a real townsman at heart, gave way and accepted a drink from a flask and some snacks. He bent over the baby and called it little baby names, while the child looked up calmly at the huge face with its big blue eyes and broad reddish beard.

It was not quite true, as they said, that the little one was christened then and there on the *kapia*, but it is true that they stayed there a long time talking, drinking and proposing many toasts. It was not until late in the afternoon that the whole gay company made its way up to Mejdan and the church was opened and the *kum*, stuttering and unsure of his words, renounced the devil in the name of the new townsman.

'It was so we christened *kum* Peter, may he remain safe and sound. He has now passed his fortieth year and as you see has lacked for nothing,' old Mihailo ended.

Everyone accepted another coffee and a glass of plum-brandy, forgetting the reality of the moment which might sweep them all away. All talked more freely and easily. Somehow it now seemed clear to them that there were other things in life, more joyful and human things, than this darkness, fear and murderous shooting.

So the night passed and with it life went on, filled with danger and suffering but still clear, unwavering and true to itself. Led on by ancient inherited instinct they broke it up into momentary impressions and immediate needs, losing themselves completely in them. For only thus, living each moment separately and looking neither forward nor back, could such a life be borne and a man keep himself alive in hope of better days.

So the day broke. That meant only that the artillery fire became more intense and the senseless and incomprehensible game of war continued. For in themselves days no longer had either name or sense; time had lost all meaning and value. Men knew only how to wait and to tremble. Save for that, words, work and movements had all become automatic.

So, or similarly, did men live in the steep quarters below the Fortress and at Mejdan.

Below, in the market-place itself, few citizens had remained. From the first day of the war there had been an order that all shops must remain open so that the soldiers in passing could make minor purchases, and even more to prove to the citizens that the war was far away and presented no danger to the town. That order had remained in force, no one knew why, even now during the bombardment, but everyone found some good excuse to keep his shop closed for the greater part of the day. Those shops which were near the bridge and the Stone Han, like those of Pavle Ranković and Alihodja, were closed all day for they were too exposed to the bombardment. So too, Lotte's hotel was completely deserted and closed, its roof had been damaged by shell-fire and the walls pitted with shrapnel.

Alihodja only came down from his house on the hill once

or twice a day to see if everything were in order, and then returned home.

Lotte and her whole family had left the hotel on the first day after the bombardment of the bridge began. They crossed to the left bank of the Drina and took refuge there in a large new Turkish house. The house was some way from the road, sheltered in a hollow and surrounded by dense orchards from which only its red roof emerged. Its owner with all his family had gone to the villages.

They had left the hotel at dusk, when as a rule there was a complete lull in the bombardment. Of the staff, the only one who remained was the loyal and unchanging Milan, an old bachelor but always immaculately turned out. For a long time past there had been no one for him to throw out of the hotel. All the others, as often happens in such circumstances, had fled as soon as the first shell whistled over the town. As always, in this transplantation also, Lotte had controlled and arranged everything, personally and without opposition. She decided what was most necessary and most valuable to take with them, and what to leave behind, what each should wear, who was to carry Deborah's crippled and feeble-minded son, who was to look after Deborah herself, weeping and sickly, and who take care of the portly Mina, who was out of her mind from fear. So, taking advantage of the darkness of the hot summer night, all of them – Lotte, Deborah, Zahler and Mina – crossed the bridge with their few belongings and the sickly child on a pushcart, with their cases and bundles in their hands. After thirty years the hotel was now for the first time completely closed and remained without a living soul in it. Darkened, damaged by the shell-fire, it already looked like a ruin. They too, as soon as they made their first steps across the bridge, aged or weak, crippled or fat, bow-legged or unaccustomed to walking, suddenly seemed like Jewish refugees who had been walking all the roads of the world in search of refuge.

So they crossed to the farther bank and came to the big Turkish house to spend the night. There too Lotte arranged everything and put everything in order, their refugee luggage and themselves. But when it was time for her to lie down in that strange half-empty room, without her things and her papers with which she had spent her life, her heart failed her and for the first time since she had been conscious of her own existence, her forces all at once gave way. Her scream echoed through the empty Turkish house, something that no one had ever heard or suspected could exist. Lotte's weeping was terrible, heavy and stifled like that of a man, uncontrolled and uncontrollable. The whole family was overcome with astonishment. At first there was an almost religious silence and then a general weeping and wailing. For them the breakdown of Aunt Lotte's forces was a heavier blow than the war itself and the flight and the loss of home and property, for with her it was possible to surmount and overcome everything but without her they could think of nothing and do nothing.

When the next day dawned, a brilliant summer day, filled with the singing of birds, with rosy clouds and heavy dew, instead of the one-time Lotte, who up to the day before had controlled the destinies of all her family, there remained huddled on the floor a weak old Jewess who could not look after or care for herself, who shivered from reasonless fear and who wept like a child, not knowing how to say of what she was afraid or tell what it was that pained her. Then another miracle took place. That old, cumbersome, drowsy Zahler, who even in his youth had never had a will of his own but had been content to let Lotte guide him as she did all the rest of the family, who in fact had never been young, now revealed himself as the real head of the family, with much wisdom and resolution, capable of making the necessary decisions and with enough force to put them into practice. He consoled and looked after his sister-in-law like a sick child and took care of everyone as she had done right up to the day before. He went down into the town during a lull in the bombardment and brought necessary food, goods and clothing from the deserted hotel. He found a doctor somewhere and brought him to the sick woman. The doctor diagnosed that the sick old woman had had a complete nervous breakdown, and said that she should be taken somewhere else as quickly as possible, outside the area of military operations, and prescribed some drops. Zahler arranged with the military authorities to get a cart and transport the whole family first to Rogatica and then to Sarajevo. It was only necessary to wait a day or two until Lotte was fit to travel. But Lotte lay as if paralytic, wept at the top of her voice and muttered in her picturesque and mangled language disconnected words of utter desperation, fear and repulsion. Deborah's unlucky child crawled around her on the bare floor, looked inquisitively into his aunt's face and called to her with those incomprehensible cries which Lotte had once understood so well and to which she did not now reply. She refused to eat anything or to see anyone. She suffered terribly from strange hallucinations of purely physical suffering. Sometimes it seemed to her that two planks beneath her suddenly opened like a trapdoor and that she fell between them into an unknown abyss and that, save for her own screams, there was nothing to save her and support her. At other times it seemed to her that she had in some way become huge, but light and very strong, as if she had giant's legs and powerful wings and ran like an ostrich, but with steps longer than from Višegrad to Sarajevo. The seas and rivers splashed under her tread like puddles, and towns and villages cracked under her steps like gravel and glass. That made her heart beat fiercely and her breath come in gasps. She did not know where that winged race would take her nor where it would stop, she only knew that she was escaping from those deceiving planks which opened beneath her with the speed of lightning. She knew that she trod down and left behind her a land in which it was not good to stay and that she stepped over villages and great towns in which men lied and cheated with words and figures. When their words became involved and their figures entangled, they at once changed their game, as a conjuror changes his scene, and contrary to all that had been said or was expected, guns and rifles advanced with other, new men with bloodshot eyes with whom there could be no conversation, no compromise and no agreement. Faced with this invasion she was suddenly no longer a powerful and giant bird that ran, but a weak, defenceless poor old woman on the hard floor. And these people came in hordes, in thousands, in millions; they shot, they cut throats, they drowned people, they destroyed without mercy or reason. One of them was bending over her; she could not see his face but felt the point of his bayonet pressed on that spot where the ribs separate and a person is softest.

'Ah . . a . . a . . a . . aah! No, don't! Don't!' Lotte woke with a shriek and tore pieces out of the thin grey shawl that covered her.

The little cretin squatted there, leaning against the wall, and watched her with his black eyes in which was more curiosity than fear or sympathy. Mina burst in from the next room, reassured Lotte, wiped the cold sweat from her face and gave her water to drink into which she carefully numbered the drops of valerian.

The long summer day over the green valley seemed endless, so that one could not remember when it had dawned or believe that it would ever be dusk. Here in the house, it was warm but not oppressive. Steps echoed in the house; other citizens kept arriving from the town or some soldier or officer wandered about. There was food and fruit in abundance. Milan brewed coffee continually. It might all have seemed like some extended festival visit to the villages, had it not been for Lotte's despairing scream which broke out from time to time and the sullen thunder of the guns which sounded in that sheltered hollow like howls of rage which showed that all was not well with the world, that universal and individual misfortune was nearer and greater than it seemed in the wide serenity of the day.

That was what war had done to Lotte's hotel and its occupants.

Pavle Ranković's shop was also shut. On the second day of

the war Pavle, with other prominent Serbs, had been taken as a hostage. Some of them were at the station where they answered with their lives for the peace, order and regular communication of the line, while others were not far from the bridge, in a small wooden shed at the far end of the square where on market days the municipal scales were kept and where the local *octroi* was paid. There too the hostages had to answer with their lives, should anyone destroy or damage the bridge.

Pavle was sitting there on a café chair. With hands on knees and bowed head, he looked the perfect picture of a man who, exhausted after some great effort, had sat down for a moment's rest, but he had been sitting there motionless in the same position for several hours. At the door two soldiers, reservists, sat on a pile of empty sacks. The doors were shut and the shed was dark and oppressively hot. When a shell from Panos or Goleš whistled overhead, Pavle swallowed and listened to hear where it fell. He knew that the bridge had been mined and thought of that continually, asking himself whether one such shell could ignite the explosives should it penetrate to the charge. At every change of guard he listened to the non-commissioned officer giving instructions to the soldiers: 'At the least attempt to damage the bridge, or at any suspicious sign that such a thing is being prepared, this man must be killed at once.' Pavle had got used to listening to these words calmly as if they did not refer to him. The shells and shrapnel, which occasionally exploded so near the shed that gravel and pieces of metal struck the planks, disturbed him more. But what tormented him most of all were his long, his endless and unbearable, thoughts.

He kept thinking what was to happen to him, to his house and his property. The more he thought, the more everything seemed like a bad dream. In what other way could all that had happened to him in the last few days be explained? The gendarmes had taken away his two sons, students, on the first day. His wife had remained at home, alone with her daughters. The great warehouse at Osojnica had been burnt down before his eyes. His serfs from the nearby villages had probably been killed or dispersed. All his credits over the whole district – lost! His shop, the most beautiful shop in the whole town, only a few paces from where he was now, had been shut and would probably be pillaged, or set on fire by the shells. He himself was sitting in the semi-darkness of this shed, responsible with his life for something that in no way depended on him; for the fate of that bridge.

His thoughts whirled in his head; tumultuous and dis-ordered as never before, they crossed and mingled and were extinguished. What sort of connection had he with that bridge, he who all his life had paid no attention to anything save his work and his family? It was not he who had mined it, nor had he bombarded it. Not even when he had been an apprentice and unmarried, had he ever sat on the *kapia* and wasted his time in singing and idle jokes, like so many Višegrad youths. All his life passed before his eyes, with many details which he had long ago forgotten.

He remembered how he had come from the Sanjak as a fourteen-year-old boy, hungry and in shabby peasant sandals. He had struck a bargain with old Peter to serve him for one suit of clothes, his food and two pairs of sandals an-nually. He had looked after the children, helped in the shop, drawn water and groomed the horses. He had slept under the stairs in a dark, narrow cupboard without windows where he could not even lie down at full length. He had endured this hard life and, when he was eighteen, had gone into the shop 'on salary'. His place had been taken by another village boy from the Sanjak. In the shop he had got to know and understand the great idea of thrift, and had felt the fierce and wonderful passion in the great power that thrift gave. For five years he had slept in a little room behind the shop. In five years he had never once lit a fire or gone to sleep with a candle beside him. He had been twenty-three when Peter himself had arranged a marriage for him with a good and well-to-do girl from Čajniče. She had been a merchant's daughter and now both of them saved together. Then came the time of the occupation and with it livelier trade, easier gain and lower expenses. He made good use of the profits and avoided the expenses. Thus he was able to get a shop and began to make money. At that time it was not difficult. Many then made money easily and lost it even more easily. But what was made was hard to keep. He had kept his and every day made more. When these last years came and with them unrest and 'politics', he, though already advanced in years, had tried to understand the new times, to stand up to them and adapt himself to them, and to go through them without harm and without shame. He had been Vice-President of the Municipality, President of the Religious Community, President of the Serbian Choral Society 'Concord', main shareholder of the Serbian Bank and member of the executive committee of the local Agricultural Bank. He had tried his best, according to the rules of the market-place, to make his way wisely and honestly between the contrary influences which increased daily, without allowing his own interests to suffer, without being regarded with suspicion by the authorities or brought to shame before his own people. In the eyes of the townsmen he passed for an inimitable example of industry, commonsense and circumspection.

Thus, for more than a half of a normal human existence he had worked, saved, worried and made money. He had taken care not to hurt a fly, been civil to all and looked only straight ahead of him, keeping silent and making money in his own way. And here was where it had led him; to sit between two soldiers like the lowest of brigands and wait until some shell or infernal machine should damage the bridge and, for that reason, to have his throat cut or be shot. He began to think (and that pained him most of all) that he had worked and worried and ill-used himself all in vain, that he had chosen the wrong path and that his sons and all the other 'youngsters' had been right, and that times had come without measures or calculations or which had some sort of new measures and different calculations; in any case his own calculations had been shown to be inaccurate and his measures short.

'That's the way of it,' said Pavle to himself, 'that's the way; everyone teaches you and urges you to work and to save, the Church, the authorities and your own commonsense. You listen and live prudently, in fact you do not live at all, but work and save and are burdened with cares; and so your whole life passes. Then, all of a sudden, the whole thing turns upside down; times come when the world mocks at reason, when the Church shuts its doors and is silent, when authority becomes mere brute force, when they who have made their money honestly and with the sweat of their brows lose both their time and their money, and the violent win the game. No one recognizes your efforts and there is no one to help or advise you how to keep what you have earned and saved. Can this be? Surely this cannot be?' Pavle asked himself continually, and without finding any answer went back to the point whence his thought had started – the loss of all that he possessed.

Try as he might to think of something else, he could not succeed. His thoughts returned continually to the point where they had started. Time crept by with mortal slowness. It seemed to him that the bridge over which he had crossed thousands of times but had never really looked at, now lay with all its weight on his shoulders like some inexplicable and fateful burden, like a nightmare but in a sleep from which there was no awakening.

Therefore Pavle went on sitting there, huddled on his chair with bowed head and shoulders. He felt the sweat oozing from every pore under his thick starched shirt, collar and cuffs. It fell in streams from under his fez. He did not wipe it away but let it stream down his face and fall in heavy drops to the floor and it seemed to him that it was his life that was draining away and was leaving him.

The two soldiers, middle-aged Hungarian peasants, remained silent and ate bread and ham sprinkled with paprika; they ate slowly, cutting off with a small penknife first a piece of bread and then a slice of ham as if they were in their own fields. Then they took a mouthful of wine from an army canteen and lit their short pipes. Puffing away, one of them said softly:

'Eh, I have never seen a man sweat so much.'

Then they went on smoking in complete silence.

But it was not only Pavle who sweated such bloody sweat and lost himself in that sleep from which there is no awakening. In those summer days, on that little piece of earth between the Drina and the dry frontier, in the town, in the villages, on the roads and in the forests, everywhere men sought death, their own or others', and at the same time fled from it and defended themselves from it by all the means in their power. That strange human game which is called war became more and more intense and submitted to its authority living creatures and material things.

Not far from that municipal shed a detachment of an unusual army was resting. The men were in white uniforms with white tropical helmets on their heads. They were Germans, the so-called Skadar detachment. Before the war they had been sent to Skadar (Scutari in Albania) where they were to maintain law and order together with detachments from other nations, as part of an international army. When war broke out, they had received orders to leave Skadar and place themselves at the disposal of the nearest Austrian Army command on the Serbian frontier. They had come the evening before and were now resting in the hollow which separated the square from the market-place. There, in a sheltered corner, they awaited the order to attack. There were about 120 of them. Their captain, a plump reddish man who suffered from the heat, had just been cursing at the gendarmerie sergeant Danilo Repac, cursing him as only a senior officer of the German army can curse, noisily, pedantically and without any sort of consideration. The captain was complaining that his soldiers were dying of thirst, that they had not even the most necessary supplies, since all the shops nearby, which were probably full of everything, were shut despite the order that all shops were to remain open.

'What are you here for? Are you gendarmes or dolls? Must I die here with all my men? Or must I break open the shops like a robber? Find the owners at once and make them sell us provisions and something worth drinking! At once! Do you understand what that means? At once!'

At every word the captain grew more and more flushed. In his white uniform, his close-shaven head red as a poppy, he seemed to burn with anger like a torch.

Sergeant Repac, astounded, only blinked and went on repeating:

'I understand, sir. At once. I understand. At once!'

Then, passing suddenly from his cataleptic stiffness to frenzied action, he turned and hurried from the market-place. It seemed as if the sergeant, approaching too close to that captain flaming with anger, had himself been touched by that flame, which made him run, curse, threaten and beat all round him.

The first living being whom he met in the course of his mad rush was Alihodja, who had just come down from his house to cast an eye on his shop. Looking closely at the once familiar '*wachtmeister*' Repac, now completely changed, rushing towards him, the astonished *hodja* asked himself whether this savage and maddened man was really the same '*wachtmeister*' whom he had watched for years, calm, dignified and humane, passing in front of his shop. Now this sombre and infuriated Repac looked at him with new eyes which no longer recognized anyone and saw only their own fear. The sergeant at once began to shout, repeating what only a short time ago he had heard from the German captain.

'God in heaven, I ought to hang all of you! Weren't you ordered to keep your shops open? For your sake, I have had to . . .'

And before the astonished *hodja* was able to utter a word, he slapped him hard on the right cheek so that his turban slid from his right ear to his left.

Then the sergeant rushed frenziedly on to open other

shops. The *hodja* set his turban straight, let down his door-shutter and sat on it, almost out of his mind from astonishment. Around the shop crowded a swarm of strange-looking soldiers in white uniforms such as he had never seen before. It seemed to the *hodja* as if he were dreaming. But in these times when slaps fell from heaven he no longer felt really astonished at anything.

So the whole month passed, in preliminary bombardment of the bridge and in the firing from the surrounding hills, in suffering and violence of every kind, and in the expectation of worse misfortunes. In the first days the greater number of the citizens had already left the town which now lay between two fires. By the end of September the complete evacuation of the town began. Even the last officials were withdrawn, by night along the road which led over the bridge, for the railway line had already been cut. Then the army was withdrawn little by little from the right bank of the Drina. There remained only a small number of defence squads, a few engineers' units and some gendarme patrols, until the orders came for them too to retire.

The bridge remained as if under sentence of death, but none the less still whole and untouched, between the two warring sides.

CHAPTER XXIV

DURING THE NIGHT the sky clouded over as if it were autumn; the clouds clung to the tops of the mountains and lingered in the valleys between them. The Austrians had taken advantage of the darkness of the night to effect the withdrawal of even the last detachments. Already before dawn they were all not only on the right bank of the Drina but on the heights behind the Liješte chain, out of sight and out of range of the Serbian guns.

At daybreak there was a fine, almost autumnal, rain. In that rain the last patrols visited houses and shops in the vicinity of the bridge to see if there were anyone still in them. Everything was as if dead; the officers' mess, Lotte's hotel, the ruined barracks and those three or four shops at the entrance to the market-place. But in front of Alihodja's shop they came upon the *hodja* who had just come down from his house and let down his door-shutter. The gendarmes, who knew the *hodja* as an eccentric, warned him most seriously to shut his shop at once and leave the market-place, for any longer stay in the vicinity of the bridge was most 'dangerous to life' and strictly forbidden. The *hodja* looked at them as if they were drunk and did not know what they were saying. He wanted to reply that life had been dangerous for a long time past and that everyone was more or less dead already and only waiting his turn to be buried, but he thought better of it, taught by the bad experience of the last few days, and merely told them calmly and naturally that he had only come to take something from the shop and would return home at once. The gendarmes, who were evidently in a hurry, warned him once more that he should move away as soon as possible, and went on across the square to the bridge. Alihodja watched them marching away, their footfalls

inaudible in the dust which the morning rain had turned
to a thick, damp carpet. He was still watching them as they
crossed the bridge, half concealed by the stone parapet, so
that they could see only their heads and shoulders and the
long bayonets on their rifles. The first rays of sunlight struck
on the heights of the Butkovo Rocks.

All their orders were like this, severe, important and yet
basically senseless, thought Alihodja, and smiled to himself
like a child who has outwitted his teacher. He lifted the
door-shutter enough to let him get inside and then let it
fall, so that from the outside the shop appeared to be shut.
Alone in the darkness, he wriggled his way into that little
room behind the shop where he had so often taken refuge
from the obtrusive world, from conversations that poisoned
and bored him, from his family and from his own worries.
He sat down on the small hard chair and crossed his legs
under him and sighed. His inner self was still troubled by
outward impressions, but he soon became calm and balanced
again. The narrow room quickly filled with the warmth of
his body and the *hodja* felt that sweetness of solitude, peace
and forgetfulness which made of the close, dark, dusty little
room a place of endless paradisiacal gardens with green banks
between which murmured invisible waters.

In the darkness and closeness of this narrow space he
could still feel the freshness of the morning rain and the
sunrise outside. Outside there was an unusual silence which,
for a wonder, was not broken by a single shot, a single voice
or footfall. Alihodja was flooded with a feeling of happiness
and gratitude. These few planks, he thought to himself, were
enough, with God's help, to shelter and save a true believer,
like some wonder ship, from every misery and care to which
there seemed no solution and from the guns with which the
two enemies, both infidel and each worse than the other,
were fighting their duel over his head. There had not been
such a calm since the opening of hostilities, the *hodja* thought
joyously, and silence is sweet and good; with it returned,
at least for a moment, a little of that real human life which

had recently grown weaker and weaker and which, under the thunder of the infidel guns, had completely disappeared. Silence is for prayer; it is itself like a prayer.

At that moment the *hodja* felt the stool under him rise upward and lift him like a toy; his 'sweet' silence was shattered and suddenly transformed into a dull roar and a great smashing that filled the air, tore at the eardrums and became universal and unbearable. The shelves on the wall opposite cracked and the things on them leapt at him as he at them. Ah, shrieked the *hodja*: or rather he only thought that he shrieked for he himself no longer had voice or hearing, even as he no longer had any place on the earth. Everything was deafened by sound, shattered, torn up by the roots and whirled about him. Improbable as it seemed, he felt as if the little tongue of land between the two rivers on which the town was built had been plucked out of the earth with a terrific noise and thrown into space in which it was still flying; that the two rivers had been torn out of their beds and drawn upward to the skies, only to fall once more with all their mass of waters into the void, like two waterfalls which had not yet been halted or broken. Was not this *kiyamet*, that last Day of Judgment of which books and learned men spoke, in which this lying world would be burnt up in the twinkling of an eye, like one stubs out a spark? But what need had God, whose glance was enough to create and to extinguish worlds, with such a chaos? This was not divine. But if not, how had human hands such power? How could he, so astonished, so deceived, so overwhelmed by this terrible blow which seemed to destroy, break up and suffocate everything down to man's very thought, give an answer to this? He did not know what power it was that bore him up, he did not know where he was flying nor where he would stop, but he knew that he, Alihodja, had always and in everything been right. Ah, shrieked the *hodja* once again, but this time with pain for that same force that had lifted him up now threw him roughly and violently back again, but not to the place where he had been but to the floor between the wooden wall and the overturned stool. He felt a dull blow on his head and a pain under his knees and in his back. Now he could tell only by ear, like a sound separate and distinct from the universal thundering, that something heavy had struck the roof of the shop and that, there behind the partition, had begun a clashing and breaking of wooden and metal objects as if all the things in the shop had come alive, were flying about and colliding in mid-air. But Alihodja had already lost consciousness and lay motionless in his little room, as if it were indeed his coffin.

Outside it was by now full day.

He could not have said even approximately how long he lay there. What roused him out of his deep unconsciousness was a light and at the same time the sound of voices. He came to himself with difficulty. He knew very well that he was lying there in complete darkness and yet through the narrow entrance a ray of light reached him from the shop. He remembered how the world had been filled with sound and uproar in which a man's hearing was deafened and his entrails melted within him. Now there was silence once more, but no longer like that silence that had seemed to him so sweet before the cataclysm that had thrown him down where he was now, but like some evil sister of it. How deep was this silence he best realized by some weak voices which, as if from a great distance, were shouting his name.

Realizing that he was alive and still in his little room, the *hodja* extricated himself from the mass of objects that had fallen on top of him from the shelves, and rose, groaning continually and uttering cries of pain. Now he could hear the voices from the street clearly. He went down and crawled through the narrow opening into the shop. It was littered with fallen and broken objects, all in the full light of day. The shop was wide open, for the door-shutter, which he had left leaning but unlocked, had been knocked over by the blast.

In the chaos and disorder of scattered goods and damaged objects that lay in the centre of the shop was a heavy stone about the size of a man's head. The *hodja* looked up. Clearly the stone had flown through the air, breaking through the weak roof of wooden shingles. Alihodja looked again at the stone, white and porous, smooth and clean-cut on two sides but sharp and crudely broken on the other two. 'Ah, the bridge!' thought the *hodja* but the voices from the street summoned him even more loudly and peremptorily and would not let him think.

Bruised and still only half-conscious, the *hodja* found himself face to face with a group of five or six young men, dusty and unshaven, in grey uniforms with forage-caps on their heads and peasant sandals on their feet. All were armed and wore crossed bandoliers filled with small, shining bullets. With them was Vlado Marić the locksmith, but without his usual cap, wearing a fur hat and with the same cartridge belts across his chest. One of the men, clearly the leader, a young man with thin black moustaches and a regular face with fine features and fiery eyes, at once addressed the *hodja*. He was carrying his rifle over his shoulder like a hunter and had a thin hazel switch in his right hand.

'Hey, you! Do you usually leave your shop wide open? If anything is missing you will say that my soldiers have pillaged it. Do you expect me to look after your goods for you?'

The man's face was calm, almost without expression, but his voice was angry and the switch in his hand was raised threateningly. Vlado Marić came up and whispered to him.

'Very well, then. Perhaps he is a good and honest man, but if I find he has left his shop yawning wide open again, he will not get off so easily.'

The armed men went on their way.

'Those are the others,' said the *hodja* to himself, looking after them. 'Why should they light on me as soon as they come into the town? It seems that nothing can change in this town without the whole lot falling on my head!'

He stood in front of his damaged shop, mouth open, with heavy head and broken body. Before him lay the square which, in the early morning sun, looked like a battlefield, scattered with large and small bits of stone, tiles and broken branches. His gaze turned to the bridge. The *kapia* was there where it had always been, but just beyond the *kapia* the bridge stopped short. There was no longer any seventh pier; between the sixth and the eighth yawned a gulf through which he could see the green waters of the river. From the eighth pier onward the bridge once more stretched to the farther bank, smooth and regular and white, as it had been yesterday and always.

The *hodja* blinked his eyes several times in unbelief; then he closed them. Before his inward sight appeared the memory of those soldiers whom he had seen six years before, concealed beneath a green tent, digging at that very pier, and he recalled the picture of that iron manhole which in later years had covered the entrance into the mined interior of the pier, and also the enigmatic yet eloquent face of Sergeant-Major Branković, deaf, blind and dumb. He started and opened his eyes again, but everything in front of him remained just as it was before; the square, scattered with large and small blocks of stone, and the bridge without one of its piers and a yawning gulf between two roughly broken arches.

Only in dreams could one see and experience such things. Only in dreams. But when he turned away from this improbable sight, there stood before him his shop with the great stone, a tiny part of that seventh pier, among his scattered goods. If it was a dream, it was everywhere.

Further down the square he could hear shouting, loud words of command in Serbian and steps hurriedly drawing nearer. Alihodja rapidly put up his door-shutter, locked it with a great padlock and began to make his way home, uphill.

Earlier too it had happened to him that while he was thus going uphill his breath had failed him and he had felt his heart beating where it should not have been. For a long time past, from his fiftieth year, he had found the hill on which his house was built steeper and steeper and the way home longer and longer. But never so long as it was today when he wanted to get away from the market-place as quickly as possible and get home as soon as he could. His heart was beating as it should not have, his breath failed him and he was forced to halt.

Down below there, it seemed, they were singing. Down below there, too, was the ruined bridge, horribly, cruelly cut in half. There was no need for him to turn (and he would not have turned for anything in the world) to see the whole picture; in the distance the pier cut short like a gigantic tree trunk and scattered in a thousand pieces and the arches to left and right of it brutally cut short. The broken arches yawned painfully towards one another across the break.

No, not for anything would he have turned round. But he could not go forward, uphill, for his heart stifled him more and more and his legs refused to obey him. He began to breathe more and more deeply, slowly, in measure, each time more deeply. That had always helped him before. It helped him now. His chest seemed to grow easier. Between the measured deep breathing and the beating of his heart he established a sort of balance. He began to walk once more and the thought of home and bed stimulated and drove him on. He walked painfully and slowly and before his eyes, as if it moved along in front of him, was the whole scene with the ruined bridge. It was not enough to turn one's back on a thing for it to cease to goad and torment one. Even when he shut his eyes he could still see it.

Yes, thought the *hodja* more animatedly, for he was now breathing a little more easily, now one can see what all their tools and their equipment really meant, all their hurry and activity. (He had always been right, always, in everything and despite everybody. But that no longer gave him any satisfaction. For the first time it did not really matter. He had been only too right!) For so many years he had seen how they had always been concerning themselves with the bridge; they had cleaned it, embellished it, repaired it down to its foundations, taken the water supply across it, lit it with electricity and then one day blown it all into the skies as if it had been some stone in a mountain quarry and not a thing of beauty and value, a bequest. Now one could see what they were and what they wanted. He had always known that but now, now even the most stupid of fools could see it for himself. They had begun to attack even the strongest and most lasting of things, to take things away even from God. And who knew where it would stop! Even the Vezir's bridge had begun to crumble away like a necklace; and once it began no one could hold it back.

The *hodja* halted again. His breath failed him and the slope suddenly grew steeper before him. Again he had to calm his heartbeats with deep breathing. Again he succeeded in recovering his breath, felt himself revive and walked on more quickly.

So be it, thought the *hodja*. If they destroy here, then somewhere else someone else is building. Surely there are still peaceful countries and men of good sense who know of God's love? If God had abandoned this unlucky town on the Drina, he had surely not abandoned the whole world that was beneath the skies? They would not do this for ever. But who knows? (Oh, if only he could breathe a little more deeply, get a little more air!) Who knows? Perhaps this impure infidel faith that puts everything in order, cleans everything up, repairs and embellishes everything only in order suddenly and violently to demolish and destroy, might spread through the whole world; it might make of all God's world an empty field for its senseless building and criminal destruction, a pasturage for its insatiable hunger and incomprehensible demands? Anything might happen. But one thing could not happen; it could not be that great and wise men of exalted soul who would raise lasting buildings for the love of God, so that the world should be more beautiful and man live in it better and more easily, should everywhere and for all time vanish from this earth. Should they too vanish, it would mean that the love of God was extinguished and had disappeared from the world. That could not be.

Filled with his thoughts, the *hodja* walked more heavily and slowly.

Now they could clearly be heard singing in the market-place. If only he had been able to breathe in more air, if only the road were less steep, if only he were able to reach home, lie down on his divan and see and hear someone of his own about him! That was all that he wanted now. But he could not. He could no longer maintain that fine balance between his breathing and his heartbeats; his heart had now completely stifled his breath, as had sometimes happened to him in dreams. Only from this dream there was no awakening to bring relief. He opened his mouth wide and felt his eyes bulging in his head. The slope which until then had been growing steeper and steeper was now quite close to his face. His whole field of vision was filled by that dry, rough road which became darkness and enveloped him.

On the slope which led upwards to Mejdan lay Alihodja and breathed out his life in short gasps.

ABOUT THE INTRODUCER

MISHA GLENNY is a former central Europe correspondent for the *Guardian* and the BBC. His books include *The Rebirth of History: Eastern Europe in the Age of Democracy*; *The Fall of Yugoslavia: The Third Balkan War*; and *The Balkans: Nationalism, War and the Great Powers, 1804–2012*.

ABOUT THE TRANSLATOR

LOVETT FIELDING EDWARDS (1901–84) was born in Nova Scotia, Canada, and moved to the UK as a child. After taking a degree in Slavic Studies he became a journalist and war correspondent. Based in Yugoslavia for many decades, he wrote a number of travel books about the country. He made his first English translations as a POW in Italy during World War II, and went on to translate many works of fiction and non-fiction from Serbo-Croat, Italian and French. Edwards was personally acquainted with Andrić, and his translation of *The Bridge on the Drina* – still the only one in English – brought the author to prominence in the West.

CHINUA ACHEBE
The African Trilogy
Things Fall Apart

AESCHYLUS
The Oresteia

ISABEL ALLENDE
The House of the Spirits

MARTIN AMIS
London Fields

THE ARABIAN NIGHTS

ISAAC ASIMOV
Foundation
Foundation and Empire
Second Foundation
(in 1 vol.)

MARGARET ATWOOD
The Handmaid's Tale

JOHN JAMES AUDUBON
The Audubon Reader

AUGUSTINE
The Confessions

JANE AUSTEN
Emma
Mansfield Park
Northanger Abbey
Persuasion
Pride and Prejudice
Sanditon and Other Stories
Sense and Sensibility

THE BABUR NAMA

JAMES BALDWIN
Giovanni's Room
Go Tell It on the Mountain

HONORÉ DE BALZAC
Cousin Bette
Eugénie Grandet
Old Goriot

MIKLOS BANFFY
The Transylvanian Trilogy
(in 2 vols)

JOHN BANVILLE
The Book of Evidence
The Sea (in 1 vol.)

JULIAN BARNES
Flaubert's Parrot
A History of the World in
10½ Chapters (in 1 vol.)

GIORGIO BASSANI
The Garden of the Finzi-Continis

SIMONE DE BEAUVOIR
The Second Sex

SAMUEL BECKETT
Molloy, Malone Dies,
The Unnamable

SAUL BELLOW
The Adventures of Augie March

HECTOR BERLIOZ
The Memoirs of Hector Berlioz

THE BIBLE
(King James Version)
The Old Testament
The New Testament

WILLIAM BLAKE
Poems and Prophecies

GIOVANNI BOCCACCIO
Decameron

JORGE LUIS BORGES
Ficciones

JAMES BOSWELL
The Life of Samuel Johnson
The Journal of a Tour to
the Hebrides

ELIZABETH BOWEN
Collected Stories

RAY BRADBURY
The Stories of Ray Bradbury

JEAN ANTHELME
BRILLAT-SAVARIN
The Physiology of Taste

ANNE BRONTË
Agnes Grey and The Tenant of
Wildfell Hall

CHARLOTTE BRONTË
Jane Eyre
Villette
Shirley and The Professor

EMILY BRONTË
Wuthering Heights

MIKHAIL BULGAKOV
The Master and Margarita

EDMUND BURKE
Reflections on the Revolution in
France and Other Writings

This book is set in BEMBO which was cut
by the punch-cutter Francesco Griffo
for the Venetian printer-publisher
Aldus Manutius in early 1495
and first used in a pamphlet
by a young scholar
named Pietro
Bembo.